S[illegible]ER GAME

The Mercer's House Book 3

A Regency Romance

by Mary Kingswood

Published by Sutors Publishing

ISBN: 978-1-912167-44-9 (paperback)

V2

Cover design by: Shayne Rutherford of Darkmoon Graphics

Author's note:

this book is written using historic British terminology, so *saloon* instead of *salon*, *chaperon* instead of *chaperone* and so on. I follow Jane Austen's example and refer to a group of sisters as the Miss Wintertons.

A Summer Game: The Mercer's House Book 3

A family in trade moving up in the world. A family of landed gentry stepping aside for them. And the sons and daughters caught in the middle.

Angie Fletcher is the lively, mischievous daughter of the family. All she wants in her life is music and dancing, plenty of pretty new bonnets, and perhaps just the occasional trick played on her tolerant family. She's been unusually well-behaved during the season in London, in dread of the least transgression curtailing all those glorious balls. Now the family is off to Bath, and freedom - surely a little game won't hurt? But Bath residents are not as forgiving as Angie expected, and she soon finds herself in deeper trouble than she could have imagined.

Mr B Appleby is a man of strict routine, and even stricter principles. His orderly life was disrupted when his uncle married and cut him out of his expected inheritance. He's not quite sure what to do with his life, but perhaps something will turn up. He has no chance of marrying now, but he doesn't care about that - women are flighty, frivolous creatures, not worth noticing, and especially that irritating Fletcher girl, even though she dances like an angel. But then a miracle occurs - an anonymous letter from a secret admirer. There is one woman in Bath who values him, after all. But who can it possibly be? Who would be so daring?

This is a complete story with a happy ever after. A traditional Regency romance, drawing room rather than bedroom. Book 3 of a 6 book series.

Isn't that what's-his-name? Regular readers will know that characters from previous books occasionally pop up, or are mentioned. The Fletchers stay in the Bath home of the wealthy Leo Audley, previously seen in *The Chaperon.* There is mention of Elliot and Evie Armitage, their ward Violet Barantine, and the Tranter brothers, seen in *The Orphan* and also in *A Spring Dance.*

About the series: A family grown rich in the wool trade. The landed gentry they've displaced. And the gentle daughter whose beauty will open the door to an even greater prize - the nobility.

The Fletcher family is moving from Yorkshire to a mansion in the south of England. After generations in trade, can they escape their roots and be admitted to the leisured world of the gentry?

Their new home is Chadwell Park, in Hertfordshire. **The Mercer's House.**

Book 0: The Mercer: the rich merchant and the poor widow. *(a novella, free to mailing list subscribers).*
Book 1: A Winter Chase: the wild daughter and the reluctant clergyman.
Book 2: A Spring Dance: the flirtatious son and the prim paid companion.
Book 3: A Summer Game: the mischievous daughter and the strait-laced gentleman.
Book 4: A Michaelmas Truce: the cross spinster and the even crosser bachelor.
Book 5: An Autumn Courtship: the intellectual son and the flighty socialite.
Book 6: A Christmas Betrothal: the beautiful daughter, the unhappy son and the lost lover.
Want to be the first to hear about new releases? Sign up for my mailing list at marykingswood.co.uk.

Note: hi-res versions of the family trees are available at my website under Extras.

Table of Contents

The Fletcher Family......7

The Plummer Family......8

The Heaman and Corsfield Families......9

The Landers Family......10

1: The Royal Crescent......11

2: The Pump Room......23

3: Arrivals......34

4: Making Friends......45

5: Saturday......57

6: Sunday......69

7: Escort......81

8: Lady Mellish Holds A Card Party......92

9: Departures And More Arrivals......103

10: An Admirer......116

11: An Outing To Lansdown......131

12: Piquet And A Spinet......144

13: Cards And Conversation......157

14: Plans And A Sermon......168

15: Word Games......182

16: An Outing To Midford Castle......194

17: A Popular Man......206

18: In The Garden......220

19: Dinner At The Royal Crescent......233

20: A Ball At The New Assembly Rooms 245

21: An Invitation 259

22: Camaraderie 273

23: An Evening With The Sylvesters 287

24: Circumspection 298

25: A Chivalrous Hero 309

26: Of Duty 321

27: A Betrothal 332

28: An Apology 344

29: A Grand Gala 357

Thanks for reading! 373

About the author 376

Acknowledgements 377

Sneak preview: Book 4 of The Mercer's House: A Michaelmas Truce: Chapter 1: An Unexpected Arrival 378

The Fletcher Family

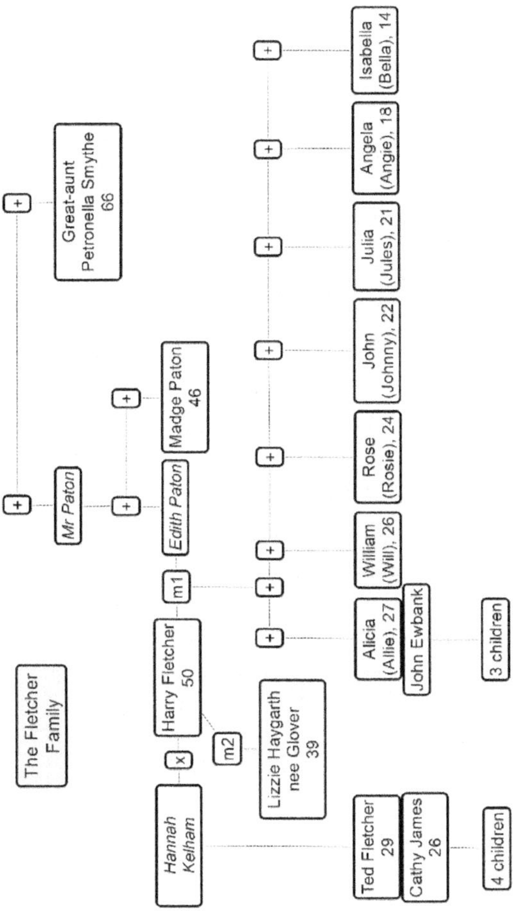

The Plummer Family

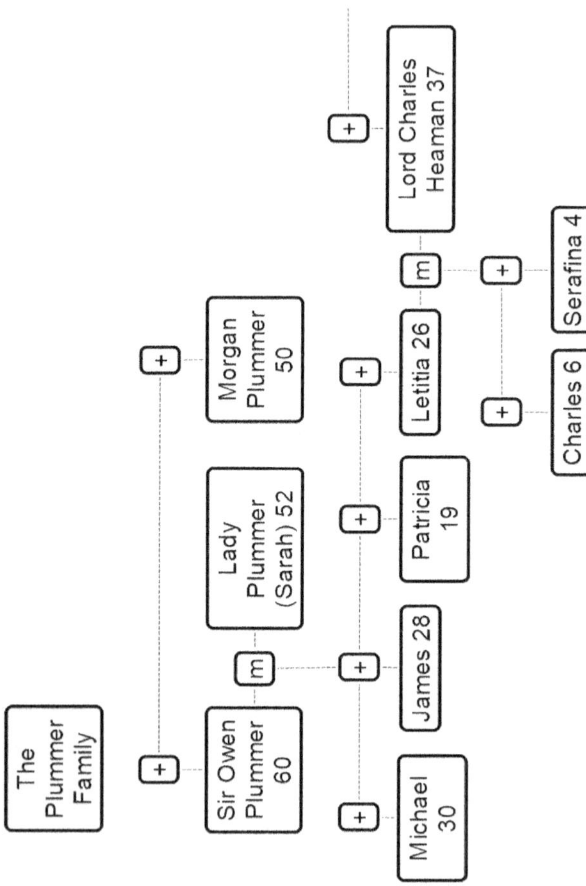

The Heaman and Corsfield Families

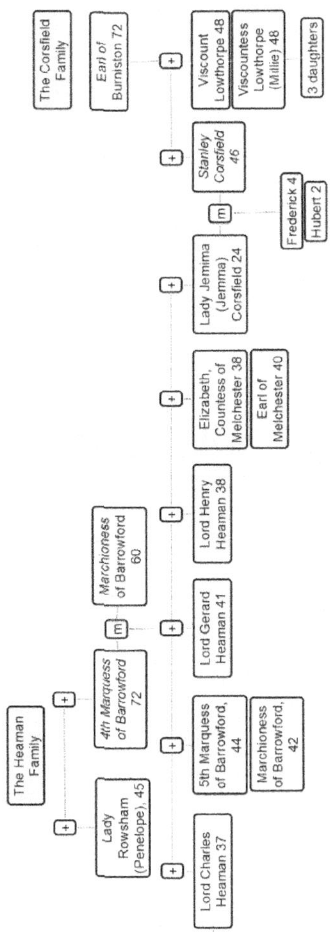

The Landers Family

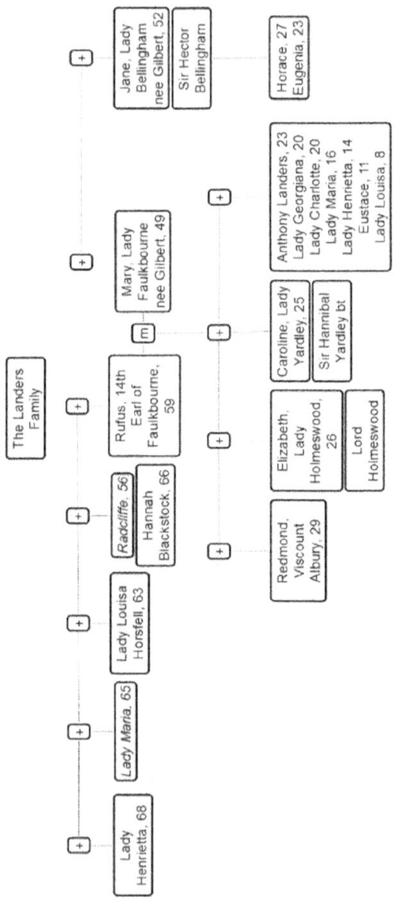

1: The Royal Crescent

ON THE ROAD FROM LONDON TO BATH, THE FIRST DECADE OF THE NINETEENTH CENTURY

JULY

As soon as the town of Devizes was behind them, Angie began to look out for the mile posts in good earnest. She had to crane her neck at every one to read the distance remaining to Bath, counting down the miles one by one.

“Eighteen... ooh, a canal! Look, Rosie, a canal. Seventeen... another canal. Or is it the same one? Sixteen... ooh, a bridge! What are we crossing over? A river, it must be a river. Fifteen...”

Her sister said nothing, merely smiling, but that was Rosie’s way. She was not a great talker.

Aunt Madge groaned. “For pity’s sake, Angie! Can't you be quiet for a few minutes? We’ll be there soon enough.”

“I beg your pardon, Aunt,” Angie said, meekly, but how could she help her excitement, when they were not to be deposited at their estate deep in the country, but were to spend a whole month discovering the delights of Bath?

For a few miles, Angie tried hard to be quiet, merely bouncing in her seat whenever the carriage passed a mile post, and silently pointing at objects of interest as they passed through Melksham, but then her excitement burst out again. "Six miles," she whispered to Rosie. "Five... only five more miles! Half an hour, do you think? It cannot be much more, I am certain. We are almost there, Rosie."

"We can't arrive too soon, as far as I'm concerned," Aunt Madge said in a faint voice.

One by one the turnpikes opened for them, and then there were fine new houses along the road, first on one side, then the other, and then both, with churches and other great buildings mingled with them, and even Angie fell silent in awe at the beauty of the City of Bath. It was not as large as London, nor could it boast the quantity of great buildings of the Metropolis, but everywhere in Bath was order and symmetry and perfection of form, and all in mellow golden stone that gently bathed weary travellers in its glowing warmth.

"Oh, this is lovely!" Angie cried out, and even Aunt Madge, crotchety as she was and with an incipient sick headache, agreed with her and smiled a little.

Soon they were turning this way and that through crowded streets, and then their carriage drew up outside a long terrace on a steep road. From the front carriage, Angie's elder brother, Will, leapt out to assist his betrothed to alight, as one of the front doors opened and an elderly woman emerged, beaming. That must be Eloise's aunt, with whom she would live until her marriage to Will.

How strange it was, even now, to think of Will as a married man! Will, who had treated women as amusing but replaceable creatures, flitting from one to another like a fashionably dressed bumble bee. But so it was. The Fletcher family's sojourn in London to find a husband for Rosie had left her as free as air, and it was Will who faced the depressing prospect of parson's mousetrap. Angie shivered at the thought of it. Married! Who in their right mind would wish to be staidly married instead of remaining in blissful liberty? Yet Will seemed delighted at the prospect. Love did strange things to people.

Soon, Will had pressed a final impassioned kiss on Eloise's gloved hand, she, her luggage and her aunt had vanished into the house, and Will was aboard again. The little procession of carriages moved off, passing down a wide street of very elegant houses, through a circle of even more elegant houses, along a narrower street and then — oh glory, the majesty of the Royal Crescent! Angie had heard of it, of course. Everyone had heard of the Royal Crescent, the finest row of houses anywhere in England, it was said. But the prospect before her was so splendid that even she was reduced to awed silence, her mouth agape. In front of her was a semi-circle of houses of perfect symmetry, overlooking a green field sloping away towards trees and the lower part of the town. It was magnificent.

"Well," Aunt Madge said. "My goodness."

"Oh, I shall like living here," Angie whispered. "What a pity we are only here for a month."

They were expected, and servants streamed down the steps to receive them. Not their own servants, and not hired, either, but the well-trained staff of the wealthy Mr Audley, whose house this was. He was presently residing at his country estate and so had rented the house to them for a few weeks for Will to arrange his marriage to Eloise, and for the rest of the family to postpone for as long as possible the time when they must be buried in the country again.

Inside, the house was as elegant as the exterior. On the ground floor, a dining room, morning room and library, and above it a drawing room overlooking the green, and a withdrawing room with a view over their own gardens. Above that, two floors of bedrooms. The housekeeper had assigned rooms for them, and even Aunt Madge could find no fault with the dispositions. Pa and Mama had the largest room at the front, with its own dressing room, Will had a dressing room too, to accommodate his vast wardrobe, Rosie and Angie shared a big room at the back, and Aunt Madge had a front room on the top floor, with the best view of any of them.

"Well, I suppose it will do," she sniffed, because heaven forfend that she should ever admit to being pleased about anything.

There was tea in the drawing room, and an array of more interesting drinks for the men, and then everyone was dispatched upstairs to rest before dinner.

"Travelling is so exhausting, is it not?" Mama said. "We shall all lie down for an hour or so to recruit our strength before the dressing bell."

The sisters trooped upstairs, and Rosie obediently removed her gown and lay down on the bed, but Angie was not in the least exhausted. She wanted to wander about the house, to examine their new surroundings in minute detail, perhaps to find a pianoforte to play, but it was difficult to disobey a direct order from Mama. Their stepmother was not a martinet, but she had a way of looking at one that made one feel very small and guilty, even for minor transgressions. Sometimes, Angie wished she were like Julia, their newly married sister, who did precisely what she wanted and never worried about it.

"Do you think we shall have much amusement here?" Angie said. "Everyone says Bath is very stuffy and old-fashioned, so it is likely to be very dull, do you not think?"

"I do not mind a little dullness," Rosie said. "London was so tiring with all the evening engagements we had, but here we know no one and will receive no invitations. Oh, to do nothing but a little walking here and there, just as we used to do at home — that will be lovely."

"But no dancing, Rosie! The season is over here, just as it is in London. How sad to be in Bath and have no assemblies to attend — whatever shall we find to do?"

"Shopping!" Rosie said at once. "The shops here are very good, Eloise says, and more conveniently located than in London. And we must go to the Pump Room. Everyone goes to the Pump Room."

Angie pulled a face. "To drink the waters? Ugh! Do you remember when Sir William Fessell discovered a mineral spring on his estate? The waters were foul, utterly foul. I was very ill afterwards."

"I do not know why, for you spat it out at the first mouthful," Rosie said. "You could not have swallowed a drop. Are you going to rest, Angie? Mama said—"

"But I am not in the least tired! I shall creep about and explore, I think."

"Mama will not like it."

"Then we must make sure she never knows of it," Angie said serenely.

She crept from the bedroom onto the landing. From the room next door, Pa's valet, Enoch, emerged, his arms full of shirts. Quickly, Angie put one finger to her lips, and Enoch smiled as he passed by in silence, and down the stairs. He had been part of the family for years, so he understood.

Should she follow him, and explore the principal rooms? But the servants were moving around down below, and she could hear Pa's voice, too. No secrecy that way. Up the stairs she would find Aunt Madge, but having spent two days in the coach with her, and shared a room with her at Newbury, Angie was glad of a reprieve. But half way up the stairs was another door, and that was intriguing. Doors hid many secrets.

Creeping on stockinged feet up the stairs to the half landing, gingerly she twisted the knob. Soundlessly it turned and the door opened on well-greased hinges. Inside was a small room, no more than ten feet wide and long, with a single shuttered window, the air dusty and stale. In the dim light, Angie could see a clutter of mismatched furniture, as if unwanted and dumped out of sight here. There was an old chaise longue, the silk covering faded to colourlessness, several chairs, a small table and a stack of hat boxes piled almost to the ceiling.

Silently she pushed the door shut. Weaving carefully through the mélange of furniture to the window, she pushed the shutters aside, and raised the sash window. Cool air flowed in. Gratefully she climbed onto the window seat and leaned a little way out.

From directly below, she heard Pa's voice directing the servants and the grunts of the footmen shifting furniture about. Pa was making an office for himself, a retreat from the feminine world of Mama, his two daughters and Aunt Madge. He would have a desk in there where he could sit and write his letters, comfortable chairs for himself and Will, a backgammon table and a decanter of brandy. Not that Pa drank a great deal of it, but sometimes when the cares of the world pressed on him or the mutton was badly cooked, brandy mellowed his mood and restored his good humour.

Further below were the usual kitchen noises, a pan clattering onto the fire, a bucket of vegetables set down with a clang, the calls of the cook or sounds of coal being shovelled. The garden was a long, narrow strip of greenery, with a straight path at one side and a more meandering affair on the other. At the far end, she could see movement as the coaches were stowed away. Beyond the stables and coach house, there were rows of chimneys in neat lines, and then only emptiness and a few trees.

Voices on the stairs made her freeze. Aunt Madge, cross, as usual, berating someone. Then the softer voice of a maid, low and apologetic. A rush of footsteps on the stairs, and then silence fell again.

Angie sighed with pleasure. It was not so much fun as the attics and hidden stairs at their Hertfordshire house, but it would do. Her own secret place where she could hide things — or herself, if need be.

There was nothing she liked better than a secret.

~~~~~

Mr B Appleby stared at the dish in front of him.

"What precisely is this?"
~~~~~

"Buttered eggs, sir."

"Where is my porridge, Higgins?"

"Ann's most profound apologies, sir, but the oats are finished and there were none to be had yesterday. Mr Evans has promised to send some today without fail."

"None to be had? Not a pound of oats to be found anywhere in Bath? Can it be possible?"

Higgins audibly sighed. "You *said*, sir, that only Mr Evans may supply the house with dried goods."

"But I did not mean— Well, never mind. It is a pity, for Evans is usually so reliable, and we have always had our oats from him. However, I must have my porridge for breakfast, so perhaps we might modify the instruction. Only Mr Evans may supply the house with dried goods, *unless* he has none of a particular item available, in which case you may go elsewhere. For today, I shall try the buttered eggs. You have my toast and preserves, I trust."

"Of course, sir. Just coming, and the coffee also."

B was left alone with his buttered eggs. Surely he could eat something different for once? Other people varied their routine without the world ending. How foolish he was!

If only there were porridge...

Sadly, these little misunderstandings occurred all too often. Probably it was his own fault, for not being specific enough in his orders, and he never liked to chastise them. Higgins, Ann and Mary did their best, he supposed, but it was a pity his uncle had taken the best servants with him when he married and moved away.

The thought of his uncle made him sigh. B was but eight and

twenty, but sometimes he felt much older. He was serious as a man should be, and not, he hoped, susceptible like his uncle, who had been swept off his feet at the supposedly mature age of fifty by a pretty face and winning ways into a belated state of matrimony. B was happy for them, naturally, and wished them well in their new life, but how reckless of his uncle to throw over a settled and ordered life for the ephemeral prospect of... love? Whatever that was. Had they not lived in perfect harmony, uncle and nephew, for almost twenty years? And now his uncle was gone to be happy with his bride in their new house, leaving his nephew in sole possession of the house in Gay Street, and the three remaining servants.

He took a mouthful of buttered eggs, pulled a face and pushed the plate away.

Higgins sidled back into the room. That was the only way to describe his manner, and B at once suspected some other kitchen disaster, beyond the porridge. Not the toast! It would be too bad if there was nothing worth eating to be had.

The toast appeared, however, and the three dishes of preserves — raspberry, bramble and apricot, arranged in the proper order — set in front of him, and the coffee was poured. But there was something amiss, he knew it.

"What have you done, Higgins? You had better make a clean breast of it at once, you know."

Higgins wriggled uncomfortably. "This came for you, sir." He fished a crumpled note from a pocket.

B absolved him of manhandling the note as soon as he saw the hand by which the direction was written. His uncle. No one else produced such careless lettering, leaning this way and that, like woodland after a gale has passed through.

"Thank you, Higgins."

Unfolding the sheet and smoothing it out, he read the contents with a sinking heart.

'My very dear nephew, The Fletchers have arrived. Mrs A and I mean to call upon them at twelve, to show them the delights of Bath. It would be a kindness if you could attend us. MA'

He sighed. *'It would be a kindness'*, indeed! Not to him, it would not be. He liked his routine in the mornings — his visit to the Abbey for morning prayers, and then to the Pump Room for his glass of the healthful waters, the Lower Rooms for his walk, a visit to one of the circulating libraries, followed by a couple of hours in the garden before dinner. But no, it must be given up for the Fletchers, whoever they were. From the north and in trade, he rather thought. Well, there were plenty in Bath whose origins were lowly, and he would despise no one on that account, but still, he did *not* like having to dance attendance on them. Not without more notice, anyway. His days were carefully planned, and it was most unsettling to have his arrangements overturned at the drop of a hat.

He ate his toast and drank his first cup of coffee. Then a fruit bun, followed by his second cup of coffee, and since he had been deprived of his porridge, he permitted himself a second fruit bun and a third cup of coffee. Then he dressed for the outdoors, and set off up Gay Street to the Circus.

At his uncle's house, Moyles must have been looking out for him, for the door opened as he crossed the entry to the front door.

"Good morning, sir. Warm out, is it?"

"Very warm. And how are you today, Moyles?"

"Very well, sir, thank you kindly for asking. The master and mistress are in the breakfast room, sir."

The breakfast room. So they were still eating, and by the time Mrs Appleby had arranged her dress for the outing, and bidden the child a fond farewell, half the morning would be gone.

"I shall await them in the library."

"Very good, sir."

At least there was reading material in the library, and paper and ink, should he need to make notes, and he was able to while away the time somewhat productively for perhaps a half hour, until the door opened with a little drift of feminine perfume.

"May I come in?" Her face was anxious, as it usually was when she looked at him.

"Of course, madam." He rose politely. He was always polite to her, yet somehow she never seemed at ease with him.

"I do wish you would call me Calantha."

"That would be disrespectful to my uncle's wife."

She dimpled in a sudden smile. "You could always call me Aunt. Then I could call you Nephew, as Maurice does."

Aunt! A woman who was barely one and twenty! She was pretty, he supposed, if one liked hair of an indeterminate brown, height somewhere between tall and short, and eyes the colour of— What colour were her eyes, anyway? Blue, he thought. Or some sort of grey... but with a hint of green. Almost brown, in fact.

She had wandered over to the window, rattling away about

these Fletchers they were to see. What was she saying?

"...the elder has fifty thousand pounds. There now, Barry." He winced. "A very pretty fortune, if you can get it."

"Please do not call me that," he whispered.

She wrinkled up her nose in puzzlement. "But it is your name! I must call you something."

"It is *not* my name. Mr Appleby. That is my proper name."

"But it is also my husband's name, and so terribly confusing. I know you dislike your Christian name, but I was cursed with a silly name, too, and I do not make a fuss about it, do I? Calantha is a far sillier name than Barry. Why do you not change it, if you dislike it so much? You could be John, say, or Thomas, or some other sensible name."

"The name I was baptised with is the name I have," he said stiffly. "It cannot be changed."

She was about to argue, but B's Uncle Maurice arrived at that moment. B had never called him that to his face. Names were so important. He was always *'Mr Appleby'* or merely *'sir'*. To others, he talked about *'my uncle'* or *'the elder Mr Appleby'*. It worked well enough.

His uncle slapped him genially on the shoulder. "Well, m'boy, here you are at last. Are you ready, Cal? Then shall we go?"

At last? As if he had not been kicking his heels for some time waiting for them to be ready.

With such insouciant words, the uncle set off with his usual swagger, his wife tripping light-footed behind him, while his much put-upon nephew, with a weary sigh, brought up the rear.

2: The Pump Room

Their first visitors! Angie jumped up from her chair and twirled about the room with glee. Mama was excited too, although in her restrained, Mama-like way. Aunt Madge sniffed, but that was just her usual manner. Rosie smiled, but then she always smiled.

The men were not there. Will had gone out early to see Eloise, and that alone was proof of the altering effects of love, for normally he would not even be dressed at this hour. Pa had woken early and gone out for a walk. How he loved his walks! But the ladies of the Fletcher household sat at ease in the splendid drawing room, with its view over the ha-ha and lawns, reading and rereading the cards the butler had brought them.

'Maurice Appleby, Esquire'... 'Mrs Maurice Appleby'... 'Mr B Appleby'.

"Eloise's sister," Mama said, although they all knew who Mrs Appleby was. The younger sister who had married a man old enough to be her father. "Who is this Mr B Appleby? A son?"

No one knew.

"Mr and Mrs Maurice Appleby, and Mr... er, B Appleby," the butler said, opening the door.

Angie lost interest in Mr and Mrs Appleby almost at once, for they were exactly as expected — an older man, although well-preserved, like Pa, and a girl three years older than Angie herself, yet already married and the mother of a son. Both had a decided air of fashion, although somewhat out of date. Angie had spent several months in London amongst the finest dressers in England and had developed a sure eye for fashion. The lady's bonnet, however, with its jaunty silk flowers and tiny feathers, was a triumph.

The third member of the group, the intriguingly named Mr B Appleby, was introduced by the older man as his nephew. He was about Will's age or perhaps a little older, but not above thirty, and was more interesting to Angie's mind. Why no Christian name? And was he a gentleman? He had the look of an attorney… or perhaps a clergyman, of a particularly repressive form, for he wore head-to-toe black, with an old-fashioned tricorne hat. He wanted only the Geneva bands to pass for an archdeacon in any cathedral in the country. His face was solemn, almost frowning, as if he disapproved of the Fletcher ladies in their bright summer gowns.

Bows and curtsies and enquiries upon health were exchanged, and everyone sat down. Mrs Appleby sat beside Mama and Aunt Madge, asking about their journey and the horrors of travelling, a subject to which both ladies responded with enthusiasm. The elder Mr Appleby's gaze slithered between Angie and Rosie, before settling on Rosie. Angie was used to that. Rosie had been an accredited beauty since her fourteenth birthday, when old Sir William Fessell had flirted outrageously with her, and Angie could not blame any man for preferring her company above any other.

The younger Mr Appleby had taken a seat across the room,

even though there was one near Angie, and at first she was inclined to be glad of it, for he looked such a stern man that there could be no prospect of pleasure in conversation with him. But then it occurred to her that it might be a punishment to him to be forced to talk, so she crossed the room to sit beside him.

"Have you always lived in Bath, Mr Appleby?" she began.

"No, I was born in the rectory at High Wilton, about twelve miles from Bath. I moved here when I was eight."

"So your father was the rector there?"

"Yes. Until he died. Then I moved here." Perhaps he felt that these brief answers were too feeble to qualify as conversation, for he visibly tried to exert himself, sitting up a little straighter. "Have you been to Bath before, Miss Fletcher?"

"No, never. It is so beautiful, is it not? London is nothing to it, nothing at all. Oh, London is bigger, certainly, and perhaps more spectacular on that account, but nothing can compare with the elegant manner in which the houses are arranged here. Perfect terraces and crescents, and we saw a complete circle yesterday — so beautiful! And so much openness. We have green fields at the front and views over open country to the rear. It is vastly more pleasant than London, where one feels so hemmed in. Do you not feel it so?"

His face softened at her words, the stern look fading away. "I confess I like Bath very well, but then I have never been to London, so cannot compare the two."

"What, never? Goodness! Should you like to go?"

He looked surprised. "Not at all. I hear a great deal of London from my friends, with whom I correspond, but nothing they say inspires a wish to visit the place. Why should I go there? Or to any other town? Everything I might need is here in Bath, and more conveniently to hand than in a sprawling place like London."

"Everything?" Angie said, amazed. "But the shops! So many fine shops there, and entertainments of every kind. Why, in London we could dance every night of the season, if we wished, and I am sure that cannot be said of Bath."

"Frivolities," he said, the stern look returning instantly. "But it is only to be expected in one of your age and sex. It would do you young ladies much good to apply yourself to serious reading, but you would rather dance or waste your time buying endless bonnets and furbelows."

"I would indeed rather dance," Angie said at once, her chin rising at this open disparagement, "for what could be more agreeable than to move to music? I have not danced for five whole days, and I was never more miserable in my life. It is excellent exercise. I should be dancing now while Rosie plays, if I had my way, but Mama said we must sit quietly because Will is to bring Eloise and her aunt to call upon us, except that it was you who came instead. And I do not think shopping for clothes is frivolous at all, sir. We must all wear garments of some sort, and they may as well be pleasing to look at as not. If function were the only consideration, we might all wear sackcloth, might we not? But no one wears sackcloth who can afford better, you must agree with that, for you do not wear sackcloth yourself. Your own clothes are expensively made, even if the unrelieved black makes you look like an attorney. As for ladies, we must display ourselves well to bring credit upon Pa, or so Mama says, and although I do not agree with everything she says, on this subject I think she is absolutely correct."

He looked startled at this diatribe, but it had wiped the stern look away once more. "You should perhaps consider—" he began stiffly, perhaps offended to be told that he looked like an attorney, but the doorbell rang below, and Angie jumped up to rush to the window.

"Decorum, if you please, Angie," Mama said. "Sit quietly until Bryant announces our callers."

"It is only Will and Eloise," Angie said. "We do not stand on ceremony for family, do we?"

Mama gave her one of her special looks. *Sit down and be quiet*, it said, as clearly as if she had spoken the words. Angie sat, although she took care to choose a seat as far as possible from the disagreeable Mr B Appleby.

"Mrs Henry Greenwood, Miss Whittleton," the butler intoned.

Will shepherded the ladies into the room. Eloise, the future Mrs Will, was a tall lady with a figure that Angie could only envy. She and Rosie were both small and too thin for fashion, but Eloise was charmingly shapely. She was taller than her sister, Mrs Appleby, although now that she saw them together, Angie could see the resemblance between them. It was not so much the face itself as the smile, and the way their lips moved as they spoke.

Mrs Greenwood, Eloise's aunt, was a plump woman with a merry face who greeted them as old acquaintances, shaking Mama's hand and planting kisses on Angie's and Rosie's cheeks, and then giving them a hug, too.

"Well, now, look at you two lovely young ladies! Eloise didn't exaggerate a bit when she said you were beauties, both of you.

And how did you enjoy your first season in London town, eh? Enjoyed yourselves hugely, I'll wager. All the young men would have been at your feet, I don't doubt."

"Rosie was the success of the season," Mama said with simple pride. "The Incomparable, they called her."

"Is that so, indeed?" Mrs Greenwood said. "You'll have had offers a-plenty, I don't doubt, yet here you are still free. That's a crying shame, that is."

"There *were* a number of offers, it is true," Mama said proudly, "but the one we hoped for... well, he was obliged to go out of town before the season's end, but perhaps next year..."

"Oh, one in particular you'd set your heart on, was there?" Mrs Greenwood said, her eyes huge with curiosity.

"Lord Albury," Mama whispered. "Heir to an earldom. A most agreeable young man."

Rosie had gone fiery red, head lowered. Inwardly, Angie raged on her sister's behalf. Poor Rosie! She had been greatly pursued in London, it was true, both for her fortune of fifty thousand pounds and for her beauty, but Mama was determined to marry her to a title, and Viscount Albury fitted her requirements to a nicety. Yet Rosie had been far from falling in love with him. Not a single one of all her many admirers over the years had ever stirred her heart.

Mrs Greenwood lifted Rosie's face with a hand under her chin. "Ah, no need to look conscious, miss. With looks like yours, you'll be used to admiration and being talked about, I'll be bound. Broke a few hearts in London town, I dare say, and now you're come to do the same to our young men here. We are not so busy as during the season, 'tis true, but we'll find you plenty of beaux, never fear."

"Oh, I do hope not," Rosie whispered in Angie's ear, as soon as Mrs Greenwood's attention moved on. "I am so tired of beaux."

After the bustle of greetings, there was the even greater bustle of fetching bonnets and gloves for their walk into town. Their visitors wished to show them the principal sights of Bath, and Angie was by no means reluctant to be outside, for the house was stuffy despite the many open windows and surely even the dust of the street would be preferable?

There were nine in their party, for Aunt Madge declared there was still too much to be done in the house to be *'gallivanting all over town'*, as she put it, so she stayed behind. Will escorted both Eloise and her aunt, the elder Mr Appleby claimed Rosie, and Mrs Appleby was deep in conversation with Mama, leaving the younger Mr Appleby to offer his arm to Angie.

"Thank you, but there is no need at all for that," she said. "I am more than capable of walking without support, and indeed far prefer to be able to move freely."

"It is not a matter of what you prefer," he said stiffly. "It is only proper for a lady to lean upon a gentleman."

"Then I prefer to be improper," she said with a light laugh, skipping off after the others.

Their way led them down streets which would soon become familiar, Angie supposed — Brock Street, followed by the perfect circle which she discovered was called the King's Circus, where Mr and Mrs Appleby lived, down Gay Street where the younger Mr Appleby lived, and then past the famous shops of Milsom Street, the pavements thronged with a multitude of people, where Angie had to be dragged away from the most ravishing bonnet in a shop window.

"Frivolities," muttered Mr Appleby, but Angie only glared at him, wondering just what he had against bonnets.

"There is a better shop in Brook Street," Mrs Appleby murmured in her ear. "Mrs Lovelock's — the most delicious confections imaginable."

The tiny feathers nodded gently as she spoke, as if in agreement. Angie smiled in delight. Here was an ally!

There was no time to visit the shops, for they were bound to the Pump Room, to add their names to the book of distinguished visitors. These names would be reported in the newspaper, they were told. Mama was excited about that, in her composed way, for she had never before been sufficiently distinguished that her coming to a place was worthy of mention in a newspaper.

"All visitors put their names in the book at the Pump Room," Eloise told them. "It saves the trouble of leaving cards to announce one's arrival. Anyone who knows you will see that you are in Bath and will call upon you."

"We have no acquaintances at all in Bath," Angie said. "It will be just like London, where we knew no one and could go nowhere, just at first. It was weeks and weeks before we received *real* invitations."

"But you know *us*," cried Mrs Greenwood, "and we know everyone else. I give you my solemn promise, my dear, that within a week you'll know everyone of consequence in Bath, and your hall table will be so laden with invitation cards that you'll hardly know what to do with yourselves. You may play cards every night, if you so desire."

"But no balls, I dare say," Angie said glumly.

"Not at this time of year, no, but after the rigours of the season, you young ones must be fagged to death. You'll enjoy a rest, I am sure, and a chance to recruit your strength for the winter to come. You must be sure to take the waters every day. Very healthful, it is, both to drink and to bathe in, and far better than the nasty stuff they have elsewhere. Malvern and Harrogate are nothing to it, nothing at all."

The Pump Room had only recently been refurbished to the heights of elegance. Angie had to admit that it was an impressive place, more like an assembly room than anything else, even boasting a group of musicians playing in the gallery. Her step lightened, as her feet instinctively tried to dance. Unlike an assembly room, however, crowds of people walked about here and there, talking loudly enough to almost drown out the music, and nobody danced. It was dispiriting.

Mrs Greenwood had spoken nothing but the truth when she said that she knew everybody, for she was soon engulfed in a circle of well-wishers, and making a multitude of introductions for Mama and Rosie. Eloise had taken Will off to meet a group of her friends on the far side of the room, and Mr and Mrs Appleby drifted away, too. Only the younger Mr Appleby clung to Angie's side, unwanted but persistent, or perhaps he did not quite know how to be rid of her.

"Should you care to try the waters, Miss Fletcher?" he said politely.

She pulled a face, and for the first time his expression

softened into something that might, in charitable eyes, be called a smile, but he only said gravely, "It is reputed to be a very healthful drink."

"I am sure it is, but since I find myself to be in perfect health today, I cannot be in need of any additional healthfulness."

"Very logical, I am sure. But if you will not try it yourself, will you at least accompany me to the pump while I enjoy my daily glass?"

Angie would happily have dispensed with his company, but she could not find a polite excuse for refusing such a civil request, when he was making the effort to be agreeable to her. Accordingly, she followed his weaving route through the groups standing about or promenading, arriving at the small carved fountain which dispensed the health-giving waters. A large number of people stood beside the rail, all with glasses in their hands, as a sedan chair decanted another willing imbiber.

"There is rather a press of people," he said, frowning. "I should not like you to be crushed. Will you take a seat while I obtain my glass of water?"

He directed her towards a row of seats against the wall, where only two elderly ladies sat, heads together, busily gossiping. As Angie approached, the two heads lifted as one, quizzing glasses were raised, and she was examined from head to foot. Knowing herself to be becomingly dressed in the height of fashion, and therefore with nothing at all to be concerned about, she smiled, bade them a good morning and sat as far as she could from them. Within seconds the heads were lowered and the whispering recommenced, although they glanced often at her. Angie was amused rather than offended. Newcomers were bound to be of intense interest. It was just so in Sagborough, too, and must be the same in any town.

With leisure now to observe the assembled promenaders in the Pump Room, it was dispiriting to find so few of her own age. Naturally a spa town would attract the elderly and infirm, that was to be expected, but surely there would be a few young people, too? Bath looked likely to be a very dull experience, if not. She could see only one young lady of almost her own age, sitting under the clock with a much older woman.

A small disturbance arose near the door, as the chair which had brought a passenger to the pump was preparing to depart again, but there seemed to be some dispute over the next fare. A very fat woman was arguing loudly with a quietly-spoken man. But the argument was over almost at once, for the gentleman bowed gracefully, and offered his hand to assist the fat lady into the chair. With a heave on the poles from the chairmen and a regal wave of one lace-fringed hand from the lady, she was conveyed out of the room.

Almost at once another chair arrived to deposit its passenger, and the gentleman was swift to secure it. He then went directly to the young lady and the older woman, escorting the latter into the chair, and himself preparing to walk alongside it with the young lady. In the business of arranging the older lady in the chair, and instructing the chairmen, Angie for the first time had a clear view of his face.

She knew him! Of all the people to see in Bath, he was the least likely, for it was Lord Albury, one of Rosie's suitors from London. Oh dear! Now all Rosie's hopes of a respite from the attentions of suitors were at an end.

3: Arrivals

"Lord Albury? Are you sure?" Rosie said, her face pinched with anxiety.

They were dressing for dinner, this being the first opportunity all day for the sisters to be alone.

"Of course I am sure!" Angie said. "We saw enough of him in town, and I danced with him almost as much as you did."

"But what is he doing here? He has not come... because of me, has he?"

"No, no, I am sure he has not. He was escorting an older woman and a young lady."

"A young lady? Then perhaps he is courting her and will leave me alone!" Rosie cried.

"Perhaps, but she is very young, younger than I am. Rosie, you must not be alarmed. He is here on business of his own, and although we will not be able to avoid meeting him, remember that he chose to leave town. That was a very clear signal that he had given up his pursuit of you. I am not convinced he was ever serious about it, frankly, but Mama made so much of him that she imbued his attentions with perhaps a greater importance than they warranted. He called on Will originally, you know, because his brother is a friend of Johnny's. Then he felt obliged to stand up with you when we met at balls. But he stood up with me, too, remember, and many others, and although he was unfailingly polite, I cannot believe that he ever contemplated matrimony at all. So if we meet again here, it will simply be as acquaintances, nothing more."

"But Mama will push me towards him," Rosie said. "I do not dislike him, not at all, for there is nothing about him to dislike, but I do not wish to marry him. That would be so if he were a plain Mister, and his title makes no difference at all to me."

"Or to any rational person," Angie said, giving her a quick hug. "Mama will have to be told, but have no fear, I shall protect you from the terrifying prospect of the Viscount Albury. Now, shall I wear the blue or the yellow tonight?"

~~~~~

Two days after their own arrival in Bath, Rosie's friend Belinda Jupp arrived from Yorkshire in some style, in a post chaise and four, accompanied by her brother, Ricky, a maid, a footman and a mountain of luggage. Belinda was Rosie's oldest and dearest friend, and the continued existence of both could not be assured, it seemed, without a visit of several months' duration. She had always planned to visit for the summer, but the prospect of a few weeks in Bath was too enticing to be missed.

Belinda was the antithesis of her friend, being tall and rather plain of face, and a great chatterbox, but the two complemented each other wonderfully, and it was with Belinda, rather than her sisters, that Rosie shared her innermost thoughts. No sooner had
~~~~~

she arrived in a flurry of tears and embraces, than Rosie had whisked her upstairs for a long exchange of confidences.

The rest of the family were left with Ricky Jupp, who sat at his ease in the drawing room as if he quite belonged there, and was not merely an apothecary from a provincial northern town dressed in a new coat, the dust of travel not entirely obscuring the high shine on his boots. It was odd to see him here, Angie decided. Most unsettling. He was part of the scenery of Sagborough, their former home, where his father was the town's principal apothecary. Ricky was an apothecary, too, working in his father's shop or riding off to outlying farms and villages. His conventional uniform was brown — a plain worsted coat with matching breeches, winter and summer alike, mud-stained boots and a battered tricorne hat. He had dressed up for dinners and balls, of course, but Angie had never thought of him as anything but an apothecary.

Now she saw him with new eyes. When he had first entered the room and stood beside Will, it was almost as if Ricky were a gentleman. He had not Will's height, but his shoulders were just as broad and he was even more handsome. Even a sister's partiality could not make Will outshine him in that way. As to dress, Will had London style and would always stand out for that reason alone, but Ricky's coat of blue superfine which fitted him like a glove, tight pantaloons and smart hessians would not disgrace him in any company, no matter how grand. Angie was impressed.

"So you've taken over Thomas Wilkes' old shop, I hear," Pa said, having been drawn from his office to greet the newcomers and hear all the news from Sagborough. "That used to be a thriving business, but Wilkes has not been able to manage the work for a while now. He should have let it go years ago, or taken on a partner, maybe."

"Aye, that's what I thought, too, but seemingly he and Pa had an arrangement from years back," Ricky said, sipping Madeira as if he did it every day of the week. "Pa always had it in mind for me, and we got possession on Lady Day. Mind you, there's a lot of work to be done, both to the shop and the house above it. It will be a while before I can move in. Michaelmas, possibly."

"Then you'll have your work cut out to build the business back up to what it was," Pa said.

Ricky laughed easily. "Aye, but the market square is such a central location. We'll be run off our feet on market days."

"We? Not taking on an apprentice already, surely?"

Another laugh. "Just a boy, to help with deliveries, at first. I've got one of the Patterson boys from Canal Street. But next year, I'll take on an apprentice... expand a bit."

Mama's smile was a trifle strained, for she would normally expect to meet an apothecary in his shop, not in her own drawing room. She was more conscious of the social strata than the rest of the family.

"Shall you stay long in Bath, Mr Jupp? I dare you will be needed at the shop, with improvements under way," she said.

"Oh, Pa's taking care of all that," Ricky said airily. "I can stay for a few days... till Monday... maybe Tuesday. I'll go back on the mail, so it will be quicker than it was coming south. Couldn't expect Bel to be rattled about on the mail, but it will suit me well enough. And you needn't worry about putting me up. I've sent my man to bespeak a room at a hotel we passed on the way in."

Mama looked relieved, but Pa said, "Hotel? Nonsense, lad!

You'll stay here and that's the end of it. We can find a room for the lad, can't we, Mrs Fletcher?"

"He can share with me," Will said. "Then he can tell me all the *real* news from Sagborough."

He grinned and Ricky grinned back. "Aye, I'll do that, but the only news there at the moment is the number of broken hearts among the ladies since the announcement in the *Gazette*. How could you do it, Will? To ignore all our fine Yorkshire lasses and betroth yourself to a southern girl — for shame! But I can't wait to meet her. She must be a very special lady to draw *you* into parson's mousetrap."

"She is!" he cried eagerly. "She is wonderful, Ricky. I know she is at home just now. Why not stroll over there and you can meet her?"

They went off directly to visit Eloise and her aunt. Angie bent her head industriously to her needlework, waiting for Mama to speak her mind, for she would not like an apothecary staying under her roof, and being shown off to their grander acquaintances as if he were a gentleman. But although she pursed her lips slightly, she said nothing, reaching for her embroidery frame and calmly picking up her needle.

Aunt Madge sniffed. "Well! He dresses very fine for an apothecary, all of a sudden."

"He always dresses well on social occasions," Pa said mildly. "I've never seen Ricky shabbily turned out when he's in company. He knows how to present himself to the world. That hat of his is as fine as any of Will's, I'll warrant. And to both of you, I'll say this — I know you don't like him staying here, but Gerry Jupp's one of my oldest friends. Lord, we were at school together and got into scrapes together and got married within a month of each other, so I treat his children as if they were my own, and I trust you'll do the same."

Mama laid down her embroidery and gazed at him calmly. "I do not mind Belinda, Harry, for she has pretty manners and knows not to prattle about her father's shop, and besides, she puts a sparkle in Rosie's eye and that is all to the good. But I do *not* want Ricky Jupp putting a sparkle in her eye. That would be fatal. Back in Sagborough, we most often saw him in his working clothes and no one could forget his occupation, but here, where he has nothing to do but follow the girls about and enjoy himself, and dressed up like a dandy as he is... well, I do not want Rosie to be distracted by him, that is all."

"It's only for a few days, Lizzie love," Pa said. "I think the better of him for coming here with Belinda and not leaving her to travel with only the maid and a footman. Very proper in a brother, that is. Besides, now that Rosie's seen *real* gentlemen, aye, and lords, too, she's not likely to think Ricky's the top of the trees, is she?"

"Rosie is very tender-hearted," Mama said. "One cannot be too careful with girls of such excessive sensibility. Happily, there is no one of importance in Bath just now."

Angie could not let that pass. "Mama..."

"Do not interrupt your elders, Angie. It is a bad habit of yours."

"I beg your pardon, Mama, but Lord Albury is in Bath."

There was a long silence, as the eyes of all three turned on Angie.

"*Lord Albury?*" Mama said hoarsely. "Why? And how do you know of this?"

"I saw him at the Pump Room yesterday, just as he was leaving with an older woman and a young lady. He did not see me, or any of us, I should think, or he would have spoken to us."

"And you did not think to mention this sooner? We were out shopping all morning and might have run smash into him at any moment, and think how that would look. We must find out where he is staying and Will must call upon him, then we can—"

"No," Pa said, with the tone of voice that brooked no argument. "If we bump into him, and he chooses to acknowledge us—"

"*Chooses* to!" Mama squeaked in outrage.

"Aye, for he might not, if he's with ladies. Or he might just give us a common bow in passing. It is entirely up to him, Lizzie. We mustn't presume upon the acquaintance. He's a viscount, after all, and whatever hopes you once harboured for him and Rosie, that's all finished now. He's in Bath for reasons of his own, so we'll leave him be, and no going behind my back on this. Angie love, does Rosie know about this?" Angie nodded. "Well, let's hope he goes away soon, before he starts raising ideas again."

Mama could hope no such thing, but she wisely said nothing and picked up her embroidery again.

~~~~~

It was raining when B walked up Gay Street to the Circus to dine with Uncle Maurice and his wife. He had an umbrella to shelter him from the worst of the weather, but his stockings would be splashed, he knew that. It could not be helped, for he could hardly
~~~~~

call out a chair for such a short distance. Not that Uncle Maurice would care. He never bothered to dress properly for dinner anyway, thinking that pantaloons were acceptable evening wear. Only the rules of the Assembly Rooms forced him into silk breeches and stockings.

B, however, took pride in holding to the old-fashioned ways. Breeches and stockings, both for day and evening wear, only the material varying. A tricorne hat for daytime and a *chapeau bras* for evenings. It was still commonplace in Bath, and only those careless of their appearance, like his uncle, or following the whimsical dictates of fashion, like Mr William Fletcher, abandoned such good practices.

He was on time, so he was ushered into an empty drawing room. His uncle had never been on time for anything, and one never expected punctuality from ladies, so he was not surprised. The butler was not surprised, either, furnishing him with two newspapers, several books and a glass of ratafia.

Eventually, Mrs Appleby emerged from her toilette wearing one of her brightest gowns. She owned a curious mixture of dresses, some in respectable greys and browns and dark greens, and some in garish colours with frivolous flounces and bows, although how she decided which to wear for any particular occasion was a mystery.

"Well now, what do you think of them, now that you have met them?" she said, perching herself beside him on the sofa so closely that he felt obliged to slide further from her.

"What do I think of whom?"

"Why, the Fletchers, of course! Are they not exactly as Eloise described them in her letters? I almost feel that if we had met them in the street as complete strangers, we should have known them at once, just from her descriptions. Do you not think so? And the sisters are so pretty! I declare, I never saw a more lovely pair in my life, and their gowns! Oh my, such elegance! That would be London, of course. I have seen some of Eloise's gowns that Lady Carrbridge had made for her, and I never saw anything so fine in my life. Why the sleeves on one of the ball gowns— But you do not want to hear about gowns, I imagine. Tell me at once, what do you think? Will one of them do?"

"Do? Do for what?"

"For you to marry, of course! Now, do not protest and say that you had no thought of matrimony in your head, for I should not believe you. The elder has the face of an angel, and fifty thousand pounds. All the girls are to get twenty from their father, but the elder girl will have an additional thirty from a rich aunt. She is demure enough even for you, Barry — I mean, Mr Appleby. But the younger is very pretty too, and has twenty thousand. "

"And is not demure at all," B said at once. "An impudent child, I thought her. As for the elder… I do wish you would give up such match-making schemes, madam. I am a grown man, and can manage my life perfectly well without your assistance. I am not ungrateful, I assure you, and I know you have my best interests at heart, but I must be left to determine my own future."

"Yet you do nothing about it," she said softly. "Here you are, two years after Maurice married me, and a whole year after baby Roger cut you out of the inheritance, and you have made not the least push to set your life on a different course. You cannot imagine how guilty that makes me feel. If I had not come along—"

"Am I to marry to assuage your guilt?" he said, but softened the words with a smile.

She tapped him playfully on the wrist with her fan. "No, of course not. I did not mean it so, as I am sure you are aware. But I worry about you, Barry — oh, I beg your pardon, I forgot. Mr Appleby. You must have something to live upon, now that you are not to inherit, and that means either a career or a rich wife. Ah, Maurice, there you are. You will support me, I know. Can you not convince Bar— your nephew that he must make a push to secure his future, and would not one of the Fletcher girls be ideal for him?"

"Now, now, Cal, I will not have you worrying yourself over the boy, for it puts those tiny lines across your forehead that I so dislike." Her husband bent to kiss the offending forehead, then smoothed away imaginary creases. "You know how much I dislike you to fret over anything, my precious girl."

She blushed and simpered, but said, "That is all very well, my dear love, but he must exert himself just a little."

"Something will turn up," he said airily. "He will get a living soon, I should think. The bishop knows of his situation and assured him he would bear him in mind, and he has powerful friends of his own. Have you written to that fellow who works for Portland, my boy?"

"I have."

"There, you see? All that education is bound to pay off eventually. One meets so many useful people at Oxford. Gracious, I am sharp set today. What do you have for our dinner tonight, my dear one? Something delicious, I wager, for you are such a clever little housewife, and it is not your fault if the kitchen boy sometimes forgets to turn the spit, is it?"

"Well, it is to be hoped that he has not forgotten tonight, for it is loin of veal, your favourite, and a chine of mutton for the other remove, which I know will please Bar— your nephew."

A chine of mutton. B's spirits lifted a fraction. A decent meal erased a lot of irritations. She was a kindly soul, his uncle's wife.

4: Making Friends

Angie was enchanted with Bath. Unlike London, where one was obliged to take the carriage for the smallest excursion, in Bath everywhere was within easy reach of anyone with energy for walking. One might visit a milliner, a haberdasher, a perfumery, a circulating library and a glove-maker, and yet have walked barely a hundred yards. It was delightful.

There was the Pump Room, too, where everyone of consequence gathered almost every day to meet friends. Belinda and Ricky Jupp had to be taken there, naturally, to taste the famous waters and to walk round and round the room, to see and be seen, and even Pa wanted to see the spectacle, although he was more interested in the Roman Baths.

Now that Mama knew of Lord Albury's presence in Bath, she was in a flutter of anticipation to meet him again. Great was her disappointment, therefore, as they made their first perambulation of the Pump Room, to find that he was not there. There were other acquaintances there to stop and talk to, however, and greet as if they were friends of long-standing, and had not been introduced only yesterday.

Despite Mama's reservations about Ricky, handsome young men were in such short supply that he was instantly a person of great interest to the residents of Bath, and several of Mrs Greenwood's friends enquired about him and promised to include him in their invitations, should he still be in town. It was no surprise that Rosie should attract attention, too, for she could not help being the most beautiful face in town. There were not many eligible young men presently in Bath, but those few clustered about her like bees drawn to honey.

With so much stopping to talk, Angie soon wearied of the dawdling pace, and settled on a seat near the orchestra where she could enjoy the music and tap her feet and imagine herself dancing. From there, she saw a sedan chair carried directly to the pump where the waters were dispensed. And the two people in attendance, a gentleman and a young lady, she recognised instantly.

At once she turned her head a little, so that she should not appear to stare at them, and closed her eyes, concentrating on the music. After a little while, and she could not quite say how, she became aware of... something. Some slight change in the air. She opened her eyes.

Lord Albury was standing before her, his expression anxious. "Oh, you *are* awake! I was not sure... I did not quite like to disturb you."

"Lord Albury." She rose and curtsied to him.

"Miss Fletcher. This is a delightful surprise! I had no idea you were in Bath, or had any intention of being so. Have you been here long?" His words were all affability, but his expression was oddly hostile.

"We arrived two days ago, my lord. My brother is here to arrange his marriage to Miss Whittleton, whose home this is, and we are here to bear him company."

"Ah! Your brother... and Miss Whittleton... of course." The expression lightened a little. "And... and are you *all* in Bath? All of your family?"

"My father and stepmother, my aunt, and my sister Rosie, as well as two friends from Yorkshire. They are somewhere about the room."

"Ah. And you are all well? Not exhausted by the rigours of the season?"

"Redmond! Do attend for a moment," came an imperious voice.

He turned, saw the older woman frowning at him, nodded his acquiescence. "Forgive me, Miss Fletcher, but I must see to my aunt."

"Of course, my lord."

With a quick bow, he was gone. Angie tried to resist the temptation to watch the three, the aunt and the two younger people, but her strength of purpose was not tested, for a noisy crowd moved in front of her, blocking her view.

Pa settled with a sigh on the seat beside her, a glass of the famous waters in his hand. "Well, this is nasty stuff so it must be doing me good." He pulled a face and took another sip, then held the glass out to her. "Do you want to try it, flower?"

"Not for the world, Pa. I cannot at all see the purpose in it."

"Why, it's to improve the health."

"And is there anything amiss with your health that requires improvement?"

He scratched his nose thoughtfully. "Do you know, there isn't a thing, beyond a slight stiffening of the joints, which is hardly surprising in a man of fifty. I cannot see the purpose in it myself." Reaching behind him, he tipped the contents into the pot of a plant which stood there. "Well now, Miss Mischief, and how do you think you'll like Bath? Not going to be bored, are you, after all the excitement of London?"

"Oh, it will be a little quieter, I dare say. It is such a pity there are no assemblies at this time of year."

"I should have thought you'd have worn out your dancing slippers, with all the balls you went to in London," he said.

"I would just dance in my stockings," she said.

He chuckled. "So you would, flower. But, Angie... I hope you won't start playing any tricks on us if Bath is a bit tame for you. No more hiding things, and getting everyone in a pother, eh? Not like you did when we first moved south."

"Oh, no, Pa," she said seriously. "I was so upset that Mama thought it was the servants, and threatened to dismiss them all without references because of it. It was just a little game, something to amuse myself, but I never meant to cause trouble. I never do. I shall not do anything of the sort again, I promise you."

"That's a good girl. Keep yourself out of trouble, that's the way. Ah, now there's the man who's going to show me around the baths."

So saying, he rose and disappeared into the crowds. Angie sat on, watching the women as they drifted past, weighing up their clothes... drab... drab... positively horrid... not bad... oh, that one was fashionable... drab... drab... But no one came to speak to her, and nothing interesting occurred.

She soon grew restless at the inactivity, and jumped to her feet to re-join the crowds walking about the room. There was a general movement in one direction to avoid collisions, but the pace was slow and she found herself walking more briskly on the outside of the crowds, for her feet responded to the rhythm of the music and she could not constrain herself to walk more slowly. She passed Lord Albury's aunt, now seated near the pump with a glass in her hand, talking animatedly to two women of her own age. Lord Albury was not there, but the very young lady sat beside them, looking wistfully about the room. She caught Angie's eye and smiled. She was very pretty! Her features strongly resembled Lord Albury's, and somehow they seemed to suit her better than they did her brother.

Angie smiled back but her pace had soon left the young lady behind, and when Angie reached the end of the room and turned to look back, she was already lost to view.

Within moments, however, she saw Lord Albury, who was talking to Mama and Rosie, while Belinda and Ricky stood respectfully a little aside. Mama was smiling, with that gleam in her eye that showed she was excited. Eligible gentlemen, especially those with a title, always excited her.

"Your family is acquainted with Lord Albury?" said a voice by Angie's side. The stern Mr Appleby.

"Oh... good day to you, Mr Appleby. Yes, we met him in London. Do you know him well?"

"Not at all. That is to say, we are not acquainted, but he is one of our more notable visitors this summer, so I know who he is, naturally."

"Do you know the two ladies whom he accompanies here? An older one and a young one."

"The older lady is Lady Louisa Horsfell, his aunt on his father's side, one of Bath's more important residents. The young lady is his sister, Lady Maria Landers, who is paying her first visit to Bath. She is to come out in a year or two, so she is making delicate forays into society in advance of the occasion."

"Delicate, indeed, since she seems to spend her time in company with her aunt's friends. I hope she has better entertainment in the evenings."

"I would not know," Mr Appleby said. "I do not move in such exalted circles. Excuse me, I must procure my glass of water. May I tempt you, Miss Fletcher?"

She politely declined, and with a formal bow, he left her. Lord Albury and her family had vanished again, swept away by the tide of promenaders, but another circuit brought her past the spot where Lady Maria sat with her aunt. This time, she smiled more broadly, and gave a quick wave of one hand to Angie. The older ladies had moved on, but Lord Albury was there, deep in earnest conversation with his aunt. The aunt looked up and caught Angie's eye before she turned back to Lord Albury, but Angie could not read the expressions on their faces. Lady Maria seemed disposed to be friendly but her aunt and brother were inscrutable.

Angie grew bored with walking round and round. Finding a quiet seat near the orchestra, she sat and soaked up the music. Oh, if she could only dance!

A shadow fell across her. Lord Albury again, smiling down at her.

"Miss Fletcher, once again I disturb your reveries, but I should very much like to take this opportunity to talk to you, if I may."

"Of course, my lord," she said but she was surprised by it. Whatever could he have to say to her privately?

He took the seat next to her, and turned to her at once. "Do not be alarmed, I beg you, for I have nothing to say that your parents might not hear, if they were present, but I cannot speak before your sister, so I come to you, instead. Miss Fletcher, you will have seen the company I keep here — my aunt lives in Bath for her health, and for a few weeks it is my pleasant duty to visit her and accompany her on her social round. My younger sister, Maria, is with me on this visit and it is for her sake that I speak now. She is but sixteen, and a shy creature, not confident in society just yet, and Bath in the summer is not well-provided with suitable companions for her. She very much wishes to be introduced to your family so that we might enjoy outings together and do all those things that one must do in Bath — walk in Sydney Gardens, make an excursion to Wells, ride in the hills — I am sure you know the sort of thing. My aunt is agreeable to the idea, and I must tell you, Miss Fletcher, I cannot think of any family better equipped to take Maria to its generous heart than yours. You are all so friendly and accommodating, that I cannot doubt that Maria would benefit greatly from acquaintance with you, and I do not think you would be disappointed in her society, either."

"I am sure we should not," Angie cried. "She looks like a sweet girl."

"She is, the sweetest imaginable. But you will appreciate my difficulty. I was privileged to get to know your sister a little in town, and it seemed to me that she was not comfortable with the high expectations placed upon her by her situation. Her beauty and gentle nature, combined with her large dowry, made her an object of intense interest to many men. That interest is something I understand very well, being subject to it myself. As the heir to a great title, I have been subjected to a parade of eligible young ladies since I was sixteen years old. I am always glad, therefore, to leave town at the end of the season and be free from such badgering, and I imagine your sister feels the same. It would please me greatly, therefore, if we could meet merely as acquaintances in Bath, without any expectations on either side."

"How thoughtful you are, Lord Albury," Angie said, "and I do not doubt that Rosie would be happy to have things on such a footing, but I cannot answer for Mama."

He laughed, and his rather ordinary face lit up momentarily. "Oh, as to that, Mamas always have expectations of matrimony when any likely couple happen to be within a quarter mile of each other, so I do not regard that in the least. But your sister has her friend with her now, and you and your brother in attendance, and there are no assemblies where we will be obliged to stand up together, so I dare say we shall not do more than exchange bows and a few words about the weather when we happen to meet. But I should be very glad to introduce my sister to you very soon. She is sorely in need of congenial company of her own age! My aunt is almost ready to return home, but I will bring Maria to call upon you later today, if you approve."

"That would be delightful, Lord Albury."

He rose, bowed politely over her hand, and returned to his aunt.

Almost instantly, Mama was looming over Angie. "What did he say?" she hissed excitedly. "Did he mention Rosie at all?"

"He wishes to introduce his sister to us," Angie said, hesitating to say more. To Rosie she might talk about meeting the viscount as mere acquaintances, but Mama would not believe it. Lord Albury himself seemed unconcerned about that. *'Mamas always have expectations of matrimony when any likely couple happen to be within a quarter mile of each other,'* he had said. It was Rosie he wished to reassure, so that she would neither be in hope of a declaration nor be worn down by the fear of it.

"His sister? Well, that is a good sign," Mama said, smiling. "What a piece of luck, meeting him here, for we had not the least idea of it. I hope he will not think we followed him here with the sole intent of throwing Rosie in his way. That would be mortifying. Still... his sister. That is an excellent acquaintance for you girls."

"Yes, Mama," Angie said meekly.

~~~~~

When they returned home, Bryant's eyes shone with pleasure. "There have been several cards delivered while you were out, madam," he said, directing two footmen with practised ease. "And Miss Paton is entertaining four callers in the drawing room."

"Four callers?" Even Mama was surprised by that.

"Persons by the name of Sylvester, madam. Friends of a Mr Plummer, I believe."

"Oh, the Plummers. Well! Goodness, so many cards... let me see... a musical evening... a card party... a whist party... oh, dinner, excellent... another whist party. Bath residents are very fond of whist, it seems."
~~~~~

"No balls, then," Angie said sadly. "No informal evenings with the carpets rolled up. And not the least sign of an assembly before October at the earliest."

"Poor Angie!" Mama said sympathetically. "How you love to dance. But we are only here for a month or so, after all, and perhaps we can hold a ball when we return to Hertfordshire."

This was not so encouraging as Angie would have liked, so she subsided into silence, and followed Mama and Rosie up the stairs.

They found Aunt Madge in the drawing room, a bemused expression on her face, entertaining with cake and wine three ostentatiously dressed young men and an even younger woman who all bounced to their feet, scattering cake crumbs everywhere, and rushed across the room.

"Mrs Fletcher! Mr Fletcher! The Miss Fletchers!" they cried, almost in unison, then in a babble of voices, "So delighted to meet you at last! We have heard so much about you all. How are you liking Bath? Have you found out all the amusements to be had here? We shall make sure you never have a dull moment!"

Angie laughed, for despite their peacock-like appearance they sounded just the people to liven up their stay in Bath, but Mama said briskly, "One at a time, if you please! You are friends of the Plummers, I understand?"

"*James* Plummer, who was—"

"—such an old friend—"

"—from Eton and then—"

Mama held up her hands. "No, no! Shall we start with a proper introduction? You are—?" She pointed at the eldest of the men, a rather flamboyantly dressed fellow.

With a florid bow, he said, "Randal Sylvester, son of Lord Trescowe, at your service, ma'am. These two wastrels are my cousins, Lambert and Digby Sylvester, and the charming lady with the rosy cheeks is Mrs Lambert."

Mama made the introductions for the Fletchers, and with some difficulty persuaded the Sylvesters to sit down again, for all of them showed a distracting inclination to bob up at the least provocation and gambol about the room, speaking with sweeping gestures as if on a stage. They stayed only ten minutes more by the clock, but to Angie, it seemed that a whole hour's worth of information had been poured into her brain in that time. She had learnt about outings to Wells, to Lansdown, to Midford, to Glastonbury Abbey, to Longleat and Badminton and Stanton Drew, and the gloriously named Wookey Hole. She discovered there were breakfasts held in Sydney Gardens, and there would be a gala in August with fireworks and an orchestra to celebrate the birthday of the Prince of Wales.

When the Sylvesters had finally bounced out of the room, they all flopped, exhausted, onto the nearest chair.

"I'm retreating to my office," Pa said firmly. "I need a little peace and quiet, and a very large brandy. Tell Will where I am if he gets back from his courting before dinner. Or at all," he added, half to himself.

The detritus of the visitors had barely been cleared, and the company settled themselves for a long chat with Belinda and Ricky to catch up with Sagborough news, when Bryant returned.

"Lord Albury and the Lady Maria Landers, madam."

After the whirlwind of the Sylvesters, the Landers were an oasis of calm. Lord Albury had impeccable manners, and he now sat between Mama and Aunt Madge making himself agreeable to both, an easy task with Mama, but even Aunt Madge was soon smiling and nodded her approbation of his conversation.

Lady Maria had none of her brother's polish, but Angie and Belinda between them drew her out a little, although she blushed and hung her head often. It would have been better, perhaps, for Rosie to befriend her, for she was shy in company too, but she was absorbed in a long discussion with Ricky, and said little to the visitors.

Lord Albury ended the visit after the correct fifteen minutes, but since Mama had extracted from him the precise times when he accompanied his aunt to the Pump Room each day, it was to be supposed that they would contrive to meet often. She could not suppress her smiles of delight for the rest of the day.

5: Saturday

Saturday brought the Fletchers their first dinner engagement, and everyone was invited, even the Jupps. Mama thought it a little early for new acquaintances to be issuing invitations, but Mr Appleby the Elder would not be denied.

"Why, we regard you quite as family," he cried, when he called to deliver the invitation personally, "when my dear wife is soon to be a sister to Mr Will Fletcher. We do not stand on ceremony with *you*, you may be sure, so we would have you take your pot luck with us as soon as may be, and Saturday is the first day we have available. You will not deny us the pleasure of your company, I am sure, not when we are so looking forward to knowing you all better."

Such good humour must override strict propriety, even for Mama, who decided that *'pot luck'* was sufficiently informal to overcome her scruples. Pa was not quite so keen on a pot luck dinner, for he liked very much to have the soup removed with a good solid roast or two, and plenty of fish and fowl on the table, too, but he disliked to offend anyone offering the hand of friendship. He need not have worried, for the Applebys' idea of a pot luck dinner was rather splendid, the long table filled with dishes, and enough meat even for Pa's appetite.

Angie was not greatly interested in meat, or food of any sort, but she was vastly interested in people. Thus it was a disappointment to find herself sitting next to Eloise's aunt, Mrs Greenwood, whose loud voice and pointed discourse on the matrimonial prospects of everyone as yet unwed were not welcome to many of those present. Her most fevered speculations centred on the presence in Bath of Lord Albury.

"The very man who was so enamoured of your sister, is it not so, Miss Angie? This is very promising, to find him here in Bath after you knew him so well in London town. He's been here a few weeks attending his aunt, but now that he's discovered you, he'll be on your doorstep day and night, I make no doubt of it. There will be a wedding before the summer is out, you mark my words, and what a great match for Miss Rosie — an earl! Well, his father is, and he will be one day."

Poor Rosie, sitting across the table from Mrs Greenwood, not able to say a word yet unable to avoid hearing it all, was in agonies of embarrassment, and only Ricky's efforts to distract her enabled her to maintain her spirits tolerably well. Mama, sitting on the other side of Mrs Greenwood, made valiant attempts to deter her, not because she disagreed with such pleasant speculation but because she thought all public conjecture vulgar.

But Mrs Greenwood would not be deterred. "I never took much notice of Lady Louisa before — quite an invalid, poor soul, and hardly leaves the house except to take the waters, but I must look the family up in Debrett's. Perhaps there is a younger brother for you, Miss Angie, eh? What do you say to that?"

Angie had no interest in marrying the younger son of an earl, or anyone, but she preferred Mrs Greenwood to turn her thoughts in that direction rather than distressing Rosie, so she encouraged this line of thought eagerly. She even invented a lovelorn admirer left behind in Sagborough to excite Mrs Greenwood's tender feelings in a healthier direction. Nor was it so far from the truth, for Angie had not been devoid of admiration, even though she had neither Rosie's looks nor her serene manner.

When, eventually, the lady's attention turned fully on Mama, Angie turned to her other dinner companion, the lugubrious Mr Appleby the Younger, who was not much of a conversationalist but was at least less irritating to the nerves. He was also polite, in a ponderous way.

"Will you have one of these calves' ears, Miss Fletcher? They look most appetising."

"Do you think so? I should sooner have the asparagus, if you can reach the dish over there. This is a lovely house, is it not? Most elegant, although not so fine a prospect as we have at the Royal Crescent."

"Few houses in Bath have so fine a prospect as the Crescent," he said, the asparagus dish suspended in mid-air. "That is one of the sacrifices one makes for the convenience of living in a town, that there is little open space to be enjoyed. However, both this house and my own in Gay Street have gardens that abut the Gravel Walk and Barton's Field, so we may still enjoy the benefits of the country, to a degree."

"Is that why you chose your house in Gay Street, for the proximity to open space?"

His face, always closed and forbidding to Angie's eyes, now took on a positively frosty look, as the asparagus dish lay, forgotten, in his hand. "That house was not my choice, Miss Fletcher. It was, and remains, the property of my uncle. We lived there together in perfect harmony for many years until his marriage two years ago. Now I alone remain."

"Oh, how sad!" Angie cried. "To live alone — how dreadful for you. Have you never thought of marrying, to relieve your loneliness?"

"It is extraordinary to me that a young person such as yourself can think only of matrimony, and cannot conceive that a man may be content with no company but his own. I have no wish to marry, Miss Fletcher."

"That must be a disappointment to the ladies of Bath," she said, unable to resist teasing him a little. "How many hearts have you broken with this resolve to remain a bachelor, sir?"

"None at all, madam, I assure you," he said, with such stiffness that she almost laughed at him. This was fun! She had spent months in London behaving in ladylike ways and not playing any of her little games, but he was too easy a target.

"Oh, but you must have admirers," she said, eyes wide, her tone innocent. "A fine-looking man like you, and a house to live in, as well. There must be any number of ladies setting their caps at you."

He spluttered a little, but answered robustly, "Not one, and I should not care for it if there were."

"For shame, sir! It is ungallant in you to speak so, for just think if some hapless young lady were to fall desperately in love with you, as might easily happen. How romantic that would be! Do not say that you would spurn her out of hand. Surely you would at least take a moment to consider whether your happiness might be improved by an alliance with a devoted and affectionate woman."

He frowned, and if Angie were more timid, she might have quailed as he growled, "No man would be better off allied to a woman so fanciful as to imagine herself in love with him."

"Imagine? You do not believe in love, sir?" she said, astonished. "That is singular indeed!"

His expression softened. "Between a husband and wife, long married, a steady affection is to be desired, certainly, but in persons not yet married, and especially in women, love is a poor guide to matrimonial happiness. One should look rather for similarity of temper, as well as eligibility of rank and wealth."

"How dull that sounds," Angie said, smiling sweetly at him. "Falling head over heels in love must be far more romantic, I should think. For myself, I should far rather choose a husband because I could not bear to live without him than because he was *eligible*. As for similarity of temper — where is the fun in that? I should like a husband I can quarrel with in good earnest from time to time. If he agrees with me on every question, I should be bored with him within a twelve month."

"You are only proving my point, and very thoroughly," he said, stabbing the air with a free finger. "Young ladies think far too much of love, in my opinion. It is no wonder, I suppose, since your heads are filled with all manner of nonsense, and your days are filled with gaiety. I would guess that your only reading is of novels."

"Oh, no, you are quite wrong," Angie said, innocently. "I read any number of other things — *La Belle Assemblée,* the *Lady's Magazine—"*

"Precisely," he said triumphantly. "Not a serious book opened from one year's end to the next, I dare say. If all young ladies would undertake a course of improving reading, and accept the judgement of their fathers as to the most suitable husband, they would be a great deal happier."

At this point, Angie caught her father's eye. He raised one eyebrow at her, as if to say, *'No games, Miss Mischief'*. Sighing, she supposed he was right. Mr Appleby was a worthy man, even if all his disapproving talk of *'young ladies'* made him sound just like Great-uncle Rowley in his dotage. It was cruel to tease him so... and yet... so very, *very* tempting.

"Do set the calves' ears down, Mr Appleby. It is like to spill if you hold it at an angle like that."

"Oh... oh yes." Then he looked at the dish in bewilderment. "Calves' ears?"

"You very kindly procured the dish for me, if you remember," Angie said, with her most innocent expression. Would he be convinced? It was a trick she had played on any number of eager young men, distracted by her attention. A very little flirtation was sufficient to make most men forget what they were doing.

Mr Appleby the Younger was not such a man. "Asparagus. You asked for asparagus, Miss Fletcher."

"Did I? Are you sure?"

"Quite sure. Do you want some or not?"

She sighed. There was no amusement to be had with a man who was so unaffected by a little — a *very* little — flirtation. He had not a romantic bone in his body. "Thank you, but no. I have sufficed, I believe. Mrs Appleby has provided us with a magnificent dinner."

He glared at her, before replacing the asparagus dish carefully back in its proper place on the table, adjusting its position minutely to line up with its neighbour, and then turning pointedly towards Eloise on his other side.

It was a relief when the ladies withdrew to the drawing room. Angie loitered hopefully near the pianoforte, leafing through the music. It was a fine instrument, and new, as every item of furniture in the house seemed to be, and she longed to play it, looking up eagerly when Mrs Appleby approached her with her ready smile.

"We shall have some music later, perhaps, but there is still too much conversation for anyone to attend to the instrument. Shall we sit down?" She gestured to a pair of chairs set at a little remove from the others. Rather surprised, Angie sat.

"Miss Fletcher," she began in an undertone, "may I ask you... a question?"

"Of course."

"Did you... were you... is it possible that you encountered my father in town?"

"Mr Jeremy Whittleton? I did, yes."

"Oh." Her eyes widened. "Because Eloise will say very little about it except that... he is married again, and I should very much like to know something more. He has been abroad for so many years that we have quite lost touch."

"I am not sure what I might tell you in addition, for I know very little about it," Angie said warily. "His appearance quite overset Eloise, that much I know, and she is so imperturbable as a rule."

"Oh yes! No warning, and he had been gone for so long — thirteen years! It is no wonder she was surprised. But his new wife — did he say aught of her? How they met, for instance? It must have been so romantic!"

Angie floundered. How could she say what she knew to be the truth, that Mr Jeremy Whittleton had abandoned his wife and young family to run away with his mistress? He had only returned now because his first wife, mother to Eloise and Calantha, had died and left him free to marry his mistress and return to society. Cautiously, she said, "I never spoke to him myself, Mrs Appleby."

"Oh, what a pity," Mrs Appleby said. "But will you not call me Calantha? We are to be sisters very soon, are we not? I know Eloise is talking of an early marriage to your brother. May I call you Angie? Eloise told us so much of you in her letters from London that I feel I know you intimately already. Shall we have some music now?"

~~~~~

B sipped his port, watching the other gentlemen clustered at one end of the Applebys' long dining table. Will Fletcher had taken the seat beside Uncle Maurice, and the two were talking animatedly about horses — Fletcher hoped to hunt during the autumn and was planning to buy a string of hunters. Uncle Maurice had never hunted, but he held strong opinions about horseflesh, so it was a subject which enlivened him.

Across the table, Jupp the apothecary and the elder Mr Fletcher were talking of their home town in Sagborough, with the easy camaraderie of old friends. Jupp's father hoped to be elected mayor, seemingly, and the conversation centred on his prospects and the support or otherwise of people B had never met, and was
~~~~~

unlikely ever to meet.

With no interest in either conversation, B's thoughts could roam at will, and for some unfathomable reason, they drifted towards the person of Miss Angela Fletcher. Something about her irritated him intensely, although he could not say what. Or *why*, which was more to the point. She was pretty, of course, with hair that framed her face in gentle curls, bright eyes that sparkled with animation, and lips... oh, her lips! He could imagine that many men would be driven to the brink of insanity by such luscious lips. It was fortunate, then, that he was unaffected by such fleshly considerations. *Entirely* unaffected. Not affected in the slightest.

"... pleasant, whatever they are. Mr Appleby, sir?"

B jumped. The elder Fletcher was smiling at him from across the table. "You are addressing me, sir?"

"I was. I remarked upon your state of abstraction, although it seemed to me from your expression that, whatever the cause of your ruminations, it must be something very pleasant."

"Far from it, I assure you," he snapped. Then, because he could not quite shake his thoughts into other channels, he said, "Your daughter has some odd ideas, sir, but then she is very young, still. One cannot expect wisdom in such very young ladies."

"Angie, you mean? Aye, she's but eighteen, and declared herself too old for the schoolroom three years ago. I worried about her then, you may be sure, for she's a romantic child and I feared she would entangle herself with someone unsuitable, and be desperate to marry him. But she's given me no cause for alarm in that way."

"She's like Rosie — they both love to dance too much to want to marry," Jupp said.

"I do not see the connection," B said.

"Why, a married woman has no reason to dance," Jupp said, smiling. "Her place is amongst the matrons. Rosie and Angie both adore dancing, and won't willingly give it up."

For a moment, B rather envied Jupp. He was the sort of cheerful fellow who made friends wherever he went, with his good looks and easy confidence. As an apothecary, he was not only making a living but was able to do some good. He had his settled place in the world, which B had not.

"Then they are typical of young women, in preferring the frivolous over more worthwhile pursuits."

"Let them enjoy themselves while they may," Fletcher said, with a slight shrug. "They will settle down soon enough once they have families of their own to worry about. I love to see them happy, and dancing is a respectable activity, after all. I dare say you enjoy a dance yourself, Mr Appleby."

"Indeed, I do not. I prefer less energetic pursuits — reading aloud, logical debate, chess or other games of skill."

"You'd get on well with my other son, Johnny," Fletcher said. "He's an intellectual, too, although he likes to dance as well as study, and he rides and shoots and all those other gentlemanly pursuits. Do you enjoy such activities, sir?"

"I have no need for them, not here in Bath," B said. "I can buy all the game and fish I require. Nor do I often ride, for I keep no horse."

"Then how do you take your exercise, sir?" said Jupp. "I neither shoot nor fish, but I should be lost without my horse, and as for dancing, what could be finer? For is it not an enterprise that may be enjoyed by men and women together? There is nothing so grand as an assembly, with the females in all their finery and partners enough for everyone who wants one."

"I had far sooner stay at home with a book," B said. "Assemblies and balls are nothing but excuses for a man to make a spectacle of himself. In young women, such a display of graceful feminine charms is accepted, but in a man it is undignified."

Jupp actually laughed at him. "You talk about young women as if you're not young yourself, Mr Appleby. You can't be much older than I am, and I'm twenty-five."

"I am eight and twenty," B said with dignity.

"Eight and twenty, and preferring a book to a ball," Jupp said, shaking his head. "You poor, poor fellow."

B disliked intensely having his habits jeered at in this way, but he disliked an argument even more, so he made no response and the conversation around them shifted into other channels.

Eventually, Uncle Maurice rose to join the ladies. Music drifted down from the drawing room as they ascended the stairs, and he recognised Eloise's sweet, clear voice. Well, music would be better than the provoking conversation of the dining room.

As soon as they entered the drawing room, Uncle Maurice bounced across to his wife, and before B could even sigh in resignation, the cry of, "Dancing! We must have dancing!" went up from them and was taken up generally. Mrs Fletcher offered to play for the dancers, and the footmen set to with a will to move furniture and roll up the carpets. And that was the end of all rational discourse.

"Shall we play whist?" Mrs Greenwood said briskly. "Miss Paton, Mr Fletcher, may I entice you to join me? Mr Appleby, I am sure you will oblige us, for I know you do not dance."

"Of course, ma'am," B said politely, himself fetching the card table and opening it out, while Mr Fletcher gathered chairs.

Mrs Greenwood moved a candelabrum nearer, and sat down, the cards in her hand. "Penny points, everyone?"

"As you wish, madam," Mr Fletcher said, holding a chair for Miss Paton.

It was a tedious end to a dull evening. But in the pause between games, as Miss Paton was shuffling, B happened to glance across at the dancers. It was only a simple country dance, such as might be enjoyed by any group of farmers gathered to celebrate the harvest or a wedding. The dancers were energetic, laughing and bouncing their way through the movements.

But one was different. He could not quite say how, except that there was an air in her movements, in the graceful way she held her arms and head, in the suppleness and delicacy with which she danced. And her expression! Her very face exuded an unearthly serenity as she moved. It was as if she were in some other place altogether, had become one with the music. He had never seen anything like it. When the evening ended, he stumbled home in the dark, his head filled with her ethereal form.

Miss Angie Fletcher. Angela. An angel in very truth. But only when she danced. By the time he had reached his house and let himself in, he had reminded himself sternly of all her multitude of faults, and was satisfactorily out of charity with her once more.

6: Sunday

Angie woke to a still silent house. It was daylight, but Rosie and Belinda were still fast asleep beside her in the big bed, and there was no sign of the servants yet.

Restlessly, she slid out of bed and went to the window, gazing out over the garden to the coach house and beyond it, to gently smoking chimneys and distant hills. She was always fidgety the morning after an impromptu dance. A ball, which often lasted until three or four in the morning, was enough to exhaust her, but a few informal dances, and especially one with insufficient gentlemen, so that she had to sit out every other dance, left her still lively and fizzing with energy. She knew that she would not sleep again, but nor could she sit quietly waiting for Rosie and Belinda to wake up. She had to do something! She could not venture downstairs to the drawing room where the servants might discover her, but there was a secret place...

Creeping across the room, she carefully turned the knob to open the door, and slipped out onto the landing. Up the stairs on the half-landing was the little room she had discovered before, a maid's room once, perhaps, but now a lumber room. But when she opened the door, she found the room transformed. The old furniture and hat boxes had gone, replaced by a narrow bed, a small table and chair set in front of the window and a press squeezed in behind the door. Only the faded chaise longue remained from the original furnishings.

Angie was enchanted, for now there was space to move... to dance! It was not a large room, but she did not need a ballroom for her movements. A few feet, that was all she needed for her steps, and clear air to raise her arms. Music rose unbidden in her head, and so she danced, utterly absorbed, until she heard Lester's heavy tread going up the stairs, taking Will his washing water. Soon after, Sarah knocked at the sisters' bedroom door below. Time to start the daily round, although today would be a little different, for it was Sunday.

The Fletchers walked to St Swithin's church, where they could use the pew paid for by the Audleys, who owned the Royal Crescent house. Their numbers were smaller than expected because Will had gone to escort Eloise and Mrs Greenwood, and Aunt Madge had one of her sick headaches. It was curious how often these occurred on a Sunday morning.

The procession that set out from the Royal Crescent was rather an odd one. Pa and Mama walked in front, naturally, and then Ricky, with Rosie on one arm and Belinda on the other, chattering away. Rosie had offered to walk with Angie, but she had no wish to break up such a happy group, so she walked behind them alone and a little forlorn. With no other sister to walk beside her, and neither of her brothers bringing up the rear, she felt oddly exposed. Even the servants had gone ahead of them. Still, the walk was a pleasant one, despite this, for the sun was shining, lighting up the warmth of the Bath stone, and Angie was filled with happiness after her dancing and could not be downhearted.

St Swithin's was a fine new church, their pew a good one and they had the pleasure of nodding to several acquaintances. The sermon was a little too long for a girl so active as Angie, but eventually the congregation was released into the sunshine again, falling into chattering groups, as friends caught up with a week's news. There were smiles all round, except from Mr Appleby the Younger, who wore his usual unsmiling countenance as he passed Angie by.

"Why does he disapprove of me so?" Angie said in an undertone to Eloise, who stood beside her.

"He disapproves of all women," she replied in the same low tone. "Young women in particular. He thinks we are all flighty and unreliable, but then he has some cause to think so."

"Oh?" Angie was deeply curious, but hardly liked to ask directly. Happily, Eloise was ready to divulge every detail.

"Did you know that he was his uncle's heir for many years? The elder Mr Appleby had never wished to marry, and so when his nephew fell to his care, he decided to make him his heir and raised him thus, from the age of eight. The nephew was therefore brought up to be a gentleman, undertaking the usual forms of education but taking no profession. He was regarded as one of Bath's most eligible bachelors, for his uncle is a very wealthy man, and in time there was an understanding with a young lady. It was not quite a betrothal, but it was certainly an accepted thing that one day the uncle would settle some money on his nephew directly and they would wed.

"But then we arrived — Calantha and I and our mama, to live with Mrs Greenwood. Maurice — the elder Mr Appleby, that is — flirted with Calantha, as he flirted with every pretty young lady, and we all thought it would fizzle out in time. Calantha assured the younger Mr Appleby that she had no designs on his uncle. But then... well, you know how that story ends."

"Indeed. But it was — it *is* — a love match, is it not?"

"Oh yes. They fell very much in love, and there was not a thought given to poor Mr Barry Appleby. Within a year, the baby arrived, and he lost his inheritance and then his future wife."

"His young lady abandoned him? Just because he had less money? That is despicable! She could not have cared very deeply for him if she could behave so callously."

"For myself, I do not blame *her*, for they could not live on nothing. It is Maurice whom I blame. He is the one who has left his nephew penniless, after all. He is rich enough to set him up in a profession, but he has done nothing. Mr Barry has taken Holy Orders, but he has no living or prospect of one, and so he waits. If he were a different sort of man, he would either set out on the path to independence for himself, or he would find an heiress... your sister, perhaps. Or you, come to that. But instead he continues just as he always has, drifting along, as if he is waiting for something to happen to him. And maybe it will, if he waits long enough."

Angie was filled with compassion for poor Mr Appleby the Younger, who had lost all his expectations and must now make his own way in the world. No wonder he looked so unfriendly sometimes, and especially with young ladies. Anybody would be cross who had been treated so barbarously, and by his own uncle. To have been heir to a great fortune, and betrothed, or nearly so, and to have it all snatched away from him. It was like having a ball promised and then denied — possibly even worse. Angie could not quite imagine any vexation so great as the deprivation of a promised ball, but she conceded that losing all a man's prospects might be almost as bad. Poor, poor Mr Appleby!

The man himself sidled up to them. "Sunday school, Miss Whittleton? Or are you too busy just now with your wedding plans for such activities?"

"I am looking forward to it," Eloise said.

"You have a Sunday school here, Mr Appleby?" Angie said. "We had one in Sagborough, too. It is a splendid idea, and generous of you to teach the children to read and write."

"We teach the *boys* to read and write," he said loftily. "The girls have no need of penmanship. The ladies teach them sewing and other useful skills."

"No need?" Angie said. "Whatever makes you think they have no need?"

"Because they will either go into service or they will marry. In either case, they will be told what they have to do, and will have no occasion to read or write."

"If a girl goes into service knowing such skills, then she has the possibility to rise to a high level — housekeeper, perhaps, or cook in a large household. An illiterate girl cannot do so."

"She may be taught, if she is in a position to rise so far," he said, "but a scullery maid can have no possible need to read or write."

"How is she to write home to her family?"

"Why, she may ask one of the senior servants to write on her behalf, naturally," he said.

"How can she read the Holy Bible or the Prayer Book?"

"She may listen as it is read to her, or learn the words by rote in church, as has been done since time immemorial."

"You have an answer to everything, but that does not make you right, sir!" Angie said stoutly. "Girls are entitled to learn to read and write if they wish just as much as boys, and nothing you say will convince me otherwise. A person, be she ever so humble, may aspire to better herself if she has access to books and newspapers. At the very least, she cannot be imposed upon if she is able to read, and if she marries, she may help her husband with his work and teach her own children, so that they, in their turn, may improve their lot in life. I see no disadvantage to the idea of every child learning to read and write and understand basic arithmetic."

"The purpose of education is solely to fit the recipient for his or her position in society," Mr Appleby said with unimpaired assurance. "A labourer's son may aspire to a trade and a tradesman's son may aspire to commerce, so a modest degree of education confers some benefit, but a working man's daughter will never be anything other than a servant, or a wife and mother, and will not aspire to a future which requires education. For the higher ranks, a broader education is necessary. A gentleman must manage his estates, and a lady must not only manage her household and family, but must also be a support to her husband's rôle in society. That is why every young lady should devote some time to serious study, and not give herself wholly to frivolity." He looked directly at Angie as he spoke. "I shall see you within, Miss Whittleton. I dare say you will not wish to be bothered with the Sunday school, Miss Fletcher."

"I should be delighted to help," Angie said, piqued at this glib dismissal. Only when he had moved away did she curse her unruly tongue. "Hmm. How long is Sunday school?"

"Two hours, but there is a half hour for breakfast as well."

"Oh, well, at least I shall not miss breakfast," Angie said disconsolately. "And perhaps I shall improve my standing with Mr Appleby by helping. Goodness, he is severe upon us, is he not? My life is not *wholly* given over to frivolity, is it?"

But when she told Pa and Mama she planned to stay, Mama seemed to echo Mr Appleby's, asserting that it would be good for her to channel her thoughts into a more serious direction.

"Your head has been filled with gaiety and amusement these last few months, Angie," she said. "A little effort put into helping those less fortunate than yourself will not go amiss. When you marry, you will be expected to set the example in your parish. Now, do not be pulling a face like that. You will marry soon enough, once Rosie is settled, but only when you have set aside a certain degree of... oh, shall we say levity that characterises your attitude. Life is not a game, Angie, and soon enough you must apply yourself to making an eligible match. Now that we are moving in a higher level of society, you will meet any number of suitable young men."

"That sounds very dull," Angie said.

Mama laughed. "It is not in the least dull to have your own establishment, I assure you, and enjoy all the respectability of the married state. I know you have a romantic turn of mind, but do not despise the practicality of having enough money to live upon. Poverty is most unpleasant, I can tell you, so be sure to do nothing which might give a gentleman a disgust of you. Which reminds me, Rosie tells me you were not in your bedroom when she awoke. This creeping about the house at all hours will not do, you know."

"I only went into the little room on the half-landing," Angie said. "Such a sweet little room, and all fitted up as a bedroom now. May I have it for myself, now that Rosie has Belinda to keep her company?"

"That room is intended for Johnny, whenever he arrives from Cambridge."

"Johnny can share with me," Will said, overhearing this exchange. "It is what I am used to, and I shall like to have his company these last weeks before I marry. Let Angie have that room, Stepmother, so that she can plot her mischief in secret."

"That is precisely what I am afraid of," Mama said, but Will only laughed and grudgingly Mama agreed that the room might be Angie's.

Sunday school was rather fun, Angie found. The girls, almost twenty in all, sat in two pews at one end of the church, arranged by age, with aprons or shirts to sew, woollen waistcoats to knit, or hose to darn, according to their abilities, all while they listened to improving sermons suitable for females. It might have been boring, but under cover of the sermonising, a great deal of whispering went on as the girls talked to each other, or to the ladies instructing them. Mrs Gravestock, one of the ladies who helped the Sunday school, had a daughter who was simple-minded and talked constantly in a low murmur, so whenever one of the gentlemen helping with the boys at the other end of the church called out, "Too much chatter, Mrs Gravestock," she would trill back, "Beg pardon, sir, but 'tis only Rebecca." And whoever was reading the sermons would speak a little louder, the better to cover the whispers.

Occasionally, Angie glanced across to where the boys sat, and although the boys themselves could not be seen above the pew walls, she could see Mr Appleby and several other gentlemen, as they instructed the boys. Sometimes, when there was a lull in the girlish chatter around her, she could hear the low rumble of the men, or the higher voices of the boys, reciting their lessons.

Once she was sent to make an enquiry of Mr Appleby, and as she approached the pew, she saw with astonishment his face wreathed in smiles as he talked to the boys around him. Why, he was a handsome fellow indeed when he looked so, and so much less forbidding! But then he became aware of her approach, and as he looked up at her, his expression changed to something more serious — not hostility, perhaps, but there was a certain wariness in his face.

"Yes, Miss Fletcher?"

"We have finished the sermon you set, sir, and Mrs Gravestock would like to know what we are to read next, if you please."

His gaze raked her up and down momentarily. "*'On Modesty of Apparel'*, Miss Fletcher."

"Very good, sir."

She curtsied demurely, and returned to the girls' pews, but inwardly she seethed. How dared he criticise the clothes she wore, which were perfectly modest, for she had no garments that were otherwise. Mama would not allow it, for she was most particular about such matters.

"Rosie may wear evening gowns a little more revealing, for she is six years older than you," Mama had said, "but you are only eighteen and your watchword must be modesty in all things,

Angie, until you are up to snuff in society."

Modesty in all things. So there was nothing for Mr Pompous Appleby to complain about. No, his Christian name began with a B. Mr Boring Appleby. Bombastic. Barbarous. Black-hearted. Block-headed. Bigoted. Bothersome... yes, definitely that. Although why he should bother her at all was a mystery.

After an hour, everything stopped for breakfast. The children were given bread and cheese to eat in their pews, watched over by Mr Appleby, while all the other adults repaired to the parsonage for a somewhat more substantial repast.

"You are very quiet," Eloise murmured to Angie after a while. "Are you regretting offering to help?"

"Mmm? Oh... no, not at all. I am trying to make out Mr Appleby's character, that is all, for I find him confusing. He seems to dote upon the boys, yet has no time for females at all. That cannot all be set down to a single unfortunate experience. There must be some deep-rooted dislike of the female sex, to produce such decided opinions."

"To my mind, there is nothing more to it than an unfamiliarity with females," Eloise said. "His mother died when he was born, and his uncle's was a bachelor household for many years, so he has never gained that comfortable state of amity with females that one acquires from sisters or aunts or cousins. He is uneasy with women, particularly young, pretty ones, like you. And like Calantha, I should add. With me, he has never been quite so prickly, for I am not pretty enough to threaten his peace of mind."

Angie pondered this, and decided it made sense. "But however did he become betrothed — or almost so?"

Eloise laughed. "That is a good question, which has puzzled me greatly. According to Aunt Beth, when he was seen as his uncle's heir, he attracted women as a candle draws moths, all vying for his attention. There was one in particular, a Miss Meek, although she was not at all meek, to my mind. Very pert, she was. No one quite knows how it came about, but it was accepted that they would one day wed, although she would not push matters any further without some settlement from his uncle. And so, when Calantha put the inheritance out of Barry's reach, the lady drifted away from him and married elsewhere."

"How horrid for him! I almost feel sorry for him, except that he dislikes females so. Is there no female of whom he thinks well?"

"None of the young ones," Eloise said, smiling. "He is more respectful of older women."

"He has been thwarted in love, and now he resents all young women," Angie said. "And yet, if he could but fall in love again, think how much improved his life would be! He could not be bitter if he had a lover. He told me he had no wish for admirers but surely in such a case he would be longing for *one* such, at least. I wonder if—"

Eloise raised her eyebrows. "Angie? You are not dreaming up any mischief, are you? You have something of a reputation for it, I know."

"Has Will been telling tales of me? How disloyal in a brother!" Angie said, laughing. "What has he said of me?"

"His exact words were, *'She has been abnormally docile in town, so watch out when she gets to Bath, for there is bound to be an outbreak of trouble.'* Is there any truth in it?"

"That I was abnormally docile in town? Oh yes! But Mama impressed upon us the importance of not getting into any trouble that would reflect badly on Rosie, so I was very good, I assure you. Besides, we were dancing almost every night and what could be more delicious? If I had so much as scratched my nose the wrong way, Mama would have sent me home, and that I could not have borne! But here... it is difficult. I am easily bored, that is the trouble, and then I start scheming to amuse myself."

"So long as your scheming does not adversely affect anyone else, I see no harm in it, but I would not have you tease poor Mr Barry Appleby. He is too serious a man to take such interference lightly, and might be offended by it. Better to turn your talents in a more receptive direction — Mr Randal Sylvester, perhaps? He was watching you in church, I noticed."

"Was he?" Angie said.

But she was not much interested in Mr Randal Sylvester, for her thoughts were bent in a different direction. It was tricky, to be sure. How on earth was she to make Mr Barry Appleby fall in love? Not with her — heavens, no! But there must be someone who would attract him, and think how much happier he would be! He was so sad, and she could not bear anyone to be sad, not if she could do anything to cheer him up. If he could be just a little bit in love, how different he would be. It was a charming idea, and she would find a way, of that much she was certain.

7: Escort

B had patronised the same tailor for twenty years, ever since he had first arrived in Bath and his uncle had taken him to be measured. Every year since, he had gone there in spring to be fitted for three new coats, one for day wear, one for evening and one for Sunday, and the same in autumn, with the addition of a greatcoat. His uncle had long since moved on to a younger, more fashionable man, but B liked old Mr Hartup. He trusted him to provide just what he wanted, with no attempt to squeeze him into some outlandishly fashionable and uncomfortable style, or to embellish a plain coat with garish buttons or unnecessary furbelows. When, in the fullness of time, old Mr Hartup should retire, or perhaps drop down dead at his sewing table one day, needle in hand, his son, young Mr Hartup, could be trusted to continue in precisely the same manner.

A tear in the sleeve of a favourite coat had brought B to Mr Hartup that morning, and although he could have sent his manservant to attend to the matter, he was suffering from an unaccustomed outbreak of uncertainty, and he knew that Mr Hartup would settle his mind, as he always did.

"Do you think I look like an attorney?" B said, eyeing himself in a full-length mirror.

"Not at all, sir," Hartup said politely, looking up from an examination of the torn sleeve. "You look like a gentleman. I should not allow any of my customers to look otherwise."

"No, of course you would not, but black is such a dull colour, is it not? And it is so frequently worn by attorneys and others of similar ilk."

"And men in Holy orders, sir, such as yourself," Hartup said. "It is also reputed to be the choice of arbiters of style, such as Mr Brummell." He looked speculatively at B. "However, Mr Brummell also favours a range of other colours — all tastefully dark, but perhaps not quite so..."

"Drab?" B said.

"Not that, no indeed, sir," Hartup said quickly. "Black is a most distinguished colour in a material of superior quality, but rather *prosaic*. A little colour elevates a gentleman's attire above the ordinary, in my view, and when combined with a waistcoat of some contrasting shade, imbues the wearer with a most refined presence, sure to draw admiration."

"Hmm. I should not wish to look like a dandy," B said.

"No, indeed, sir," Hartup said soothingly. "Happily, your innate good taste will always prevent such an outcome. If I may perhaps show you a most desirable superfine in a very tasteful shade of bottle green, most appealing, and, if I may say so, very flattering to a gentleman with so fine a complexion as yours. It is not everyone who could wear such a colour to advantage, but you, sir, I venture to suggest, are one of the few."

B was not immune to such flattery, and even though he knew

the man to be buttering him up to make a sale, he allowed himself to succumb. What harm could it do? A single new coat, and the lightly embroidered waistcoat he was persuaded to order with it, was not so very radical. He could afford it. He still had his uncle's very generous allowance to live on, and his expenses were few. One day, if ever he were to obtain preferment in the church, he would have only his tithes to live upon and would have to practise greater economy, but for now, money was not in short supply.

Outside the shop, his mind still on his new purchase, he walked round the corner into George Street and ran smash into Mr Fletcher with his irritating daughter. The daughter who may not be angelic in other ways, but danced bewitchingly like an angel, a small voice in his brain reminded him.

Fletcher only laughed at the collision. "My goodness, Mr Appleby, you are in a great rush today. Where are you off to in such a hurry?"

"Mr Fletcher. Miss Fletcher. My profound apologies. I was not attending to my surroundings as I ought. As to where I am bound… not the Abbey today, so the Pump Room is next on my itinerary."

"Do you always visit the same places in the same sequence?" Miss Angela said.

"As far as possible, yes. It is logical."

"So you would never do anything on impulse?"

Having just impulsively ordered a new coat and waistcoat in the middle of summer, and not in his habitual black, B could not honestly answer in the affirmative, but nor did he wish to admit to such rashness before that young lady, whose expression might be innocent but who he was sure was trying to provoke him. Fortunately, he was not obliged to answer her.

"Now, flower, don't tease Mr Appleby," Fletcher said. "Take no notice of her, sir, if you please, for she will tie your tongue in knots if you let her. We will not delay your plans, for if you would but direct us to a reputable supplier of books and periodicals, then you may be on your way with no further hindrance."

"A bookseller? I most often obtain my requirements from Quarman's, just a short distance from here. Why, you might even see the door from here — the blue one with the engraved arch above it, do you see it? Pray allow me to escort you there, sir, and introduce you to Mr Quarman himself, for I fancy you will receive every attention from him once you are known to be an acquaintance of mine."

"That is uncommonly good of you, Appleby," Fletcher said.

B threaded his way through the crowds thronging the pavement and across George Street to Quarman's door. The shop was one of the largest in Bath, housing an extensive circulating library with all the latest books, journals and newspapers, as well as such supplies as might be needed by those inclined to write letters or accounts or even music. It was, perhaps, his favourite place in all of Bath, after the Abbey and his own church, for it boasted myriad dark corners where a man of unsociable but bookish disposition might hide himself away for hours at a time. It was no inconvenience to him to introduce the Fletchers to Mr Quarman, and to show them all the offerings of the establishment.

Fletcher was soon making enquiries of Mr Quarman on the subject of interest to him — something to do with reservoirs and water pipes, of all things — so B found himself with only Miss Angie in his train. She was pleasingly interested, however, and made no provocative comment when he took her to the mercifully small section that housed novels.

"I suppose this is where you will obtain your reading matter," he said.

"Not at all," she said, smiling up at him. What a trusting smile she had! "I rarely read a book of any sort, but when I do, it is generally poetry."

He could feel his eyebrows rise. "Poetry?"

"Oh yes! So romantic, poetry, is it not?" She heaved a sigh of pleasure. "So much *sensibility* in a single word or a particularly felicitous phrase." Before he could deal with this most misguided opinion as it deserved, her mind flitted away, as the female mind was wont to do. "This is a very dark and gloomy place. What is the especial attraction that makes this particular circulating library superior to any others? Is it the largest?"

"It is one of the largest," he said, with punctilious correctness. "Also it has a greater than average catalogue of more serious tomes."

"Fewer novels and volumes of poetry, I collect," she said, gazing up at him with wide eyes. She looked so innocent, and yet he was sure she was not to be trusted. Why, even her father had said as much.

"Certainly fewer novels," he said. "Poetry... there is much to be said in favour of poetry, in some cases. But the unique feature of Quarman's is just in this small room here. Do you see these shelves of boxes? A resident of Bath who subscribes here may also subscribe to his own personal box, as I do. This is my box here." He laid a proprietorial hand on its polished wooden surface. At the front, a card with his name and address was tucked into a brass holder. "Any book I wish to borrow I may place in here, and it will be wrapped and delivered to my house the same day. It is such a convenience not to have to wait at the counter to be attended to, or to carry my acquisitions with me. Also, any book or journal which I have ordered may be sent to me the day it arrives. Ah, there is your father. Let me return you to his care."

But he found that Mr Fletcher was by no means ready to leave the interesting volumes he had discovered. "I wonder, Appleby... hmm, it's an imposition, I know, but since Angie's been wanting to meet her friends at the Pump Room long since, and you're bound that way yourself...?"

"Of course. I should be delighted to escort Miss Fletcher."

A flash of something — irritation, perhaps? — crossed her face, but she instantly recovered. "How kind of you, sir," she murmured, eyes demurely downcast.

She refused the proffered arm, as he had expected, but she walked at a steady pace, not dawdling as so many women did, so it was no hindrance to have her beside him. She was pleasingly silent, too, as they made their way down Milsom Street, clearly feeling no need for conversation. Oddly, she hummed a little as she walked, so low as to be almost inaudible, and her manner of walking was an up and down motion on the balls of her feet, almost as if she were dancing. Perhaps she was humming along to herself in her head, her steps as graceful and elegant as if she were in a ballroom.

He was struck with a most peculiar desire to see her dance again, dancing *properly*, with her slender arms raised, her delicate fingers perfectly positioned. So many young ladies looked like circus elephants when they danced, and although they had clearly been taught the correct movements, they executed them without any true feeling for the dance. It was the company, indeed the proximity, of young men which energised them, whereas Miss Angie Fletcher simply enjoyed the dance for its own sake.

It was an illuminating insight into her character, and it was some minutes before he reminded himself sternly that she was just another frivolous young woman, no matter how beautifully she danced, and he should beware of giving her any attention beyond the calls of politeness.

~~~~~

Angie was glad to reach the Pump Room, to be free of the stern-faced Mr Appleby who looked at her so disapprovingly. But a glance around the room brought home the unwelcome fact that there was no one of her acquaintance present. Mr Appleby, who was sadly punctilious in such matters, insisted on staying with her until her friends should arrive. To avoid sitting with him, which might look rather particular, Angie walked about the room, following the general direction of the other promenaders, but Mr Appleby strode beside her, matching her pace precisely. If her steps slowed down, so did his. If she sped up, so did he. It was like nothing so much as being followed by a persistent fly which would not be swatted away.

"Do you not wish to partake of your usual glass of water, Mr Appleby?" she enquired, in dulcet tones. "I am quite content to walk alone while you do so."

"That is very thoughtful of you, Miss Fletcher, but there will be time enough for that when I have handed you into the care of
~~~~~

your friends. Your father has charged me with your protection, and I would not wish to appear derelict in that pleasant duty."

His solemn expression conveyed no pleasure in it, but she could not fault his politeness.

After a while, he said in unusually gentle tones, "Should you care to sit beneath the gallery and listen to the music, Miss Fletcher?"

"Why do you suggest such a thing? Do you believe me to be tiring, for if so, I assure you I am not in the least tired."

"I suggest it because on our last two circuits, you have slowed almost to a halt near the musicians. It occurred to me that, until your friends arrive, the music is the greatest attraction for you in the room."

His tone was unexpectedly friendly, but she read reproof into his words, nevertheless. Was he telling her she was neglecting him by not speaking? Or — a more realistic thought, perhaps — that he wished to deposit her on a bench so he could pursue his own interests? In her reply, she chose her words carefully. "When I am alone, I do like to sit near the musicians, it is true, so that I may enjoy the music while I watch the company go by. I should be very happy to do so today, so that you may go and talk to your friends."

He almost smiled. "May I confess, Miss Fletcher, that there is no one here to whom I particularly wish to talk."

"No one?" She was astonished. "But you must know everyone in Bath, all the residents, anyway. You surely know most of the people here today. Indeed you do, for you have been acknowledging them as we pass by."

"Yes, but I have no desire to talk to them. *'How are you, sir, since I saw you yesterday? And will it rain today, do you think? Do you go to the colonel's card party tonight?'* And the next day, exactly the same again, except a different card party."

She smiled a little, but said, "The words may be the same, sir, but in the people themselves there is always some change that is of interest."

"Is there? A lady might have a new bonnet, you mean? You follow the fashions, I believe."

"Oh, as to that... the bonnet itself may or may not be interesting. It is *why* she wears a new bonnet that intrigues me. Is there a new sparkle in her eye? Then perhaps she is falling in love. Or is she sad? Perhaps the bonnet is to cheer herself after a disappointment. You see? It is the story behind the bonnet that is interesting. And now you may tell me that it is just romantic nonsense, Mr Appleby, and I should bend my mind to more serious pursuits. You would be quite right, of course, but I find people so endlessly fascinating."

To her surprise, he did not chastise her for her frivolity. He even smiled a little, looking far less forbidding. "And are your insights accurate? If you notice a sparkle in a lady's eye and suspect an attachment, do you later discover that you were quite right?"

"Ah, I am very sorry you asked me that, for now I must confess that I am almost invariably wrong. I had no idea that Will was falling in love with Eloise, for example, and to be fair, they did not behave at all in a lover-like manner. In fact, they acted at all times as if they disliked each other most cordially, and then they astonished everyone by becoming betrothed, and then they astonished everyone even more by unbetrothing themselves. And now they are betrothed again and deep in love and I cannot make head or tail of it, I assure you. So if ever I say to you that a certain lady has a new bonnet and must therefore be in love, you may be quite confident that it is nothing of the sort."

She half expected some admonishment from him, but instead he answered her seriously. "Even if you are sometimes wrong... or often wrong, it is an interesting point you make, that by observing such seemingly trivial changes in a person's outer appearance, one might detect an inner change also."

To Angie, a new bonnet was by no means a trivial matter, but she chose not to argue the point, merely saying, "Do you not choose your garments according to your current disposition? I certainly do. After the sobriety of Sunday, I always like to wear something colourful on Mondays. And sometimes, if I am a little down for any reason, I wear something bright and pretty to cheer myself up. But of course, you always wear the same colour, do not you? That must make it a great deal easier to decide what to wear. Oh look, there is Lord Albury with Lady Maria! Should I wave? Oh, they have seen us."

There was no sign today of the elderly lady in the sedan chair, only the two young people. Lady Maria smiled widely at Angie as they approached.

"Miss Fletcher, how glad I am to see you today!" she cried. "It is so awkward knowing no one, do you not think? At least..." She blushed suddenly. "Knowing no one of my own age, I mean, for naturally we have a great many acquaintances in Bath, but all friends of Aunt Louisa's, you see. Are your family not with you? There is no indisposition, I hope? But *you* are well, I can see! How lovely you look today. I think the Bath air agrees with you. Have you visited the baths yet? That is where Aunt Louisa has gone today. Every Monday she immerses herself in the Abbey Baths, which she says eases her pains wonderfully although I have not noticed any improvement myself."

"Very good, Maria," her brother murmured. "Miss Fletcher, you cannot appreciate how beneficial an effect you and your family have had on Maria, who is become quite fluent these days."

She blushed an even deeper red. "Oh! Am I talking too much, Red? I am only excited to have a friend of my own age. Oh... may I call you my friend, Miss Fletcher? Am I too presumptuous? I beg your pardon if I am too forward."

"I should be very happy to be your friend," Angie said at once. "You are not the only one to lament the lack of persons of her own age, you know. Apart from my sister, that is, and now that she has Belinda with her, who is likely to stay for the whole summer, I feel a little *de trop*, for they are such close friends, and have been for years. It would please me greatly to be friends with you."

"Thank you!" cried Lady Maria, blushing again in excitement. "Then shall we walk about the room together? You must tell me what the season is like for I may be making my appearance next year and I confess, I am *terrified!* Is it quite horrid? My sisters tell me so. Oh, Red, you must go away, for Miss Fletcher and I cannot talk if you are by."

"And Mr Appleby may go and drink his glass of water," Angie said. "Thank you for your escort, sir. I am most grateful."

She curtsied, he bowed. Lord Albury, equally dismissed, bowed also. And then Angie tucked her arm into Lady Maria's and, with a sigh of contentment, settled down to a long, detailed discussion of balls and fashions and shopping and theatres and routs and evenings at Vauxhall Gardens and all the many and varied delights of a season in London.

8: Lady Mellish Holds A Card Party

When he finished dressing that evening, B went through to the now unused bedroom that had once been his uncle's. Unlike his own, it was fitted with a long cheval glass and he gazed now at his reflection. He had ventured to don the satin embroidered waistcoat he had worn for his uncle's wedding two years ago, which his uncle had bought for the purpose.

"I will not have you looking as if you have wandered in from a funeral, not for this of all days," he had said. "For every other day of the year you may wear whatever you please, but for my wedding you will be cheerfully dressed, in compliment to my lovely Calantha, and you will smile, nephew, and pretend you are happy about it."

"I *am* happy about it," B had protested.

"So you say, but the first child will deprive you of your inheritance, and neither you nor I expected that. For myself, I was quite happy with my freedom, as the bee is happy to wander from flower to flower and never thinks to settle on just one when there are so many others to choose from, but Cal has quite won my heart and nothing will do but marriage. I am sorry for it, for your sake, but you will find some alternative, I am certain of it."

"I shall take Holy Orders at Easter."

"Yes, yes, a country living somewhere, the very thing! In fact, truth be told, that sort of quiet life will suit you better than managing estates and dealing with bailiffs and so on, I dare say. Just the thing for a bookish fellow like you. There you are then, nothing to worry about, is there?"

It was fair to say that Uncle Maurice had indeed not worried about it, or even thought about it from that moment onward, and whenever anyone should mention to him the uncertain future of his displaced heir, he would wave an arm airily and suppose that a living would turn up, sooner or later.

B seldom thought about it, either, truth to tell. Following his ordination, he had written to the bishop, and to those of his acquaintance as might have livings in their disposal, and there did not seem to be much else he could do. Occasionally, when he saw a vacancy for an attorney advertised, or heard of a position as secretary to some great man, he had wondered if such a career would be within his capabilities. But that would involve all manner of upheavals and disruption to his orderly life, and a strange resistance clutched his heart at the thought of it. How he hated change! Somehow nothing was done and the moment passed by, and he meandered aimlessly on, aware that his life was drifting slowly past him but seemingly unable to do anything about it.

Now he gazed at his reflection in the glass and wondered what he was doing with his days on earth. He had early eschewed his uncle's hedonistic way of life, so there were no women, no drunken revelries, no long nights at the gaming tables. He kept to his books and his church activities, his morning round of Abbey and Pump Room and circulating library, his afternoons in the garden, his evenings of card parties and concerts in the season. And for the first time, with the words of Miss Angie Fletcher still ringing in his head, it all felt rather dreary. She had contrived to draw him into a lengthy conversation about clothes, of all things, a topic which had never interested him in the slightest before. Had his life been so colourless?

Colourless... would a little colour make him different? *'If I am a little down for any reason, I wear something bright and pretty to cheer myself up.'* So she had said, but would that work for him, too? If he wore this frivolous waistcoat, would it cheer him up? Or would it simply make him another frippery fellow, like his uncle?

There was only one way to find out. He minutely adjusted his cravat, drew the holland cover back over the cheval glass and went to find his evening cloak, gloves and hat. And a cane. His uncle had left several behind, so perhaps he should carry a cane, for once. No, that was a step too far. Just the waistcoat, for now.

Lady Mellish's drawing rooms were already well filled when B arrived at Queen Square. A few people loitered on the stairs and in the ante-room, chatting to friends before they entered, for they knew that their hostess expected strict attention to the play once seated at a card table, but B went straight past them with no more than a nod here and a quiet greeting there. He wanted only to sit down and play, and not have to indulge in trivial chit-chat. Miss Angela Fletcher, no doubt, would want to linger, seeing who was wearing a new gown which might denote a romance or a disappointment. The thought amused him, but he would not know how to read such signs as she did.

Lady Mellish bustled over to him at once. "Ah, Appleby! Just the man I need. Would you be so obliging as to make up a four over there with Colonel and Mrs Plaxton and Mrs Gravestock? Ah, here are the Fletchers just arriving. Excuse me, if you will."

He nodded his agreement, and she rushed away. Lady Mellish was a wealthy widow with a fine estate near Taunton, where she kept a gaggle of quarrelsome relations in subjugation. She fled often to Bath, ostensibly to take the waters for her health, although there never seemed much amiss with her. Possibly it was the company she craved, for she held frequent card parties with extravagant suppers, inviting everyone she knew or met in the Pump Room. As a result, she was spoken of as a splendid woman, and was generally well-liked, although a few who transgressed in her eyes and were cut from her invitation list murmured to their friends that she was an unfeeling and censorious creature, who would do well to take her excess of piety back to Taunton.

B made his way speedily to the place indicated for him, although horribly conscious of the quizzing glasses raised in honour of his waistcoat. He knew it was a mistake! He should have listened to his own instincts. But at least he would have his back to most of the room, so perhaps it would not be too much remarked upon. How he hated to be the focus of attention.

As he took his seat, he could hear the greetings behind him as the Fletchers entered the room. He sighed with relief that he was not confined to a table with the beguiling Miss Fletcher. Beguiling? Why had that word popped into his head? Irritating, that was what she was. Annoying. Vexing. Bemusing. Bewildering. Bewitching... No, that was all wrong. Infuriating. Exasperating. Enchanting—

"Are you playing, Appleby, or are you going to stare at those cards all night?"

"Oh... I beg your pardon, Colonel. I was not paying attention. Let me see... trumps are...?"

"Hearts, Mr Appleby, hearts," Mrs Gravestock said in long-suffering tones.

Gradually, as the last arrivals drifted in, the two rooms given over to cards settled into steady play, with only a low murmur of conversation. Footmen moved silently about, refilling glasses and replenishing dishes of sweetmeats. Now and then, one table or another would break into restrained celebration or subdued groans, but there were no noisy round games to disturb the even tenor of the evening. Lady Mellish took her card games seriously.

Colonel Plaxton and Mrs Gravestock took them seriously too, but Mrs Plaxton spent the time between hands, quizzing glass in hand, gazing around the room avidly.

"What think you of the mercers, Mr Appleby?" she whispered, during an interval while her husband struggled to add up the scores.

"The mercers, ma'am?"

"The Fletcher family. He is a mercer, is he not? From somewhere in the north, I understand. One of these manufacturing towns that have sprung up to entice the honest working man into the mills. Trade." She shook her head to signal her disapproval of trade. "Although they seem pleasant enough people."

"Fifty thousand," Colonel Plaxton said, unexpectedly looking up from his numbers. "That is what the elder girl has, and a real peach she is too, if I am any judge. Which I flatter myself I am, even at my advanced years. She'd do very well for you, Appleby. Get you out of a tricky situation, eh?"

"Yes, but *trade*," Mrs Plaxton said, a little more firmly. "That would never do for Mr Appleby, my dear, for the good name of the family to be sullied by such an association. It is all very well for the son to marry Eloise Whittleton, for the Whittletons are a very long-established family, most respectable, so it is a very good match for *him*. But Mr Appleby is a man of standing in society. A man should not look beneath him for a wife, he must always look for a wife who will raise him higher, one whose connections will be of benefit to him in years to come. Now, Lady Maria Landers... there is a possibility, if you like, Mr Appleby. An earl's daughter! Who could possibly make you a better wife?"

"Almost anyone, I should think," the colonel said sharply. "A man cannot live on connections, after all. If Appleby still had expectations of his uncle, then an earl's daughter would suit him admirably, but although the Landers have high rank, there's little money to throw at a younger daughter. Five thousand, if she's lucky — that is the word. Appleby would do better to aim for the Fletcher girl and her fifty thousand."

"But surely his uncle will do something for him, in time?" Mrs Plaxton said. "He has two estates, so—"

"And he has a son of his own, and may have more," the colonel said sharply. "Really, Dolly, you say the most absurd things, sometimes. Do not voice your opinion on matters you do not understand. Appleby, it is your deal."

To all this, B said nothing. He strongly disliked being talked about as if he were not present, but he would not stoop to comment on any of it. As if he were not perfectly well aware of his own dilemma! He was of the same mind as the colonel, for he had long since resigned any hope that his uncle would settle any money on him. It had been much talked of amongst the Bath gossips when his uncle had married and more so when baby Roger had arrived, and there were those who argued strongly that a man ought in common justice to make proper provision for his former heir, now ousted and left to fend for himself.

B himself could see both sides of the question. He would have liked to be independent of his uncle's charity, but any settlement would deprive little Roger of a portion of his inheritance, and who knew how many more children there might be to feed and clothe and educate and find careers or husbands for? It was not to be thought of. Besides, he was deeply grateful to his uncle for taking him in as a boy, and educating him. There was no justification for expecting more from him.

But what, then, was he to do? Perhaps an heiress would solve his problem rather neatly. Fifty thousand pounds... he made some rapid calculations in his head. Perhaps two thousand a year, with care. More than enough to live as a gentleman in Bath.

When he had dealt the cards, he ventured to turn his head just enough to look at Miss Rose Fletcher. To his annoyance, she had her back to him, but sitting opposite her, and looking directly at him, was the irritating Miss Angela Fletcher. She saw him looking, smiled widely at him and gave him a little wave.

Annoyed to be caught out, he at once turned away, and then played so badly that Mrs Gravestock felt compelled to remonstrate with him.

Supper was the usual squeeze, for Lady Mellish never quite grasped that if one invited forty people to enjoy one's table, one should in common courtesy provide forty chairs. Instead twenty-four people sat in relative comfort in the dining room, while the remainder, being the fittest and youngest, stood about, hindering the footmen or cluttering up the hall. The food, he had been told, was excellent, but since he could never partake of it fully, he could not honestly say whether he agreed or not.

He filled a plate as best he might with food which could be eaten with his fingers, and edged his way out to the hall again. It was unfortunate that the first people he saw were Miss Fletcher and Miss Angela, and the two friends from the north. Nor was there any avoiding them.

No sooner were the civil greetings got out of the way than Miss Angela cried, "What a charming waistcoat, Mr Appleby! How well you look in it. I do believe you should wear such garments more often. It suits you admirably."

"You mean it makes me look less like an attorney," he said, rather crossly, for he should have anticipated her interest.

"Well, yes, although there is an attorney at home who wore the most garish waistcoats... at home in Yorkshire, I mean, not Hertfordshire. Do you remember, Rosie? Not Mr Bertram, for he was always soberly dressed. Oh, you must know who I mean, the one whose brother has the warehouse on Bridge Road where we bought that ravishing gold spangled muslin two years ago."

"Gorton," put in the young man from the north. What was his name? Jupp, that was it. "Gorton's is where you bought the gold spangled muslin, for you told me so when I admired the dress."

"Oh yes! Mr Gorton's brother, who is also Mr Gorton, of course! You must remember him, Rosie. He wore such vivid embroidered silk waistcoats and such a quaint style, that they must have been his father's."

"His grandfather's," Jupp said. "He said they were too good to throw away, and he liked them. But I don't think Mr Appleby is much interested in Mr Gorton, Angie. Have you had good fortune with the cards, sir?"

"Mixed," B said. "I am a guinea or so in pocket, I believe. How about you?"

"Oh, we have not been playing for *money*," Miss Angela said. "Not when it is just the four of us. It would not seem right, somehow."

More people emerged from the dining room passing between their little group, and then more Fletchers emerged and distracted Miss Fletcher and the two northern visitors. B found himself pushed a little closer to Miss Angela and with no one else near enough to draw into the conversation.

He was about to make an excuse to disappear, when she leaned forward, one hand on his coat front, and whispered, "Of course, now I shall be entirely taken up with trying to work out what it means. It must mean *something*, of that I am sure, for I never saw you in anything other than black before. I wonder if waistcoats fulfil the same function for you as bonnets do for me? When I feel happy I wear a bonnet with flowers upon it, or pretty flower colours, perhaps — rose pink and cream and delicate blues. When I am sad, I wear bright colours — poppy red or jonquil or emerald green to cheer me up. When I am really in the dismals, I have an old violet cap that I wear. But it might be different for you. Did you put it on because you were in an unusually lively mood, or are you in the dismals and trying to cheer yourself up? Or are you...?"

She smiled up at him with mischief in her eyes. Such pretty eyes... No, this had to stop. "Am I what, Miss Fletcher?" he said, in what he hoped was a discouraging manner. But nothing appeared to discourage her.

In a melodramatic whisper, she said, "*In love*, Mr Appleby. Or courting, perhaps. Do you have marriage on your mind? I do hope so, for I should so like to see you happily wed, like your uncle, and as Will and Eloise will be very soon."

All his annoyance came rushing back. "Why on earth should you care about such a thing? Of what concern is my happiness to you, Miss Fletcher?" Then, realising to his horror that that might sound as if he was asking if she had formed an attachment to him, he panicked. That would never do! In terror, he rushed on. "You are quite wrong, in fact. The waistcoat signifies only that... that... I felt like a change, that is all. Nothing more than that. There is no significance to it, so you waste your time trying to uncover one."

"Oh." Her face fell. "That is disappointing. It is so sad to see you always alone, that I was quite excited for a moment. I was in such high hopes of an affair of the heart."

High hopes of an affair of the heart? Was it possible that she was... *flirting* with him? For a moment, horror struck him dumb, followed by blind, unthinking rage.

"There is no affair of the heart. None whatsoever. I am not in love, not courting, not thinking of marriage, nor have I the least intention of ever falling into such a trap. You are a troublesome chit, Miss Fletcher, and it is very wrong of you to torment me in this way."

Setting down his plate with a crash on the hall table, he stormed back upstairs to the drawing room.

~~~~~

Angie watched him go, rather bemused. *Torment* him? Was she a torment to him? Oh dear. Yet all she hoped was to put a little spring in his step and a twinkle in his eye. He need not marry if his mind was so firmly against it, but a touch of love, that would be just the thing to lighten him up. He was too gloomy, too miserable a person altogether. Too unyielding.

Yet she had seen the softness of his expression when he looked at his Sunday school pupils, and occasionally at her, too, so she knew there was a gentle, kindly man hidden behind the gruff manner. Beneath that forbidding exterior lay a beating heart that would surely respond to the right woman. A romantic entanglement, just a small one, nothing serious, would be the making of him.

And yet, how could it happen? He lived in Bath with its seasonal flood of visitors, yet ever since the inaptly named Miss Meek no woman had captured his heart. No one from the endless succession of beauty and wealth and high rank had swayed him. No quiet little miss, as bookish as himself, had persuaded him to share his library. He had found no practical person to manage his house so that he might devote himself to his books. He remained true to the memory of the pert Miss Meek, who clearly embodied his ideal of womanhood. A little bitter, perhaps, but ever faithful.

He was a hopeless case! She should leave him to his endless acquisition of books and the convenient box in the circulating library.

And that was when the idea popped into her head, out of nowhere. She smiled mischievously. It was a perfect plan, and he would never, ever guess.
~~~~~

9: Departures And More Arrivals

Ricky had intended to leave on Monday morning, but first Lady Mellish's card party, then a dinner for the Applebys and finally another, rather less formal, card party with the Sylvesters delayed him. He might have stayed even longer, had not his sleeping place been required for Johnny's visit from Cambridge. Johnny arrived on the incoming mail coach on Thursday morning, and Ricky was to depart on the same coach as it returned to town that afternoon.

Angie could not decide whether she was most glad or sorry to see Ricky go. On the one hand, Rosie and Belinda were distraught at his departure, but on the other, he was a reminder of all that the Fletchers had left behind when they had moved south to Hertfordshire. They were landed gentry now, possessed of the estate of Chadwell Park, and their world was very different from that of an apothecary.

Angie liked Ricky very much, but it was strange to see him mingling with the gentry in the Pump Room or strolling up Milsom Street with Rosie and Belinda on his arms, or sitting down to cards in the drawing room of a baronet's lady, a little part of their familiar old home brought into their new world. For all the fun she was having in the south, she still missed Yorkshire, and Ricky brought that pain into sharp relief.

It was all very well for him! For a little while he was a gentleman, yet soon he would go back to Sagborough, don his worn brown coat and apron, and become an apothecary again. He was like Pa, still with a foot comfortably in either world, whereas the rest of the family could never go back. They had become adapted to the gentry.

That was especially so of Will and Johnny. They had both received the education of gentlemen, first at Harrow and then at Cambridge, so they looked and sounded and behaved like everyone else in this new society the Fletchers now inhabited. There was not the least hint of Yorkshire in their voices, and they talked of the usual interests of young gentlemen — horses and country sports, clubs and politics, clothes and curricles. Not a word about business or industry.

Johnny being Johnny, he was not remotely interested in their social round or their new acquaintances, but as soon as he had removed the dust of travel, he set off for the booksellers.

"Who will come with me, to direct me to the best of the libraries?" he said cheerfully to the ladies collected in the drawing room.

"We are to pay some morning calls," Mama said rather stiffly. "Lady Mellish, Lady Louisa Horsfell, if she is well enough to receive us, Mrs Jardine, the Miss Bensleys. We shall be back in time to bid farewell to Ricky."

"May I go with Johnny, Mama?" Angie said. "I can show him Quarman's, which Mr Appleby the Younger recommended. It is one of the biggest booksellers in Bath, he says, and has a great many of the learned volumes that Johnny will appreciate."

"You are not normally so keen to visit book shops, Angie," Mama said in suspicious tones.

"I had rather be with Johnny than visiting Lady Mellish," Angie said at once, and with absolute truth.

Mama laughed. "Very well. Rosie and Belinda will accompany me on my calls, for they enjoy such occasions more than you do. It is a great trial to you to sit still for the requisite fifteen minutes, is it not?"

Angie meekly agreed to it, and was allowed to fetch her bonnet and gloves, and depart with Johnny, who set off towards the town at a great rate.

"Must we walk so fast?" she said, running to keep up with him. "I shall be greatly dishevelled when we arrive, if so."

He at once stopped, and turned to face her. "Beg pardon, little sister. I forgot you have not my long legs. But if I am to walk at a dawdling pace, you must tell me all that you have been doing, for I know nothing. One letter from Rosie to say you had arrived and one from Mother, mostly about the house, and nothing at all from Will."

"He spends all his time with Eloise."

"Ah, yes. Too busy a-wooing his lady to have time for his brother. *'Wooing is hot and hasty like a Scotch jig--and full as fantastical.'* He will have no time for any of us now, I dare say. I am happy for him, and very glad he did not end up with some grand society lady."

"What about you?" Angie said slyly. "Do you not envy him his happiness? Just a tiny bit?"

"Lord, no! I am perfectly content at Cambridge with my books and my lectures and my Fellowship. I should have to give all that up if I marry, and there is not a woman alive who would compensate me for the loss. How about you? Plenty of beaux here in Bath, are there?"

She pulled a face. "None at all... at least, Lord Albury is here, and Mama did think he was dangling after Rosie in London, but it came to nothing in the end, and he is not pursuing her now."

"Then what is he doing here?"

"Visiting his aunt, the Lady Louisa Horsfell, with his sister, the Lady Maria Landers. We have seen a little of them — I like Lady Maria very much! She is very shy — worse than Rosie, if you can imagine such a thing. We see a great deal of the Applebys, for Mr Maurice Appleby is married to Eloise's sister. Oh, and the Sylvesters. They are a very strange family! They are friends of James Plummer, but I am not very sure that they are quite the thing. They took us to a breakfast in Sydney Gardens the day before yesterday, and that was quite pleasant, I suppose, although we had nothing to eat until past noon and Pa was so cross by then, you cannot imagine. But the whole time, Mr Randal Sylvester was trying to flirt with all the ladies, even Mama, quite outrageously so. Ricky kept him away from Rosie and Belinda, and Pa was protecting Mama, but I could not evade him. It was most unpleasant."

Johnny frowned. "Why did Will not see the fellow off?"

"Oh, Will was not there. He was looking at carriages with Eloise, and could not spare the time."

"Well, I shall be around for a few weeks, so I shall look after you, little sister," he said, from the lofty heights of his twenty-two years.

They had passed through the Circus, where Angie pointed out the Applebys' house, and then down Gay Street where the younger Mr Appleby's house was, before turning onto George Street.

"Ah, this is more like it," Johnny said, looking about him with satisfaction. "That is a fine looking bookseller just there. Shall we try that one?"

"No, no, we must go to Quarman's. It is only a little further. You will be pleased with it, I am certain."

"Very well, little sister," he said equably.

Quarman's was dark, but Mr Quarman emerged from the gloom, remembered Angie and was introduced to Johnny, who was instantly whisked off to some dusty corner of the shop where lurked the impenetrable tomes he favoured. Angie wandered about, looking at the journals first to see the fashions, and then ambling from room to room in a seemingly aimless fashion. But eventually, by a circuitous route, her steps led her to the small room wherein lay the private boxes of Bath residents. And there was Mr Appleby's... A quick peek inside showed her two books waiting to be parcelled up and delivered. With deft fingers, she scooped a sliver of paper from her reticule, slid it between the pages of one of the books and closed the lid of the box. Then, on silent feet, she slipped out of the room.

Johnny finished more quickly than she had expected.

"Heavens, I thought we would be settled here for the whole

morning," she said, closing the journal she had been flicking through. "Are you being thrown out for being an infernal nuisance?"

"Not in the least," he said with a grin that made him look twelve again. "Customers are never infernal nuisances. I have told Mr Quarman my particular field of study and he is to collect some volumes that might be of interest."

"What is your particular field of study this year? Beetles again?"

"No, fossils. Ammonites, in particular. Cephalopods. Snake-stones. They are fascinating, you know, and I am certain there is more to them than merely the preserved remains of living creatures or plants. There must be some purpose to them, and I mean to find it out. There is a professorship of mineralogy which would suit me very well... in the fullness of time, naturally. I am by no means fit for such an elevation yet. Or the professorship of natural and experimental philosophy. That would be interesting, too, although I think I would not qualify. I am from the wrong county for it. Or botany, perhaps. I am very fond of botanic studies."

Angie let him muse on, as they left the shop to re-enter George Street. A fine carriage passing at a rattling pace threw up such a quantity of dust that several passers-by fell to coughing. Happily, a slow-moving wagon brought the carriage to a halt, and the cloud of dust diminished enough for Angie to distinguish the face within.

She gave a squeak of surprise and stopped dead.

"What is it?" Johnny said. Then, following her gaze, he went on, "You know that fellow?"

"It is Mr Whittleton! Eloise's father... oh, but she will not want to meet him, I am sure. We must warn her!"

"Where will she be? At home?"

"I have no idea! The Pump Room... if we go to the Pump Room, she might be there, or if not Mrs Greenwood, or Mrs Appleby, and one of them might know where she is. There will be *someone* there who knows."

"Then let us go there at once."

As they walked, Johnny striding along and Angie half running beside him, he said, "I should have thought Miss Whittleton would be accustomed to her father's presence in her life by now. Surely they met many times in town."

"Not exactly. The first time she saw him—"

Laughing, he said, "I know about the first time — Miss Whittleton swooned on the spot. Hardly surprising, when she had not seen him for a decade or more."

"Thirteen years!" Angie said indignantly, "and not the least idea whether he was alive or dead, then he simply turns up at a ball. With his new wife, if you please, who was his—" She stopped abruptly, for the word *mistress* was not one to be bandied about on the street. She went on in a low hiss, "Who is a most immoral person. With *children!* Before he married her! Is that not abominable?"

"It is certainly irregular behaviour," Johnny said laughing. "One disapproves, naturally, but at least he has married her in the end." Angie squeaked in annoyance at that, and he raised his hands in surrender. "Yes, yes, abominable, quite abominable. But Miss Whittleton must have encountered him since the swooning incident. Whittleton and his wife are in the Carlton House set, I believe, so they would be received everywhere."

"I cannot say on that point. There were many engagements where they were not present at all, but we did see them sometimes... certainly Eloise has *encountered* her father. They attended the same events from time to time — balls, routs, large events of that kind. But they never exchanged a single word. She did not wish it, he chose not to draw attention by pressing the issue publicly, and no one had the bad manners to invite them to dinner together or anything of the sort. But here in Bath—! There will be no avoiding them. What can he be thinking, coming here to Eloise's own home town? We all thought he was gone to Brighton to amuse himself with the Prince of Wales and his cronies until the shooting season opens. What business can bring him here?"

"Family business?" Johnny suggested. "Perhaps he is here to see his *other* daughter."

"Oh! Calantha Appleby! Oh, Lord," Angie said. "She has never seen him. Just imagine if she should meet him on the street or at the Pump Room, without warning? We shall have another swooning! Quickly, we must get word to both of them, Eloise *and* Calantha, so they are not taken by surprise."

They hurried on to the Pump Room, where they were at least partly successful in their quest — Mr and Mrs Appleby were there, although it took some time, and considerable ingenuity, to detach them from the crowd of particular friends which surrounded them. But eventually Johnny drew Mr Appleby aside to whisper the news to him, hoping he would find a way to inform his wife discreetly of the arrival of her long-lost parent.

Mr Maurice Appleby was not a man much given to discretion.

"Cal? Cal, my love, here is news indeed. Your father is this moment arrived in town. Miss Angie has seen his carriage."

Angie winced, but Mrs Appleby screeched loudly and clapped her hands, and since there was no sign of a swoon, it was to be supposed that she bore the news with greater fortitude than her sister.

"We must go and see him *at once!"* she cried. "My dear, we must! Our other engagements must be given up, for surely my father takes priority. Was his wife with him, Angie?"

"I did not see her, but then I had but the merest glimpse of Mr Whittleton before the carriage moved off again."

"Surely she is with him, so newly married as they are. So romantic!" she sighed. "My dear, let us delay no more, but go at once."

"But you cannot know where they may be staying," Angie said. "Or if they are staying at all. Perhaps they are merely passing through."

"Oh, they will be staying at the York House Hotel," she said airily. "Everyone stays there, after all. Come, my love, let us go there at once."

Mr Appleby was by no means loath to go, and so, with a little string of followers, they left the Pump Room and set off to beard Mr Jeremy Whittleton in his den.

"Do you want to go?" Johnny said in a low voice to Angie. "I cannot think they will want so many people with them when they finally meet the gentleman."

"No, indeed, and we must find Eloise, to warn her," Angie said. "We will try Lansdown Road."

"Lord, I never expected such excitement in Bath," Johnny said cheerfully. "Such a sleepy sort of hole, everyone said so, yet here is scandal a-brewing before I have even been here half a day."

"Scandal? I suppose it is. What fun!" Angie said.

They retreated from the Pump Room, seeing no sign of the Applebys or their entourage, and sped on, Johnny's long legs setting the pace, towards Lansdown Road.

They were fortunate in finding Eloise and Mrs Greenwood at home, and Will was also there, naturally, for he was seldom far from Eloise's side.

"You will never guess who I have seen!" Angie burst out, before she had properly got inside the house. "Your father, Eloise. His carriage passed us by on George Street, and paused long enough for me to see his face clearly, although I cannot say if Lady Penelope is with him. Calantha thinks they may be gone to the... the York Hotel? Is that the right name?"

"York House Hotel," Mrs Greenwood said. "That is the best hotel in Bath, and she is very rich, they say. Or I suppose *he* is very rich, now. Eloise?"

"Calantha knows?" Eloise said faintly.

She had gone very pale, and now she sat down abruptly. Will sat beside her, one arm protectively around her waist.

"We found her in the Pump Room and told her. She seemed... excited," Angie said.

"There was no swooning," Johnny said, grinning.

"Hush!" Will said, frowning. "Calantha knows nothing of her father's misbehaviour, so naturally she is pleased at the prospect of meeting him. Whereas Eloise..." He turned to her, his voice softening. "You need not see him, my love. We may go directly to Hertfordshire, if you wish. Everything is in train here for the wedding, after all, and there is much to do in Hertfordshire — Orchard House to be got ready for us to live in, for one thing. I can have the carriage at the door in an hour."

"Oh, Will! You would do that for me?"

"Of course, my love. There is nothing I would not do to ensure your comfort and happiness," he said with such heartfelt simplicity that Angie felt tears prickling. If only she had a man who loved her so well! How glorious it would be to be so cherished.

"Perhaps before you fly within the hour, we should ascertain whether he is to stay in town, and is not merely passing through on his way elsewhere," Mrs Greenwood said.

"Then let me do so at once," Will cried, leaping to his feet. "I shall go to the York House Hotel and enquire, and you may consider, my love, what you will need to do if we are to decamp to Hertfordshire — packing, informing your acquaintances, and so forth. Aunt Beth, you will come with us, if we go? There is no one at Chadwell Park just now apart from my youngest sister and her governess, so Eloise will need you as a chaperon. I can stay with James and Julia, if you feel it best for me not to be under the same roof as Eloise. I shall be back directly. Johnny, do you wish to come to the hotel with me?"

"I am escorting Angie... or she is escorting me, I am not sure which it is."

"Let us all go," Angie said at once, agog with curiosity to see Mr Jeremy Whittleton and his wife again.

It was a short distance from Lansdown Road to the York House Hotel, which they found full to overflowing, the entrance hall abuzz with a great crowd all chattering excitedly, heads nodding together, the ladies' plumes making them look like a flock of exotic birds.

Will forged a path through the mêlée to the couple in the centre of the crowd, a well-dressed and handsome pair of middle years, laughing genially with their friends.

"Whittleton!" Will called.

The man turned a puzzled face towards him. "Yes, my friend?"

"May we talk privily, sir?"

"I have no time at present. If your business is urgent—"

"What are you doing here, Whittleton?" Will burst out. "Did you not distress Eloise sufficiently in town, that you must follow her here?"

"Eloise? Oh... you must be... Lord, I have forgot your name. My dreadful memory, you know. But how can my presence here distress her? I confess, my unexpected appearance in town startled her, but she has had time to grow accustomed, eh? And my *other* daughter... may I not see her? And my little grandson? Must I forego all familial visits in case Eloise should be upset?"

He spread his hands wide, a smug smile on his face, and looked round at the circle of onlookers, who nodded approvingly.

It was too much, and to Angie's mingled horror and delight, Will lost his temper altogether, fists clenched as if he would like to do more than bandy words with the impudent fellow.

"No, but you might write to inform your daughters of your intention to resume the rôle of a father, a rôle you deserted for thirteen years, sir, to the great detriment of your wife and four young children, who were left to shift for themselves for all those years. Your behaviour was unforgivable, nor have I seen a shred of remorse in you for your neglect of those who depended upon you. You may do as you please and go where you please, naturally, but I must ask you to give due notice in future if your movements might bring you within my betrothed's society, so that she may make immediate provision for quitting the place. She is a lady of great sensibility and it would pain her deeply to be obliged to give her own father the cut direct. Good day to you, sir. Madam."

With a punctilious and excessively graceful bow, he spun on his heel. The astonished crowd parted silently for him as he stalked past them and out onto the street.

10: An Admirer

Angie was so thrilled by Will's unprecedented display of masculine contention that she skipped home to the Royal Crescent fizzing with excitement. It was only when she recited her dramatic tale to the rest of the family that she realised the seriousness of the situation. Rosie and Belinda promptly burst into tears, Mama cried, "Oh no!" and Aunt Madge rose to her feet with a set expression on her face.

"I'll go and see about the packing."

"Packing?" Angie said. An awful dread fell upon her, settling like a ball of lead in her stomach.

"We can hardly stay here now, can we?" Aunt Madge said. "The whole point was to help Will and Eloise prepare for their marriage."

Angie was awash with misery. It was the end of all pleasure. Even without a single ball to enjoy, Bath had so many delights — the shops! The Pump Room! Sydney Gardens! And dinners, card parties, people to meet and talk to and tease, sometimes. And she would like to continue her plan to make Mr Appleby fall in love, or at least brighten his life.

Happily, Pa scotched these fears at once. "What, leave after ten days when I've paid for this house for a full month? Not likely!" he said, chuckling. "And I've an option on a second month, too, so if you girls are enjoying yourselves we can stay on. Will can go off and hide away in Hertfordshire if he likes."

Angie breathed again.

"Well, *I* shall go," Aunt Madge said. "Someone has to manage the servants, for I am sure Mrs Greenwood has no notion how to run an establishment of that size. You can stay here and enjoy yourselves if you wish, but I know my duty."

So saying, she stalked out of the room, head high.

"May we stay? Truly?" Rosie said. "Mama?"

"I am willing, but it is for your father to say."

"Certainly, if it pleases my lovely ladies," he said genially.

"Thank you, Pa!" Angie cried, throwing her arms around him and hugging him tightly. "Thank you, thank you, thank you! You are the very best of fathers."

"Aye, well, you've more chance of staying out of mischief here, where there's plenty going on, than in the country. You *are* staying out of mischief, aren't you, flower?"

"Of course I am, Pa. How could I get up to mischief in Bath?"

"If Aunt Madge were here, she would say you could get up to mischief anywhere, little sister," Johnny said, ruffling her hair and tugging a curl.

"Ow! Well, she is *not* here, is she?"

"Now, now, children," Pa said, smiling at them. "Rosie love, what about you? Are you enjoying Bath? You could go home too, if ever you want to escape."

"I am very happy here, Pa, especially now that Belinda is come."

"Your admirers not bothering you? We've been here a whole ten days, yet not one impassioned gentleman has begged for my permission to pay his addresses to you."

Rosie blushed. "No one is bothering me, Pa. I was a little out of my depth in London, it is true, and I very much disliked being described as the beauty with the fortune, as if there were nothing more to me than my face and a large dowry. London society was very frivolous, I found, always hopping from one thing to the next, and it was hard to get to know anyone properly... a person's true character, I mean. It was all show. Here our acquaintances are of a very different nature, and our engagements of a more restrained type. Bath society is very congenial, and it is agreeable to have a smaller number of friends whom one meets almost every night at card parties."

"It is a pity there are no balls at this time of year," Mama said with a sigh. "Card parties are all very well, but Rosie shows to such advantage at a ball."

"And Angie, too," Rosie said at once. "No one dances as well as she does."

"Aye, very true," Pa said, "and as to the matter of balls, there may be some pleasing information on that head before long."

The ladies all gasped with delight, and Angie spun round in joy. A ball! Nothing was wanting to make Bath perfect except a ball.

"Who? And where?" said Mama. She was not given to displays of emotion, but her eyes gleamed more than usual, before narrowing suspiciously. "And how do you know about it, Harry?"

He tapped his nose and chuckled. "Ah, wouldn't you like to know, eh? I have my sources, Mrs Fletcher. I have my sources." And he chuckled again.

~~~~~

B had spent his customary two hours in the garden, one hour with the vegetables, weeding and then picking raspberries and peas, and then a second hour in the herb garden, with more weeding and finally cutting roses for the house. He grew few purely ornamental plants, but the rose was the perfect flower, blooming in a variety of tasteful colours and filling the house with perfume. Nor were they especially hard to grow, for he disapproved of any plant which had to be cajoled into life and shielded from adversity. If a plant could not robustly withstand the deprivations of wind, rain, frost, hail and sunshine, it had no business putting itself forward as a suitable variety for a garden.

By the time he had completed these tasks and readied himself for the evening, his parcel from Quarman's had been delivered. Having perhaps a quarter of an hour in hand before he must leave for his dinner engagement, he took it through to his small study at the back of the house. Had he wished, he could have made use of his uncle's larger and more commodious study overlooking the street, but it still bore all the signs of his uncle's tenure. The scratches and ink marks on the desk, the books carelessly left higgledy-piggledy on the shelves, the drawers still full of forgotten bills and letters — it could never be *his* room when his uncle's much more forceful character dominated.
~~~~~

He far preferred his own much neater domain. A small desk, two shelves for his books, not yet filled, a chair beside the fire. The desk was clear, apart from an inkstand, a leather pad to write on and a tray of letters from his numerous friends scattered about the country. That was his Sunday task, to reread these glimpses into the lives of others, their eccentric families, their wives and children, or their grand employers, all the trials of their daily existence. Then he would reply with his own small doings, unembellished, rather dull. The only blemish intruding into the orderliness of the room was the line of boxes of his father's books along one wall, and never opened in twenty years.

Retrieving his knife from a desk drawer, he cut the string and then unwrapped the little parcel. Two books, one of sermons by Hugh Blair and the other a collection of poetry, including a favourite by John Dyer. Smiling in anticipation of his bedtime reading, he flicked gently through the pages.

A small leaf of paper fluttered to the floor.

Puzzled, he bent to retrieve it, realised it was a letter of some sort, and in a woman's hand, too, and thrust it hastily back into the book. Whoever had previously borrowed the book must have left it there inadvertently. It was nothing to do with him. He could not possibly read it...

Could he?

Of course he could not! What an unthinkable intrusion. But what on earth was he to do with it? It was not his to dispose of, and yet he could hardly return it to its owner without reading it. It was bound to have some indication of its author, and it was hardly likely to be of an intimate or embarrassing nature, not when it had been so carelessly abandoned. Most likely a duty letter, thrust aside in relief when some better entertainment offered.

He could imagine just how it would read. *'Dearest Mama, Bath is dreadfully thin of company and we have not had two days together without rain. Yesterday we attended a card party at Laura Place. George's chest is a little better already. I hope you and Papa are well. Your loving daughter, Emily.'* All over Bath, in a hundred shabby lodging houses a hundred Emilys were writing thus every day of the week. Or perhaps it was less dutiful and more urgent. *'Dear Papa, Please send more money, Obediently yours, Emily.'* Or it might be even more prosaic than that. *'Dear sir, Please supply me with another dozen pairs of the silk stockings with cotton feet, such as you provided in October last. Mrs G Smith.'*

What harm would it do to read it? He smiled, opened the book and retrieved the note.

'To the estimable Mr B A, Pray forgive me for writing to you in this unorthodox manner, but I have for so long watched you from afar and can no longer remain silent. You are of all men the most worthy. Your virtue in all things combined with your modesty and good nature must be honoured by all who know you, including one who is most sincerely, An admirer.'

B stood as if turned to stone, his mouth open in shock. Impossible! Yet there it was, held in his own trembling fingers. He could barely believe it.

Who? That was his first thought, quickly followed by — how? How had some person secreted this note into one of his books? This second mystery was speedily resolved. Quarman's was patronised by half the population of Bath. Any of them might know of the boxes in the little room.

As to who... his mind was blank. It was indubitably a lady, that much was clear from the elegant form of the letters and the quality of the paper. It was torn across, as if it had been written on paper printed with an address, but the printed portion had been ripped away. A lady of quality, then, with engraved writing paper.

The image of Miss Angela Fletcher rose unbidden in his mind, for he had himself shown her the box, and very recently, too. But surely *she* could not have sent his letter, for she had barely been in Bath much above a week, and could hardly have written *'I have for so long watched you from afar'*.

Higgins came into the room just then, starting when he saw B there. "Beg pardon, sir, but I thought you'd be away by now."

"What time is it? Good Lord, I shall be late!"

Folding the note quickly and stuffing it into an inner pocket, he departed in haste, racing up Gay Street to the Circus. He need not have bothered, for Uncle Maurice and Calantha had not noticed his absence, being entirely taken up with two other guests, who were cooing over little Roger.

"Ah, nephew, there you are. Come and meet Cal's father and stepmother, Lady Penelope and Mr Jeremy Whittleton. This is my nephew, Barry Appleby."

B flinched at the name, but bowed and said all that was proper. At least, he hoped that he did. His brain seemed curiously defective at that moment, so full of *An Admirer* that there was no room to spare for Calantha's errant father, returned with a smile and a string of light-hearted banter to be accepted back into the family fold. B felt as if he were floating, somehow detached from all that was going on around him. He sat through dinner, saying nothing, then followed the others the short distance around the Circus to the card party of the evening.

He could not play whist, of that much he was certain. He was too befuddled for any serious concentration, and would only be a trial to his partner. Luckily, the Ansteads were less concerned than some Bath residents about serious card play, and more interested in ensuring that their guests had an amusing evening. There would be at least one round game, therefore, where B could sit quietly and lose money without anyone noticing his abstraction.

As soon as he could escape the effusions of his hostess, he slunk through the room to join a noisy game of speculation already in progress. It was such a simple game that he could pretend to be absorbed in the play while his thoughts roamed far away. The letter sat heavy in his pocket, like a cannonball, heavy and primed to explode. He could not feel it, but he was constantly aware of it. He could think of nothing else.

'You are of all men the most worthy... virtue... modesty... good nature...' He tried to be so, certainly, but no one before had ever suggested that he had succeeded. Not his father, nor his uncle, either.

'You must be esteemed by all who know you.' That, at least, was untrue. No one esteemed him, or even respected him. He was sure he was much laughed at behind his back, by those who thought about him at all. Even Jupp the apothecary had jeered at him. Until now, he would have said with absolute certainty that not a single person had ever *admired* him. Not even Miss Meek, who had been widely thought to have an understanding with him. She had admired his uncle's fortune, that was all.

So who could it be? Was it Miss Hayward who had penned the letter? She often stopped to speak to him after church. Or one of the Miss Branscombes, who had tried to get him to dance with her once, although he could not remember which one. Or their cousins, the Miss Laceys. But no young maiden would be so forward as to write such a letter to a man. It must be an older woman, a spinster. A widow, perhaps. A married woman? Could it be Mrs Lacey, who so often sat beside him in the Pump Room as they drank their glasses of water, and smiled at him frequently? But if so... what on earth was her motive in writing to him? She could not mean—?

"Careful, Mr Appleby! Your cards might fall."

The voice was familiar. His gaze was drawn across the table, where a heart-shaped face surrounded by delicate curls smiled at him.

"Your hands appeared to shake," she said in concerned tones. "Are you quite well, sir?"

"Oh. No... yes... Thank you... quite well. Thank you... for your concern, Miss Fletcher."

No, impossible! Mrs Lacey was a respectable married woman, she would never... would she?

He pulled himself up sharply. This would never do! He must concentrate on the cards, for he was bidding almost at random.

Supper came as a welcome relief. He followed the crowd down to the dining room, took a glass of something from a statue-like footman with a tray, and propped himself against the wall. The middle Miss Branscombe had always been rather forward, so perhaps— But no, he rather thought she was betrothed to the sallow-faced fellow who talked incessantly about horses.

"Good evening, Mr Appleby. What do you make of the new arrivals?"

With an effort, he dragged his mind back from its wanderings.

The annoying Miss Fletcher again. Again he wondered whether she was his mystery writer, for it was precisely the sort of foolish and wild thing that a thoughtless girl like her would do. They were all romantically inclined, girls of her age, barely out of the schoolroom and prone to fall violently in love at the least provocation, or none at all. She would think nothing of writing to the object of her desires, with all propriety tossed out of the window. A girl who would spurn a gentleman's proffered arm to walk unfettered down the street would be hampered by no moral scruples, he was sure.

What had she said... something about arrivals? "Of what arrivals are you thinking, Miss Fletcher? Scores of people arrive in Bath every day."

"Why, Mr Jeremy Whittleton and Lady Penelope, of course. Have you met them yet? They are here, but so surrounded by the curious that it is impossible to get near them."

Whittleton. Lady Penelope. He could see why the gossip-mongers might be energised by such people, bathed in scandal as they were. "I dined with them at my uncle's house."

"Oh!" Her eyes were round. "You *dined* with them. And what is your opinion of them?"

"I have no opinion of them."

"What, none at all? You must be aware, sir, that they are persons of the greatest interest to most of Bath on account of their interesting history. When it is known that you have dined with them already, you will be thoroughly quizzed to reveal their every utterance. Failing that, it will be the food. Did they compliment the soup, sir? Did they take the fish or keep to flesh? Did their tastes lie in lobster and sturgeon or rabbit and pigeon pie? All of Bath awaits this information with bated breath."

He was about to respond sharply when he caught something in her expression — a kind of innocence mixed with amusement. She was teasing him, he realised. And yet, she was not laughing *at* him. She was sharing a joke, perhaps, expecting him to understand it and to be amused. It was an odd concept, but he rather liked it.

"I am sorry to be the bearer of bad news," he said carefully, hoping his tone sounded sufficiently light, "but all of Bath must be disappointed, for I noticed none of it. It was a dinner like any other dinner, in no way remarkable. I cannot even tell you what I ate or said myself, still less the Whittletons. But Mrs Appleby seems happy to see them."

Miss Fletcher frowned. "She does, and yet I wonder at it, when he abandoned his family for so long. He sent no word at all, so they had no idea whether he was alive or dead. How horrid that must be!"

"I understand," he said cautiously, for he disliked repeating gossip, "that she believed him to be engaged on some secret mission for His Majesty."

"Oh, then no wonder! Such a romantic tale of one's father. Other girls have fathers who do nothing at all except sit about all day with a book in one hand and a glass of wine in the other. Just think how glorious it must be to have a swash-buckling and mysterious father instead, who is never seen and therefore leaves one free to spin any tale one likes about him."

"Both types of father are reprehensible," he said savagely. Then, seeing her eyes widen at his tone, he went on more temperately, "There is a kind of neglect in both and I cannot disregard such dereliction of duty. As to Whittleton, for myself, I could not accept him back without a qualm. I am far more of Miss Eloise Whittleton's mind, that what he did was unpardonable and that he should not even be received in good society."

"Yes, indeed," Miss Fletcher said. "Still, society is fickle, and easily swayed by rank. She is the daughter of a marquess, and a great favourite of the Prince of Wales, it is said, and they are married at last, so everyone pretends they are respectable now. Except Eloise. And Will, of course. They are gone to Hertfordshire, and will stay there until the Whittletons are gone from Bath and it is safe to return."

"Gone?" he said, astonished. "So abruptly?"

"Within two hours of hearing of the Whittletons' arrival. Will accosted the pair in the entrance to the York House Hotel, and told Mr Whittleton roundly that Eloise would not meet him, that he was taking her out of town because it would pain her to give her own father the cut direct."

"Great heavens! Did he so?"

"Indeed he did, and I assure you, it is the most exciting thing I have seen since we arrived in Bath. This town is far too staid for me. But then, I imagine that is why you like it so much. In any event, Will and Eloise have left in tremendous haste, together with Mrs Greenwood and also Aunt Madge, who is most disgruntled to find that the Audleys' servants are too efficient to grumble about, so she is gone back to Chadwell Park, where they are satisfactorily slovenly and need a great deal of supervision."

He recognised the teasing tone in her voice this time. "You exaggerate, I am sure, but perhaps it is as well that Miss Whittleton has left Bath. There will be a great deal of talk for a while, and she would not be comfortable to be subjected to that. Whereas her sister..."

"You do not approve of Mrs Appleby," Miss Fletcher said, her head tipped, bird-like, to one side.

"Why do you say that?"

"Because she is a flighty young woman, like me, and you disapprove violently of me."

She smiled up at him so guilelessly that for a moment he was taken aback. "Disapprove?" he said startled. "No, indeed, I—" Then he remembered her father's words. *She will tie your tongue in knots if you let her.* He laughed, pleased to see her eyes widen in surprise. "You like to be provocative, I think, Miss Fletcher. However, I am minded not to be provoked this evening."

She laughed gaily. "Now, that is most unhandsome of you, sir, and very... um, provoking! Ah, we are returning to the card tables. Shall you do better this time, do you think?"

B hesitated. Another hour sitting opposite Miss Angela Fletcher? He was not sure he could bear it. She was a distraction from his brooding, but it was not a distraction he found congenial. There was something unsettling about her, although he could not make out precisely what it was. It was not simply that she was young and pretty, for he had long been immune to such superficial and transient attributes. Her pert manners he thought deplorable, and she was as frivolous as all young women. But something about her disturbed him, even if it was impossible to pin down.

"I shall go home, I think. I am not accustomed to losing quite so much in a simple game of Speculation, so I must nurse my wounded pride with brandy and a book of sermons."

"Ah, yes, the very thing to cheer you up, a book of sermons," she said solemnly. "Good evening, then, Mr Appleby. We shall meet again before long, I am sure, for unlike Eloise, I have no plans to run away from Bath. I am enjoying myself far too much."

He bowed, and crept away to the cloak room while there was a general movement back up the stairs. By the time he emerged, the hall was empty apart from the hall boy, who silently opened the door for him and closed it behind him with a soft snick.

He was too restless to go home at once, and the night was filled with a soft warmth, the moon suffusing the air with silver light. He rounded the Circus, and strode down Brock Street, still a-bustle with sedan chairs and walkers, and then round the quieter Royal Crescent. From there it was but a short distance down to the Gravel Walk. That, too, was still busy with couples and groups in evening dress, laughing together as they made their way home or perhaps were still en route to a late party. A few people gave him a cheerful "Good evening!" and he responded mechanically, without noticing who he greeted.

He was lost in thought again, but this time his focus was less on his letter and more on the troubling Miss Fletcher. Had she been longer in Bath, he would have suspected that hers was the pen responsible for his letter, for she was hare-brained enough for such a scheme. He had himself shown her his box at Quarman's, too. But those few words — *'for so long I have watched you from afar'* — removed her from all suspicion. A little over a week could hardly be described as *'for so long'*. Besides, if she were such a great admirer, would there not be some sign of it? Some excitement in her, when he was nearby? He could recall no such signs.

Yet she was always around, somehow. No matter where he went, she was there, and irritating him like a... like... hmm, a splinter, perhaps. A minor pain yet impossible to ignore. How on earth was he to remove the splinter, that was the question. Miss Fletcher could not be plucked out of his mind with tweezers, nor could he escape from her by leaving Bath, as Eloise Whittleton had done. But she would not be there for long. By mid-August, the gentlemen would be wanting to stride about the countryside and shoot things and away the Fletchers would go, disappearing from his life for ever, leaving only a wisp of memory.

He reached the gate into his own garden and was striding up the path to the rear door when he saw the joke. *'The very thing to cheer you up, a book of sermons',* she had said. He chuckled, and at that moment he realised exactly why Miss Angie Fletcher unsettled him so much.

She made him want to laugh. It was a most unfamiliar sensation.

11: An Outing To Lansdown

While the Fletcher ladies waited for further news of the ball, there were a multitude of other activities planned. The travelling coach had taken Will and Eloise away, and the town carriage had gone back to Hertfordshire, since it was not needed in so compact a town as Bath, but the barouche had arrived, the weather was now settled and there were numerous pleasant outings within a short drive of the town.

Lord Albury was the instigator of the first such expedition, a gentle drive up to Lansdown for the ladies with the gentlemen riding, to admire the view, followed by a picnic.

"It is not far, but my aunt is not well enough to venture further, and I believe the outing will do her good," Lord Albury said, when he and his sister came to the Royal Crescent to issue the invitation. "With the weather so warm at present, it will be agreeable to leave behind the close atmosphere of the town. The air is very clear and fresh on the downs. We should be delighted if you could join us. I do hope you are not planning to follow Mr William Fletcher to Hertfordshire just yet, for Maria would be sorry to lose her new friends so soon."

"We plan to stay for the month agreed with Mr Audley," Mama said. "It appears that Will and his future wife are settled in Hertfordshire, and will call the banns there later this summer, so there is no constraint on our time. Besides, the girls are not yet ready to bury themselves in the country, and we all enjoy Bath society." She smiled at Lady Maria as she spoke, but Angie knew that her thoughts were on Lord Albury as well. "We are very happy to accept your invitation."

"Excellent news. Do any of you ladies ride?"

"No," Mama said at once, for although they could all ride passably well, she considered it more dignified for a lady to make such excursions only in a carriage. "My daughters, Miss Jupp and I will take the barouche. Lady Maria, do you ride with the gentlemen?"

Lady Maria blushed to be so directly addressed, and stammered some unintelligible reply.

"My sister rides very well at home," Lord Albury put in smoothly. "She has a favourite mare and knows the paths well, but it is a different matter to ride a hired hack on unfamiliar ways. She has chosen to drive for this outing."

"That is very wise," Mama said. "Mr Fletcher feels just the same but we have no room for a fifth person in the barouche, so he will be obliged to ride. For myself, I always feel that one may admire the view better from a vehicle, without the distraction of managing a horse. You will be able to bear your aunt company, Lady Maria."

"If Mr Fletcher would truly prefer to travel in the barouche," Lord Albury said, "Miss Angela Fletcher might perhaps join Maria and my aunt. I trust Miss Fletcher will forgive me for not giving her due precedence over her sister on this occasion, but I am sure she would prefer to accompany Miss Jupp."

Rosie blushed and nodded, Mama agreed to the arrangement with alacrity and so it was settled. It was unfortunate, perhaps, that the Sylvester family called as these details were under discussion, and Lord Albury could not avoid including them in the invitation, and somehow the Applebys were included too, not forgetting Mr Whittleton and Lady Penelope. In the end three vehicles set out to climb the hill to Lansdown, with six gentlemen on horseback, making such an impressive cavalcade that even Mama was reduced to happy silence, only a wide smile and frequent sighs of contentment marking her pleasure in the occasion.

Lady Louisa's carriage took the lead, avoiding the worst of the dust, setting a stately pace. Angie found it rather agreeable to have her back to the horses, for it gave her a splendid view over the rooftops of Bath, its mellow stone glowing in the sunshine, with numerous church spires rising above the chimneys, and the Abbey the most splendid sight of all. Unfortunately, Lady Maria sat beside her aunt, facing forwards, and Angie's companion on the rearward seat was Mrs Lambert Sylvester, who chattered incessantly.

"Look, look, I can see St Swithin's. Or is it the Walcot Chapel? There is the Cleveland Bridge. What a pretty tree. Do you see, Angie? Such delightful blossom. I declare I could look at it for ever. Did you see that strange looking man? Did you ever see such an odd hat? I declare I never saw such a thing in my life. I should be mortified if Lambert wore anything so very odd. Did you see it, Angie?"

"I did, Mrs Sylvester."

"Oh, but you must call me Hermione, such friends as we are. Goodness, your brother looks very fine on horseback. I do declare, Lady Maria can scarce take her eyes from him." Leaning forward, she said loudly to Lady Maria, "Do you not think Mr John Fletcher looks splendid?"

Lady Maria blushed fiercely. "Oh, yes, Mrs Sylvester."

"Do call me Hermione. Yes, such a fine figure. How lucky you are, Angie, to have two such charming and handsome brothers. I wish Lambert were so well provided with brothers."

Here she paused for Angie to make some complimentary remark about Mr Digby Sylvester, but neither he nor his cousin Randal nor Lambert himself inspired any admiration in Angie's breast. She chose not to take the hint, and Mrs Sylvester was obliged to undertake the appropriate praise herself. It was no more than four miles to Lansdown, but to Angie it felt like the longest four miles in the world.

The servants had arrived before them, or at least Lady Louisa's and the Royal Crescent servants had arrived. Neither the Applebys nor the Sylvesters had offered their own servants. Mrs Maurice Appleby had promised to bring a hamper of food, but the Sylvesters had not even done as much. Presumably they deemed the condescension of their company a sufficient contribution to the happiness of the day.

A small pavilion had been erected to shield the ladies from the sun, complete with chairs and a small table, with rugs set out on the grass for those of the party prepared to endure the rays. At first everyone walked about, looking at a monument to a fallen soldier from the Civil War and admiring the view over the Bristol Channel. Angie dutifully trailed after the others, taking care to avoid Mrs Sylvester, to allow her ears to recover from the onslaught.

She quickly found that she needed to avoid Mr Randal Sylvester, too, for he seemed inclined to flirt with shocking ineptitude. Angie was not averse to a little delicate flirtation, full of subtlety and hidden meanings, but Mr Sylvester had not a subtle bone in his body.

"What a pretty gown," he said. "Shows off your charms to perfection, eh? I know how you ladies like to tempt us poor susceptible men with all your attractions."

"Indeed," she said. "I practise on the instrument every day for that very purpose."

"Eh? Instrument? Oh — ha ha! Very good, Miss Angie. Very good. What a little tease you are! A tease in every way, for look how daintily you walk, so that your skirts sway about in that very enticing way."

"I cannot help the way I walk, sir," she snapped, wearying of such poor sport.

Lady Louisa soon tired and retreated to the pavilion, where a padded chair and footstool had been brought for her, and many of the party followed her to the shade, where flasks of lemonade and ale, cooled by a nearby stream, were broached. The Sylvesters and Johnny had got up a game of battledore and shuttlecock on a patch of open ground, but Angie was not minded for such an energetic game on a hot day. What she would have liked above all things was to sit with Rosie, whispering together about this and that, but Rosie had Belinda to talk to now. Angie sat, parasol raised against the sun, watching her sister strolling about contentedly with Belinda. Angie had never been without a sister to talk to before, and it was oddly unsettling.

Soon there was a summons to eat and everyone gathered at the pavilion, the older ladies on chairs and everyone else disposed on rugs or on the grass. There was a great chattering on all sides, for the Sylvesters were their usual ebullient selves, and Mr Whittleton and Lady Penelope were minded to compete with them in loudness and quantity of inconsequential chattering. Angie liked inconsequential chattering as much as any girl of eighteen summers might, but with such an excess of it about, it was a relief when most of the party drifted away again, the energetic back to their game and the others to walk about.

Angie felt she should walk too, but the walkers were all in neat pairs, and she could not see a situation where she would not be *de trop.* In the pavilion, there were strawberries and cream to eat, lemonade to drink, and no Randal Sylvester with his heavy-handed compliments. Besides, Lord Albury and Lady Maria were in attendance on Lady Louisa, talking intriguingly about their house and its many imperfections. Altogether, she could not see that her pleasure would be increased by walking about in the afternoon heat.

"You are very fortunate, Miss Fletcher," Lord Albury said, after running through a long list of problems at Chaseley Court, "in having a modern house which is not falling down around your ears. Chadwell Park was built just a few years ago, I understand."

"Twenty-five," Angie said, reaching for the strawberry bowl. "It is very modern, it is true."

"That is the perfect age for a house, in my view," Lady Louisa said. "All the little teething problems overcome, and the garden established. And do you like living in Hertfordshire, my dear?"

Angie reluctantly laid down her spoon. "I say nothing about Hertfordshire, which is a fine county, I am sure, and cannot be blamed for not being Yorkshire, the finest place under the sun, but I do not particularly like to be buried in the countryside, with no shops and no balls, and the same narrow range of people to be seen."

Lady Louisa laughed. "You Yorkshire folk are fiercely proud of your homeland, which is commendable, but perhaps it is the change which daunts you in Hertfordshire, and not merely the lack of shops. After all, your family has seen a great many upheavals in a few short months — your father's remarriage, for instance, which is bound principally to affect his daughters. Then there was the move south to very different society, and now one of your sisters is recently married and your elder brother is treading the same path. It is hardly surprising that you are a little nostalgic for Yorkshire."

Angie considered that. "It is true that all our lives have changed, yet I cannot but feel it is for the better. Even if I do not greatly care for the countryside, I should not like to move back to Sagborough, not after seeing other places."

"Ah yes, the shops! Anything one may require may be had in London."

"True, and the balls, the parks, the *people!"* Angie cried, with a shiver of delight. "There is always something of interest. But London... I felt very small and insignificant there. Now Bath, on the other hand, is the perfect size, and one may meet all one's friends at the Pump Room every morning."

Lady Louisa smiled. "My sentiments precisely, my dear. I far prefer to be here, even though I have a snug little estate of my own in Devon. It will be for Eustace, one day, of course. He is the youngest of the boys, so it works very well. Albury will have Chaseley Court and the London house and I know not what else, and Anthony will have the Westmorland estates, if he can ever prise them from my sister-in-law Hannah's hands, of course. And Eustace gets my little place, such as it is. Mind you, he is only eleven so it will be a while before he has need of it."

For a while, they were silent, Lady Maria watching the game of battledore and shuttlecock some distance away, Lord Albury chewing a grass stem and Lady Louisa gently fanning herself. Angie pondered the strangeness of the world, where one family could own so much property. Three sons, all with houses, estates, money to support them without labour. How much must their father be worth? What must his income be? Pa's fortune must be nothing to it. And yet their seat, Chaseley Court, seemed likely to fall down around their ears at any moment. She reached absent-mindedly for the strawberry bowl again.

Lady Louisa snapped her fan shut. "Albury, I believe Maria would like you to accompany her to watch the players at battledore and shuttlecock from a closer vantage point. Do not concern yourself with me, for Miss Fletcher will keep me company, at least for as long as the strawberries last." She sighed. "I used to be able to eat strawberries and cream all day myself when I was younger, and still be as dainty as you. Not any longer, however, as you may observe." She patted her ample stomach, with a chuckle. "There now, Maria will be able to admire your brother so much better from over there. She displays admirable taste, for I have rarely seen a handsomer fellow. He is at Cambridge, I understand? Will he take a profession afterwards, or will he become a gentleman of leisure like his elder brother?"

"He intends to stay at Cambridge," Angie said. "He has a Fellowship now."

"But he will give all that up when he marries, no doubt?"

"He does not plan to marry."

"Now that is a waste of a fine young man, to bury himself amongst dried up academics. I sincerely hope he repents of such a career and makes a young lady duly grateful. Oh, not Maria. She is but sixteen, and has barely begun to take notice of the male sex. Her fancy will pass over half a dozen young men before she settles on one, I dare say. Do you not find it so, Miss Fletcher? Are you the sort of girl who falls in love two or three times every year?"

"I do not think I have ever been in love," Angie said. "Not *truly* in love, anyway. In my first season in society, I imagined myself in love half a dozen times, at least. A gentleman had only to smile in my direction and I was smitten. There is a certain distinction in being violently in love, especially with a man who has never even noticed one. A girl may be satisfactorily heartbroken, and everyone is so very sympathetic. It is most gratifying, but it grows tedious after a while and it becomes necessary to be more selective. Happily, one cannot be around Rosie for long without learning to distinguish between honourable men and those who merely play games. Since then, I have *admired* certain men, naturally, especially those who dance well, but I never met a man yet who encompassed all the manly perfections."

"No more have I," Lady Louisa said, "and I have been an admirer of the male sex for decades longer than you have. In my experience, no man is perfect. Every one of them has flaws and the more perfect he seems on the surface, the worse the flaws hidden beneath."

"That is very profound," Angie said. "I had not thought of it in quite those terms, but it is very likely so. Perhaps what I should have said is that I have not yet encountered a man who encompasses all the manly virtues that I require for happiness. He must be handsome, for one thing, for I could not bear to look at a plain man for the rest of my life. And he must be rich, to keep me in comfort, for that is what I am used to and I am afraid, selfish though it is, I do *not* want to spend my life economising. And he must dance divinely, because dancing is so important, is it not? And now you may smile and tell me that when I *do* fall in love, all such considerations will fly out of the window, for so Mama says."

"No, I shall tell you no such thing, for on the question of money, you are absolutely correct. A man need not be *very* rich, for a competence will do, so long as it is enough to live upon, but there must be money or life will be miserable indeed. However much in love one is, one must still eat, after all. As for handsome, well, that is not a matter to worry about, for when you see a man gazing at you with utter adoration in his eyes, he will be excessively handsome to you, you may be sure, however plain others may think him. But dancing? Now there I agree with your mama. It is immaterial."

"Not to me," Angie said fervently. "I can never love a man who does not dance, and dance well."

Lady Louisa smiled, and there was a faraway look in her eye, as if she was in some other place altogether, or perhaps some other time. How strange it must be to be old, Angie reflected, to look back over one's life and remember being young and full of energy and dainty, and forget for a while that one is old and fat and not at all well.

Within moments, Lady Louisa had recovered. "Ah, there is

your sister again, by the trees. I am glad to have met her, having heard so much of her great beauty. One is inclined to dismiss such tales as exaggeration, but in this case, the reality is every bit as lovely as rumour suggested. You must feel it, I make no doubt, for in any other company you would be accounted a very pretty girl indeed. But next to your sister... well, life is hard sometimes. I suffered likewise, for although I was the eldest, I was never considered more than passable and my two younger sisters were great beauties. But there, although it was a great trial to me in my youth, time settles all scores, for one of them is now so stout she cannot leave her own apartments and the other is dead, so I suppose I have the last laugh."

"I have never been jealous of Rosie or her beauty," Angie said at once, rather startled by the suggestion.

"No? Then you must be a virtuous girl indeed."

"Oh, I make no claim to virtue! You see, I am the fourth daughter, Lady Louisa, and there are many benefits to being... oh, let me say *overlooked.* My eldest sister, Allie, was — *is*, indeed — an argumentative soul, who would dispute any point where she felt herself to be in the right, and persist until the end of time. Since she invariably believed that she *was* right, you may guess how that went. Then there was Rosie and her beauty, although there is far more to her than that, but no one bothers to look beyond her face. And my third sister, Julia, was always in some scrape or other. Last summer she fell into the canal at Sagborough. Well, she was pushed, in truth, because it was market day and some young loobies were making game of her, to which she took exception and pushed the leader into the water. Whereupon his friends pushed her in too, which was just as well for their friend, for he could not swim and would have drowned if Julia had not fished him out. But you see, with all the attention on my elder sisters, no one took any notice of me, and there is a great deal of fun to be had if one is out of people's thoughts."

Lady Louisa chuckled merrily. "How very true! I will not enquire as to the nature of the fun, but I hope we will know each other well enough in time that you might let one or two titbits slip. Do you play whist, Miss Fletcher? And your sister also?"

"We do, although not well. If you want a *good* game—"

"No, indeed, I do not." She shuddered. "Heaven preserve me from keen players, who focus all their attention on the cards and consider any conversation a grievous distraction. Now, I like a great deal of conversation with my whist, and care not whether I win or lose. If you and you sister have no other engagement tomorrow evening, would you take pity on Maria and me, for Albury is to dine out, a gentlemen's affair, and we shall be very dull, just the two of us. If you and your sister would care to come to me in Queen's Parade after dinner, we might have a very pleasant ladies' evening of cards and supper. My carriage will take you home again. You will forgive me if I do not invite Miss Jupp on this occasion, but five would make for a very awkward number for whist."

"I do not know of any engagements, but—"

"Then I shall talk to your mama and arrange things. And now, since the strawberries are no more, perhaps you would be so good as to find Albury and let him know that I shall be glad to return home as soon as it might be arranged."

"You are tired!" Angie cried, leaping to her feet. "I beg your pardon for not attending as I should."

"Nonsense! It is true that on any other day I should have been enjoying my afternoon nap long since, but I have been so well entertained that I have not missed it in the slightest. Still, we have been here for some hours in the sun, and perhaps it would be wise for all of us to retreat to shelter now, and recruit our strength for the delights of the evening. You have something amusing planned, I trust?"

"Oh, yes, but there will be no dancing," she said sadly. "London was too big, too noisy, too disordered for my taste, but we were able to dance almost every night. It was bliss."

"Well, do not despair, Miss Light-feet, for a little bird tells me you may soon get your wish, and I promise you this — if it comes off, then I shall be there to watch you dance."

12: Piquet And A Spinet

The second letter was almost more of a shock than the first. For some reason, B had assumed that the few short sentences he had already received had relieved the author's desire to communicate her feelings. She had told him of her admiration, and what more was there to be said?

A great deal more, as it transpired. This second letter, tucked neatly between the pages of one of Homer's lesser works, was much longer.

'My very dear Mr B A, May I call you so? It is presumptuous of me, but you fill my mind so completely that I feel such an address to be not entirely unwarranted. By day you are in my thoughts, and by night in my dreams. Never have I felt such regard for any man as I do for you, sir. Other men are frivolous fools by comparison. They flirt and jest and pay me absurd compliments, yet they move me not. How shallow they are! I despise them utterly. They attempt to purchase my affection with their nonsense, yet my heart remains untouched. For them, it might as well be made of stone. Only for one man does it melt. It is you, my dear sir, with your unparalleled rectitude who inspires me to call myself, Your greatest admirer.'

B shivered. This was plain speaking! He could scarcely imagine himself — his dull, uninteresting self — inspiring such thoughts. It had always seemed improbable that he could inspire affection in any right-thinking woman. He looked at his uncle, so lively and irresistibly charming in women's eyes, and knew that he could never compete. He had no witty repartee, no light manner of flirting with a lady. It was not in his nature. After Miss Meek had married Mr Romney, B's uncle had clapped him cheerfully on the shoulder and said, "Not to worry, nephew. There will be a woman for you in time, I am certain of it. Look at me — never thought to see myself caught in parson's mousetrap, but there we are."

That was true enough. Uncle Maurice had never intended to marry, for why should he when women threw themselves at his head without a scruple in the world? Every season brought its influx of free-spirited widows to Bath, and they delighted in flocking around him. So wanton and wild as they were! It was horrifying.

As for himself, B had not supposed there would ever be another woman interested in him, not after Miss Meek had revealed herself to be driven purely by mercenary considerations. Now he wondered what his mysterious admirer had in mind — marriage? Or something else? Or perhaps she was content to admire him from a distance. Whatever her motives, it was gratifying to receive such admiration... affection... perhaps even— No, he would not name it. Unless she herself spoke of it, he would not assume. Let it be as she said, admiration, and nothing more than that.

But he was no nearer to knowing who his admirer might be.

~~~~~
~~~~~

One evening, Angie was ready for bed, but was sitting by the open window looking out over the dark garden. Beyond it, a lamp flickered above the coach house, and here and there lights glimmered far away up the hills behind. She could hear the steady murmur of Belinda's voice from the room she shared with Rosie. Sometimes the murmur died away, as Rosie answered in a tone too low for Angie to hear. She wondered what they were talking about together, but then she had never known the answer to that. Even as girls, the two had been inseparable, heads bent together, whisper, whisper, whispering all day long, and now half the night, too.

Part of her wished she could be there, too, whispering with them, but Belinda's constant chatter left no room for Angie's own thoughts, such as her plans for Mr B Appleby. Was he any happier now that he had received two letters of affection? How she wished she could watch as he discovered them, to see his expression and know his reaction. Was he pleased? Outraged? Indifferent? She had noticed no change in his demeanour and it irked her so much to see him gloomy and unhappy. Surely a third letter would spark a response? Just one more, and then if he was still glum and unsmiling she would give him up to his misery, the poor man.

A knock on the door drew her from her abstraction. Pa's head, resplendent in a tasselled nightcap, appeared.

"Not asleep yet, flower? Good. May I have a word?"

"Of course."

He closed the door carefully behind him and sat on the only chair. "This is a pretty little room, and you have it all to yourself. Do you like not having to share?"

She was not sure how to answer that. "I shall have to get used to it, Pa. Julia is married now, and Rosie cannot be far behind."

"Aye, perhaps. But what about you? Does anyone take your fancy? One of the Sylvesters, perhaps? The one who's a lord's son?"

"Randal Sylvester? He is a dreadful rattle, Pa. I hope you did not come here only to talk about the Sylvesters, for I cannot find them interesting."

"No, no. I like them no more than you. Angie love, how should you like to visit a friend of mine?"

"I was not aware that you have friends here, Pa. A new friend?"

"Aye, he is, but you've heard of him. Mr Bravington, who owns the house we leased in Grosvenor Square. I should like to buy it from him, so that we have a London home all year. It will be much more comfortable for us to have a permanent place there, instead of renting for the season and then staying in hotels and the like when we are there at other times."

"Are we likely to be there at other times?" Angie said, surprised.

"Why not? Chadwell Park is all very well, but Ware is such a small town, not a quarter the size of Sagborough, and nowhere near the same provision of shops. We're so close to London we could go there instead, and any time we like if we have a house there, whenever the roads are fit for travel. Now, we could manage with a smaller place, I dare say, but the Grosvenor Square house has that lovely big drawing room, big enough for a ball, and I do like to see my lovely young ladies dancing. Besides, your stepmother likes it, and that's enough for me to like it too.

Bravington has no need of it now, but will he sell it to me? He won't, no matter how much I offer him. So I thought to try a different tack. I'll take you and Johnny along, and you can charm him with your pretty ways and Johnny can play piquet with him, for it's not my game at all and Bravington is as keen as mustard. What do you say?"

"I should like to meet him, Pa, if it would help."

"Ah, you're a good girl, Angie love. But not a word to your mama, mind. It's to be a secret until I've got a deal in my hand."

Mama was not one to harbour suspicions against her husband, so when he told her openly at breakfast the next morning that he was taking Angie and Johnny to call upon a business acquaintance, and he hoped that would not overset her plans, she merely smiled and said that it was quite all right, for she had Rosie and Belinda for company.

There was not far to walk to Mr Bravington's house, for he also lived on Royal Crescent. A very elderly manservant admitted them, and showed them into the first room off the hall. In their own house, the equivalent apartment was the dining room, but here it was fitted up as a fine library, every inch of wall space filled with laden shelves, and several smaller bookcases scattered about the room, too.

Mr Bravington, resplendent in a high powdered wig and a scarlet velvet coat with enormous cuffs, sat beside a low fire, a rug across his knees.

"Mr Fletcher, Miss Fletcher, Mr John Fletcher, sir," the manservant intoned.

"Ah, Fletcher! Good of you to call. And two of your young

people — a welcome sight in my dull life. Forgive an old man for not rising to greet you, Miss Fletcher, but the knees are not all they might be these days. Well now, what a pretty bonnet, but I do so like to see a lady's hair in all its glory. Will you indulge me, my dear?"

Angie smiled, and deftly unfastened the bonnet, laying it on top of a pile of books on a table nearby. "There, sir. Is that better?"

"Much, much better." He nodded, eyeing her with a twinkle that was not entirely avuncular. "You have a look of your father about you, but your brother's features are quite different. Very different indeed." He looked thoughtfully at Johnny.

"I am said to favour my mother, sir," Johnny said.

"Then she must have been a remarkably handsome woman, that is all I have to say about it. And the black hair — is that hers, too?"

"That is my gift to Johnny," Pa said. "My hair was just as black in my youth, but without the curls, sadly."

Mr Bravington chuckled. "We all had darker hair in our youth, and in greater abundance. So you are the younger son, eh? Have you a career in mind, or do you plan to marry an heiress?"

Johnny merely smiled. "I have no plans to marry any woman, rich or poor. I am a Fellow at Cambridge, and there I intend to stay."

"College?"

"St John's."

"Wrangler?"

"Third. Best in my college."

Mr Bravington nodded. "Very good. I was Fifth. Pembroke. Welcome, young man. Well, sit, sit, all of you. Yelden, some claret for the gentlemen and... what do you drink, my dear? I doubt we have any ratafia in the house. There might be some sherry in the cellar."

"Claret will do very well," Angie said. "I would not put your servants to the trouble of scouring the cellars. I should be glad to have some cake or a biscuit, however."

"Excellent! But here we have a four for cards, if you would indulge me, all of you."

"I have a better suggestion for you, sir," Pa said. "Angie and I are but indifferent card players, but Johnny will take you on at piquet, if you wish it."

"He is a good player, is he? I confess it is not so easy to find anyone to give me a good game these days." Mr Bravington rubbed his hands together in glee. "Bring that little round table over here, young man, and pull your chair a little closer. Well, such a treat!"

Pa sat beside them to watch the game, but they played fast and after sipping the wine and nibbling a biscuit, Angie grew bored. She was drawn across the room to a table where stood a beautiful spinet. Smiling, she ran her hands over its polished wood and then, very gently, the keys. How she longed to play it! To hear the music, to imagine herself dancing once more... She leafed through the box of sheet music nearby, hearing the tunes in her head, her feet forming the steps of their own volition.

"Will you play for us, little lady?" Mr Bravington called out from across the room. "A little music would be just the thing."

"May I? It is a beautiful instrument."

"It has a lovely tone," he said. "It was my sister's, but it has not been played these many years, not since she died."

There was no stool, so Angie stood at the instrument and carefully played a few notes, then began a favourite tune, her fingers moving expertly. The advantage of standing, she found, was that her feet could continue to move. The spinet was sadly out of tune, but it was still a pleasure to play, the sound soft in the large room.

When she paused for a moment, she heard a low chuckle behind her. "You had sooner be dancing, I think, little lady," Mr Bravington said.

"Indeed I would! There is no pleasure in life greater than dancing."

He chuckled again. "Perhaps. But you will soon have the chance, for there is to be a ball very soon."

"So Pa says!" Angie spun round in delight. "Do you know something about it, sir, for Pa will tell us nothing, nothing at all."

"Not only do I know about it, but the ball is at my instigation," he said. "Many years ago, when my sister and her husband lived in this house, she held a ball at the Rooms every year to celebrate her birthday. Naturally, the habit lapsed when she died, and when I lived in London, I saw no need for it. Now that I have returned to Bath, I hope to revive the custom while I am still well enough to attend such an occasion, but it does rather depend upon my nephew. This house is his, in fact, for he inherited it from his mother, although I have the right to live here until I am carried out, and he has a fine estate in Cheshire and no need of it. I have invited him and his wife, and as many of his in-laws as care to accompany them, to come here and arrange matters for the ball. They have intimated a certain interest, but have not yet confirmed, so there is a degree of uncertainty at present."

"That would be so splendid!" Angie cried. "Bath is almost perfect, and all that is wanting is the possibility of a ball, or some kind of dancing. But I am distracting you from your game, sir. I beg your pardon."

"You are, but it is the pleasantest kind of distraction imaginable," Mr Bravington said, his eyes twinkling. "So delightful to have a pretty young lady call upon me. I hope you will visit me many times during your stay in Bath, Miss Fletcher, and play for me, too. But now, if young Mr Fletcher will agree to stay on, I believe you and your father may leave us to our cards."

"Of course, sir," Pa said, rising and reaching for his hat. "Johnny, keep mentioning the house in Grosvenor Square, for I've not given up the idea yet."

Mr Bravington shook his head, making his wig wobble slightly. "You are a persistent man, Fletcher. No wonder you were so successful in business."

"Aye, I was, because I dealt fairly with everyone. I'll give you a good price for it, and no haggling. Or a long lease, if you truly won't sell. That would suit me as well. Think about it, Bravington. And now I'll bid you good day."

On leaving Mr Bravington's house, Angie and her father turned their steps inevitably towards the town. "The Pump Room?" Pa said.

"Why not?"

"No shopping today?"

"Not today. I overspent a trifle in town, so I am eking out my pennies until next quarter day."

"I can always let you have a little more," Pa said genially. "I like to spoil my lovely ladies, you know."

Angie tucked her arm in his. "I know you do, Pa, but it is better for me to keep within my allowance. Ma was always very strict about it, and Mama is just the same. She says that economy is a good habit to learn, since one never knows when one's circumstances may change, and although I do not think it very likely that you will lose your fortune at the gaming tables or anything of the sort, I can see the point."

"How very sensible you're getting, flower. I hardly know you when you talk of learning good habits in that way."

That made her giggle again. "To speak truth, I bought so much in town that there is not a thing I need just now."

He chuckled too. "Now, that's more like the Angie we all know. But did you wear yourself out in London, with all that junketing about? It's a rackety sort of place, to my mind, and likely to burn anyone to the socket."

"It was a little overwhelming, after Yorkshire, I admit," Angie said. "Too big, too many people, too much of everything, and no Pump Room where one may meet all one's friends. I do like Bath, very much. I almost wish we could stay here and not return to Hertfordshire."

"There is an easy solution that that problem, flower. You will just have to marry a Bath man."

She spluttered in indignation. "There is not one who would

not be torture to me to marry, I swear it." She stopped dead. "Pa, why is a footman leaning out of that window, do you suppose?"

They had made their way down Brock Street and turned into the Circus when they were arrested by the extraordinary sight of a footman in livery and wig leaning perilously out of an upper window, waving vigorously.

"Sir! Sir and madam, please to step inside," he called.

"Oh, it is Mr and Mrs Appleby's house," Angie said.

A moment later, the front door opened, and Mr Appleby the Elder rushed out to them.

"Mr Fletcher! Miss Fletcher! Will you not step inside for a moment? Mrs Fletcher and Miss Rose Fletcher and her friend are presently within."

"Oh well, if Mrs Fletcher is there," Pa said equably.

They allowed themselves to be led into the house and up the stairs, where they found not only the Fletcher ladies and Belinda with Mrs Appleby, but also Mr Whittleton and Lady Penelope Whittleton. The latter looked bored, but her husband was cooing over the Applebys' baby who was sitting on the floor.

"Is he not enchanting?" cried Mr Whittleton, almost before the civilities were got out of the way. "Is he not the most delightful infant? I adore children — always have. It tore me apart, Cal, to miss so much of your growing up. I missed you every single day."

"Did you, Papa?" Calantha said, her eyes brimming with tears. "I missed you too, naturally, but I know it could not be helped."

"No, indeed. Nothing for it, unfortunately. I never wanted to leave you behind but... you know how it is. Sometimes, one is pulled in two directions at once. But now, *now* there is no reason for me to go away ever again. Do you know what I should like, dearest Cal? I should like to settle in Bath to be near you and your delightful son, and perhaps, with God's grace, I shall live long enough to watch him grow up, as I was never able to watch *you* grow up. Would that not be wonderful?"

"Oh, Papa, I should like it of all things!" Calantha cried, throwing her arms around him as best she could without spilling the glass of Madeira he held. "That would be *wonderful!* Do you not agree, Maurice? And there is a house in Lansdown Crescent that would be perfect for you, absolutely perfect. They have such large gardens there, you see, ideal for a growing boy to run about. We could even find a house to share. Would that not be blissful?"

She prattled on in this manner for some considerable time, while neither Lady Penelope nor Mr Appleby offered a word in support of the scheme. As Mama's visit had exceeded twenty minutes, she soon afterwards rose to leave.

"Do come for dinner," Calantha gushed. "Tonight, if you do not mind taking pot luck."

"We have engagements for this evening," Mama said.

"Tomorrow, then. You must come tomorrow. I want everyone to get to know Papa and Lady Penelope. Do come!"

"I cannot accept without knowing what other engagements we may have," Mama said firmly. "Do send an invitation, and then I shall be able to determine the matter."

And with that she swept out of the room, her lips set in the thin line that signalled disapproval. Angie rather disapproved, too.

Not of Calantha, for she was not to be blamed for her innocence of her father's history, but there was only sanctimonious falseness in Mr Whittleton's professions of familial affection. It was all nauseating humbug.

13: Cards And Conversation

Angie looked forward to the evening with Lady Louisa and Lady Maria with keen anticipation. For one thing, she had Rosie to herself again for a while, without the additional company of Belinda Jupp. Belinda was a good sort of girl, and Angie liked her very well, but she was not restful to be with. Not that she would have chattered as much as usual had she been invited, for she was very much in awe of Lady Louisa.

"She's a *real* lady, and Lady Maria too, and I've no idea what to say to such people," she had said. "I never had fancy governesses like you to teach me the right way to curtsy to them and how to address them. Do I call her *'my lady'* or *'Lady Louisa'?"*

"Oh, it should always be *'my lady',"* Rosie said. "Anything else would be disrespectful."

"Mama says that social equals may call her *'Lady Louisa'* or *'ma'am',"* Angie said.

"But we are *not* her social equals!" Rosie said, rather shocked.

"I am certainly not!" Belinda said, laughing.

"But Rosie and I are, odd as it seems! We are landed gentry now, after all. We dine with such people, and they with us. Lady Louisa has invited us to play cards with her, so *she* views us as social equals. Not her equal in rank, obviously, but we are not so very far below her. *We* may address her as *'Lady Louisa'."*

"I should never dare," Rosie whispered.

Angie laughed. "Oh, Rosie, I believe you! Why, you even call our butler *'Mr Keeble'*."

"I know," Rosie said. "That is silly of me, but somehow I cannot quite bring myself to call him *'Keeble'*. I cannot accustom myself to having a butler at all, or a housekeeper, either. It seems very grand, to me."

"You'll have to get used to being grand yourself when you marry a lord, Rosie. I can't wait to call *you 'my lady',"* Belinda said, which effectively silenced the conversation.

Pa and Johnny escorted the sisters to Lady Louisa's house on their way to some male card-playing fastness recommended by Mr Bravington.

"I expect you will be throwing away more than my entire year's allowance at the tables tonight," Angie said as they walked briskly down Gay Street in the deepening dusk, stepping around the lamp lighters.

"I hope we'll end the evening in pocket," Pa said, with a broad grin. "We should take a few guineas off them, unless Johnny's completely lost his touch. What it is to have a clever son!"

Lady Louisa lived on Queen's Parade, another row of elegant town houses, of which Bath seemed to have an inexhaustible supply. Rosie and Angie were received by the manservant, who led them upstairs to the softly-lit drawing room, the card table set out ready. Music drifted out to greet them.

Lady Maria jumped up from the instrument, her face shining with pleasure. "Here you are! How splendid. I have been *so* looking forward to this evening and knowing you better."

That set the entire evening on a charming footing, for there could be no formality after such words. In no time, Lady Louisa was calling her guests by their Christian names as if she had known them since infancy, and Lady Maria swiftly followed suit. Only Rosie hesitated to abandon the protocol, although she called Lady Louisa *'ma'am'* once or twice without blushing too deeply.

Lady Louisa had not misled them when she said she preferred to talk rather than playing cards. In almost every hand, she set down her cards and leaned across the table to whisper in confidential tones some rumour or story of one of Bath's residents. She had only lived there since her widowhood, some seven years ago, but Bath was such a small, gossipy place that she knew everyone, and knew everything about them.

After a while, and very tentatively, Angie asked about Mr Appleby the younger.

"Now there is a man who has suffered a grave injustice," Lady Louisa said, laying down her cards. "Brought up from childhood to consider himself his uncle's heir and a future man of property — of *considerable* property — and then to be left dangling, with neither career nor prospects. But there, Maurice Appleby always was a slippery sort of a fellow. Very much an eye for the ladies, and not with marriage in mind, until he met Calantha Whittleton. A charming man, of course, but that type always is, smirking here and there and talking sweetness to the whole world, but not in the least dependable. When he married and cut out his nephew, he should have settled some money on him there and then, or helped to him to a career. I said so at the time, and I say so still."

Picking up her cards again, the play resumed for another trick or two, before she went on, "He's a serious fellow, the nephew, so the church would suit him very well. He preaches an excellent sermon. Have you heard him? No? He writes his own, too, and very thought-provoking they are. Not ponderous, like the regular fellow, or shouting at one, like some of these great men who preach occasionally. It is a great pity he cannot find a parish somewhere. One might have thought his uncle to be rich enough to have bought him a preferment somewhere, but no. *'Something will turn up,'* he says brightly, but how is that to happen unless he makes a push to ensure it *does* turn up? No, it is a travesty. I sincerely pity the young man, and wish I were placed to do something for him, but my jointure is in the hands of trustees. There is little I can do, except mention him at regular intervals to such of my relations as have livings in their gift."

"That is exactly my opinion, also," Angie cried. "It is abominable how he has been cast off in that dreadful way, when he has no other prospects at all."

"Has he no other relations who might help him?" Lady Maria said. "Presumably he inherited nothing from his father?"

"Not a penny piece, by all account," Lady Louisa said. "His father was a country parson with no property of his own, so there was nothing to bequeath to his son. Naturally he expected his brother to provide for the boy, having no son of his own at that time, and so it seemed, for many years. A pity Appleby ever looked at Calantha Whittleton, if you ask me."

"Oh, but surely he should not be obliged to give up his own hopes of happiness?" Rosie said. "Mr Appleby — the uncle, that is — could not help falling in love, I am sure. It is not a matter over which anyone has any control, and he could not disappoint Miss Whittleton in order not to disadvantage his nephew. For they are very much in love, are they not?"

Lady Louisa patted Rosie's hand. "You are a romantic, are you, my dear? Do you think every marriage must be a love affair? It is wonderful if it should be so, of course."

"Oh no, indeed I am not so foolish," Rosie said, with surprise in her voice. "For everyone to marry only according to their own inclinations and the dictates of their heart would lead to all manner of ills. There must be prudence, and regard for eligibility and suitability. And one must consider also the obligations imposed upon one by family. A duke's daughter should not marry a coster-monger, nor a coster-monger's daughter a duke. It would be quite wrong! One must marry to please one's family and the proper order of society, in the first instance, and I suppose money is a consideration too. But Mr Appleby, the elder Mr Appleby, has no family to think of and sufficient money to please himself, and Mrs Appleby is not at all unsuitable. So I do not see why they should not marry if they wish to. But it is very wrong to cut out poor Mr Appleby, the younger Mr Appleby, altogether. How does he survive? He must have some income, surely?"

"He has the house and an allowance from his uncle, but only until he finds an alternative. It is very unsatisfactory." Picking up her cards again, she cried, "There! My trick, I believe, and the game. Shall we have some supper now?"

The supper tray was brought in, and Angie was relieved to see that it was not at all elaborate, as she had so often seen in

London. The board carried only cold meats and a raised pie, with the usual pastries and bread and butter, with tea to drink.

After the tea things had been removed, Lady Louisa showed no inclination to return to the card table. Instead, she poured herself a glass of port and settled down for what she called *'a proper coze'*.

"How did you enjoy your season in town, Rosie? You were a great success, I hear."

Rosie blushed, of course. She blushed so easily. "Everyone was very kind," she said, in her soft way. "We were very fortunate in invitations, so we attended a great many balls."

"You danced the minuet!" Maria said, eyes gleaming. "I read of it in the *Morning Post*. Miss Mimms, our governess, permits us to read the society reports so that we will know what to expect. Lady Pinner's ball, was it not? I remember it because Redmond was there, and Miss Mimms said—"

"Enough schoolroom chatter, Maria," Lady Louisa said repressively.

"Oh!" Maria blushed a fiery red. "I beg your pardon, Aunt. I almost forgot."

"There, there, child. You have been under the thumb of your governess for so many years that it is hard to adjust to the wider world. Do remember in future that you must never mention your governess or your lessons in conversation. No one wants to hear such childish concerns, least of all gentlemen."

"Yes, Aunt. I shall remember."

Lady Maria was reduced to silence by this admonishment, and Rosie so felt for the girl that she blushed and lowered her head, too. It was left to Angie to answer Lady Louisa's questions on their activities in London, although she could not resist asking one, too.

"Did you have a season, Lady Louisa?"

"Oh, yes, but it was — goodness me, forty… no, forty-five years ago now. Times were very different, and a gown was a *gown* in those days, all hoops and gold embroidery and yards and yards of brocade, not like these flimsy modern affairs. We had to be pinned into them. And the hair! Vast, and ornamented with ships in full sail, or fruit. My mama was particularly fond of cherries. Of course, one could remove the whole contraption at night, which was so comfortable. And then the next morning, hours of work to be dressed again. Such a different time, when half one's day was spent in merely the act of dressing. But I do not think the season was quite so rackety as it is now. The roads were so bad that no one travelled in the depths of winter unless for a dire emergency, so we went up to town in the autumn and stayed the whole winter and into spring. There was not this cramming everything into a few weeks that one sees nowadays. One could take one's time and get to know a gentleman. And of course, Mama and Papa hovered over every event, watching who I danced with or even spoke to. Your mama guided you through the season, Angie, but not your papa, I think? I do not recall any mention of him in the newspapers."

This was such a curious point to raise that Angie was immediately wary. What could Lady Louisa mean by it? But there was no secret about Pa's activities in London.

"Pa felt that he could not mingle in society — not the sort of society Mama hoped we would encounter. He is uncomfortable with it, for his background is not gentry, and he knows no one he might talk to at a London ball. He always came to the assemblies with us at home... I mean, in Yorkshire, because he had many friends there, but in London his friends are all in the City."

"And so he left it to your mama to steer you through the Beau Monde. I see. Yet he accompanies you to the Pump Room."

"Oh, Bath is different!" Angie cried. "The Pump Room is... well, it is where everyone goes, high or low, is it not?"

"True, and—"

The door opened, and Lord Albury entered with a smile.

"Good evening, Miss Fletcher, Miss Angela. Aunt, Maria. I trust you have all had a pleasant evening."

"Albury? Heavens, are we dreadfully late, or are you back earlier than I expected?"

"A little early. I was not minded to stay any longer."

"Ah, well, it is not so late as I had supposed, but still, I must see you girls safely back to your mama. Gledhill? Ah, there you are. Have the carriage brought round at once."

But before the butler could carry out this order, Lord Albury said smoothly, "Unless perhaps the ladies would prefer the refreshment of walking the short distance to the Royal Crescent? The air is pleasantly cool now, and I should be very happy to offer my escort. Or if my aunt has exhausted you, the carriage is at your disposal. What shall it be, Miss Fletcher? It shall be however you wish."

Angie glanced at her sister, who looked suddenly anxious. She knew precisely why. If she accepted the carriage, it might be seen as a rebuff to Lord Albury and Mama would be cross about that. Yet if she agreed to his escort, he might view it as encouragement. But Angie knew what she wanted.

"Rosie, would you mind very much if we walked? A little exercise before bed would be just the thing to help me sleep. But if you prefer the carriage—"

"No, no. I should be happy to walk, if it would not inconvenience Lord Albury..."

"Nothing would please me more," he said, and there was nothing in his tone to suggest that this was any more than a polite form of words. He was a consummate gentleman, with nothing in his manner to distress a lady, even one so sensitive as Rosie.

So it was agreed, and within a very few minutes they were bidding Lady Louisa and Lady Maria farewell, and stepping out into the night air of Bath. It was not precisely cool, but fresher than during the day, and Angie was immediately invigorated, taking two or three deep breaths with the utmost satisfaction.

"Will you take my arm, Miss Fletcher? Miss Angela?"

But Angie could not bear to be so constrained. "Forgive me, but I prefer to walk unfettered. Rosie will be glad of your aid, I am sure."

"Of course. Miss Fletcher?"

Blushing, and reduced to inarticulacy, Rosie leaned her hand on his arm and they began their walk, Angie bouncing alongside them, for the most part. Occasionally she skipped ahead, but then recalled that Rosie would not wish to be left alone with Lord Albury, and slowed her steps.

As she walked, she pondered the evening — Lady Louisa's affability, the odd questions she sometimes asked and then the timely reappearance of Lord Albury. It was almost as if — but no, surely these matters had not been orchestrated... had they? Lady Louisa's questions gently probing beneath the surface of the Fletcher family, and then the reluctance to return to the card tables, whereupon Lord Albury reappeared, just in time to escort the ladies home. She had thought he had dropped his interest in Rosie, if indeed he had ever had any, for his attentions in London had been not at all particular. And then he had said explicitly that he had no matrimonial intentions. But there was an air of manipulation in the way he had returned at precisely the right moment, and earlier than expected. It was odd.

But if he had any thought of courtship, he gave no cause for alarm, even for Rosie's delicate sensibilities. He maintained a light patter of remarks, but his words were so unexceptionable that Angie forgot them as soon as they were uttered. He was surely the blandest and least interesting man in the Kingdom, and if he had not the prospect of an earldom in his future, would have nothing at all to attract notice. They arrived at their house without incident and even Rosie felt able to bid farewell to the viscount without more than a slight blush to her cheeks.

~~~~~

B quaked whenever a parcel arrived from Quarman's, although whether it was fear or anticipation uppermost in his mind he was hard-pressed to say. Still, every parcel was opened without delay and every book within examined with a rapidly beating heart. Great was the disappointment when nothing was concealed within, and great was the excitement when, finally, a paper fluttered to the floor.

The third letter changed everything.
~~~~~

'My dearest one, Have you worked it out yet? I am sure you must have bent your great mind to the question of my identity, and perhaps even now you have deduced it, and smile to yourself in glee at the knowledge of my secret. Or perhaps you still wonder, and examine every lady of your acquaintance for the brightened eye and slight blush of consciousness that would reveal all. Are you still curious as to why I approach you thus, surreptitiously? That at least you should understand. In this world we live in, openness on the female side is condemned. We must wait patiently for the object of our desires to notice us and make the approach, but if he does not notice us, what then are we supposed to do? Must we give up all possibility of happiness and remain silent forever? It is too cruel, and I cannot submit to it. My feelings may not be held in check any longer. My dearest, most wonderful friend, allow me to tell you how greatly I love you. All my hopes are in your hands. One word, one glance from you, and I shall know whether those hopes may one day be realised or whether I must prepare myself for sorrow and despair. In the greatest anxiety, I await some sign from you to your humble but adoring, Secret Admirer.'

Love. She had at last used that word. Somewhere in Bath was a woman who loved him, no, who *adored* him, and not because of his prospects of inheriting a fortune. She could only love him for himself, quiet and diffident as he was. A woman known to him had penetrated the barrier of disinterest he showed the world, and had found something beneath it worthy of her regard.

He was *loved*. For the first time in his life, he was loved unreservedly for himself, beyond all question.

But who on earth was it?

14: Plans And A Sermon

Mama could not avoid the dinner with Lady Penelope and Mr Whittleton, since Pa expressed an interest in the evening, and there was no gainsaying the head of the household, whose interest in a good dinner outweighed her scruples about the immoral scions of the nobility. She did not like it, however, and she ordered Johnny to keep a close eye on his sisters.

"Make sure Mr Whittleton stays away from them, and Mr Maurice Appleby, too, for they both have wandering eyes and must be kept far from innocent young ladies. Happily, the Sylvesters will not be there, so Angie need not spend the evening evading Mr Randal."

"What about Lady Penelope?" Johnny said. "Must she be kept away from innocent young ladies, too?"

"She is the daughter of a marquess," Mama said calmly. "Whatever she may have done, she certainly knows how to behave with propriety in public. It is gentlemen of whom the girls must be wary, not a lady of rank, and I am sure we shall find that she conducts herself in a manner beyond reproach."

In this assessment she was correct, for nothing could have

been more decorous than Lady Pen's behaviour. Her gown was both elegant and demure, her voice was well-modulated and her conversation aimed to please. Her husband, too, was more restrained than usual, and apart from a florid compliment or two for each lady, kept his badinage to himself.

They sat down twenty-four to dinner, which was rather a squeeze, but no one minded, the meal was accounted an excellent one, and the conversation was lively. Only Mr Appleby the Younger sat mute and serious amidst his more animated companions. It was a disappointment. Clearly Angie's letters had not raised his spirits as she had hoped.

When the ladies withdrew to the drawing room, Angie waited hopefully for music to be called for, but no one seemed minded for it. She sighed and found herself a seat in a far corner of the room, one where she could not see Rosie and Belinda whispering together, and laughing from time to time. It was very lowering to have all one's sisters taken from one. With Allie and Julia married, and Bella still in the schoolroom, Angie had depended on Rosie for company in Bath. Not that she begrudged the two their close friendship, but she would have liked a friend of her own. Lady Maria Landers would have been perfect, but she was not there.

Still, there was entertainment in watching the expression on Mama's face as she was compelled to talk to Lady Penelope with apparent civility. Mama was equal to it, naturally, for putting on a polite face was her strongest accomplishment, and only those who knew her well would appreciate the effort it cost her.

Before too long, Mama made some excuse to move away, and Lady Penelope looked about for her next target. Angie was not quick enough to avert her eyes, and so she had the doubtful pleasure of seeing that lady bearing down on her with a smile.

"Well... Miss... um"

"Fletcher. Angela Fletcher."

"Of course. Goodness, I am so hopeless with names. In the Tsar's court, you know, with all those foreign names, I was quite lost. I never had the least idea to whom I was speaking, but it never seemed to matter. I smiled at them and fluttered my eyelashes, and they forgave me my transgressions. If I had been a man, I dare say I should have been called out a dozen times, but men are so silly around women, are they not? Make them think you are panting for them, and you will have every one of them at your feet."

"How did you manage the Russian language?" Angie said, feeling she ought to drag the conversation back to safer channels.

"Heavens, no one speaks the peasant language! No, everything at court was in French, a far more civilised language, if you ask me. I suppose English must be accounted civilised, too, but it has not the elegance of French."

"Are you pleased with Bath?" Angie said, a little offended by the reluctance to accord English its proper place in the pantheon of languages.

Lady Penelope laughed throatily. "What a well-brought-up child you are, sticking to the approved subjects of conversation like a good girl. Am I pleased with Bath? Not especially. It is a dull old place, if you want my honest opinion. London, now... that is my natural home. Brighton is delightfully lively, too, although this time— But never mind that. Bath it is. At least we have found a place where we can play cards properly. I assure you, I was quite in despair at first, for there was nowhere we could truly enjoy ourselves, but then Maurice introduced us to Willow House, and we can play there every night with our friends. The Wherrets, the Ansteads, the Sylvesters... they all play there. Most agreeable. Wildly expensive, of course, but the best places are never cheap."

Angie could not quite see why, when there was a card party every night of the week, and often more than one to choose from, anyone would need to go anywhere else, and be charged for the experience, but she said politely, "If you find Bath so dull, I wonder you left Brighton at all."

"Oh... there were reasons," she said, waving a hand vaguely, so that a waft of exotic perfume filled the air. "Bath is not so bad, if one has a few amiable companions to liven things up, but so many of them are dreadfully staid and stuffy. Do you not find it so?"

"Oh, yes!" Angie said with feeling. "They are all so... so *respectable."*

This sent Lady Penelope into peals of laughter. "Indeed! For what could possibly be worse than a *respectable* person, eh? Who is the most respectable person in Bath?"

"Lady Mellish," Angie said promptly. "Very pious."

"Oh, piety! I have no time for piety," Lady Penelope said, wrinkling her dainty nose. "And what of the men? Who is the stuffiest and most respectable gentleman? There must be one, at least, who is without fault."

"Mr Appleby the Younger," Angie said without a second's hesitation. "He is stuffy perfection personified, and disapproves thoroughly of me."

"And of me too, I make no doubt. And the best of it is, that he is here tonight, so I can have a little fun with him."

"I beg you will not. It would be unkind to vex him in that way," Angie said, alarmed.

Lady Penelope laughed again, and agreed to it with perfect affability. And when the gentlemen emerged from their port-filled interlude in the dining room, she set out with single-minded determination to engage Mr Appleby the Younger in conversation. He tried to move away from her, his expression pained, but she pursued him around the room, and only the arrival of the card tables put a stop to her sport.

Watching her, and seeing his acute discomfort, made Angie remember the many times she had herself set out to tease Mr Appleby. She had even justified it in the same way, as a little fun. But she could see now that it was not fun for him, not at all. Poor Mr Appleby. Guilt rose up inside her, and she thought uncomfortably that her letters might be an even greater vexation. He had accused her once of tormenting him, and she began, for the first time, to glean some inkling of what he meant.

~~~~~

B set his mind seriously to work out who might be sending him these letters. It was imperative he find out, for there could be nothing more fatal than to accidentally say something which might be taken as encouragement. A woman who was so wanton as to write letters to the object of her desire without the certainty of marriage or a betrothal was not a rational person, and there was no knowing how she might react if he so much as smiled at her. *'One word, one glance from you...'* she had said, but how could he prevent himself from saying that word or giving that glance if he
~~~~~

had no idea who she was?

He ran systematically in his mind through all the ladies of his acquaintance, bearing in mind that she had described herself as his friend, but he could not identify a single one who had ever displayed a *'brightened eye and slight blush of consciousness'.* Even those who were only slightly known to him passed under review, but at the end of it he had to declare himself baffled.

Yet he had to resolve the question. It was a peculiar but exquisite form of torture to know himself to be an object of affection, to have inspired the deepest feelings in *someone*, and not have the least idea who it might be.

How could he find out? He could hardly ask anyone outright, nor did he have any samples of writing with which to compare. It was a conundrum. Throughout dinner that evening and then cards afterwards, his mind returned to the problem again and again. When Higgins had left him that night, B reached for his Bible to read a little before he surrendered to sleep, and perhaps the word of the Lord would guide him, and bring him counsel.

The Holy Book fell open at Proverbs. *'Death and life are in the power of the tongue: and they that love it shall eat the fruit thereof',* he read.

The power of the tongue... There was indeed power in words, and not merely those of the tongue, for look how a few written words had disturbed the even tenor of his life. And not far away, his eyes fell on another line, *'The heart of the righteous studieth to answer: but the mouth of the wicked poureth out evil things'.*

The mouth of the wicked... The woman who wrote those letters had a wicked pen, more correctly, but it certainly poured out evil things. To declare her love to a man — a man who was not her husband! Where was the maidenly modesty and gentle reticence that should characterise the female sex?

But his thoughts had shown him the way forward. He now knew how to discover the identity of his mysterious admirer. With a smile of satisfaction, he closed the Bible, and knelt beside the bed to say his prayers.

~~~~~

Angie was not long in returning to Mr Bravington's house, armed this time with her tuning fork. He professed himself delighted to see her, but she thought he looked less well than before.

"Are you sure I do not disturb you, sir? Tuning an instrument is hard on the ears."

"But the results will be worthwhile, I trust. You will play for me before you go?"

"Of course, until Johnny arrives to play piquet with you."

"Ah. Excellent."

It was no easy task to tune an instrument so long neglected, but the effort was worthwhile, for the spinet had an exquisite tone. Angie played for more than an hour, and it was hard to say who enjoyed the time more. Mr Bravington had tears of joy in his eyes.

"Ah, child, you are well named, for indeed you play like an angel. Such ability! I never heard a better player."

"You are kind, sir, but it is clear you have never heard my future sister-in-law perform. She is both a better player and a better singer. It is true that I have in the past been much praised for my musical performances, and was greatly puffed up in my own
~~~~~

consequence as a result, but Eloise casts me sadly into the shade. It is very lowering."

Mr Bravington chuckled. "I doubt anyone would put *you* in the shade, young lady. I have heard of Miss Whittleton's talents, but I do not often venture out in the evenings, and so have not been anywhere where she might be heard. But after such a pleasant morning, I am afraid I must be the bearer of bad news. There is to be no ball. My nephew and his wife cannot spare the time to come to Bath, and naturally I cannot make the arrangements myself."

"Oh but if that is all, *we* could arrange it for you!" Angie cried. "Mama is wonderfully clever at such things. Is it to be at the Assembly Rooms? Then Mr King will help."

"Do you truly think your mama would do it? There is a great deal of work involved."

"Mama would adore the work, I assure you. Besides, you cannot be so hard-hearted as to deprive us of a ball after dangling such an enticing prospect before us. It is all that is wanting to make our stay in Bath perfect."

"Very well, young lady. If your mama is willing, then she may arrange this ball for me. I confess, I should very much like to see *you* dance."

"And so you shall, sir. So you shall!"

Angie at once launched into a cotillion, humming the music as she danced across the room, and only stopped when Johnny arrived to play piquet.

"Everyone has gone on to the Pump Room, little sister, but I am to escort you there, if Mr Bravington will be so good as to delay our game for a little while."

"No, no! There is no need for that," Angie cried. "You two must have your cards. It is no distance to the Pump Room, and I can walk there by myself."

"I do not think—" Johnny began, but Mr Bravington waved an airy hand.

"My man will accompany you, Miss Fletcher. A lady of your tender years and station in life must always have an escort, but it need not be your brother."

The footman was an imposing fellow the size of a tree, so Johnny conceded that he might be an acceptable escort and Angie was permitted to leave. To Angie, used to walking everywhere with one or more of her sisters or brothers, there was something rather freeing in walking about the streets with only a footman keeping the correct three paces behind. For one thing, there was no need for conversation, so Angie could hum to herself without distractions. For another thing, if she stopped at a shop window to admire a particularly fetching straw gypsy bonnet with blue ribbons, as anybody might, a footman would not say impatiently, "Come *on*, Angie! Do you intend to stand about all day?"

Sadly, there was a major drawback to this happy state of affairs, in the dandified person of Mr Randal Sylvester, who bounced into view as she admired the said bonnet. For a moment, she toyed with the idea of giving him the cut direct, but he gave her no opportunity.

"Miss Fletcher! What a delightful surprise," he exclaimed, making her a florid bow. "The very person I most hoped to see today. *'Randal,'* I said to myself as I tied my cravat this morning, *'if there is one person above all others whom it would thrill me to meet today, it would be Miss Angie Fletcher.'* Not that I mean any insult to your lovely sister, for who could denigrate such beauty? Certainly not Randal Sylvester, oh no! But she has not your liveliness, my dear Miss Fletcher, and if there is one thing a man admires more than beauty, it is liveliness of spirit. I must have liveliness, Miss Fletcher, I positively must, and here in your person is the very ideal of womanhood. You are the shining light of Bath society, the paramount—"

"Do you always talk to yourself as you tie your cravat?"

"What? Oh... well, sometimes, you know how it is."

"No. How is it, Mr Sylvester?"

He smiled weakly. He really was a very stupid man. "Well now... Ha ha! How you like to jest, Miss Fletcher. But come, let me escort you to your destination. A lady should not be unattended, even in Bath, and especially not one so—"

"I am not unattended, Mr Sylvester." She gestured towards the footman, staring at nothing in particular not six feet away, and pretending not to listen.

"Oh, a manservant! I do not regard that as a proper escort for a lady. Allow me to accompany you to wherever you may be going." Flapping his hands at the footman, he went on, "Off you go, fellow. You are no longer needed."

"I take my orders from my master," the footman said, adding belatedly, "sir."

"Well, I cannot prevent you from trailing along behind us, if you insist, but keep your distance, mind. I should not want anyone to suppose that I am not capable of defending a lady in a fight."

"Are we going to encounter a fight?" Angie said mildly.

"Should I have armed myself with my parasol? Or a sword stick, perhaps?"

"It is only a figure of speech," Mr Sylvester said testily. "Lord, how you do take a fellow up, sometimes. Now, do take my arm, Miss Fletcher and let us get moving. We cannot stand about in the street all day."

He held out his arm, and when she hesitated, grabbed her hand and placed it firmly on his. She removed it at once.

"Thank you, but I do not need your support," she said, moving off down Milsom Street so swiftly that he was momentarily left behind.

"Wait! Wait!" he cried, rushing after her. "Well, you are a most ungrateful girl! Slow down a little, I beg you. How can I keep up with you when you rush away like that? Where are you going, anyway?"

"I am going to the Pump Room and you may accompany me there if you must, Mr Sylvester, but pray do not imagine me to be some feeble creature who would fall over without a man's arm to lean upon."

For a few moments he was silenced by this forthright speech, but the irrepressible Sylvester nature soon reasserted itself. By the time she reached the Pump Room and met the rest of her family, Angie was heartily sick of Mr Randal Sylvester.

~~~~~

As Angie had anticipated, Mama hurled herself into the business of organising of Mr Bravington's ball with all the rigour of a military campaign. Within twenty-four hours, she had discussed the arrangements with Mr Bravington, booked the Upper Assembly
~~~~~

Rooms for the occasion, had sent notes to musicians, flower suppliers, a servants' registry and an array of bakers, pastry cooks, grocers, ice cream makers and sundry other purveyors of comestibles, and had covered the large desk in the library with lists. She was so caught up in making lists, that she never thought to ask just why Pa had been calling on Mr Bravington in the first place, so she had no suspicion he was trying to buy the Grosvenor Square house.

"Aren't you glad we came to Bath?" Pa said smugly, as proud as if he had had the idea of a ball himself. "Now my lovely ladies will be able to dance again. Just as long as you don't wear yourself out with all this work, Mrs Fletcher."

She laughed at that. "Work? This is pure pleasure, I assure you. Now, what colour should we have for the flowers, do you think?"

"Do you have to pick just one? Flowers come in so many pretty colours," Pa said.

She smiled sadly, and shook her head at such a want of sensibility. "True, but one must have a *theme*, Mr Fletcher. One colour to dominate, and then a scattering of others to contrast or blend, just as when choosing trimmings for a bonnet."

Pa's eyes promptly became unfocused. "Well, if there is to be talk of bonnets, I can have nothing further to add to the conversation, my dear. I shall leave you to your plans."

"Yes, do," she said cordially, her eyes already turning back to her list. "Cream, I think... with pale peach."

With reluctance Mama set aside her lists for Sunday but Pa insisted that she have at least one day free of planning. Meekly, she agreed to it, but she was unusually silent on the walk to church, her mind still contemplating her lists, for every now and then she muttered to herself, like an incantation.

Church brought a surprise, for when the congregation settled itself resignedly for the sermon, usually a long, dreary affair, Mr Appleby the Younger ascended the steps to the pulpit. Angie had forgotten that he was an ordained clergyman, for normally he sat in his uncle's pew, just another worshipper. Now, in his Geneva bands and surplice, his serious face looked rather fitting, and effective, too, for Angie was immediately consumed by guilt. What degree of sin was it to tease a sober man of God with impassioned love letters? And what punishment would God impose for such wickedness? Spots on her face, perhaps. Toothache, or... oh, the horror! A broken leg, so she could never dance again! She bowed her head in remorse.

For a while, she scarcely attended to the sermon itself, but gradually the words seeped into her consciousness. Mr Appleby's voice was not strident, but it was authoritative and held his audience spellbound. *'The word of God... the mouth of the wicked... the power of the tongue...'*, and a great deal more in the same vein. Words... words held a power, and should not be used lightly or wantonly, whether spoken or written. He was emphatic on this last point. "Take the utmost thought before committing a single word to paper, for you know not what injury you may do to your immortal souls thereby," he said, gazing down at the congregation from the height of the pulpit. "To the females amongst you in particular I say this — write no word of evil, for you above all must be unblemished, your virtue untouched. *'Who can find a virtuous woman? for her price is far above rubies.'*"

His tone was not condemnatory, rather he sounded like Pa

sometimes did when Angie had got into a scrape — sorrowful and disappointed. That was worse than anything, in Angie's mind. Guilt already held her in its icy grip, but now she was truly penitent. If she could have taken back those letters, she would have done it in a second. She had meant no harm, only to bring a little pleasure into his sad life, but she should not have done it, she knew that now. How wicked she was!

The sermon went on, moving into less particular themes, but Angie could not doubt that what she had heard was aimed directly at her. *'Take the utmost thought before committing a single word to paper, for you know not what injury you may do to your immortal soul thereby',* he had said, and what else could it possibly mean? She kept her head low, and tried very hard not to cry.

15: Word Games

B watched the congregation carefully as he came to the important part of the sermon. From his vantage point in the pulpit, high above the congregation, he could see into every box pew. Surely one of the ladies present would show some sign to indicate that she understood him? He had reckoned without the attributes of the fashionable bonnet. Some, it was true, wore small caps that did nothing to conceal their faces, but too many hid behind wide brims or obtrusive feathers. A lady with modestly lowered eyes was invisible to him, and he could see nothing of her expression. If any mouth opened wide in shock at his words, or any eye shed a silent tear, he knew nothing of it. He left the church quite despondent. How was he to uncover his mysterious admirer now?

Lady Mellish accosted him almost as soon as he emerged from within. “An excellent sermon, Mr Appleby. You have a great way with words, if I may so express myself.”

B dutifully smiled at this modest witticism. “Thank you, ma’am. Too kind.”

“I like a man who can say what needs to be said without that hectoring tone so many preachers have. And you understand that young women must be kept in order. Some of them nowadays behave in the most shameless ways, but when they hear such words of wisdom, and spoken with all your own firmness of character, perhaps one or two of them will draw back from their wicked ways."

"One must hope so," B said, although only half attending, his mind still running on his letters.

"Do you have a living yet, Mr Appleby? Or hopes of one?"

"I do not."

"Hmpf. I cannot think what the bishop is about, not finding you something long since. But I may be able to do something for you, which will also benefit myself. There is a chapel at my estate at Hessenford, but the chaplain left last Candlemas. I have been looking about me since then for a suitable candidate of the required moral standard. I should like to offer you the position. Should you care to come with me when next I return to Taunton? You can put the fear of God into my daughters-in-law and instil proper principles into the children, for otherwise they will continue to run wild and in a few years will be all but ungovernable. Two hundred a year, daily prayers, a Sunday service and such marriages and baptisms as may be needed. Some tuition for the boys, perhaps, before they go to school. An apartment within the house. What do you say, Appleby?"

B could hardly breathe. A chaplaincy! Two hundred a year! Accommodation, and his meals, presumably. He stammered out his gratitude as best he could, his fluency deserting him.

"Good, good. But say nothing to anyone just yet, for I do not want the boys to hear of it through idle chatter. I shall have to sweet-talk them, because they will be against it. They are against everything I propose, but it is still my house and they must abide by my wishes. They can do whatever they like after I am gone. Good day to you, Appleby."

She strode away, leaving him rather breathless. Well! Finally he would be beholden to no one, would be his own man at long last. Lady Mellish had chosen him personally, as being of the required moral character. A pillar of rectitude. How gratifying, to have his respectability recognised and rewarded. He was humbly thankful for her confidence in him.

So why did he feel so... so *odd.* But he knew why — he would have to leave Bath. That was a blow for he could remember no other home. He would lose his friends, his daily routine, the familiar shops, his beloved garden... Everything would be different.

But he must not think of the disadvantages. He would have a new home, he told himself sternly. He would grow accustomed. There would be a garden at Hessenford, and presumably he could work in it, if he wished. He must be grateful... he *was* grateful...

And yet... it would not be *his* garden. He would have no control over what he could grow, or how, and the gardeners would see it as interference. Then there was the salary. Two hundred a year. Not an inconsiderable sum, but less than he had now, and not enough to marry on. Another oddity... he had never particularly wished to marry, so why did that concern him? Yet it did.

There was no time to ponder the matter further, for once Lady Mellish had moved away, the rest of the congregation felt entitled to draw near to shake his hand and thank him, with varying degrees of sincerity, for his sermon.

"Very original," Mr Fletcher said. "I shall think of you every time I take up my pen, sir."

"Most uplifting," his wife said, frowning at him.

Miss Fletcher and her friend were too engrossed in their own conversation to speak to him, and the Fletcher son moved past with a nod and a smile, but Miss Angela Fletcher stopped before him, her face riddled with anxiety.

"Did you mean that, sir?" she said. "About... about wickedness? Because that seems very harsh indeed for nothing but *words*. Surely it is what we *do* that matters, not what we *say?"*

She seemed so distressed that he answered her in his gentlest tones. "It is perhaps not the wisest course to argue theology with an ordained clergyman, Miss Fletcher. Words matter very much."

She blushed fiery red, nodded and scuttled away.

The congregation had scattered and B was on his way home when he stopped dead in the middle of Gay Street, causing two women approaching to giggle together, and step off the pavement to go around him.

Of all the women in the congregation at St Swithin's, only one had shown any sign that she had been deeply affected by his words, and it was the last one he had expected. Miss Angela Fletcher.

It was hard to believe, but *Angela Fletcher* was in love with him!

That changed *everything.*

~~~~~

Angie could not face the Sunday school, so she went home with
~~~~~

the rest of the family and spent the rest of the day in a bout of unusually serious reflection. She was not a person who thought very deeply about anything beyond bonnets and balls, but now she was forced to face up to her own iniquities. With the best of intentions, she had done a wicked thing and now she had no idea how to make things right again. Or perhaps she never could.

Her naturally ebullient spirits whispered that it was not so bad. Surely a few letters, written with benevolent intent, were not so serious a transgression? She badly needed someone to talk to, but there was no one. Rosie, who would have wept and reassured her instantly that she had done nothing so very wrong, would have been the ideal person to confide in, but she was always with Belinda.

Will would have been her next choice. He would have ruffled her hair, and said, "Lord, Angie, take no notice of Appleby. He is naught but a prosy fool," and they would have laughed about it together. But Will was far away in Hertfordshire, and who else was there? Not Johnny, who would shrug and turn back to his book. Not Mama, who would tell her she was a foolish girl who should know better, and would probably send her home! Before the ball! No, such an outcome could not be borne.

Pa, now... Pa was always sympathetic. He would sigh, and say he was disappointed in her, but he would not send her home. No, for he would do something far worse — he would insist that she go straight to Mr Appleby, confess all and apologise, and the humiliation would be beyond enduring. She could not! She *would* not!

"Are you quite well, flower?"

Pa's voice made her jump. "Oh, yes. Perfectly well."

"You've been looking at that page for a half hour or more, and such a serious look on your face. It's not like you, Angie love."

"I wish we could have some music," she said plaintively, for the instrument would soothe her far more than her own thoughts.

Pa chuckled. "Aye, I don't like the Sabbath much myself. Can't do this, can't do that, nothing but sermons or the Bible to read. Not but what there's always something interesting in the Bible, but I'd rather have a hand of cards after dinner, to be truthful."

"We are all a little out of spirits after Mr Appleby's sermon," Mama said. "I do not know how it is, for he never once raised his voice, but his words have been echoing in my head all day. Shall we have our tea now, and be in our beds early?"

Pa's face brightened. "What a splendid idea, Mrs Fletcher, since there's nothing worth doing downstairs."

Johnny looked up from his book and laughed, although Angie could see nothing funny in what Pa had said. She wondered if she would ever feel like laughing again. She escaped to her bedroom at the earliest opportunity, and said her prayers with unusual sincerity. Then she curled up under the blankets in a miserable huddle, and cried herself to sleep.

~~~~~

A night's repose restored much of Angie's optimism. No one knew of her great sin, and even if it was as grave as Mr Appleby suggested, she had the rest of her life to atone for it. She would be very, very good from that day forth. There would be no more games, no more tricks played, no more teasing, no matter how gentle. There would *definitely* be no more letters. She would be a model of maidenly decorum. She would even follow Mr Appleby's
~~~~~

advice, and start a course of improving reading.

With this resolution made, she bounced down the stairs for breakfast, spent an hour with Mr Bravington's spinet and then enjoyed the silent escort of the tree-like footman to the Pump Room. Lady Maria rushed across to her as soon as she set foot through the door.

"There you are, Angie! I was beginning to wonder if you were coming today. Do you want to walk or shall we find a quiet corner? For I have had some very good news — my sister Georgiana is betrothed! At last! We were beginning to think that poor Hugo would never come up to scratch, but at last he has, and they will be married by Christmas. Three years he has been hovering around her, can you believe it? The first season she came out, he was so attentive, everyone thought it would be a match, but he went away without offering and the next year he was not in town at all. But this year, he was back and again everyone thought he would offer for her. But he dashed off before the end of the season without saying a word. Poor Georgiana went into such a decline, Mama says. But then just last week he turned up at Chaseley quite unexpectedly, went straight in to talk to Papa and offered within the hour. He had been hoping for an inheritance from a great-uncle, and now it has come through. Is it not wonderful?"

"Wonderful that his inheritance came through, but also wonderful that she waited so long," Angie said. "I should certainly not wait three years for a suitor to come up to scratch. He was very lucky that no one else snatched her away from him."

"Oh... well, as to that, there were never great queues waiting to snatch up Georgiana, or Charlotte, either. Mama gets so cross with them, for nothing ever pleases them. But the best of it is that now I shall be able to come out next year, instead of waiting another year. Not that I am looking forward to it, for I think it will be horrid, but it is better to get it over with sooner rather than later. That is what Patty says — our old nurse. *'Take your medicine at once, dearie, and then 'tis done with.'* That is what she always says, although I cannot quite capture her accent."

Angie, who could not imagine how the pure felicity of a season in town could ever be compared with a dose of medicine, homed in on one point which puzzled her. "But what does your sister's marriage have to do with your come-out?"

"Oh, because Mama said she positively refused to have three unmarried daughters in town at once. So if Hugo had failed again, she would have given Georgiana and Charlotte one more year, and after that they would have had to stay at home. Or perhaps two more years and then Henrietta and I could come out together. It is very trying to have so many sisters, I can tell you."

Angie's eyebrows rose, for she found her sisters very far from trying. "How many do you have?"

"There are seven of us, and Mama says it is a great test of her ingenuity to find husbands for so many. I almost wish I did not have to marry, but if I do not, then Henrietta and Louisa cannot come out. Louisa is so lucky, being the youngest, for she need not marry at all, if she dislikes the idea."

Angie was unsure how to respond to this insight into the ways of a peer's family. She and her sisters had come out when they had wanted to, with no question of the younger kept back until the elder ones were married. She herself had left the schoolroom at fifteen, and not a soul had suggested she should stay there while Rosie and Julia were still unwed. She would have liked to see them try! As if anyone could keep her from the York assemblies!

Fortunately, she did not have to respond to Lady Maria, for there was a surprising diversion. Mr Appleby the Younger entered the Pump Room looking as smug as a cat in a roomful of mice. He smiled, he greeted acquaintances affably, he was in all respects a changed man.

"Whatever has happened to him?" Angie said, rather awed by this transformation.

"He does look different," Lady Maria said. "I like him better without his surplice."

"Perhaps he has had an inheritance, too," Angie said. "He must have wealthy relations somewhere, surely. A great-aunt in... oh, Garforth, perhaps. An uncle in... um, Uckerby."

"A cousin in Colchester," Lady Maria said. "A great-uncle in Grantham. A... hmm, what else? It cannot be a close relation."

"A *second* cousin from Scarborough," Angie said triumphantly. "A third cousin from Thorpe."

"A fourth cousin from... I cannot think of anywhere with an 'F'! Oh, Folkestone, of course."

They would have continued in this vein for some time, except that Lord Albury came to reclaim his sister, and for a while Angie was left alone in her seat. This gave her time to watch Mr Appleby more closely. He was sitting not far from her, drinking his glass of water. Whenever she looked at him, he was watching her, but he instantly turned his gaze in a different direction. She looked away, then when she next glanced across, he was watching her again. And this time he smiled. It was unnerving, that smile. It made him look... well, handsome. Agreeable. Approachable. Perfectly normal. It was astonishing.

No one who knew Angie would call her shy, and normally she would have relished the opportunity to tease Mr Appleby for staring at her so. Yet after his sermon yesterday, she dared not attract his notice. So she sat unmoving, and resisting the urge to look at him, or even to go there and ask him what he was about.

Instead, to her confusion, he came to her.

"Miss Fletcher?" he said, bowing. "Are you quite well?"

"Why yes... thank you... I... I am perfectly well," she said.

"Your feet are not moving to the music today," he said, and he smiled — again he smiled at her! "I have been considering what you said after the service yesterday, and I should not wish you to worry unnecessarily. I cannot think that you have done anything which might put your immortal soul in peril. In fact, I am quite sure of it. Pray set your mind at rest, for I am *certain* you need not regret any words, spoken or written."

He bowed, smiled yet again and bade her good day. She watched him move away rigid with shock. *'You need not regret any words, spoken or written'.* Written words. He knew! He must know that she had sent those wretched letters. Oh, what on earth must he think of her!

She caught herself sharply. Why was she even concerned about such a thing? What was his good opinion to her? She cared not a jot what he thought of her, and it was too bad of him to occupy her thoughts in this way. She had wasted far too much time on the wretched man as it was, and all to bring a little happiness into his life. And what was her reward for her benevolence? She was berated from the pulpit and reduced to a quivering wreck by *his* words. Words *do* matter, just as he had said. And then — the nerve of the man! — he actually told her, in the most patronising manner, not to worry about it! He was abominable! Well, then, she would *not* worry about those stupid letters at all. If he could denounce them in ringing terms one day and then tell her she need not regret them, so be it. She need not consider the matter again.

While she was engaged in these ruminations, Randal Sylvester gambolled across the room to her. "Did you see?" he hissed in an urgent whisper, sitting down beside her. "Appleby! Whatever can have occurred to put him in such good humour?"

If there was anything worse than Mr Annoying Appleby and his condescension, it was Mr Silly Sylvester. Angie could not quite hide her displeasure at being thus interrupted.

"Who knows what is in his mind?" she snapped. "He is a closed book to me."

"But he spoke to you, and you are wondrous great with him," Mr Sylvester persisted. "Come, dear lady, do tell, for I am sure he must have said something to you. To everyone else, his utterances were merely commonplace, but his expression as he talked to you — so earnest, and yet so cheerful — whatever his good news must be, I am certain he imparted to *you* what he would not say to *me*."

Angie could not tell him the truth, naturally, but if she simply refused to say anything, he was perfectly capable of pestering her until she heartily wished to throw him in the river. Besides, the opportunity to tease him was too great.

Leaning forward conspiratorially, she whispered, "He did, of course. Shall I tell you? No, I should not."

His eyes gleamed. "Oh, but you must! My dear Miss Fletcher, have pity on my wondering mind and tell me *everything*."

"Oh, very well, but you must not speak of it to a single soul.

It is a stupendous secret. He has been left a large sum from his second-cousin in Scarborough, who had a seizure while swimming in the sea. He was a single man with no other successors, so he left him his silk warehouse, his stable full of stallions, all his sadly departed sister's sketches and his silverware."

"Gracious!" Mr Sylvester said, eyes round. "How much is Appleby worth, then? What would his income be?"

"Can you not guess? Six thousand a year."

"Well, I never! A man of means, then. But no house? Or an estate? Not even a pretty little cottage somewhere?"

"Of course not!" she said sharply. "Nothing but a small shack, naturally. Lord, you are slow this morning, Mr Sylvester. Excuse me, if you please, but I must seek my mama now."

He bowed as she rose and strode out into the crowds milling about the room. Such a stupid man! Her wit was wasted on him.

16: An Outing To Midford Castle

B felt curiously light, like thistledown floating over the meadows. *Angela Fletcher loved him!* It was extraordinary. He could scarcely believe it, yet he could not doubt the evidence of his own eyes. Her confusion, her distress after his sermon could not be misunderstood. She it was who had written those heartfelt letters, speaking of her admiration, her affection, her love.

For the whole of Sunday, he drifted in a dream, not at all sure what to make of it but quite unable to think of anything else. Even Lady Mellish's kindly offer of a chaplaincy paled into insignificance beside the overwhelming discovery that, for the first time in his life, he was truly loved for himself. Not even Elspeth Meek, persistent as she had been, had cared about anything beyond his expected fortune, but Miss Fletcher could have no such considerations. He had no money or great rank to attract her, and in person he was unremarkable, so her love must be the truest kind, entirely disinterested.

How flattering it was! She was so young, so pretty, so full of life... yet she had surrendered her heart to him, of all people. She had spent the spring in London, where surely she had met some of the most attractive men in society — men like his uncle, with smooth manners and seductive words to entice gullible young girls. Men like Randal Sylvester with his convivial ways. Yet she had not succumbed, but had turned her eyes elsewhere, onto his own unworthy person. He could not be ungrateful, naturally, but she was beyond his reach. Her wealth and beauty and manifold charms rendered her ineligible for his humble self.

At this point in his musings, he was brought up short. Her manifold charms? Had she any charms at all? A few days ago he would have said not. He had thought her flighty and empty-headed, as all young women were, and her manners were impertinent. He had despised her thoroughly. Yet he could not now summon his previous righteous indignation against her. Any girl of eighteen who fell so desperately in love as to write impassioned letters to the object of her affections was greatly to be pitied, especially as there could be no question of her hopes being fulfilled. He was not in a position to marry, and might never be so. Lady Mellish's offer would make him independent of his uncle at long last, but he would still be subject to Lady Mellish's goodwill.

What might marriage be like? With Elspeth Meek, he had never been remotely tempted. He was not, he hoped, so shallow as to be deterred by the pasty skin, dumpy figure and teeth better suited to a rabbit, but her shameless pursuit had horrified him. Where was the maidenly modesty he could admire? Where the submissiveness a well-brought-up female should display? Where the desire to improve herself? She had told him openly that she had never read a book in her life, and had no wish for female accomplishments, or *'all that boring nonsense'*, as she described it. Art, music, skill with a needle, any kind of learning — she eschewed it all in favour of determined hedonism, and he could never respect such a woman.

But Angela Fletcher was not like that. Yes, she pursued pleasure as much as any young woman, and she was a little short of maidenly modesty, it had to be said, but her response to his sermon showed there was hope of improvement. She was accomplished, too, able to play and sing... and dance! He still shivered at the memory of her dancing, like an angel come to earth. She was not at all angelic in other ways, but he could forgive her much for her musical aptitude. It was not frivolous to spend years perfecting her performance on the pianoforte. And she was easy to talk to, he had to admit. One did not struggle to converse with her. There was a teasing wit to her that, if he were honest, he rather enjoyed.

When he entered the Pump Room on Monday, she was almost the first person he saw, giggling with Lady Maria Landers, no doubt infecting her ladyship with her own irreverence. Such an innocent. She may not be a deep thinker, but she was so young that she must be forgiven her childish giddiness. He was so grateful for her freely-given affection that he could be charitable, even benevolent towards her. The light-heartedness inside him was entirely due to her influence.

He greeted a few acquaintances, then received his usual glass of water. It was while he was sipping it dutifully that he noticed Miss Fletcher, now alone, watching him. He glanced away quickly, for he did not wish to give her an ounce of encouragement in her benighted passion for him. *'One word, one glance from you...'*, she had said, and he dared not risk it.

Yet she looked so forlorn, sitting there quite alone, and her feet not even dancing away to the music, all by themselves, as they usually did. He was struck with guilt for his sermon of yesterday, which had clearly terrified her. That, at least, was something he could correct. He rose, crossed to where she sat and gave her a few words to set her mind at rest.

Then he left the Pump Room and made his way towards the Lower Assembly Rooms for his usual perambulation, and allowed his mind to wonder just what it would be like to be married to Miss Angela Fletcher.

~~~~~

AUGUST

On Tuesday, there was an outing to Midford Castle and Farleigh Castle. B was disinclined for it, but his uncle insisted and he could not think of an excuse to escape. It was the worst kind of outing, for his uncle had collected together the most random selection of people, with no thought given to compatibility. The Fletchers, of course, for they were almost family, because of Eloise, and through them Lord Albury and his sister. Whittleton and Lady Penelope could not be excluded, and somehow the Sylvesters contrived an invitation. Then Uncle Maurice's particular friends the Ansteads must be included, and the overpowering Mrs Hayward and her daughter overheard some of the discussion in the Pump Room, and invited themselves.

"We were planning just such an excursion ourselves, weren't we, Dora?" Mrs Hayward said in her artificially bright way. "Why, we were only discussing the idea at dinner last night. *'Midford Castle,'* I said to Mr Hayward. *'We must go to Midford Castle before the weather turns,'* I told him, for it always does turn in August, doesn't it? Have you noticed? It always takes a turn for the worse
~~~~~

in August, so we must go very soon. What about next Tuesday?"

She was right about the weather, for the long, dry spell finally broke with showers overnight and B woke to ominous grey clouds in the morning. He was hopeful the excursion would be called off, but his uncle was made of sterner stuff and apart from the switch from open to closed carriages for the ladies, and the provision of shawls and umbrellas, the outing proceeded exactly as planned. Only two of those invited cried off. Lady Louisa Horsfell declared herself not fit enough for such a long outing, and Calantha Appleby felt the swaying of the carriage would not be agreeable in her present delicate condition. But everyone else met in the Circus, ready for a day of pleasure.

Luckily the rain held off as they departed from Bath in a train of four carriages, with five gentlemen on horseback. In his aunt's absence, Lord Albury rode in the carriage with his sister, accompanied by Miss Hayward and Miss Angela Fletcher.

B watched the latter carefully, drawing alongside the carriage rather often to examine her expression. He had never taken a great deal of notice of her before, but now that he knew how much she loved him, he felt a stronger interest in her. His concern was purely platonic, naturally. Whatever the strength of her feelings, there was no attachment on his side, not the least in the world. He merely felt a degree of responsibility for her welfare, no more than that. And if he had spent two nights imagining a life as her husband, that was merely normal curiosity in a man of his age.

He wanted to reassure himself that she was not downhearted in her unrequited love, but he could not convince himself of it. When he recalled her previous behaviour, he had thought her a vivacious sort of girl, with a teasing twinkle in her eye. Now she seemed serious, unlike her usual self. She wore a vivid blue bonnet, and he tried to remember whether that signified that she was happy or not. He could not remember, having taken little notice of her light chatter before, but he would be glad to be sure that she was happy.

Midford Castle was soon reached, an odd looking building and not at all medieval, for it was no more than thirty years old. It was unoccupied, but a steward had been persuaded to let them in and show them around. B would have offered his escort to Miss Angela, but Randal Sylvester was there before him, so he followed them from room to room, overhearing a great deal of nonsense from the gentleman and barely a word from the lady. Yet she made no effort to be free of his attentions, so he must suppose she enjoyed them.

B soon found he had a companion of his own. In one of the rooms, he found Miss Hayward sitting quietly with her mother.

"There, now, Dora!" Mrs Hayward cried. "There is Mr Appleby, who will help us, I am sure. Mr Appleby! Poor Dora is finding the tour rather tiring. May I prevail upon you to offer her the support of your arm?"

Dora simpered and blushed and attached herself to him at once, before he could speak a word.

"My pleasure, ma'am," he said, rather bemused by this enthusiasm. "If you are tired, Miss Hayward, allow me to escort you back to your carriage."

"Oh no, Mr Appleby. I should not like to miss the remaining rooms of the castle. I shall go on very well with your help."

"Then let us follow the others," he said, too polite to enquire where Mr Hayward had disappeared to, and why he was not around to support his daughter.

Miss Hayward was not shy, so she kept up a patter of conversation, mostly with her mother, who stayed close to them. Since Miss Hayward barely rested more than the tips of her fingers on his arm, B concluded that she was not excessively tired. She walked slowly, however, so Miss Fletcher and the garrulous Mr Sylvester were soon far ahead of them. After a while, B looked out of an upper window, and saw them on the terrace below, she sitting, head down, on a low wall while he strode about, declaiming his point with sweeping gestures of his arms.

They came to a bedroom, where Uncle Maurice was holding a large audience spellbound with a tale of a previous owner, whose wife had supposedly run off with a footman. Miss Hayward's fingers dropped as she listened, mesmerised, thus releasing B momentarily. He crept to the window and saw Miss Fletcher now alone, her head still lowered, her shawl clutched forlornly around her.

He saw Mr Hayward in the crowd, so with a quick word to pass the ladies into their father's care, he made a hasty escape down the stairs and out to the terrace. She was still alone, lost in her own thoughts.

"Miss Fletcher?"

She started, then looked up at him. "Oh... Mr Appleby."

Was that a blush on her cheeks? Perhaps it was the *'slight blush of consciousness'* of which she had already warned him. He was oddly touched. She was so young and defenceless that he wished with all his heart that he could protect her from the hurts of life.

"Are you warm enough, sitting out here? The wind is a trifle too chilly for comfort."

"I do not regard it, but thank you for your solicitude."

"But you should not be alone. May I sit with you for a while?"

"Of course."

She gazed at him with bright eyes, as clear as spring water, and he had the strangest feeling, as if he could see clear to her heart. Yet her tone was flat, most unlike her usual effervescent self. What could he say to cheer her up? He had not the happy knack that some men possessed of conversing lightly. Scouring his mind for some subject of common interest, he could not shift his mind from Sunday, his sermon and her quaking response.

"We missed you at Sunday school," he blurted, realising even as he spoke the words that it was not the most felicitous subject. "Several of the children asked where you were." She gave him a wan smile, so he blundered on. "It was my fault, I know. That sermon..." Another foolish subject! How inarticulate he was becoming.

"Do you often preach?"

"Perhaps two or three times a year at St Swithin's, and occasionally elsewhere. Only once at the Abbey."

"You write your own sermons." She made it a statement, not a question.

"I do. It is an interesting exercise, to write words to be heard rather than read." She blushed again, and he cursed his wretched tongue, to lead him directly into such an unhappy subject. He lapsed into miserable silence.

"You enjoy Sunday school, I think, sir," she said with sudden animation. "You regard the children with some affection, it seems to me. The boys, at least. I was used to think that you disapproved of everyone, but you are not so hard-hearted as you like to appear, Mr Appleby."

Hard-hearted? Was that how she saw him? Then he noticed that little twinkle in her eye. Her face was solemn, but he knew she was teasing him. She must know he was not hard-hearted, for how could she have fallen in love with such a man as that?

"They are so innocent," he said with a little smile, folding his arms. "Such guileless creatures when they are small. I always teach the youngest boys, Miss Fletcher, for with them there is some hope of instilling proper principles into them. By the time a child is nine or ten, he has grown wise to the ways of the world, and had time to become wily and devious. Once set on that course, it is almost impossible to turn his steps aside. But a young boy who is willing to listen may be steered gently onto the path of righteousness."

"Do you not think that girls may be innocent, also?" she said. "If I have understood you aright, you are saying that a boy at a certain age may be led into correct ways, but beyond that age his character is fixed. May that not also be true of the female sex?"

"It is an interesting point," he said, a little surprised at her perception. "It may be so, but I am peculiarly unqualified to express an opinion, for I know nothing of the female sex."

She raised astonished eyebrows. "But you know any number of females, Mr Appleby. You are sitting here talking to one specimen of the sex in a perfectly rational manner, so how can you say you know nothing about us?"

He could not help smiling at her earnestness. "That is true, and perhaps I have acquired enough knowledge of the world to enable me to converse with women. But I know nothing of their characteristics, of their essential nature. My mother died when I was born, so I had not that gentle influence on me as an infant, and from the age of eight I shared my uncle's bachelor household. It has rendered me unfit to mix with the fair sex, for I understand them not."

"Whereas I grew up with three brothers, and my father, too, and any number of cousins and friends of the male sex," she said, with a swift smile that shone from her face as if a lamp had been lit inside. "They were my constant playfellows, and even when Will and Johnny went away to school and we girls were kept in the schoolroom, when we were together there was not the least constraint between us. Men and women may follow different paths in life, Mr Appleby, men out in the world of business and politics and finances, and women confined to the domestic sphere, but those paths run side by side, do they not? And we are not so very different in essence, I think. A girl may be lively or dull, quick-witted or slow, dreamy or practical, active or indolent, just as her male counterpart may be. In the end, she is her own self, to be judged for what she is, not for what is true of the generality of her sex. Would you not agree?"

That was startlingly deep for a flighty girl of eighteen, B had to admit. "I do agree," he said slowly. "You think I am not as hard-hearted as I appear, but I think *you* are not as frivolous as you appear, Miss Fletcher. You seem to devote your entire life to pleasure, but there is a more serious seam running through you, as well."

"And is the same true of you, Mr Appleby? Only in reverse,

naturally. You seem to spend your time in serious pursuits, but is there a frivolous side to you? Do you write exciting Gothic romances in your spare time? Do you play spillikins with yourself? Do you climb into the attics on wet afternoons and sing arias at the top of your voice?"

Now she was openly teasing him. It was an odd feeling, to have a chit like Angela Fletcher jesting with him, but he rather liked it. Or perhaps it was her youthful beauty and bright eyes which made him breathless suddenly, and turned his brain to mush.

"I... I am sorry to disappoint you, Miss Fletcher, but... I do none of those things. No doubt my life would be immeasurably improved if I were to do so, but I do not."

She sighed with theatrical intensity. "Ah, you are too serious a man altogether, sir. I cannot approve of *that.* Every man must lift his head from his books and his sermon-writing occasionally to enjoy the lighter aspects of life. There must be something! What do you do for amusement, sir? What pleasure delights you more than any other?"

"With you it is dancing, is it not?" he said softly. "You love to dance above all things."

"I do, indeed I do! There is no felicity in the world so great as dancing, and I would dance anywhere, at any time, if I could, even without a partner. I often dance for my own pleasure, humming the tune, and needing no one else."

"Then we are very different, for I never dance," he said. "For me, the greatest pleasures are of the mind, not the body. Chess is my great joy, Miss Fletcher. One of the masters at Winchester taught me and we played together for years. When he retired, he moved to Bath and I spent two nights a week trying every trick I could think of to best him, although I rarely succeeded. He died two years ago, and since then I have had no one skilful enough to challenge me. Unlike you, Miss Fletcher, I cannot manage without a mind to play against."

She tipped her head on one side, gazing at him with a little frown across her smooth forehead. "Is Mr Bravington not a good enough player for you?"

"Bravington? Your neighbour on the Royal Crescent? I did not know he played."

"He plays piquet with Johnny, and mostly wins, by the sound of it. He also plays chess, but, just like you, he can find no one of his standard."

"Bravington!" B said, astonished. "He lives so retired now that I have seldom met him since he returned to Bath. I confess, I had no idea he played chess — or piquet, either. I must look him up at once. Thank you, Miss Fletcher, thank you! If Bravington is all you say, then I shall be for ever in your debt. Ah, here are the others leaving the house. I imagine we shall be returning to the carriages soon. May I offer you my arm? Oh, but you do not need a man's arm, I recall. Forgive me."

"It was kind in you to offer," she said, with a little blush. "I may not need your arm, but I would be very grateful for your company, to deter Mr Sylvester. I find him… a trifle exhausting."

"It would be my pleasure."

17: A Popular Man

Angie could not evade Mr Sylvester for long. It had taken all her ingenuity to escape him even for a few short minutes, but he soon returned and thereafter clung, limpet-like, to her side for the rest of day. When they stopped at a small village for refreshments, he sat beside her. When they looked around ruined Farleigh Castle, he walked with her, expounding on the antiquity of the place, but without imparting any useful knowledge. She caught snatches of Mr Appleby's conversation with Lord Albury and Lady Maria, which sounded much more interesting, for he knew all about the family who had owned it, and drew little vignettes of them — their fortunes in the Hundred Years' War, their pride in being able to ride all the way to Salisbury on their own land, the owner who gambled away the family's entire fortune. He knew about the monuments in the family vault, too. She would have liked to ask him why some of the stone coffins were made to the shape of the person within, and why he connected that to Egypt, but Mr Sylvester whisked her away before she could do so, pontificating loudly on nothing at all.

It was a relief to escape the endless inane chatterings each time she entered the carriage.

When they reached home, and were enjoying a welcome cup of tea after the exertions of the day, Angie burst out, "Could none of you rescue me from that *stupid* Randal Sylvester? He is the most inane man I ever met, and by far the most annoying. Johnny, I was trying to attract your attention for hours, but you were too busy making up to Lady Maria."

"I was not *'making up'* to her, as you so inelegantly phrase it, little sister," he said stiffly. "I could hardly be doing so, when she is barely out of the schoolroom. I was merely doing the pretty to the young sister of a friend. Her brother Anthony is also at Cambridge, the best of fellows, and he asked me to keep an eye on her, if you must know."

"She has her elder brother here to keep an eye on her. That is what brothers are for, to look after their younger sisters who are being importuned by presumptuous upstarts who cannot take a hint that they are not wanted."

"Mr Randal Sylvester is very eligible," Mama said. "The son of a baron, after all, so he is an Honourable, and he has seven hundred a year of his own, with the expectation of more. He is a bit of a rattle, I grant you, but—"

"He is a buffoon!" Angie said impatiently.

"But very personable. I like him a great deal more than that surly Mr Appleby. The uncle is a most agreeable man, but the nephew is far too morose for my taste."

"He is not surly, or morose!" Angie cried. "He is not a chattering fool, like Mr Sylvester, that is all."

"Well, I cannot like a clergyman who preaches in the softest tones, and yet one crawls out afterwards feeling horribly guilty, even when one has done nothing at all wrong," Mama said stoutly. "I felt obliged to rewrite my letter to Berinsfield afterwards. He is an unpleasant man."

"Now that I will not have," Pa said, twirling his Madeira glass in his hand. "He's a serious fellow, I'll admit, and he doesn't rattle away like his uncle or smile at the whole world, but he's a sensible man, which is more than can be said for any of the Sylvesters. Angie, do you want me to warn Sylvester away?"

"No, no, because I cannot think he has any serious designs on me. But if you see him hovering round me, please come to my rescue, for his company is not at all agreeable to me."

Pa nodded, and Johnny added, "I shall watch out for you, little sister, now that I know you wish it, but you are usually easily able to deal with unwanted admirers, so how could we guess you needed help?"

"He is impervious to hints," she said. "He is so wrapped in his own conceit that he cannot conceive that his attentions might not be welcome. Pray do not let him sit at my table at our card party tonight."

But it was not Johnny or Pa who intercepted Mr Randal Sylvester that evening. It was Mr Appleby the Younger who smoothly enticed him to a table with Colonel and Mrs Plaxton on the far side of the room, with only the tiniest of smiles in Angie's direction as he did so.

Angie was deeply grateful, of course, but she wondered greatly at his behaviour. He now knew that she was the wicked person who had broken all the rules of propriety to write letters to him. He should be disgusted by her, and avoid her at every opportunity. Yet he had sought her out that day for a pleasant conversation, without the least hostility, and now he was going out of his way to make her evening comfortable.

Whatever could he mean by it?

~~~~~

It was not very many days before B realised that something odd was occurring, something which had not happened since his uncle's betrothal had been announced. He was once more the object of attention from a number of unmarried females.

The first sign had been Miss Hayward's strange behaviour at Midford Castle, when she had asked for the support of his arm, even though she was clearly not at all tired. Then, after supper at the Fletchers' card party that evening, he found himself expertly swept into a four by the Miss Branscombes. They had been plain, uninteresting girls when they had first come out some six years ago, and the intervening years had not improved either their looks or their conversation. They still giggled every time they spoke, and sometimes when anyone else spoke, too. To make matters worse, they had added some unfortunate habits to their arsenal. Miss Branscombe rested one pudgy hand on his arm possessively whenever she addressed him, and Miss Lucy had a horrifying tendency to lean towards him, displaying her considerable charms while doing so, and fluttering her eyelashes.

It was enough to unnerve the most stout-hearted man. B sincerely wished he had continued to play with Sylvester and the Plaxtons, but the Fletcher son had scooped all the Sylvesters into a noisy round game and B had felt himself at liberty to join a different group. It was torture, however, and no consolation that the girls were such poor players that he made over thirty shillings from them.
~~~~~

On Tuesday, his visit to the Pump Room revealed the full extent of his problem. Not only Miss Hayward and the Miss Branscombes thronged around him, but also the Miss Laceys, Mrs Kaye, who was a young widow of reduced means, Miss Paine and her cousin Miss Starling, who were known to be in Bath to find rich husbands, and three complete strangers.

All day he mulled over the situation but could think of no good reason for it. He had been of interest to ambitious young ladies when he was heir to a considerable fortune, but now? He could not imagine what drew them.

When he arrived at his uncle's house for dinner that evening, Calantha bounced into the room, beaming from ear to ear, she cried, "My dear sir, my felicitations on your good fortune."

"Thank you," he said in some surprise that news of his chaplaincy had emerged already. "Lady Mellish told you of it?"

"Lady Mellish? No, it was not her. Someone told me... I forget who, now."

"I thought it was supposed to be a secret."

"Oh, of course, I was told in the strictest confidence, naturally. Not a word will pass our lips on the subject, you may be sure. But such good news. I could not be more pleased, and no one could deserve it more than you."

"You are too kind," he said, making her a small bow, for her warmth was sincere and one could withhold no courtesy to so good-humoured a girl. "I am only pleased that I shall be independent of my uncle's charity at last."

"He does not begrudge a penny of it, you know that, but it is a satisfactory end, all the same. Ah, I hear the Ansteads arriving, so not another word about your great secret."

B passed a pleasant evening in his uncle's house, with only eight for cards and no attentive young ladies to unsettle him. There was no Miss Angela Fletcher, either, and her absence was less pleasing to him. Many times during the evening, when there was an oddity in the cards, or someone made a particularly absurd remark, he wished she were there to share the joke, or to tease him with those clear eyes of hers with the amused twinkle in them.

He supposed he looked just the same to those around him, but inside he was lighter, freer and perhaps kinder. He had always been tolerant towards men, accepting their foibles as well as their virtues, but now he looked at the women around him and wondered if he had been too harsh all these years. *'She is her own self, to be judged for what she is, not what is true of the generality of her sex.'* So Angela had said, and it was self-evidently true.

Calantha, for instance, might be a flighty creature, but she was also dotingly fond of her son, her face lighting up whenever she spoke of him, or of her hopes for the new baby. She was unfailingly kind to B himself, too. Mrs Anstead was a haughty and disagreeable woman, but she was involved in innumerable good works for the poor, had recruited her servants almost entirely from the workhouse, and was generous to her daughters' long retired governess, treating her as a sort of unofficial companion. The governess was present on this occasion to make up the numbers, a mousy little woman with frightened eyes, who played a surprisingly sharp game of whist.

When his attention turned to the final female present, Lady Penelope Whittleton, B's goodwill wavered somewhat. As the daughter of the 3rd Marquess of Barrowford and sister to the 4th, and now respectably married to Jeremy Whittleton, she was beyond reproach socially. But for many years she had been Whittleton's mistress, bearing him three illegitimate children, and such outrageous behaviour could not be condoned. It would take many charitable works or many years of repentant piety to counterbalance such iniquity.

Still, he would try to find some good in her, he decided. He would give her the benefit of the doubt. Perhaps she was now resolved on a new life of propriety, and would be glad to have her previous notoriety quietly forgotten. She was admitted everywhere in Bath as she had been in London and in Brighton, where she had been part of the Prince of Wales's set. She had left Brighton before His Royal Highness, which also spoke of a reformed character. The prince was notoriously wild, and if Lady Penelope had tired of his debauchery, it was clear that she had mended her ways.

And what of Miss Angela Fletcher? Here B quailed momentarily, for whenever he thought of her now, he could not forget that she was desperately in love with him and yet must in the end be disappointed. Poor Angela! Such a lovely young girl, to be blighted by a hopeless love affair at such a tender age. He prayed that she would recover soon from her misdirected affection.

He walked home, scarcely noticing the rain, his head full of Angela and her mischievous nature. He smiled as he walked.

~~~~~

Angie was very caught up in the preparations for Mr Bravington's ball, and was often sent round to his house with a note or a question. On one such errand, she was pleased to see Mr Appleby the Younger at the chessboard with Mr Bravington.
~~~~~

"Oh, is it working well for you both? Is Mr Bravington a good enough player for you, Mr Appleby?"

His face melted into a rueful smile. "The boot is very much on the other foot, I regret to say."

"You are too modest, sir," Mr Bravington said. "You are certainly better than any other I have found in Bath. I have been teaching your brother to play, Miss Fletcher, but although he is an apt pupil, he is as yet far short of Mr Appleby's facility with the game. I cannot thank you enough for sending him to me. We have agreed to meet twice a week, if his other engagements permit, for he is a popular fellow just now."

"I am glad to hear it," Angie said, rather puzzled. She would have enquired further about this unexpected popularity, but Mr Appleby changed the subject, so she could not discover more.

It was the following morning before Angie saw this new popularity for herself, for it was the first time for some days she had been at the Pump Room at the same time as Mr Appleby. He sat on his usual bench with his daily glass of water, with the two Miss Laceys on either side of him, and Miss Hayward hovering nearby, clearly wishing the other ladies at Jericho so she might have her turn.

Poor Mr Appleby! He looked rather bemused, saying little, while his two devotees chattered away in a noisy chorus. Angie was swept with a desire to rescue him, until she remembered that she had wanted him to be admired, so he might be tempted to fall in love. It would be good for him, she told herself sternly, to see that some young women still valued him, even though he had neither fortune nor rank.

Although… it was strange. Miss Paine and Miss Starling were

loitering, too, and she knew for a fact, since they told everyone of it, that they were looking for rich husbands, so why should they have the slightest interest in Mr Appleby?

She slowed her steps a little as she walked around the room to allow Mama to catch up.

"Mama, do you know why Mr Appleby the Younger is so popular lately?"

"Hmm? Mr Appleby...? Oh, I recall now, you were not by when Lady Penelope called yesterday. He has had some good fortune, it seems, although I cannot tell you what. Lady Penelope would have told me all about it, but she mentioned that it is supposed to be a secret, so I did not feel it proper to enquire. I expect the bishop has found him a living."

"Then why keep it secret? If it is only a living, there is no reason not to tell everyone, is there?"

"Goodness, child, how you do take a person up! That is only a guess, for I do not know at all, nor do I wish to. It would be vulgar to pursue the matter further."

This was said in such a severe tone that Rosie would have been reduced to instant tears, and would have spent the rest of the day apologising. Angie was not so lily-livered, however. Dropping a little behind Mama, she looked about her as she walked until she spied Calantha Appleby sitting rather forlornly by herself, sipping her glass of water. Angie bounced across to her and plumped herself down on the next seat.

"Good day, Mrs Appleby. I am come to you because I know you will tell me everything that Mama is too particular in her notions of propriety to gossip about."

Calantha looked up with a little smile. "Oh, yes! A little gossip would cheer me up tremendously. What do you want to know?"

It dawned on Angie that Calantha was rather pale. "I beg your pardon — you are not well."

A wider smile. "Perfectly well, merely... the usual thing at this stage. I was worse with Roger, and the end result is worth all the trouble, I assure you. Maurice wants another son, naturally. Men always want sons. For myself, I should like a daughter this time. I so long for a little girl to cuddle, with lovely long hair to brush. I always wished I had a younger sister, for Eloise was not at all the cuddling sort."

"But you have one, surely!" Angie said. "Your father has three other children, and I believe one of them is a girl... yes, I am sure of it. She is your sister — half-sister, anyway."

Calantha's eyes widened. "Three other children? Did he have another wife before he married Lady Pen, then? He never mentioned it. But how could that be when Mama was still alive?"

Angie realised she had unwittingly blundered into deep waters. She could hardly explain that the children were illegitimate, nor was it her place to do so.

Hastily, she said, "I dare say I have got muddled again. Mama is always telling me that I do not attend properly."

With a quick laugh, Calantha accepted this without comment. "What was it you wished to ask me?"

"It is about Mr Appleby — not yours, the younger one. Mama thinks he has lately had a turn of good fortune, but she does not know what."

"Oh, yes! Some distant relation we knew nothing of has left

him a great deal of money, it seems. It is a great secret, but I know I can trust you."

"But how splendid for him," Angie cried, clapping her hands with glee. Her little game with Lady Maria had actually come true — how amazing! "That accounts for his sudden popularity."

"Indeed! They are all after him now, or at least his six thousand a year. Six thousand! Can you imagine it?"

Six thousand? The exact amount she had mentioned to Randal Sylvester. A terrible sinking feeling gripped Angie's insides. He could not have taken her seriously — could he?

"Tell me," she said, carefully nonchalant, "this distant relation... where was he from?"

"The north, somewhere," she said, frowning. "A strange name... quite outlandish. Scar... something."

"Scarborough," Angie said. "His second cousin from Scarborough, who left him six thousand a year and a stable of stallions. I forget the rest. Good heavens, was there ever a *stupider* person than Randal Sylvester?"

"Mr Sylvester? What does he have to do with it?"

"Everything!" Angie cried, jumping to her feet. "Oh, I could wring his neck, truly I could. But at least I can stop all this nonsense here and now. Mrs Appleby, I must tell you that there is no fortune to be inherited. It was all a silly game, something I made up for fun. But Mr Sylvester must have believed it, and passed on the story."

"Oh, but—"

"There are Mrs Lacey and Mrs Hayward. I must tell them, before their daughters make themselves look even more foolish."

She whisked away to where the two ladies stood conversing amiably together, and watching their daughters' delicate assault on Mr Appleby and his supposed inheritance.

"Mrs Lacey, Mrs Hayward, good day to you," she said briskly, with the most perfunctory curtsy. "I am come to tell you that these rumours of Mr Appleby's inheritance are quite false. I made up the story myself, as a game, and now it seems to have been taken up as a real thing. But it is nothing of the sort, I do assure you. I would not wish you to be under any misapprehension."

The ladies exchanged amused glances. "It is quite all right, dear," Mrs Hayward said. "We do understand. You thought you had him all to yourself, but now that he has an independence he may choose whoever takes his fancy."

"And I think we all know where his fancy lies," Mrs Lacey said. "With his refined tastes, he will naturally select a wife who is as well-bred as he is."

Her friend nodded agreement. "Cultured. Elegant."

"With polished manners and every ladylike accomplishment."

Angie was too irate to hear the insults. "You cannot have understood me! There is no fortune, it is all a lie! I made it all up as a game to play on Randal Sylvester, but he believed it and spread it about as truth, but it is completely false."

They laughed, they actually laughed. "As if we would take the word of a rattle like Randal Sylvester. Naturally, we asked Mr Appleby himself, and he confirmed it."

"What?"

For a moment, Angie was too flummoxed to speak. He had

confirmed it? But why? What sort of man had the sheer effrontery to allow such an outrageous lie to stand? He seemed like such an upright person, far too proper in his ways to let anyone believe he was wealthy when he was not. Why on earth would he do such a thing?

There was only one way to find out. Angie strode across to Mr Appleby, stepping around the ever-hopeful Miss Hayward.

"What are you about, sir, to be acknowledging this nonsensical rumour? You should not be encouraging these poor dupes to dangle after you when you know the tale is completely false."

The Miss Laceys squawked in outrage, Miss Hayward began to cry and both mothers gathered protectively around their chicks. Mr Appleby gawked at Angie, more puzzled than angry, it seemed to her.

"Well, sir? What do you have to say for yourself? I should have thought you to have more scruples than to allow such deceit to stand."

He rose slowly to his feet, the glass of water still cradled in his hands. "Miss Fletcher, I have not the pleasure of understanding you. Of what deceit do you speak?"

Mrs Hayward butted in. "She is referring to the great good fortune which has recently fallen your way, sir."

"Which has *not* fallen his way," Angie said. "It was all a made-up thing — a game, that was all! Oh, why does no one believe me!"

She almost stamped her foot in frustration. It was bad enough that Randal Sylvester had taken her nonsense as fact and spread it all over Bath, but for no one to accept her word on the matter was beyond anything!

"Miss Fletcher," Mr Appleby said, staring down at her from his great height with a black look on his face. "I cannot conceive what goes on in your head. You are young and thoughtless and bound to make errors of judgement, that must be your excuse, for I can see no other reason why you should profess such a thing, or why you must concern yourself with my affairs at all. You are mistaken in supposing—"

He stopped abruptly with an exclamation, looking about him. Angie now saw with dismay that a crowd had gathered around them and a lull in the musicians' performance made the discussion all too public.

Carefully setting down his glass, he made Angie a punctilious bow. Then, with the utmost dignity, he walked away from her. As the crowd soundlessly parted and then closed up behind him, all eyes turned to Angie.

"Angela!" Mama hissed into the silence. "We are going home."

"But Mama—"

"Home."

Head lowered, Angie turned and meekly followed her.

18: In The Garden

B walked steadily through the streets. Perhaps he passed acquaintances, but he saw nothing. Breathe... stride, stride... breathe... His heart hammered away, and he briefly wondered if it might explode or become so overloaded that it would stop altogether. Breathe... stride, stride... breathe...

Gradually, step by step, his heart slowed its pace and his breathing became easier. But not until he had entered his own house and shut himself away in his small study did he feel that he might survive his ordeal. With shaking hands, he poured himself a sherry, which was all he kept in that room, and took a careful sip. Then another.

He took a deep breath, and wondered how on earth he was to endure the humiliation. Such a public spectacle to be dragged into, he whose policy had been never to draw attention to himself. Whatever was Angela thinking? And what on earth did she mean by stating in that forceful way that his appointment as chaplain was a false story? A game, she had said, as if Lady Mellish would ever do such a thing! He could make no sense of it.

All he knew was that Angela Fletcher had made a scene right

there in the Pump Room, and called him a liar. She could hardly have chosen a more public place. The girl was insane! And to think that he had begun to have softer feelings for her, to pity her unrequited love. He had even wondered if she might be right in thinking him too serious, and consider how he might lighten his manner a trifle.

Well, no more. He was just fine as he was, and she was beyond the pale. Was there ever a wilder, less restrained girl? He had thought Calantha air-headed but she was nothing to Angela.

A little more sherry and a little more reflection brought him to the opinion that his credit was good enough to survive such a scene, appalling as it was. In a few short weeks, the unruly Angela Fletcher would be gone from Bath and his life, and he could put this unspeakable episode behind him.

Higgins came in. "You're back early, sir. Is anything amiss?"

Early... yes, he was early, his whole schedule disrupted. But he had not the heart to go out again, not even for dinner. The garden... that was it, the garden would soothe his wounded spirits. "Nothing that an hour or two with my vegetables cannot mend," he said. "Tell Ann I shall be dining at home tonight."

"On a Friday, sir? But you always—"

"Eat at the Circus on Fridays. I know, Higgins, but not tonight. Run up there and let Moyles know, will you? Tell Ann not to put herself out. I shall be content with whatever she has to hand."

Higgins goggled at him. "You'll want a bit of fish, though, sir, if there's any to be had this late in the day. I'll send Mary out to see what she can find. And perhaps a leg of mutton. You'd enjoy that, I'm sure, sir."

"Whatever Ann wishes to cook. I do not care."

Higgins' jaw dropped, but he wisely made no further protest and bowed himself out of the room.

Oddly, this exchange lifted B's spirits. He could be impulsive sometimes if he felt like it, for where was the harm? And it had nothing to do with Miss Angela Fletcher, infecting him with her wayward behaviour. He finished his sherry, changed into his gardening clothes and set to work on a bed of peas, gone over now, and needing clearing so the cabbages could go in.

There was nothing like a garden for putting life's vagaries into perspective. By the time he had harvested a few shrivelled pods to set aside for next year's sowing, he had reminded himself that although Angela was still young, she had shown signs of mature thought in their conversation at Midford Castle. It was possible, therefore, that time would bring her greater wisdom and, it must be hoped, greater temperance in her behaviour.

As he piled the pea vines onto the compost heap, he recalled her flashing eyes and heightened colour as she berated him. She was too pale, as a rule, and a little rosiness about her cheeks only enhanced her beauty. That she was beautiful he had never doubted. It was a delicate, ethereal beauty, not, perhaps, to be compared to her elder sister's exquisite perfection, but when she was animated, Angela was quite breath-taking.

He leaned on his spade. *Breath-taking?* That was dangerous ground. But surely he could admire a young lady's physical form without implying... well, anything more. Admiration was not *love*... was it? Of course not! He could look at Angela and admit her to be a comely woman, yet still deplore her shallow nature and lamentable want of decorum. Surely he could.

This train of thought led him to consider his letters, and the poor besotted girl who had written them. And then — a revelation! That drama in the Pump Room could only have arisen from jealousy. Poor Angela in her hopeless passion had seen him surrounded by tempting young ladies and had been so fired with protective rage that she had created a scene, making up some foolishness on the spot, if only to draw his attention away from the boring Miss Laceys to her.

He chuckled suddenly. Was there ever anything so funny? That he — dull and uninteresting as he was — should have any young lady fired up in a jealous rage on his account, but especially one so young and beautiful as Angela. She could have any young man in Bath, if she set her mind to it, he suspected. Perhaps not Lord Albury, but anyone below his rank must surely be at Angela's feet. Yet she had looked at him, who had neither rank nor fortune nor charm to attract her.

With a smile, he set his spade to work again.

~~~~~

Seething with indignation, Angie mutely followed Mama, Rosie and Belinda home. Mama's face was set in its 'dismayed but pretending not to be' expression. Rosie was trying not to cry. Belinda was trying not to giggle. And Johnny was nowhere to be seen. What was the point of a brother who disappeared at crucial moments, anyway? He was probably buried in a bookseller's shop somewhere, oblivious to the world around him. Useless, that was what he was.

When they reached the house, Mama said at once, "Go to your room, Angie. Your father will deal with this when he returns, but I may as well tell you now that I shall expect him to send you
~~~~~

home immediately."

Rosie burst into tears in good earnest, and Belinda cried, "Oh, no! That would be too bad, for Angie to miss the ball!"

Angie knew better than to argue with Mama when she was in this mood. When Julia had been around, she had generally managed to create enough Mama-annoying mayhem that Angie could hide behind a convincing shield of innocence, but now she was fully exposed to Mama's scrutiny. Rosie was no protection, for she truly was innocent of all wrong-doing, so Angie was now the first person anyone looked to for an explanation of some mischief or other. In London, she had been careful not to put a foot wrong, for fear of being sent home and missing so many balls and wonderful things, but in Bath she had not been so careful.

Well, that was her mistake, and she would not make it again, that much was certain. But oh, the injustice of it! To be punished for something that was not even her fault, but could be laid squarely at the door of Mr Ridiculous Sylvester. If he had not passed on that silly little story, none of this would have happened.

It was almost two hours before Pa returned. Two hours of Angie pacing her room in a lather of impatience to know her fate. Two hours of wondering if her acquaintance with Calantha Appleby was sufficient to beg for a bed under her roof. Or Lady Louisa Horsfell... perhaps she would— But such schemes were foolish, Angie knew that. If Mama wanted her to be sent home in disgrace, then sent home she would be, and that was all there was to it.

But eventually, she heard the front door, and Pa's voice in the distance, and then Mama's voice, louder than usual, although the words were still indistinguishable. Then an ominous silence.

Finally, a knock on the door, and the apologetic head of Enoch, Pa's man. "Begging your pardon, Miss Angie, but your pa wants to see you in his office."

He was alone, which was a good sign. He had a brandy glass in his hand, which was less promising, but his smile when he saw her reassured her.

"Well, flower, whatever have you been up to this time? You've set your stepmother in a right pother, that's for certain, and she's not got the slightest idea why you worked yourself into a lather."

"She never asked me why, so how could she know? Oh, Pa, *please, please, please* do not send me home, for it would be infamously unjust! It is not at all my fault, I give you my word."

"Set your mind at rest on that score, Angie love. There's no possibility of you going home. The travelling carriage is in Hertfordshire, you can hardly go all that way in the barouche and no daughter of mine will travel post. Besides, Johnny or I would have to go with you, and neither of us can leave Bath just now. But that doesn't mean you can carry on as if nothing's happened. Your ma says you just flew into a passion in the middle of the Pump Room and called Mr Appleby a liar to his face."

"Well, he *is*, Pa! He must be, although it is hard to believe, for he is such a respectable man. I cannot understand why he would say such a thing."

"You don't deny, then, that you flew into a passion?"

"Oh... well... I spoke forcefully, I suppose, but I had to make them understand."

"Them?"

"Mrs Lacey and Mrs Hayward and their silly daughters. They have been fawning over Mr Appleby, thinking he has this wonderful inheritance and it is all nonsense. There is no inheritance, and they are wasting their time. But no one would believe me, and Mr Appleby himself told them it was true, seemingly, and it is not, I swear it, Pa! It was just a silly game between Lady Maria and me, but when I tried it on Randal Sylvester, he must have believed it all, and told everyone in town of it, despite me telling him not to. Oh, he is so *stupid!* I have no patience with him."

Pa laughed. "He's hardly the sharpest knife in the drawer, I'll grant you that, but you'd better explain this game to me, so that I understand it aright."

So Angie told the whole tale, from Mr Appleby's unaccountably benign countenance when he entered the Pump Room, the silly game with Lady Maria — "At least *she* understood it at once!" — and the continuation with Mr Sylvester, and then the discovery that Mr Appleby was besieged by hopeful young ladies.

"I had to do something, Pa, you must see that," Angie said. "Once I knew that it was my own nonsense being parroted all over town, I had to correct the misapprehension, surely you agree. And when Mrs Hayward said that Mr Appleby himself had confirmed the rumour — well, I could not be silent, and allow him to mislead the Miss Laceys and Miss Hayward with such a falsehood. Although... I do not quite understand why he would say such a thing."

"That's the part that concerns me the most," Pa said thoughtfully. "Appleby's too serious for my taste, but he's not a man who would ever tell a lie, I'd have thought. So there's some misunderstanding at the root of this, which we can't quite fathom. But you were quite right in thinking that the story about the inheritance should be squashed at once. I don't disagree with you there. As to the manner of it... well, there might have been more discreet ways to deal with the problem than shouting about it in the middle of the Pump Room. But as for calling Mr Appleby a liar... did he lie to you?"

"Not to me. I am only going by what Mrs Hayward said. To me he said... he said I am young and thoughtless and bound to make errors of judgement." She hung her head, subdued. "I suppose he is right about all of that. I do foolish things sometimes, and even though I mean no harm by it, and sometimes I am actively trying to do good, my efforts result in discomfort for others. I was only trying to correct a misapprehension, but I have upset Mama and you, and I cannot imagine what Mr Appleby must think of me."

"So there is only Mrs Hayward's word that he confirmed this mythical inheritance? She may be mistaken... or lying herself, who knows. It's not for us to judge. We cannot assume he has lied, and it was very wrong of you to say so, flower."

"I can see that now, Pa. What can we do?"

"Well, this rumour has to be properly squashed, but you can leave that to me, as you should have done in the first place."

"But how? No one would believe me."

"No, and they wouldn't believe me, either, not if I just go round saying the story is false. The one person they'll believe is the person who set this hare running — Randal Sylvester. Once he knows how he's been taken in, and how foolish he'd look if the whole story came out, I think we can depend on him to scotch the tale. But what we must do before anything else, flower, is to find Mr Appleby so that you can apologise to him. So put your bonnet back on and let's go and see if he's at home, shall we?"

"You? Not Mama?"

"Two ladies can hardly call upon a single gentleman, so if I'm to be going with you anyway, I see no need to trouble your stepmother, do you? Besides, she's rather enjoying lying down on her bed being cosseted. She has Hathaway burning pastilles, Rosie fanning her and Belinda pressing a lavender-scented handkerchief to her brow. I think we'd do well to leave her to recover her composure in her own good time, eh, flower?"

"Is she... is she very upset?" Angie said, in a small voice.

"Oh, she'll bob up soon enough, never fear. She's never had children of her own, you see, so she doesn't always see the funny side of the little scrapes you all get into."

"She would not want anything to interfere with her plans for Rosie, either, but she won't stop me going to the ball... will she?"

Pa laughed. "Angie love, I can't imagine any power on earth strong enough to keep you away from a ball."

"You joke about it, but it is not a laughing matter, Pa. You know that if Mama forbids it, I cannot go."

"You leave your mama to me, love. Now, where's that bonnet?"

The afternoon sun was warm as they made their way to Gay Street. Pa rapped on the door, and then they waited a long time before a rather harassed footman answered.

"Yes?" His voice was puzzled, as if callers were an unexpected event.

"Is Mr Appleby at home?" Pa said.

"I'll see. What name is it, sir?"

"Fletcher. Harry Fletcher."

"Please step inside while I find out."

The hall was cool after the heat of the streets, and they waited patiently, examining a series of small framed paintings on the wall. Angie could not say whether or not they had any artistic merit, but they were rather pleasant views of modest country churches.

Eventually, the manservant returned. "Mr Appleby says please to step into the garden, sir."

They followed him through the house, which was furnished in excellent taste, everything of the finest quality, although of a somewhat outdated style. It was not like Mr Appleby the Elder's house on the Circus, where every carpet, chair and candlestick was of the newest fashion.

The garden was long and thin, and every inch of it was given over to plantings, without so much as a square foot of lawn. Near the house was a profusion of herbs in orderly beds, bees humming busily, the walls covered with trained fruit trees. Beyond that lay vegetable beds overflowing with well-grown produce.

A man was digging with rhythmic energy, head down, intent on his work. He wore sun-faded knee breeches and apron, like any gardener, but had doffed his coat in the heat, and his shirt sleeves were rolled up above the elbow, revealing a pair of tanned, muscular forearms. Mr Appleby, as Angie had never seen him before.

Her breath caught in her throat. *This* was how a man should look, not spider-like in his black coat, his face disapproving, or pious in his surplice in the pulpit, but hard at work, hot, dishevelled and so unexpectedly human.

He looked up at the little procession, Higgins leading the way, then Pa and Angie following. Thrusting his spade back into the soil so that it stood upright, Mr Appleby turned to greet them, his face slightly wary. Then he caught sight of Angie, and froze.

"Miss Fletcher! I beg your pardon — I had no idea you were here too." Hastily he began to roll down his sleeves to cover those masculine arms. "Pray forgive my informal appearance, madam. If I had known—"

"It is of no consequence, sir, I assure you. I have brothers, so I am perfectly accustomed to gentlemen of informal appearance."

"Even so... but I thought it was a mere matter of business, and I knew your father would not mind. Shall we go into the house, and Higgins can bring you some lemonade while I make myself presentable?"

"No need for that, Appleby," Pa said. "We would not wish to disturb your work, and this will not take long. Don't set anyone scrambling about for lemons on our account."

"Very well, then. Shall we sit? There is a bench over here in the shade."

They sat, and Angie made her apology and explained the game she had played, first with Lady Maria, and then, fatally, with Randal Sylvester. To her astonishment, Mr Appleby actually laughed as she told her sorry tale.

"What a creative mind you have, Miss Fletcher! A stable of

stallions, indeed! But it accounts for so much that has puzzled me greatly in recent days. Several people have congratulated me on my good fortune, and it was this to which they were alluding, seemingly. And I, all unwitting, accepted their felicitations and so gave credence to the story. You see, I have indeed had a piece of good fortune lately, although sadly there are no stallions in the case, and the position is worth no more than two hundred a year."

"You have a living at last!" Angie cried, clapping her hands together in glee. "How wonderful!"

"Something of the sort, yes, but it must remain a secret for a while longer yet, so I would be obliged if you would not mention it to anyone. And especially not to Mr Randal Sylvester, who clearly cannot be relied upon to keep secrets."

"No, indeed. I wish I might never speak to him again, for he is the greatest trial to me. Mr Appleby, what are those strange berries on that bush over there? I have never seen green berries before, and yet they look very plump and juicy."

"They are gooseberries, Miss Fletcher. Have you never seen them growing before?"

"No, never, although I have eaten them often enough. I love gooseberry fool, but I never knew they grew on bushes like that. Our garden in Yorkshire was given over to apples and chickens, and I have never been into the kitchen garden at our Hertfordshire house. What are those over there? They look like onions. And what is growing under those glass covers? It surely cannot be strawberries. Do you have strawberries, even in August?"

"Mrs Appleby enjoys them, so I try to ensure there are some on the table from early summer to autumn. Would you like to look around my garden, Miss Fletcher? Mr Fletcher?"

Pa declined, preferring to sit in the shade, but Angie willingly followed Mr Appleby up and down the gravel paths between the beds, pointing to this or that, while he explained which were grown from seed and which from roots or cuttings, and all about forcing beds and pruning and the benefits of horse manure. Angie had little interest in horse manure, but she was fascinated by this animated version of Mr Appleby, full of enthusiasm and energy, his eyes sparkling, his shirt sleeves now decorously concealing those well-muscled forearms. This was a Mr Appleby she liked a great deal better than the prosy, disapproving parson. If only he were always thus!

Pa had to drag her away in the end by pointing out that Mama would be wondering if they had walked all the way to Bristol and back, but since he invited Mr Appleby for dinner, she would have an opportunity to observe whether his more likeable demeanour was maintained once he had put on his blacks again.

19: Dinner At The Royal Crescent

B was light-headed as he walked up Gay Street that evening. Too much sun, he suspected. Or possibly too much Angela Fletcher. She was bad for his peace of mind, and he could not quite work out why. Yet seeing her there in his garden, her lovely face alight with curiosity, her skirts swirling around her as she danced up and down the paths. Even when she was only moving from one place to another, her movements were so graceful, her feet so precisely placed at every step, it was like a mesmerising dance.

Watching her, he had been overwhelmed by some emotion he could not quite name. He was disconnected, living in a strange dream world, where nothing existed beyond her and himself and the garden. And all the while, as they talked of cabbages and cauliflowers and cucumbers, she was dancing, dancing, just for him. Like a fountain she was constantly in motion, never still, never quiet, but gently calming. She had cast a spell over him, and his befuddled head could not quite decide whether the enchantment was benign or not.

He should not have accepted Fletcher's invitation to dine, for a whole evening of Angela might befuddle him beyond unravelling, and yet... yet... How could he refuse? It would have been uncivil after such a splendid apology, and at least he would not have to eat alone that evening. He hated eating alone. Even though he was not a great conversationalist himself, he liked to have other people about him, to feel himself a part of society. Uncle Maurice and Calantha could be irritating, it was true, but their good-humoured banter filled the air when better conversation was lacking, and tonight he would have the chattering Fletchers to keep him cheerful.

There would be a better meal, too. Uncle Maurice had taken his cook with him, leaving B with the kitchen maid. Ann was willing enough, and could manage a plain roast or a bit of fish, but he missed Mrs Holding's light hand with pastry. Her apricot tarts were a delight to be savoured. There was no Mrs Holding at the Fletchers' Royal Crescent house, but they had one of Leo Audley's many cooks, and since Audley was one of the richest men in the south west, the meal was bound to be exquisite. Higgins had accepted the sudden change of plan with no more than a slightly reproachful, "As you wish, sir," and after all, whatever Ann had planned could just as well be cooked tomorrow.

B had chosen to wear his new bottle green coat and the embroidered waistcoat in cream silk in honour of the occasion, for he had never before dined in a Royal Crescent house, most of the inhabitants being far above him in wealth and rank. He was rather pleased with his appearance. Mr Hartup had plied his needle to good effect, and B thought he looked rather stylish, without being ostentatious.

The Fletchers were in the smaller drawing room at the back of the house, which faced north and so was a little cooler at this hour. Only the family were present, leaving him wondering if he were to be the only guest. He made his greetings to Mrs Fletcher and the three young ladies, but before he could turn to the two gentlemen, Angie laughed softly, her eyes twinkling merrily.

"A dark green coat, Mr Appleby? You are growing adventurous."

"Do I look less like an attorney?" he said.

"You look splendid, sir, as a gentleman should."

He decided at once that he would order more new coats, in blue or burgundy or... or anything but black.

Mrs Fletcher tutted at her. "Really, Angie! That is not how we greet our guests. Pray forgive her, Mr Appleby. She is in high spirits tonight, and I cannot think why, for she should be a great deal more contrite after that disgraceful performance in the Pump Room. May I say again how sorry I am that you were subjected to—"

"We've agreed that it's best forgotten, Lizzie love," Mr Fletcher said gently. "All a misunderstanding, and Mr Appleby has been most gracious over the matter."

Mrs Fletcher forced a smile, but she pursed her lips in a manner which suggested that it would not be forgotten by her, at least. Poor Angela! An apology offered and accepted should be the end of the matter, and for B it was. He could not allow her to suffer any further retribution on his account.

Recklessly, therefore, he plunged to the rescue. "Indeed, it is already forgotten, as far as I am concerned. I hope Miss Angela will always be in high spirits, ma'am. For myself, I have grown used to her lively ways and would not have her moderate them. I trust she will never do so on my account."

They stared at him in some amazement, but the two Mr Fletchers stepped forward to make their formal greetings and the moment passed. He found himself deftly steered to sit between Mrs Fletcher and Miss Fletcher, while Angela sat on the opposite side of the room, decorously plying her needle on a dainty piece of embroidery. Sometimes, however, she looked up from her work and threw him such a mischievous glance that he could not suppress a smile.

Three more guests arrived, all well known to B. Mr Clymer was a retired architect who was also an expert on the workings of the Roman baths and aqueducts. The Miss Bensleys were friends of Mrs Greenwood, as impoverished as she was, who twittered with excitement at dining in such lavishly appointed surroundings. The party descended to the dining room shortly thereafter, where the twitterings continued at an even higher pitch. The number of candles, the footmen, the plate, the magnificent chandelier — all came in for their share of excited approbation, and as for the food! So many dishes! So many rarities! Lobster! Veal! Salmon! A green goose! And such delicious ham as they had never tasted before. They tried everything and enjoyed every mouthful.

B felt sorry for poor Mr Fletcher who had the two ladies on either side of him. B felt himself to be much better placed, for he had Mrs Fletcher to one side, all polite amiability, and on the other side was Angela, with her teasing eyes. Under cover of the first flurry of servings, she leaned towards him and whispered, "My high spirits are entirely at your disposal, Mr Appleby. How delightful that I need not moderate my lively ways on your account, but even if you no longer disapprove, I fear I have not yet won over Mama and must be suitably demure when her eye is on me."

Whereupon she assumed the most innocent countenance, the very picture of demure maidenhood, yet with an undisguised look of mischief in her eyes. It was all he could do not to laugh out loud.

But then her expression became solemn. "I am trying to improve myself, however. I have taken your advice that I should read more, and of a more serious nature. I read for a half hour before breakfast every day. I find that if I read aloud while walking about my bedchamber, I can understand the meaning better."

"What are you reading?"

"A book of sermons by a Dr Deerham. Do you know him? He is from Shrewsbury. I had never heard of him, but the book was on the shelves here. And a book I found at the circulating library called *'Memoirs of Eminently Pious Women'*, which I thought would be more interesting, being about real people, but... they are so *very* pious that it makes me feel dreadfully inadequate. Which is the point, I suppose," she finished glumly.

His heart was wrung by her earnest little face, so when he answered, his tone was soft. "Such books are all very well, but I would also recommend you to vary your reading with works which are... informative, perhaps, but without being quite so pious. Books of history, perhaps..." She pulled a face. "Travel, then. There are some splendid books telling of a traveller's journeys about our own country, or foreign parts. Quite entertaining, some of them. Should you like me to find you one or two?"

"Thank you, that does sound more interesting. I should be obliged if you could find me something of that sort, Mr Appleby. Would you be so very kind as to pass me a little of the rabbit?"

"It would be my pleasure. Miss Fletcher, I believe we are a good influence on each other. You are reading to improve your mind and become a little more serious, and I am attempting to become… not frivolous, precisely, but a little less serious. I am also making an effort to see the good in everyone. Even females," he added solemnly, and to his delight, she understood his feeble jest at once, and laughed delightedly.

There followed the most disconcerting meal he had ever endured. On one side, Mrs Fletcher provided him with civil if uninspiring conversation. On the other, he was disconnected from the world again, caught up in Angela's magic, suspended in a dreamlike place where only the two of them existed. Occasionally, when Angela's attention was drawn away and he returned to the waking world around him, he noticed Mrs Fletcher watching him quizzically, but he gave it no thought. His mind was entirely taken up with Angela.

Mrs Fletcher rose. "Shall we leave the gentlemen to their port, ladies?"

So soon? Where had the time flown? Angela threw him one last playful smile, before gracefully following the little train of ladies in their shimmering silks out of the room.

The four gentlemen rearranged themselves at Mr Fletcher's end of the table. He and Mr Clymer were soon deep in a discussion of the workings of the hypocausts. Mr John Fletcher turned to B with amusement in his eyes.

"Are you interested in the Roman baths, Appleby?"

"The water in them, yes. The means by which it is produced, no, not at all. I drink the stuff, and occasionally bathe in it, but beyond that it interests me not at all. And you?"

"The same. I like to read about the Romans as much as the next man, although they indulged in rather too many wars for my liking, but I have no desire to crawl about in subterranean passages like my father. I enjoyed your sermon on Sunday, by the way. Your style is one I should like to emulate when I am myself ordained."

"You intend to enter the church?" B said politely.

"It is a condition of my Fellowship at St John's that I take Holy Orders and become a Bachelor of Divinity, in time, so I must preach occasionally. I shall not look for a living, however. My life at Cambridge suits me very well, and with my Fellowship, some scholarships, two Exhibitions and tutoring fees, I have an income in excess of three hundred pounds a year, with room and board found. It is more than adequate to my needs, for my wants are small."

B looked at the quality of Fletcher's coat, and his immaculately starched neckcloth, and wondered about that. Young men brought up steeped in wealth often found that their small wants came quite expensive in the end. But he was too polite to voice the thought, so he said mildly, "You are fortunate to possess such an independence, although you will not be permitted to marry, I presume."

"No, but that is of no consequence, since I have no inclination towards matrimony. I prefer my books, and I believe you are of the same mind, or so I hear."

That comment cut to the bone! "Even if I were minded to marry," B said cautiously, "I cannot afford it. My home belongs to my uncle, and although he maintains my allowance for the moment, it will stop the instant I find a living. It is unlikely I would ever make enough as a clergyman to support a wife and family."

A small frown marred Fletcher's smooth forehead. "I do not wish to criticise your uncle, but it seems harsh to raise you with the expectation of inheriting, and then cast you aside with nothing. Have you asked him to secure your independence? An annuity, perhaps, or even to establish you in a profession?"

"Heavens, no! I could not... and besides, he may in time have a numerous family to provide for. He should not erode his fortune for me. I do not wish it, I assure you."

Fletcher smiled. "You are more tolerant than I should be, Appleby. I should deeply resent such a disinheritance."

"And yet I do not," B said. "It is not in my nature, perhaps. I accept what comes my way with pleasure, when it is to the good, and with resignation otherwise. If I had been of a more active disposition, I should have carved out a career for myself many years ago and would not now be in this predicament. But I allowed myself to be carried by the current of life wherever it would take me, and so I cannot now complain if I am stranded on a sandbar and cut off by the tide. Whatever happens, I shall be content."

"Even if you drown, to continue your analogy?" Fletcher said.

"Even then."

Feeling it necessary to change the subject, he asked about Fletcher's field of interest at Cambridge, and listened without impatience to what could only be described as an impassioned lecture about fossils.

Music from the room above drifted down to them through the open windows. If only B could be in the drawing room with the ladies! Instead, he was trapped in the dining room, looking at the younger Fletcher's face when he would far rather be looking at his sister.

The senior Mr Fletcher said, "Now, Johnny, don't bore Appleby to death with your ramblings. All that talk of dead creatures is enough to give a man dyspepsia."

"I assure you, I am finding it most interesting," B said.

"Aye, so it is, in small doses. Now, if Will were here, he'd bore you with horses and hunting and such like, and I can bore you with Roman constructions, and if that doesn't put you to sleep, with the making of water closets, or the best means of carding wool. What is your great interest, Appleby? What subject do you choose when you wish to bore dinner guests?"

"He is a clergyman," his son said. "He can, if he wishes, bore an entire congregation on selected Sundays with a single verse of the Bible."

They all laughed.

B froze. Were they *laughing* at him? But then he saw, as clear as if she were there in the room, Angela's mischievous eyes when she said something outrageous. There it was, in John Fletcher's eyes! They were *teasing* him... it was a joke, something to laugh about. A whole family given to teasing! What a strange thought.

He gave a tentative smile. "I hope my sermons are not entirely boring, but if you want to be bored, gentlemen, I could discourse for hours on the subject of caterpillars, and the damage they do to my cabbages. Then there is carrot fly and asparagus beetle, blackflies, whiteflies and thrips, aphids and sawflies, blight, rust and scab, cankers and mildew—"

Laughing, the elder Fletcher held up his hands in surrender. "That takes the trick, Appleby. This might be a good time to join the ladies, do you think?"

Angela was at the instrument, playing a duet with her sister and singing. B stood just inside the door, watching her. She had a lovely voice, not as fine as Eloise Whittleton's, but still a privilege to hear, and she played with an easy grace, caught up in her music, oblivious to her audience. B felt a rush of pride in her, although why he should was more than he could fathom. She was not his, and would never be so.

The piece finished, there was an immediate request for another. This time Mrs Fletcher suggested that Angela should sing while her sister played. It was an enchanting performance. Unlike Eloise, who stood as still as a statue while she sang, Angela was constantly in motion, her arms taking elegant poses, her feet neatly arranged in the starting position for a dance. B could not take his eyes off her.

When the song ended, and the sisters returned to their duets, he found Mrs Fletcher standing beside him.

"She sings very prettily, do you not agree?" she said. "None of her sisters are her equal in that regard, or in performing on the pianoforte, and she is the only one of them who can play the harp. Such a treasure!"

He made some remark at random, for he had rather watch Angela than talk about her.

"Such a high spirited girl, but her liveliness gets her into trouble sometimes, as you have reason to know. Still, with her looks, she cannot help but attract admirers, so we have to be careful with her, as with all our girls. There are plenty of men, eligible in many ways, who also admire the twenty thousand pounds she will have when she marries. Naturally, Mr Fletcher will not agree to an unequal match. A man must have a considerable fortune of his own before he can look at one of the Fletcher daughters."

"That is very wise," he said, as he was clearly expected to.

"Of course, the outright fortune hunters are easy to spot," she said. "But there are also those who fall head over heels in love with one or other of the girls and then have to be gently turned away when it is discovered that they have not a feather to fly with. Mr Fletcher had to reject several of Rosie's admirers in town. It is very sad for them, but the girls cannot be allowed to marry a penniless man, no matter how great the attachment between them might be."

"Very true," he said. "One must be prudent."

"Exactly so!" she said happily, having made her point, and after a few more bland remarks, moved away.

B understood her perfectly, but then he had never harboured any hopes of marrying Angela. He might think of it sometimes... in fact, he might think of it rather often lately, but that did not mean he was foolish enough to imagine he could ever aspire to her hand.

The music ended, and the card tables came out.

"Would you be so kind as to put up with my ineptness at the chessboard?" the younger Mr Fletcher said to B. "Mr Bravington is an indulgent teacher, but I need all the practice I can get."

"Certainly, if I am not needed to make up a four at whist."

"My stepmother is minded for a round game tonight, and Pa and Mr Clymer will play cribbage."

So B agreed to it, and was rewarded by the company of

Angela, who drew up a chair to watch their game. She said little, but it was enough to have her there by his side, an attentive audience.

Clymer and the Miss Bensleys summoned chairs to carry them home, but B borrowed a lantern and made his way on foot along the Gravel Walk. It was late, and no one was about, so he saw not a soul before he entered the gate to his own garden. And there he stopped, sitting on the same bench where Fletcher and Angela had sat, where she had apologised so contritely, where she had seen the gooseberries.

So many memories! He could scarcely remember now his first meeting with her, his first unfavourable impressions, and then the letters... Was that when it had happened? No, because he had not known then who had sent them. But later, after his sermon, when he knew beyond all doubt *she* had written them, that she *loved* him... Was that the point when everything changed? Or was it in the garden, talking about gooseberries and onions?

He could not say. That part of it was uncertain, shrouded in the mists of time. But of one thing he was sure, beyond all doubt — he was hopelessly, deeply in love with Angela Fletcher. His life would never be the same.

In the darkness, surrounded by the scent of herbs and garlic and freshly turned earth, he smiled. For the first time in his life, he was entirely happy.

20: A Ball At The New Assembly Rooms

As the day of the ball approached, Angie was careful to ensure that her behaviour was beyond reproach. For all Pa's reassuring words, Mama still had the power to forbid her from attending, and that could not be borne. Everything that could be contrived to keep Mama sweet must be done. If Mama wondered where her shawl was, Angie would run off to look for it. If there were lists to be made or invitations to be written, Angie was ready with her pen. When the flower supplier warned of a shortfall, Angie offered to visit every other supplier in the town to ensure there were enough blooms on hand. And when she did not have to help, she sat meekly with her embroidery, or practised at the instrument.

Nothing more was said about her outburst, and although she avoided the Pump Room herself, Rosie and Belinda reported that the gossips no longer talked about her, for there was a new outrage in the form of a scandalous book, recently published, and reported to represent numerous characters from the Prince of Wales's set in the most unflattering terms.

"It is called *'The Errant Prince',"* Rosie told Angie, as they worked through a pile of acceptances to the ball. "It is about a prince who behaves in the wildest manner, and how he is banished to a small island with a group of his cronies."

"Yes, and dreadful things happen to all of them," Belinda said, "but eventually the prince repents and promises to be good thenceforth, and is allowed to leave the island. It is set in Italy, but of course that is just a ploy to throw people off the scent of what it is really about."

"It seems to be a most unsuccessful ploy," Angie said. "Oh, this letter is not an acceptance. Mrs Lacey asks if she might bring a Mrs Romney with her. Mama?"

Mama quickly scanned the letter. "Let me see… she says this Mrs Romney is a former resident of Bath, just arrived for a visit, who would dearly like to see her old acquaintances."

"She might see them at the Pump Room, one might have thought," Angie said.

Mama laughed. "True, and another lady… it is a pity Mrs Lacey does not have two or three agreeable young men visiting, but no matter. One does not like to be disobliging. Rosie, you may write to say that we should be delighted… the usual things. You know how to phrase it. Well, it does seem as if Mr Bravington's ball will be a modest success."

Since it was the only ball to be held in August, and since every invitation had prompted an immediate acceptance, it was hardly in doubt. Bath was not as full as it would be in the winter months, but there were enough residents and visitors to make a creditable crowd in the New Assembly Rooms.

The nearer the day came, the more an agony of fear gripped

Angie, and it was not until Mama began to decide on the gowns they might wear, and Angie was included that she breathed again.

"The very pale pink, but not the one with the fuller sleeves, for fashions are not so advanced here. The silver net over-gown, I think."

"Yes, Mama," she said, her tone quiet, but inside her heart was singing. She would dance! A whole evening of dancing, and what could be more delicious?

The evening arrived, and Angie was in a fever of impatience to be there, to hear the music, to *dance!* She could scarcely breathe for excitement. Mama and Pa went with Mr Bravington in his carriage, while Angie, Rosie, Belinda and Johnny followed in their own carriage. Rosie was in her best looks, for pleasurable anticipation always gave her a becoming glow. Belinda was almost incoherent with joy, for she had borrowed a gown from Mama for the occasion, being of too large a frame to wear anything of Rosie's or Angie's, and declared she had worn nothing so fine in her life. Johnny twitted them amiably, and hoped there would be enough gentlemen present that he would not have to stand up more than once or twice.

"For shame!" Rosie said. "You must do your duty, Johnny. Will would, if he were here. He out-danced us all in London."

"Oh, Will is a paragon in a multitude of ways," Johnny said cheerfully. "I cannot hope to compete."

As for Angie, she positively shivered in delight. There was always the fear of insufficient partners, thus causing her to sit out some dances, but since this had never yet happened to her, her uneasiness was not very great. The only real difficulty with a ball, to her mind, was that it had to end.

A throne-like chair had been arranged for Mr Bravington to receive his guests in the Octagon Ante-Chamber, and within a very few minutes of his taking his seat with the Fletchers in attendance, the first guests were arriving. Under cover of the greetings, Angie crept away through the entrance to the ballroom. It was not quite so impressive as the pillared splendour of the Grand Assembly Room at York, but who cared about pillars when there was dancing to be had? The musicians were already warming up in their eyrie above, the guests in their finery were beginning to trickle in and within a short time the ball would begin. She spun around in delight.

"Excited, little sister?" Johnny smiled down at her affectionately.

"Oh, yes!" Another spin. "Is this not perfect? A whole night of dancing! Mr Bravington is my hero."

Johnny chuckled. "Perhaps you should tell him that, when you return to your place on the receiving line."

"Oh. Is Mama cross?"

"Only very slightly. Come now, we must do our duty before we may enjoy the pleasures of the evening."

With a rueful smile she allowed herself to be shepherded back to her place in the Octagon.

The ball started badly for Angie, for she was claimed for the first two by Randal Sylvester. It was inevitable that he would ask her, however, and it was as well for his turn to be got out of the way early, so she might hope for more agreeable partners for the rest of the evening. He was not a bad dancer, and it would be no penance to stand up with him if he would only talk less, or perhaps more intelligently. As it was, after half an hour of inane chatter, her ears ringing, she was heartily glad to be solicited by a blushing youth even younger than she was, and relieved that he said not a word. He was an ungainly boy, far from an expert dancer, but she no longer cared for that, if he would spare her from Randal Sylvester.

It was while she stood in blissful silence with this young man, awaiting their time to join the movements of the dance, that she noticed Mr Appleby the Younger. He had arrived early, honouring the event with his rare smile, and thereafter had ambled about the perimeter of the ballroom, talking to one or two acquaintances and watching the dancing. She knew he would not dance, so she wondered rather at his staying where he had no occasion to be, when he could have been in the card room.

Now he was with a woman in a gown of a hideous shade of green. It was not the gown, dreadful as it was, nor the ostentatious diamond choker which drew her notice so much as Mr Appleby's face, for he looked as if he would rather be anywhere else. The woman was chatting animatedly to him, her hand resting on his left sleeve, while he had his back to the wall, his expression blank, but his eyes skittered to left and right, as if looking for a means of escape. Eventually, he made some remark to her, shook off her hand and strode away, while the unknown lady watched him go with such a triumphant expression that all Angie's curiosity was aroused.

"Who is that woman?" she hissed to her partner. "The one in green, beside the fireplace."

"Where? Oh, that is Mrs Romney."

"But who is she? What do you know of her?"

He frowned. "Nothing much. She used to live here, until she married about a year ago."

"What is she to Mr Appleby — the nephew, that is, not the uncle?"

He grinned, looking even younger, suddenly. "Lord, she jilted him, didn't she? All set to marry the poor sapskull, she was, but then he lost his prospects and she thought better of it. Lucky for him, I'd say. Who'd want to marry a face like that?"

They were swept into the dance shortly afterwards, and by the time it ended, Mr Appleby had vanished. The lady in green was still present, however, paying court to Mr Bravington, whose throne had been moved to a small dais at one end of the room. There he sat, surrounded by the dowagers and matrons, receiving the homage of his guests.

With only a tiny bit of manipulation, Angie's partner was induced to walk in that direction, thus providing a clear view of Mrs Romney. She it was who had been added to the guest list at the last minute, at the behest of Mrs Lacey. Mr Appleby's lost love. Miss Meek, as she once was, although to judge from her animation, and the way she constantly reached out to touch Mr Bravington as she talked, the name was anything but apt.

Angie had never judged anyone by their face, for who could help the way she looked? Mrs Romney was not at all handsome, but she could have improved herself vastly by wearing a more tasteful gown, and leaving off the ugly diamonds that hid her throat. Besides that, she was too forward altogether to please Angie's notions. Having seen the lady for herself, she could agree with her partner in thinking that Mr Appleby had had a fortunate escape.

She returned demurely to Mama's side and looked about hopefully for her next partner, but to her dismay Randal Sylvester appeared at her side.

"Miss Fletcher, might I entreat you once more to honour me with your hand for the next two?"

"Oh no, I cannot dance with you again, sir. It would be most improper."

He leaned close to whisper in her ear. "There are circumstances — most desirable and joyous circumstances — in which it would not be at all improper, my very *dear* Miss Fletcher."

"I cannot think of any," she said, in what she hoped was a repressive tone.

"Can you not?" he said, even more quietly. "Let us find a secluded spot and I shall show you precisely what I mean... *Angie.*"

"I did not give you permission to address me thus," she hissed, "nor will I ever do so. You are impertinent, Mr Sylvester."

She looked about for help, but Mama was dealing with a cluster of jostling aspirants for Rosie's hand, and Johnny was, as usual, nowhere to be seen. There was nothing for it, but to make her own escape.

"Look at that!" she cried, pointing.

"What? Where?"

"Over there, in the far corner. Can you not see?"

He peered into the distance, his forehead creased in bewilderment, while Angie deftly stepped behind him, then merged into a passing group of ladies and dived out of the door to the Octagon. Now where? To her left was the card room, where she would find her father, but that would be far too conspicuous. To her right was the long corridor to the entrance, with no visible hiding place. But the door to the supper room was ajar, from whence came the reassuring murmur of voices and the clink of cutlery, so she slipped into the room.

There was no hiding place here, either, but there were people, who would act as chaperons if Mr Sylvester should corner her. Servants moved about laying the tables for supper. A gaggle of women examined a sideboard filled with fruit, jellies and creams. Several men huddled round a table, holding a low-voiced conversation. But not far away sat a familiar, and rather glum, figure, head down, lost in thought. No doubt he was thinking about Mrs Romney, but he would serve Angie's purpose perfectly.

"Mr Appleby!" she cried in relief. "Just the person I need. Will you protect me from Mr Sylvester, for he means mischief, I am certain of it?"

"Of course," he said, albeit rather startled, rising from his chair. "I am entirely at your disposal, Miss Fletcher. Whatever has he done to alarm you so?"

"He wishes to take me to a secluded spot, and although I have no precise idea of what he means to do there, it is nothing good, that much is certain."

"No, indeed. What do you wish me to do for you? Throw him out of the Rooms? Knock him down?"

She giggled. "Oh, no, no! Nothing so dramatic, I assure you. May I sit with you for a while? Mama will notice I have gone missing before very long and send someone to find me, but until then, your presence will deter even the persistent Mr Sylvester."

He held a chair for her and then sat beside her, his calm demeanour soothing to Angie's ruffled spirits. Nothing bad could happen to her while she was with Mr Appleby.

"I am surprised no one in your family has managed to shield you from Sylvester," he said. "He danced the first two with you, but after that he should have been sent about his business."

"Oh, Mama would have done it, but she has Rosie and Belinda to attend to as well, and I suppose Johnny is doing his duty by the wallflowers. I did not quite like to disturb Pa when he is deep in a game. I thought you would be in the card room, too, Mr Appleby, since you do not dance."

"I am not minded for cards tonight," he said, looking a trifle glum. "I had sooner watch the dancing, even though I do not participate."

"But you are *not* watching the dancing, are you? Here you are, skulking in—"

The supper room door opened a little wider, a man's head appeared and Angie held her breath. But it was no one she knew, and since he went away at once, Angie breathed again.

"You thought that might be Sylvester?"

She nodded. "I had to play a little trick to evade him, but he will come looking for me sooner or later. Or, if I am lucky, Johnny will, perhaps. Or Mama. But you will protect me until someone arrives to rescue me."

"You are lucky to have a large family about you, looking out for your interests," he said. "It must be wonderful to have relations who care for one."

"But you have relations who care," Angie said in surprise.

"Your uncle and Calantha care very much what happens to you."

"Do they? I cannot say. I believe they show me the same casual affection they feel for any acquaintance of long standing. I am deeply grateful for all that my uncle has done for me in providing me with a home and an education, but I do not flatter myself that he would miss me very much if I were to leave Bath. And as for my father— No, let me not bore you with all of that."

"I am not in the least bored," she said, "but I will not press you if you prefer not to talk about it. Not everyone can have a father like mine, I suppose. He may seem easy going and placid, but he would fight to the death to spare any of us the least hurt."

Mr Appleby smiled then, his face instantly flooded with good humour. Never did a man appear so different when he smiled!

"I am sure he would," he said.

"What father would not do as much?" Angie said without thinking, and was mortified to see Mr Appleby's face close up at once.

"Mine would not have lifted a finger for me," he said savagely. "Ah, you think I exaggerate, but it is not so. You see, my birth killed my mother. My father lost his beloved wife of no more than a year, and in exchange gained a puling infant. He thought it a poor bargain, and I am not sure that I disagree with him. My mother was a great beauty, lively, accomplished, admired and loved by all who knew her, and I sent her out of the world for ever. It is no wonder he cared nothing for me."

"It was not your fault!" Angie said in a great passion. "How despicable to blame an innocent babe for such a thing! Why, he was as much to blame himself, for who got her with child, I should like to know?" Mr Appleby laughed out loud at that. "Well, it is true, although Mama would be shocked to hear me speak on such a subject, and to a gentleman, too. *'Decorum, Angie,'* she would say to me. *'A lady does not discuss such subjects in mixed company, or at all until she is married.'* But with two married sisters and a sister-in-law, none of whom care over much for decorum, one is bound to pick up hints here and there. As for your mother, she sounds a perfect paragon, which people always are, when they are dead. If I were to drop down this minute of an apoplexy, you may be sure that even Mama would cry and tell the world I was an angel. Which you are well aware I am not."

He laughed again, and said, "An angel would be boring, I think."

"Well, I think so too," she said, pleased. "Rosie is terribly good, always, and so very meek and obliging, but sometimes I do wish she would stand up for herself. Instead, she just drifts through life, allowing things to happen to her."

"I drift through life myself, to be quite truthful," he said. "Things happen to me, sometimes good, sometimes bad. Perhaps I should stand up for myself, but I never got into the way of it, because nobody cared what I did. My father— I *will* tell you about him, I think, and then you may judge for yourself. After my mother died, my father's grief was so severe that he went into his book room, and never came out of it, except to sleep. He took on a curate to do the parish work, and all he did, every day and all day, was to read. He would sit in his chair, a book in his hand, his spectacles perched on the end of his nose, a glass of wine beside him, and nothing disturbed the pattern of his days.

"When I was old enough, my nurse used to take me downstairs at four every day, all dressed up in my best clothes, and primed with a verse or two of the Bible learnt by heart to recite. She would knock on the door, usher me inside, and say, *'Here is your son to see you, sir.'* And my father would say, *'Not today, Nurse.'* Every day, the same words. And he never even looked up from his book."

He seemed still and composed, and his voice was even, but one hand clenched and unclenched as it lay on the table. Impulsively, Angie reached out and laid her gloved hand on his.

"That is shocking! To treat an innocent child so — it is wicked!"

He gave a rueful smile. "Wicked? That is not for me to say. Shall I tell you the strangest part of all this? When my father died and I came to Bath, a few weeks later a wagon arrived bearing twelve large boxes. He had left me all his books. It was his only legacy, for he owned nothing else. And I cannot bring myself to look at them. There they sit, those boxes, taking up far too much space in my study, and yet I cannot bring myself to open them. I suppose I should simply burn the whole lot, and be done with it. Then it would be gone, my childhood carried away with the smoke of the bonfire."

"How can you talk so?" she cried. "You love books! You cannot burn them, for it is not their fault, after all. There might be books amongst them that you want to read."

He shuddered. "I shall *never* want to read them, never!"

"Then get rid of them. Sell them to someone who wants a library — us, for instance. Johnny is supposed to be filling the shelves of our library in Hertfordshire, but he keeps buying other things — globes and inkwells and maps and an orrery, would you believe! Do you know what that is? I did not, but it is a working model of the planets, seemingly. I have not the least idea why we should want one of those, when we still have empty shelves. Johnny estimates we need two thousand books to fill the library completely, and so far he has bought perhaps fifty. Fifty! We shall all be dead before it is done."

"Well, that is the way it is usually done, you know," he said, smiling down at her. "One buys the books one wants to read, then they go on the shelves and one buys more. A good library is the work of several generations. But if your brother would like to examine my father's books and take what he wants, I should be happy to be rid of them. Miss Fletcher, I hear the music of the next dance under way, and I am keeping you from the pleasures of the ball room. Do not let me detain you."

"Will you come with me?" she said impulsively. "I know you will not dance, but I cannot leave you here to be miserable on your own. You are avoiding Mrs Romney, I know, but if you will accept unsolicited and presumptuous advice from one much younger and less worldly than you, it seems to me that it is better to face up to that which is disagreeable at once. So I have found, anyway."

"I am not avoiding Mrs Romney," he said gravely. "She is an odious woman, and I have never much cared for her good opinion."

"Never? But... I thought you were in love with her! Oh, I beg your pardon, my wretched tongue."

He laughed, and this time he was the one to rest his hand on hers. "I hope you will never guard your tongue with me. I have never been in love with Mrs Romney, and I was relieved when she married Romney. But now that she is back, and so unexpectedly, everyone is looking at me, attempting to gauge the degree of my distress, and I cannot bear to be the focus of so much attention."

"Then my point still applies," she said. "Show them you care nothing for their foolish gossip-mongering! Come and walk about the ballroom with me and we shall do each other a service — I shall distract scrutiny from you, and you will defend me from the attentions of the abominable Randal Sylvester. Well? What do you say to my cunning plan?"

For answer, he rose and held out his arm. "Shall we promenade, Miss Fletcher?"

"By all means, Mr Appleby."

21: An Invitation

It was the oddest evening B could remember. First the appearance of Elspeth Meek, very much dressed up and glorying in her married status, and now... now he could walk about the ballroom with Angie, with her sweet face beside him, just as he saw other men walk about with a lady. At first, when she tucked her arm companionably in his, he was acutely aware of her diminutive size, for she only came up to his shoulder.

But it was not long before she released her hold, and then she began to dance. There was no other way to describe the way she moved, light-footed, spinning round to face him, then turning to his other side, then another twist, her skirts shimmering about her ankles, her arms making graceful arcs in the air. And all the time, she chattered away. She talked about his garden, asking how his cabbages were coming along, even though he had sown the seed only a few days ago, and then it was strawberries or pears or asparagus...

He was mesmerised, unable to take his eyes off her, enchanted all over again as she spun her magic around him.

They had made their way almost fully around the room when

he noticed Mrs Romney. She was dancing in the nearest set, if dancing it could be called, her face red from the effort as she jigged about, her steps lumbering and heavy. He looked at Angela, feather-light and graceful, and then back at the woman he might have married, had matters gone otherwise, and almost laughed aloud. He must remember to thank Calantha for sparing him such a dreadful fate.

He could never aspire to Angela's hand, for such a lovely girl must attract far better suitors, but he was grateful to have met her and known her... to have learnt to *love* her. Soon now she would leave Bath and he would never see her again, but he was content. For a few weeks, an angel had visited him and made his life immeasurably better. Whatever his life held in the future, he would accept it equably, holding the memory of Angela in his heart.

The music subsided, the first of the two dances finished. The dancers laughed, caught their breath, chattered happily as a few latecomers joined the lines for the second dance.

"Miss Fletcher, you had sooner be amongst the dancers than standing about with me," he said gently.

"No, indeed, I—"

"The Wherrett boy is over there, gazing at you longingly. Let me take you to him, and by the time this dance is over, I shall have extracted your father from the card room to protect you from a certain encroaching young man."

She laughed, but agreed to it willingly, and young Wherrett was delighted to have so charming a partner, his eyes as big as saucers. Seeing her safe, B made his way to the card room and explained the difficulty to Mr Fletcher, who at once set off to the rescue. The price of B's solicitude for Angela was high, however. He was called upon to replace Fletcher in the four, and could no longer have the pleasure even of watching Angela dance. Nor did he catch more than a glimpse of her at supper, and only when the other card players released him was he able to return to the ballroom in time to see Angela's final steps in the Roger de Coverley. And then, in the bustle of departure, he lost sight of her altogether.

He was satisfied, however. He walked home through the quiet dawn streets at peace with the world.

~~~~~

The Fletchers were quiet as they sat down to a late breakfast that morning. Their quietness was not the result of the exertions of the evening, but because a packet of mail had arrived, redirected from Hertfordshire and London. There were letters for them all, which they perused in silence until Mama cried out in delight.

"You will never believe— Oh, Rosie, what a wonderful opportunity for you!"

"What scheme is afoot now?" Pa said, smiling at her excitement.

"This!" she cried, waving a letter aloft. "So very kind, and I was inclined to dismiss them as being of little use to us, despite being near neighbours."

Pa laughed. "I'm having a bit of trouble following you, Lizzie love. Why don't you read it out to us?"

"Oh... I do beg your pardon. I must sound like a positive zany. It is from Mrs Armitage, who was our neighbour in Grosvenor Square. Let me read you the whole of it. *'My dear Mrs Fletcher, I*
~~~~~

write to beg your aid. You will remember that my husband's ward, Violet—".

"The one with the pretty little dog!" Rosie put in.

"The one with the *well-behaved* dog," Mama said acidly, for the attempt to acquire such a dog themselves had proved to be a disaster. "Do let me finish, Rosie. *'...my husband's ward, Violet, recently married a son of the Earl of Kilrannan. Various of his relations, having braved the long journey from Ireland, are minded to stay with us until the autumn. We would like to provide them with better entertainment than our small family can supply. Mr Armitage has invited a number of his acquaintances, including some very charming young men, but we are in need of young ladies to add their beauty and accomplishments to the company. I at once thought of your charming eldest daughter, Rose, and would like to invite you to bring her to stay with us at Marsham Grove, near Epping, for a fortnight, or perhaps longer, if you should find the company agreeable. It would be very informal, with rides and outings in the countryside during the day, making our own entertainment in the evenings, all of which will I hope provide a welcome respite after the rigours of the season. Pray forgive me for not inviting the rest of your delightful family, but we are very pressed for space. Do let me have your early reply. We would be delighted to see you as soon as you can arrange the journey. Yours in friendship, Mrs Eliot Armitage.'* There! Is that not charming?"

"So you're going to abandon us and rush away to... where was it? Epping? Where is that, anyway?" Pa said.

"It is in Essex, the next county to Hertfordshire," Johnny said. "Epping is no more than twenty miles or so from Chadwell Park."

"Will Mr Tranter be there?" Rosie said in a small voice.

"Mrs Armitage does not mention names," Mama said. "He might well be, for he is Violet's brother-in-law now, but just because he offered for you in town and was refused does not mean that there would be anything awkward in his company. He is an earl's son and a gentleman, so he knows how to behave."

"He will do nothing to make me uncomfortable, I am certain," Rosie said. "Lord Albury is the same – he knows just how to set one at ease, so that he feels like a friend."

"Are you beginning to like him a little, Rosie love?" Pa said slyly. "Might we anticipate a match yet?"

"No one could possibly take him in dislike," she said, with a slight blush. "As to the rest, time will tell, but I can assure you that I am not averse to the idea. In London, I was a little overwhelmed by... oh, everything! It was so different from everything I knew, but having Belinda here, and seeing Ricky too, has helped me to see that I must leave all that behind now. Not my friends from Sagborough, naturally, but the old life... that has quite gone. I am not a child any longer, and I must look to the future and marriage. Not necessarily Lord Albury, for there are plenty of other young men in the world."

"Indeed there are," Mama said, "and this invitation to Epping is a perfect opportunity to meet some of them. Just think of it, Rosie — a whole fortnight living under the same roof with any number of eligible gentlemen, for Mr Armitage is very well connected. It is a great compliment to you."

"A compliment to her dowry, you mean," Johnny said. "You see it as an opportunity for Rosie to pick up a titled husband, but they undoubtedly see it as an opportunity to pick up a fortune."

"That is crudely put, but there is some truth in it," Mama said.

"And why not? These aristocratic families need money to keep themselves going, and while their sons might fall in love with Rosie for her looks and sweet nature, they often cannot marry without a dowry. That is why we moved south, after all, to put Rosie in the way of a better class of men."

"Higher ranking, maybe, but there are plenty of men of sterling worth in Yorkshire," Pa said reprovingly. Ma had the good grace to look abashed.

"But what about Belinda?" Rosie said. "We invited her to keep me company for the summer. I can hardly go away and leave her."

"Oh, but you must go!" Belinda said. "Don't think of me. It's far too good an opportunity to miss. I want you to marry a lord as much as anyone could. I'll go home to Yorkshire, of course."

"You'll stay as long as you please," Pa said. "Even if Rosie goes jauntering off to Epping, there's no need for you to go scampering back to Sagborough. You'll be company for Angie, after all."

Angie had no particular wish to have Rosie's friend foisted onto her. A mischievous bubble rose inside her and burst into life. "Why not go with her, Bel? Rosie will need a maid, after all."

Belinda gasped and her eyes grew round, but Mama said repressively, "We shall take Hathaway, of course. She can look after both of us. Besides, Belinda can hardly demean herself by acting as a lady's maid."

"Oh, but I should love to do it, Mrs Fletcher. I'm used to helping my sisters, and I know how to press a gown and polish boots. Oh, please, may I go? I've got some plain gowns that would be perfect."

"I should be so happy to have Belinda with me, if Angie is not to go," Rosie said pleadingly. "A friend to talk to... she could share my room."

"Whatever would people think? Really, it hardly seems—" Mama began, but Pa waved a hand and she fell silent.

"What does it matter what people think?" he said sweepingly, as Mama raised surprised eyebrows. "I don't want Rosie thrust into another crowd of grand people like she was in London without at least one friend, and no, Lizzie love, you're her stepmother, not her friend. She'll not talk to you the way she does with Belinda, it's only natural."

"Well, of course, if you approve the scheme, my objections must be set aside," Mama said frostily. "I shall write at once to Mrs Armitage to accept."

"Shall I rush down to the Saracen and bespeak a post chaise and four for you?" Johnny said, grinning. "They can be outside the door in an hour. Or, since Rosie has a thousand gowns to be packed, perhaps we can delay until dawn tomorrow."

Mama laughed, but shook her head. "We will not leave immediately, I think. Lady Louisa dropped a hint that Lord Albury will be staying for another two weeks, and it would be a pity to rush away before then, when he was so attentive to Rosie last night."

"He danced with me, Mama, that is all, as he did with others," Rosie said in her quietest voice, blushing fiercely. "It means nothing."

"But one never knows what may develop. That will give us time for our own carriage to be sent from Chadwell, for nothing is so comfortable as one's own equipage, and we can all travel together. Besides..." She hesitated, with a sideways glance at Angie. "I do not like to leave Angie here with you without a female chaperon. It is not proper." Another glance. "Angie, I do hope you are not encouraging Mr Appleby's attentions. He is not at all eligible, and your father would not want you to marry him."

This was not a topic Angie wanted to pursue, since the subject of encouraging Mr Appleby brought her dangerously close to the question of those dreadful letters, and all the remorse she now felt for ever writing them. If only it could all be forgot! Happily, her father intervened before she had to answer.

"I don't want her to marry anyone," he said, laying down his toast. "Not yet, anyway. She's only eighteen, Lizzie love, and far too young to be thinking of marriage. Let her enjoy herself a while longer. Allie was three and twenty when she wed, and Julia one and twenty, and those are sensible ages for a woman to take on a husband. I don't want any of my girls rushing into the responsibilities of marriage and motherhood too early."

"No, indeed," Mama said with unruffled calm. "I believe I said nothing to suggest otherwise, and certainly it is more important to get Rosie well settled first. But even if Angie herself is not thinking of marriage, you may be sure that many young men are looking at her and her twenty thousand pounds, and marriage is very much on their minds."

"Not everyone looks at Angie and thinks of her dowry," Pa said. "She's very well worth looking at, even without that, I'd have thought."

She blushed, lowering her eyes.

"Of course she is," Mama said, "and it is not merely our own sentiment that makes us think so, for she was so admired last night, nothing could be like it. Everyone said she was in her best looks, and several people told me, quite without prompting, that she was by far the best dancer in the room. Lady Louisa said so, and Lady Mellish, too, and they must have seen some very superior performances at court. Such a compliment!"

"Aye, and no credit to them for stating the obvious," Pa said, smiling fondly at Angie.

That made her blush even more. Such praise was hardly justified, when it was Rosie who had been surrounded by admirers all evening, Rosie who had danced with Lord Albury, Rosie who set so many men's eyes shining. But then, perhaps everyone expected such compliments to Rosie, which made them almost commonplace.

"But that is nothing to the point," Mama said. "Angie is bound to attract attention, and not all her admirers are in a position to marry. Mr Appleby is one such. Not a farthing to his name. *Most* ineligible."

"He may be poor, but he's a gentleman and a sensible man," Pa said. "He looked after Angie yesterday when she was hounded by that fool of a Sylvester, and that was my fault, Angie love, for hiding away in the card room when I should have been taking better care of you."

"My fault, too, Pa," Johnny said. "I promised to watch over the girls, and failed dismally."

"You were dancing, and that's important, too," Pa said, with a slight shrug. "I should have known that Sylvester would be a pest. Ah well, least said, soonest mended. What about these books of Appleby's, Johnny? Will you have a look at them?"

"I will, although I cannot think that the collection of a country clergyman will be what we want. There are only so many books of sermons and theological texts that one needs."

"None at all, I'd have thought," Pa said, chuckling. "If that's all he has, he can keep them. But there might be a few we could buy from him, and put a bit of coin in his pocket. But you be sure to give him a good price for them, won't you? It wouldn't do to be cheeseparing with a man of his standing."

"If I find anything worth buying, I shall give him a fair price for it, you may be sure," Johnny said.

Belinda had been bouncing with increasing impatience through this exchange. "Never mind about Mr Appleby's book!" she burst out. "Have you heard the news about *'The Errant Prince'?"*

"Belinda, it is not ladylike to repeat gossip," Mama said. "I am sure you would not want anyone to think you are one of those vulgar, chattering persons who is interested in such things. Frankly, I think the less said about it the better. It sounds a most unpleasant book, and not one that any of you girls should be reading."

"Definitely not!" Johnny said, setting down his coffee cup roughly. "It is not at all the sort of book that *any* lady should read."

"A bit warm, is it?" Pa said, chuckling.

"Very! Not at all the thing."

"For myself, I don't wish to, for I know none of the people it is supposedly about," Belinda said, "but it is not precisely gossip, for everyone is talking of it. Just imagine — the author is someone who lives in Bath! Isn't that amazing? Why, it could be someone we know, someone we see every day."

"Goodness!" Mama said. "Surely it could not be any acquaintance of ours! But who could it possibly be?"

The rest of the meal passed in fevered speculation, for they knew almost all the principal inhabitants of the town, and the thought that one of them had written a book featuring thinly disguised caricatures of some very high-ranking persons was deliciously exciting.

~~~~~

B slept later than usual, ate his customary breakfast and then strolled down the hill to a flower shop to order a posy to be sent to Angela, and another to Calantha, to whom he was particularly well disposed that morning, since her marriage had spared him the horror of marriage to Elspeth Meek. Then he left his card and a note of thanks at Mr Bravington's house. The old gentleman was still abed after the exertions of the evening before, but his man assured B that his master was in the best of spirits, and only a little tired. By this time, B had missed morning prayers at the Abbey, so he went directly to the Pump Room, where he was accosted almost at once by his uncle.

"There you are, nephew! Where have you been? Never tell me you have been lying in your bed all this time? Laid low by a mere ball, and you did not even dance, you idle fellow. No stamina, you young men. But tell me, have you read this book that everyone speaks about? You have friends in town, some in very high places — that Crabb fellow you knew at Oxford is very thick with Portland, is he not? So you must know whether the depictions in the book are at all accurate, eh?"

B struggled to make sense of this. "Are you referring to *'The*
~~~~~

Errant Prince'?" he said, hazarding a guess.

"Yes, yes, of course! What else? Everyone is talking about it, and the author comes from this very town! Is that not extraordinary? Has Crabb said aught of it? Or any of your other connections?"

"Only that the book's publication put His Royal Highness in somewhat of rage."

"Well, of course, but who do people think wrote it? They must have some idea."

"Crabb has not mentioned it recently. He has been in Nottinghamshire with the Duke of Portland since Parliament rose."

"Hmm, lips sealed, I suppose. Very discreet, although I am sure Portland knows everything about it. Ah, there is Wherrett. I wonder if he has any idea?"

He bustled away, obviously intending to press everyone of his acquaintance for information.

B sighed. "Good morning, Uncle. Yes, I am very well. And yourself? I am glad to hear it," he murmured under his breath, as he made his way to the dispensing rail for his daily glass of water. Then he found his usual seat and settled down to sip his drink.

He was alone. For the first time since news of his spurious inheritance had spread, he was unencumbered by hopeful young females. They walked past him on their circulation about the room, the Miss Laceys with Miss Hayward, then Miss Paine and Miss Starling, arm in arm, but they merely smiled at him in a bland way and continued on. It was blissful, and he sincerely hoped he would remain alone for the duration of his visit.

This thought was immediately abandoned when the door

opened to admit the Fletcher family, for there was Miss Angela Fletcher, wearing a tall blue feather on her bonnet. She, at least, was one whose company he would not spurn. She was soon swallowed up in groups of friends, too diminutive to be seen. Occasionally, as the crowds parted and reformed, he glimpsed that jaunty feather. What did it signify, that waving feather, bobbing about with every movement of her head? What was her mood, that she put on such an amusing hat? She must be happy today, cheerful and a little mischievous. The thought made him smile, and he wished he could see more of her than the feather in her hat.

But then the tide of well-wishers receded slightly, and left her visible to his gaze. Such a pleasing sight, so small and dainty and elegant, the blue feather matching her blue spencer, above a pale muslin gown. Her arms made graceful arcs in the air as she said something to her sister. So lively, and yet kind, too, to rescue him from his misery at the ball last night.

And in love with him. His heart was filled with gratitude for that love, freely given and generously revealed through the medium of her letters. They nestled even now in an inner pocket of his waistcoat. He had read them so often he knew every word by heart, and only occasionally brought them out to savour anew, unfolding them carefully, for the paper was beginning to tear along the folds.

Those letters were the proof of her love, for she cleverly gave no sign of it when they met. She was friendly, always, but not at all affectionate, nor did she employ any of the stratagems he had so often seen from other young ladies who wished to attract his notice. She was more subtle than that. But though she behaved with complete propriety when they met in public, he knew the secret concealed in her heart, for the proof of it rested against his own heart.

Her letters... so trustingly written, so *intimate*. All her feelings and dreams exposed to a man who was not her husband. As if they were betrothed... exactly as if they were betrothed.

She turned her head a little, she saw him, she smiled and waved. Then she was stepping purposefully towards him, and he was filled with warmth... with *joy*.

His Angela. His love. His betrothed.

22: Camaraderie

That day was idyllic to B. Angela only spent a brief time with him, thanking him prettily for the posy of flowers and for protecting her from Randal Sylvester the night before. She was in high good humour, she told him artlessly, after a whole night of dancing. He could have listened to her sweet voice all day, but she was called away by her stepmother.

It was unimportant. He was caught up in this new idea, that her letters meant that she was betrothed to him. A woman would never write to a man unless she were bound to him so the letters sitting in his waistcoat pocket demonstrated that bond. Even if he had not proposed marriage, and she had not accepted his proposal, still she was his in very truth.

Not that he ever could propose to her, naturally. He had no means to support a wife, not as a chaplain with only two hundred pounds a year, which made him ineligible as a suitor, as Mrs Fletcher had made all too clear. So be it. In a week or two, Angela would leave Bath, but he would still have her letters and she would still be his, in his heart.

His conscience whispered that he should burn those letters.

That was what a man of honour would do, he knew that. Yet they were too precious to him, especially as there would be no more, not after his sermon. One day, perhaps, they would be so insignificant to him that he could destroy them, but not yet.

So he went about his day with a smile on his face, and neither a tedious dinner with all his least favourite acquaintances, principal among them Lady Penelope and Mr Whittleton, nor his poor luck at the card table punctured his beatific mood.

But the next day was decidedly odd. He met Mrs Lacey and her daughters on Milsom Street, and although he stopped and bowed courteously to them, as always, Mrs Lacey glowered at him and hustled the young ladies past him without so much as a "Good day". Then at the Pump Room, several ladies turned away without responding to his bow.

As if that was not unsettling enough, he was accosted — that was the only word to describe it — in hearty fashion by Tommy Cadman, stinking of brandy, who slung an arm around B's shoulders as if they were the greatest of friends, leered at him. Or perhaps he was winking, it was hard to tell, for louche living over many years had ravaged his once handsome face.

Cadman was a lifelong friend of Uncle Maurice, and the two of them had cavorted through Bath society with gleeful abandon. Uncle Maurice had restricted his activities to the petticoat line, but Cadman had gone his length in every direction, including drink and gaming, and only a fortuitous marriage had kept him from the debtors' prison. B had long ago learnt to avoid him, and Cadman held him in equal aversion, making only the occasional sneering remark when a meeting was unavoidable. Now, it seemed, Cadman was happy to acknowledge B, and in the friendliest fashion, leaving B mystified.

The Fletchers were nowhere to be seen, so after lingering hopefully for some time, B was forced to decamp, and continue his day without a glimpse of a certain sweet face.

It was only when he reached home that the significance of Cadman's friendliness was brought home to him, for there awaiting him was a letter from Lady Mellish.

'Appleby, I regret to inform you that the position of chaplain at Hessenford is no longer available.'

Friendly overtures from one of Bath's most disreputable inhabitants and a distinctly frosty air from one of its most respectable could only mean one thing — another rumour was circulating about him, and this one far more damaging than hearsay about a spurious inheritance. Bath had always been a whirlpool of speculation and gossip, for the confined nature of its society combined with a high number of elderly residents with nothing better to do with their time made that inevitable. Never before, however, had B himself been the subject of such talk. His supposed inheritance had been a misunderstanding, easy to excuse, but this... this was a different matter. How could something so damaging as to cause Lady Mellish to withdraw her offer circulate, except by malice? And he could imagine no one who would wish him any harm.

Over the next few days, B found himself quietly viewed with suspicion by many of Bath's female residents. Few ostracised him completely, for he had been an upright member of Bath society for twenty years and most were prepared to give him the benefit of the doubt, although with some reserve in their manner. Still, fewer invitations than usual flowed in, and one lady went so far as to withdraw an invitation already issued. So sorry... mistake in the numbers... no room... sure he would understand. He understood only too well, but if there were not so many card parties or dinners as before, there were enough that he was seldom at home of an evening.

If the ladies were wary of him, he found the gentlemen unexpectedly friendly. His uncle, who had never treated him with more than casual distance, now took a greater interest in him, scooping him up at the end of decorous card parties and whisking him away to a different kind of gathering altogether. The Willow House had a large drawing room where whist or piquet or other games of skill were played, although for higher stakes than usual, but at the back of the house were rooms where riskier games like faro or hazard were available to those with deep pockets. Here B was greeted in the friendliest manner imaginable, a basket of fish pushed into his hand and invited to join any table he liked.

"What is the rate of play?" he asked his uncle.

"Only a pound for each fish, at least to start. After that, five pounds... ten... who knows? But you need not worry about it, nephew. I am happy to underwrite your vowels, you know. You need only have an amusing time."

Mindful of Angela's advice that he should be less serious and enjoy himself more, he tried the faro table for an hour. But the amounts of money changing hands distressed him, and since there was not the least skill required that he could see, he found himself bored.

Still, there was a good supper provided, with enough potent drink to put half the British navy into a drunken stupor, and he found a certain enjoyment in standing about, glass in hand, watching and listening. There were several ladies present, although none he knew, but they appeared to be on the friendliest of terms with the gentlemen. In this informal atmosphere, the normal constraints of mixed company seemed not to apply, so there was a jovial camaraderie amongst the men that B rather enjoyed. For the first time in his life, he was part of a convivial group of male friends. Besides his uncle, he encountered Cadman, the Sylvesters and the less welcome sight of Mr Jeremy Whittleton.

"Well, well, well," Whittleton said, on encountering B at the club. "The man himself."

"What does that mean?" B said, but Whittleton only laughed.

The Sylvester cousins were more forthcoming. "My goodness, the hero of the hour!" Lambert Sylvester said, pumping B's hand vigorously, while his brother Digby nodded and smiled and slapped him on the back.

"Hero? What makes me worthy of such an epithet?" B said, moving out of Digby's reach.

They roared with laughter. "So modest," Randal said. "Not everyone would call you a hero, but to us, you are. And who would ever have suspected it? Not I! You always seemed like such a sober sort of fellow, Appleby, with your sermons and your self-effacing manner and your black clothes, like a physician."

"Attorney," he said.

"What? But I always knew it was a hum. Did I not say so, Coz? Digby? *'There is more to that Appleby chap than meets the eye,'* I said, many times."

"Did you, Randal?" Lambert said. "I disremember it."

"I expect he did," Digby said. "Stands to reason. Must have done."

While B puzzled that out, Randal went on, "Well, I did. Many times. I am sure I did. Certainly I *thought* it, which is much the same thing. No one can be quite as good as all that. Anyone who appears to be entirely virtuous — well, bound to be a hum."

"Not my Hermione," Lambert objected. "She is all goodness. Not a wicked bone in her body."

"Oh, well, *ladies,*" Randal said. "Quite different, Coz. But Appleby, here... well, there was always something secretive about him."

"I have no secrets," B said at once, resolutely pushing aside the thought of his letters, tucked safely away in his pocket. "I wish you would tell me what it is that I am supposed to have done."

The three Sylvesters stared at him, then laughed again. "Come, come, Appleby," Randal said. "Dissembling ill becomes you. Your secret is out, you know, so no need to pretend. We have all read your book, after all."

Book? The dreadful truth dawned on B. He it was who was presumed to have written the scurrilous and lewd book, *The Errant Prince.* He laughed. Impossible to take such an idea seriously, when it was patently ridiculous.

"You think *I* wrote that moonshine? Truly?"

They laughed again. "Who else is so well-connected?" Randal said. "Eyes and ears in Portland's crowd, so you must know everything. Very clever, though, Appleby. Here you sit quietly in sleepy Bath, seemingly hundreds of miles from the court, yet your little epistle is as fresh as if you lived there. Ingeniously done, my friend, most ingenious, for who would have suspected so respectable a man? No one, until the home of the author was revealed to be this very town."

"But you suspected it, Randal," Lambert said. "You just said so."

"Did I? I did! Suspected *something*, at least. Always said that Appleby was too good to be true. Did I not say so many times?"

"Ah, but did you?" Lambert said. "Are you sure, Randal?"

B left them to their squabbling, and soon afterwards walked home through the dark streets, seeing no one. Occasionally the sounds of revellers drifted to his ears, and once an owl, hunting nearby. Otherwise, the night was silent.

~~~~~

For several days, B had not seen Angela, and he had begun to fret rather. She was not at the Pump Room in the mornings, nor did she attend the same evening engagements. Even at Mr Bravington's, he found that either he had just missed her, or she was expected later. Twice he called at the Fletcher's house, to be told that none of the family was at home.

On the second occasion, the butler, perhaps seeing his crestfallen face, said helpfully, "Lord Albury and the Lady Maria Landers were here, sir, and Mrs Fletcher and the young people set off to accompany them back to Queen's Parade. You might catch up with them on the Gravel Walk."

B could walk fast, but even his long legs could not catch up with the party. Instead he met them just as they embarked on the return journey, Mrs Fletcher on her son's arm, Miss Fletcher and Miss Jupp arm in arm, and Angela... Angela walked alone at the back of the group, lost in thought. His heart was wrung by her serious face.
~~~~~

Stopping to make his bow to them, Mrs Fletcher glared at him and would have moved on at once, but Angela saw him and, to his delight, her face came alive, her smile wide and her eyes... oh, those eyes! So clear and bright, afire with affection.

"Mr Appleby! Where have you been? You were not at Lady Mellish's last night and I made sure to see you there."

After that, Mrs Fletcher's disapproval could not prevail, and B turned and fell into step beside Angela. He could not recall afterwards what was said on that walk, for he knew only that his world, which had been increasingly out of kilter these last few days, was now gloriously back in alignment.

When they reached the Royal Crescent, Angela said, "Mama, may I call upon Mr Bravington? I have not seen him since the ball, and I should like to tell him how much I enjoyed it."

"You sent him a note, and Rosie embroidered him some slippers," Mrs Fletcher said, frowning, her eyes slipping to B and then back to Angela.

"But I have not thanked him personally, or played for him, and in a week's time we shall be gone, and I dare say will never return to Bath. Please, Mama!"

She hesitated, but Mr John Fletcher intervened. "The old gentleman loves to hear Angie play, and it would be a shame to deprive him of the pleasure. I shall escort Angie to the door myself."

"Oh, very well," she said, turning to usher Miss Fletcher and Miss Jupp through the open door where the butler and a footman waited patiently.

B thought it would be pleasant to visit Mr Bravington, too, so he walked alongside Angela and her brother.

"Angie, run on ahead and ring the doorbell, will you?" Fletcher said.

Willingly, she skipped away. Fletcher turned to B and said with a smile, "You did not write that dreadful book, I take it?"

B gave a laugh of pure surprise. That was straightforward dealing! "I did not."

"So Pa would have it. He said that anyone could see there is no mischief of that nature in you."

"Do you know how such an outlandish rumour started?"

"No idea, but if we knew that, we would know who actually wrote the book."

"How do you work that out?" B said.

"The author is in Bath, supposedly. How better to deflect attention away from himself than to circulate innuendo about someone else entirely? By the time everyone has worked out the deception, there will be some new scandal to gossip about. Lord, I thought Cambridge was bad for tittle-tattle, but Bath is a hundred times worse. How you can live amongst these people I cannot imagine. Are you not enraged to find yourself the subject of such outrageous lies?"

"What would be the point? My true friends, if I have any, will trust to their own judgement rather than the swirling foulness of rumour, and the rest are of no interest to me. I have lived for twenty years in Bath, Fletcher. I have seen the seasons come and go, visitors arrive and depart, scandals explode and then dissipate. The future arrives, becomes the present and moves smoothly into the past. However unpleasant or distressing, everything passes in time, and so will this."

And if he had in mind something other than rumours about a book, something beautiful and enchanting and utterly delightful, who would also soon be a part of his past, he did not say so. Angela was his secret, as he was hers, and nothing would compel him to drag it into public view.

They had by this time arrived at Mr Bravington's house, where the door stood open, and Angela was busy removing her gloves and bonnet.

"May I look at those books of yours tomorrow?" Fletcher said, suddenly boyishly eager. "My stepmother has kept us all in a whirl these last few days, but I am free again at last."

He agreed to it, and Fletcher turned away with a cheerful wave. B took that as permission to follow Angela into the house. Mrs Fletcher might suspect him, but young Fletcher was unconcerned.

Mr Bravington was resting, the footman told them. "He will be delighted to see you both," he said. "Pray wait in the library."

He ushered them in, and fussed about the windows, which were open to air the room and must now be closed again for fear of draughts. Then he withdrew to inform Mr Bravington of their arrival.

Angela had seated herself at the spinet, picking out a charming tune with those elegant fingers. B positioned a chair so he could watch her face, her expression intent as she concentrated. A week! That was all the time that remained to him. He must memorise every contour of her lovely face, every expression, every eyelash, every little twitch of those soft, red lips... such lips as would drive any man to distraction.

He could close his eyes now and still see her face, still see the hands moving over the keys, the way she held herself, the placement of her feet. Would he still remember her so clearly in a month? Or a year? Or would she gradually fade away, so that he could not quite recall the curve of her cheek or the colour of her eyes? The face of his old nurse, whose features had been as familiar to him as his hobby horse or the nursery rug, was gone now like smoke in the breeze. He could not bear to lose Angela like that! He must—

She had stopped playing, looking at him now with that little curve about the mouth and the impish gleam in her eye. "You were very far away, Mr Appleby, but I shall not enquire as to your thoughts, for Mama says it is best not to with gentlemen, for their answer might put one to the blush."

How he loved her artless way of talking! "I trust I would never say anything to put you to the blush, Miss Fletcher."

"Now that is exactly what I would have thought, but when I asked Lady Mellish last night whether you were to be of the party, she looked just as Mama does if she steps in something best kept to the stable yard, or when Julia trails mud through the house. And then she said, *'You should keep away from that man, Miss Angela, for he is not fit company for a lady.'* Which I cannot believe, for you have always been so correct with me, and preach a most affecting sermon. Even Mama said it made her feel very penitent and humble, which is a great triumph for you, for she is not either of those, as a rule. Although I should not speak so of her, should I?"

"Probably not," he said, trying not to laugh. "Lady Mellish and I are at outs just now, on account of a foul rumour circulating about me, and so she has withdrawn her offer of the chaplaincy of her estate."

"Oh, that is too bad!" Angela cried, spinning round on the stool, to face him. "Have you done something terrible?"

She spoke in a conversational tone, as if she were enquiring if it were raining out, or whether he preferred mutton or beef.

"I have done nothing wrong at all, apart from the usual trivial transgressions of which we are all guilty every day. But Lady Mellish heard the rumour and must have believed it."

"How horrible! And now you have lost the chance of being her chaplain."

"But now I can stay in Bath, as I prefer," he said.

"You love it here," she said, with sudden intensity. "I remember the first time I met you, you told me so. *'Everything I need is in Bath,'* you said. And your garden, of course. How could you bear to leave your lovely garden?"

His breath caught in his throat — she understood! She had seen his garden, heard his enthusiasm and she entered into his feelings on the subject. She understood it all! *Of course* he would hate to leave his garden, to leave his seedlings before they had reached their full growth. It was unconscionable! How should he have managed at Hessenford? Probably Lady Mellish would have looked askance at him and said, *'A chaplain is paid to attend to matters spiritual, Mr Appleby, not to grub in the earth like a peasant'*? And then he would be cut off from one of his deepest pleasures.

"I love my garden," he said, his throat unexpectedly tight. He could not have borne to lose it! Yet it was not his. For almost twenty years now it had been his comfort, his consolation for every disappointment in his life, and yet it was not his, except by the whim of his uncle. "Gardening clears my mind like nothing else on earth. No problem is as great when I have my hands in good, rich soil."

"Oh yes!" she said, leaning forward to lay one slender white hand on his larger one. Her touch ricocheted through him like a bolt of lightning, so that he almost jumped in his chair. "For me it is dancing... or music. Either of those. I can lose myself in music for hours at a time. It makes me feel alive as nothing else does. For most of my time, I am just a very small, insignificant person, of no importance to anyone outside my family, but music makes me feel I have a purpose in life."

Some slight noise made B turn his head, to see Mr Bravington standing in the doorway, supported by his footman. At once Angela jumped up, her face wreathed in smiles.

"There you are, sir! Are we disturbing your rest? Come and sit down. How are your legs today?"

She took his other arm and guided him slowly across the room to his favourite chair, then carefully tucked the rug around his legs, all the while keeping up a patter of small talk. Once he was settled, a glass of Madeira at his elbow, she knelt at his feet.

"There! Now, if you are comfortable, I can tell you how much I enjoyed the ball the other night and how grateful I am that—"

With a dismissive wave of the hand, he said, "You said as much and more in your prettily worded letter, young lady, and you know perfectly well that it is I who has most reason to be grateful for the privilege of watching you dance. Now tell me, where have you been since then, for I have missed my little pixie abominably."

"We have been taking advantage of the fine weather to go out in the barouche."

"What, every day?"

"Every day. Lady Louisa Horsfell has taken us under her wing rather, and since Mama harbours hopes of Lord Albury for Rosie, she has been nurturing the acquaintance. We have been to Longleat and Badminton and Stourhead... so many great houses! I am quite overwhelmed by them all."

"And which did you like best, child?"

"Stourhead, although not for the house which is not so grand as some, but the gardens are amazing. Pa is fired with enthusiasm and wants to improve our own grounds at Chadwell Park. He is to build a fountain, apparently." Her face drooped suddenly. "We are to return home next week, although it will be so dull there. I shall miss Bath very much, and especially you, sir."

"Nonsense, miss! You might miss my spinet, though."

"I shall! I shall miss it very much, as well as the kindly gentleman who allows me to play it. I wish I might never leave Bath so that I might play it every day."

"I wish that, too," Mr Bravington said wistfully. "Who knows, perhaps some way may be found to make it possible. But until then, play for me, my little pixie, play! Appleby, bring over the chess table, and let us have the pleasure of Miss Fletcher's music while we can."

As he silently complied, B wished with all his heart and soul that their wishes might come true, so Angela would never leave. But he could see no manner by which it might be accomplished.

23: An Evening With The Sylvesters

Angie spent almost two hours at the spinet, returning home in the beatific frame of mind that an excellent instrument and an appreciative audience always supplied. She found Mama in a taking.

"There you are, child! Where on earth have you been all this time?"

"At Mr Bravington's, Mama," Angie said, startled. "You said I might go."

"I did not mean you to be there all day. You must not make a nuisance of yourself, you know, for Mr Bravington is an elderly gentleman who needs a calm household, and you are anything but calm. No doubt he is too polite to ask you to leave. Still, you are here now. There has been a change of plan for this evening."

"Are we not to dine at Lady Louisa's after all?"

"Oh... well, as to that, yes, *we* are going, for the opportunity for Rosie is too good to miss, but you have received another invitation which I have accepted on your behalf, since you were not here to ask. You are to dine with Mr and Mrs Sylvester."

"The *Sylvesters!* Oh, Mama, no!"

"Now, now, it is very much an errand of mercy, for Mrs Sylvester's aunt is staying with them at present, and she is a great lover of music and they should like to provide some entertainment for her, even though she is not well enough to venture out in the evenings. So they asked very civilly if we could spare you, since you are quite the best performer in Bath at present. There! Is that not a pretty compliment? And you need not pull that face, for it will be only the two of them and the aunt. Neither Mr Digby Sylvester nor Mr Randal Sylvester will be present, and with Mrs Sylvester there, it will be perfectly proper. It will be good experience for you to undertake engagements on your own occasionally." With a little laugh, she went on, "They were at pains to tell me that they have a most superior instrument. Come now, cheer up! I imagine it will only be one course, and then you may spend the rest of the evening at the instrument, and not have to talk to them at all. Johnny is to take you there, and Mr and Mrs Sylvester will both walk home with you, so you see, it is all arranged in the most felicitous manner. But they dine early, so you had better go and change at once. The blue with the cream ribbons, I think. There is no need to don one of your best gowns, not for the Sylvesters."

Angie foresaw no pleasure in the evening, but dutifully she went upstairs to change. Sarah had already laid out the designated gown, rather a dull one which suited Angie's mood perfectly. She liked Lady Louisa and had looked forward to dining at her house for the first time. Now she was denied that pleasure, to be confined instead to the tedious company of Hermione Sylvester, her nodcock of a husband and an elderly lady. It was too bad. Most of the time she did not envy Rosie her superior place in the family, for she bore all the burden of Mama's expectations, and her attention, too, but it was also true that Rosie got all the fun. If there was only room for one, it was Rosie who was invited. She was the one going to Essex to stay with the Armitages, and now she was the one who would dine with Lady Louisa.

When the time came to leave for the Sylvesters' house, a sudden shower meant that she needed to take a sedan chair, and it was Pa's man, Enoch, who walked alongside her, since Johnny was not to be permitted to risk muddying his evening attire. Angie was greeted with great cordiality by the Sylvesters. Mr Lambert Sylvester emerged himself to hold an umbrella over her, and Mrs Sylvester helped her to remove her cloak.

The evening unfolded exactly as Mama had foretold. There was indeed only one course of not very enticing dishes, but Angie's ability to concoct a convincing compliment or two remained untested. Her powers of conversation were barely needed at all, for the irrepressible Sylvesters took all the work of it onto their own shoulders, requiring little more than an occasional, "Indeed?" or "Is it so?" from her. The elderly aunt, Mrs Ratcliffe, did not trouble to open her mouth except to stuff into it another heaping of whatever dish was within reach. She ate as if she had not seen food in a month, yet she was rail-thin, almost emaciated.

There was one troubling moment. Mrs Sylvester was conducting a long debate, mostly with herself but occasionally with her husband, on the prospects for rain for the Grand Gala at Sydney Gardens Vauxhall the following week, and the likelihood that the fireworks would be spoilt. Then, without a break, and almost as if the one subject followed logically upon the other, she went on, "Of course, we are all dreadfully worried about poor Mr

Barry Appleby."

Angie froze, a spoonful of the fricassée of rabbit and mushroom suspended half way to her lips. "Mr Appleby?" she said, laying down her spoon, her appetite quite taken away.

"Oh, yes. Poor man! Well, we cannot condone what he has done, of course, but still—"

"What *has* he done?" Angie said sharply.

"Aaahh!" Mrs Sylvester said, with a glance at her husband. "You *are* sweet on him! So we suspected but—"

"I am *not* sweet on him!" she said indignantly. "What an idea! I regard him as... as a friend, perhaps. What has he done? For I saw him just a few hours ago and he said nothing untoward."

They both laughed. "No, indeed, he would not speak of it, not to you nor to anyone, I dare say, but everyone knows of it all the same. I refer, of course, to a certain book that he wrote, which we will not name but—"

"You mean *'The Errant Prince'*, I suppose," Angie said coldly. "I have heard the ridiculous rumours, but it is all nonsense. Mr Appleby would never write anything so vulgar. He is too much the gentleman to stoop so low. Bath is the most dreadful place for gossip and idle tittle-tattle, and I wish you would not repeat such *stupid* speculation."

Again, they exchanged glances. "We will not quarrel over it," Mrs Sylvester said. "Eat your fricassée before it is quite cold, Angie dear. Whether he did or did not is of no consequence. What is certain is that he has fallen into... unsavoury company, shall we say. People who are leading him down the path to true vice. Perhaps now that his perfidy is revealed, he—"

"There was no perfidy!"

"—may feel himself released from all constraint, or perhaps his rejection by good society has soured him. Who knows? But Randal..." She paused, and took a long sip of wine, eyeing Angie thoughtfully. "I know you and Randal do not always see eye to eye," she said slowly, "but he is a good man, Angie, and he has your best interests at heart. And Mr Appleby's, as well. Have you not wondered why he and Digby are not here tonight? They are out looking for Mr Appleby, to try to persuade him to turn aside from the dire path on which his feet are set. He can be saved, we are all sure of it, and Randal is determined to save him."

Angie could not — *would* not — believe it of him. He was a clergyman, after all, and although not all men of the cloth were sober, hard working men, she had seen no sign of wickedness in him. Quite the reverse, for had he not railed at her from the pulpit to make her understand her own wickedness? Until this foolish rumour about the book, no one had ever had a bad word to say of him, except that he was unduly sober and dull. She had spent two hours in his company only that afternoon, and he had been his normal self, and had said nothing—

She stopped, shocked. He *had* said something! What was it? Some nonsense about his uncle leading him astray, just idle talk during the chess game while she was looking for another piece of music. He had said *he was enjoying the change!* At the time, her mind on her music, she had thought nothing of it, but now, with Mrs Sylvester's words, it made a horrid sort of sense. Poor Mr Appleby!

Mrs Sylvester rose soon after to leave her husband to his solitary port, even though Mrs Ratcliffe was still happily eating. Filling her mouth hastily with as much food as it would hold, a dribble of sauce trickling unnoticed down her chin, she scuttled after her niece, and Angie followed them, still lost in thought.

The instrument was neither a fine one nor even in tune, but it would have to do. As Angie perched on the rickety stool, Mrs Sylvester settled her aunt comfortably with a dish of bonbons and a glass of wine to hand. The old lady devoured the bonbons, tossed back the wine with unladylike enthusiasm, and promptly fell asleep. Angie played a little louder to drown out the stentorian snores.

As she played, her thoughts turned inexorably to poor Mr Appleby, caught up in yet another false rumour, and this one more harmful than a tale of a large inheritance. The question of whether this new rumour was true or not troubled Angie not at all. She could not believe it of him. Even when Mr Appleby the Elder had told her that his nephew had acquaintances well placed to inform him of the foibles of the Prince of Wales and his cronies, she could not conceive of Mr Appleby using that information in a book.

When the subject had arisen at home, Mama, always protective of Rosie's honour, had been inclined to cut his acquaintance, as many others had done, but Pa would have none of it.

"Appleby's as sound a man as ever I met," he said robustly. "I'll not believe idle gossip about him, and that's all it is, after all. If you can find any proof of his wrong-doing, Mrs Fletcher, apart from *'people say'*, then fair enough, but I'll not have it said that any Fletcher condemned a man on mere hearsay."

After that, Mama had said no more, and the subject had not arisen again. Angie had not even thought of it, although she had noticed he was not at the same evening engagements. Once she could have been sure of seeing him twice out of every three evenings, for Bath was a small town, with only a limited society. No more, however.

At one card party, she had overheard Lady Mellish say forcefully, “That man! I have been most grievously deceived in Mr Barry Appleby. First, he starts a report that he has inherited a great sum of money, and now— I hope he may be driven out of Bath altogether.”

This remark hit Angie hard. Her own foolish game, spread abroad by Randal Sylvester, was now to be laid at Mr Appleby’s door, to give credence to a less benign story. That was harsh, indeed! She wondered how Mr Appleby must feel, to have his friends of many years turn their backs on him, and all because of a silly game and a stupid lie. Poor man! Even his own uncle believed it of him, despite his nephew’s denials.

“Naturally, he would deny it,” he said airily. “But who else could it be? No one else in Bath is so well placed to know such details about His Royal Highness.”

She considered how she would feel in Mr Appleby the Younger’s place. With even his denials being disbelieved, what could he do? His reputation was destroyed, and a man — a clergyman, moreover — who sees his very honour chipped away, may feel that he has nothing left to lose. If the whole world believes him to be wicked beyond redemption, then why should he not make it so? Perhaps he truly was falling into a pit of vice.

She had not been at the instrument for long when a commotion was heard in the hall, with raised men’s voices, followed almost immediately by the drawing room door crashing open. In rushed Randal and Digby Sylvester, wild-eyed and panting, as if they had been running.

Randal's eyes scoured the room, and settled on Angie. "Thank God we have found you, Miss Fletcher!"

Jumping to her feet in sudden terror, she cried out, "What has happened? Is it Pa? Rosie?"

"What?" he said, bewildered. "Of course not! What an idea! I cannot think why—"

"Randal," Mrs Sylvester said quietly.

"Oh... yes, yes, of course. It is Mr Appleby, Miss Fletcher. He is going to— To tell truth, I am not sure where he will end up tonight if we do not stop him, and I cannot do it. He will not listen to me."

"You have been to Mrs Gravestock's house?"

"Mrs Gravestock? What has Mrs Gravestock to do with anything?"

"That is where Mr Appleby is tonight," Angie said, impatiently. "He told me so only this morning."

"Mrs Gravestock?" Randal gaped at her, frowning. He looked as startled as if he had been struck by lightning.

"He must have changed his mind," Mrs Sylvester said quickly. "I expect he decided against it, and went to Willow House instead. Is it not so, Randal?"

"Willow House! Yes, yes, Willow House. That is where he is, and bent on all kinds of mischief. I tried to remo— rem— Dash it, Hermione!"

"Remonstrate," she hissed. "I expect you tried to *remonstrate* with him."

"Yes, yes! I did, but he would not listen. Miss Fletcher, there is only one person he will listen to, and that is you. Will you come with me now to rescue him? For I cannot guess what trouble he may be in before the night's end if we cannot draw him back."

"With you? No!" Angie cried. "But the constables— Or let me send word to Pa and Johnny. I know where they will be."

"No, no time," Randal said. "If we are too late— I cannot imagine how bad things will be if we are too late."

"We will all go," Mrs Sylvester said smoothly.

A part of Angie's mind baulked at this sudden haste, and wondered why anyone needed to rescue a grown man from his own misbehaviour. Willow House was a gaming house frequented by Pa and Johnny, respectable enough even for ladies, so they said. It was hard to imagine what misbehaviour Mr Appleby could get up to in such a place.

But she was tender-hearted, and hated the thought that Mr Appleby had been driven to such desperation, and partly by her own foolishness, too. If she had not unwittingly started one rumour about him, no one would have believed the story about the book. And if all the Sylvesters would go with her, then there could be nothing wrong with that, could there? If Mama thought them suitable dining companions and escorts home afterwards, then surely they were suitable companions for a rescue mission, too.

So they all donned their outer garments and, leaving Mrs Ratcliffe still fast asleep, her chin still marked with sauce, they set out into the night. They soon turned off the streets with which Angie was familiar, entering quieter, though still respectable, streets. Nothing moved in the shadows, apart from the occasional cat on the prowl.

Soon they came into a better lit street, with sedan chairs passing, a few walkers ambling by and houses with welcoming lights over their doors. One bore a painted sign, *'Willow House'.* Two or three people were entering the front door, but Randal led them to a narrow lane at the side.

"We must go round the back," he said.

"Why?" Angie said.

He stopped so abruptly that she almost bumped into him. "Why? Why? Why do you ask so many questions? Because we must, that is all."

"We do not want to be recognised," Mrs Sylvester said.

"Exactly," Randal said. "Exactly so, Hermione. Come along, come along."

The lane led to a wider lane, fringed with coach houses. The Willow House coach house, however, held neither coach nor horses, for the big double doors stood open to reveal an informal tap room, comprising a single plank of wood on trestles to hold the barrels, and rough benches to accommodate the many men patronising the establishment. Empty barrels set on end made makeshift tables.

Randal hustled Angie past the door to the foot of a set of external stairs with a wooden door at the top. "We will find Appleby up here."

Angie was tolerably certain that this was not a place that any gently-born woman should visit, and wished rather badly that she had after all insisted on summoning Pa and Johnny. But then she bethought herself of Mama's reaction should the long-awaited dinner at Lady Louisa's be interrupted for such a reason, and perhaps Lord Albury himself would feel obliged to join the rescue party. She went hot and cold at the very idea. At least this way there was some hope of keeping Mr Appleby's fall from grace, whatever it was, a secret. There had been enough rumours about him already.

So she reasoned with herself, and since there was no point delaying, she turned resolutely to the stairs.

"We shall await you here," Mrs Sylvester said.

"You are not coming?" Angie said.

"Lambert and I can do nothing to help, and I am not as stout-hearted as you, Angie."

"I shall not go alone," Angie said at once. "You may think me as pudding-hearted as you like, but I will not under any circumstances do this on my own."

She glared at them, and Digby at once shifted to stand behind his brother. "Not me, Miss Fletcher."

"I shall come with you," Randal said, taking a stance as if he were on the stage. "I am not afraid, Miss Fletcher. Someone must have the courage to protect you. For you, I would dare anything."

"There is no need to be so melodramatic," she said crisply. Then, because she was by no means confident of his courage, she said, "Since you wish to protect me, you may go first, and ensure that it is safe for me to enter."

His mouth flapped open, as if he would protest, then closed again. Without a word, he turned and set off up the stairs. Her heart in her mouth, Angie followed him.

24: Circumspection

Angie followed Randal up the stairs and through the door. The room within was dark, lit only by a few guttering candles, and for a moment she could see nothing. As her eyes adjusted, she could see faces staring at her incuriously. A few men and women were sitting about, shockingly informally dressed, some playing cards or dice, some drinking. The room was not large, so the swiftest glance assured her that Mr Appleby was not present.

She turned to leave, but one of the men heaved himself off the chair where he had been sprawled and lurched towards her. He was well dressed, like a gentleman, but in an advanced state of inebriation.

"Pretty!" he said, and reached out for her.

Without hesitation, she slapped him hard across one cheek. He staggered, and almost fell, with an expression of ludicrous surprise.

"Tha'sh not very kind, pretty lady. Gi' me a kiss, eh?"

"You are foxed, sir! Go home and sleep it off, and stop harassing innocent females."

"Inn'cent? Here? Ha!"

He reached for her again, this time catching hold of her, and as she pushed him away from her, there was a loud ripping sound. "Now look what you have done! Get away from me, you horrid man!"

"Desist, sir, or I shall be obliged to take stern measures," Randal cried, raising his fists in what he probably supposed was a menacing manner.

To Angie, who had seen real fist fights on market days in Sagborough, his posturing was ridiculous.

"Oh, for heaven's sake!" she muttered, turning for the door and escape. As she reached the bottom, she found that the rest of the Sylvesters had vanished. It was the final straw.

When Randal reached her, she turned on him. "You set all this up, I suppose. You must have thought me such a fool, to walk right into your trap. *'Do come and play for poor Aunt Mary, who so loves music.'* That is why she slept through every piece, no doubt. *'Oh no, we must rescue poor Mr Appleby! No one else will be able to convince him.'* Except he is not even here, is he? I imagine he is safe with Mrs Gravestock all this time. And you—! You were supposed to protect me, Randal Sylvester, not thrust me into a... into a... What was that place, anyway? Why were those women wearing nothing but their undergarments? And my gown is torn, too! Wait till my father hears about this!"

"No, no, you must not tell him! Miss Fletcher, I swear, I mean you no harm, but— Where are you going?"

She had turned to walk briskly back down the lane to the front of Willow House. "Home. Back to safety and people who care about me."

"But *I* care about you. We all do."

"Oh yes, you and your nasty cousins who ran away and abandoned me in that place. You all care so much about me."

The street was empty, but within moments a sedan chair appeared. It was occupied, but Angie hailed the chairmen. "Where is the nearest stand?"

"Just round the corner, miss. I'll send one to you."

"Thank you."

Angie immediately regretted not going there herself, for standing about with the unspeakable Randal Sylvester as her only protection was a terrifying prospect. Within seconds a man had materialised out of the shadows, and although he was clearly a gentleman, he looked her up and down with an eye not all gentlemanlike.

"Evening, Sylvester," he said, his speech rather slurred. The smell of brandy filled the air. His gaze was still fixed on Angie, and the place where her gown was torn. Hastily she pulled her cloak around her. "Who is your little ladybird? Why, if it ain't Miss Fletcher! Well, well, well, had no idea you were so venturesome, my dear. My congratulations, Sylvester. Looks like you have a pleasant evening ahead of you, so I will not keep you from your delightful companion a moment longer, sir. Your servant, Miss Fletcher."

With that he tottered away down the street.

"Who was that man?"

"Cadman. Lord, now we are in the suds, Angie."

"I did *not* give you permission to use my name. Ah, my chair at last," she said, as two chairmen arrived at a run.

"Yes, but Angie— I mean, Miss Fletcher. We need to—"

"Royal Crescent, if you please," she said, stepping into the chair, and settling her skirts about her. At least she was safe now, for the chairmen would not allow anything terrible to happen to her.

They set off at a brisk pace, but Randal had not given up. He walked alongside the chair, trying to talk at first, then lapsing into puffing silence as they climbed the hill.

Angie thought furiously as the chair swayed along. She had been introduced to Mr Cadman somewhere, she could not remember where, but he had not been a regular participant at the genteel card parties and musical evenings they attended. One or two remarks she had overheard suggested he was not a person of good character. Would he tell people he had met her, alone with Randal? Very probably. No doubt everyone would assume that they had an understanding. Well, they would soon discover their mistake there.

What of the Sylvesters? Would they tell anyone what had happened? Likely not, for they were involved in it too, and it reflected badly on them. They had tricked her into going into that horrid place, and—

Why? Why would they do such a thing? She wondered greatly that she had not considered this point before, but she had been so concerned with reaching the safe haven of home that she had not thought beyond that. The Sylvesters had set up an elaborate scheme to entice her to a disreputable place, so they must have had some end in view. Was it Cadman? A witness to her humiliation, someone to spread gossip about her? But again, why?

She had reached no conclusions when Royal Crescent was reached. The butler and footman appeared instantly at the chairman's shout as they arrived outside the house, and Angie practically fell out of the chair in relief. Randal, wheezing heavily, thrust some coins at the chairmen, who grinned and took off at a run.

"Angie... Miss Fletcher!" Randal said urgently. "We must... talk."

"I have nothing to say to you."

"Just listen... Cadman... not a good man... won't hesitate to... tell tales. Very bad... for you."

Angie considered. It was still early, and no one else would be home yet, but perhaps that was a good thing. Her first instinct had been to run to Pa and tell him everything, but perhaps this whole affair might be kept from them. Randal seemed to be genuine in his concern over Cadman. Talking could do no harm, could it?

The butler had opened the door and taken a few steps towards the pavement, and now he stood, an impassive but reassuring presence, just beyond arm's length.

"Bryant, I am going to step across the road with Mr Sylvester for a few moments. I shall call for you if I need you."

"Certainly, Miss Fletcher," the butler said, with a bow.

At the railings edging the road, she turned to Randal. "Now, Mr Sylvester, tell me the truth. Was Mr Cadman part of your scheme?"

"No! I swear it, Angie, I was never so shocked in my life! The rest of it... well, you have guessed it. We thought... look, it was

Hermione's idea, that if we took you somewhere where you would be threatened... not *really* threatened, for it was all acting, like a play, Hermione said. Well then, I could rescue you and look like a hero and you would be so grateful that you would marry me."

"What!"

"Good Lord, Angie, you must know that is what I want. I never met anyone like you in my life before — so pretty and lively and dainty, and with twenty thousand, too! That would show my father that I am not so useless after all! I can get myself a wife worthy of the family name, just like Gaston. My brother, you see. The heir. So meek and obedient, following Father around like a little lamb, and marrying Drusilla Hartley because Father had arranged it with *her* father practically when they were born. Pah! But she is nothing to you, Angie. She looks like a horse, actually. And she brays... like a donkey, now that I think about it. *She* only had fifteen thousand, so that will be one in the eye for Father."

"If a good dowry is so important to you, I wonder you did not try for Rosie and her fifty thousand," Angie said tartly.

"That was my first thought," he said eagerly. "However, your mama made it very plain she wants a title, so then I looked at you, and found that you would suit me perfectly well."

Angie stamped her foot impatiently. "But you would not suit *me* at all!"

He huffed a little, and then said, "It hardly matters now, for you will have to marry me, whether you like it or not. There is no way out of it, Cadman will see to that."

Angie felt as if she had been hit in the stomach. "He would not... could he? Spread foul rumours about me?"

"He not only could, he would delight in it. There is no help for it — we must consider ourselves betrothed."

There was a queer kind of logic in what he said. Angie had already seen how quickly rumours spread through Bath society, with no hindrance. One might be as pure as the driven snow, yet a single misstep could see one condemned out of hand. Her spirits plummeted.

But she would not be in Bath for much longer. A few more days only, and then she would be gone to Hertfordshire, and could recover her equanimity in the quietude of the country. By next spring, when she returned to London, it would all be forgotten, for if Bath was quick to condemn, it was just as quick to move on to the next scandal.

Licking her lips, she thought quickly. "I see what you mean," she said slowly. "Yet my antipathy towards you is well known. It would look most odd if I suddenly betroth myself to you."

"By Jove, yes!" he cried. "That is a very good point."

"We must be circumspect," she said, improvising hastily. "We may begin to meet in public without quite so much... erm, disapprobation, and then, very gradually, after a few weeks—"

"A few *weeks!*"

"Well, a week or two, shall we say. After a fortnight or thereabouts, we may begin to—"

"But you will be leaving Bath next week. It must be settled by then — families told, announcement in the *Gazette* and so forth."

"No, no!" she said, in alarm, for a public announcement was at all costs to be avoided. "We shall let it be seen that... that we are on better terms, I shall leave Bath and then you must follow me to Hertfordshire." For it would be far easier to get rid of the irritating man there than in gossipy Bath.

"To Hertfordshire?" he said blankly. "Why?"

"Um... to demonstrate the depth of your passion for me. And then, after a time, if our feelings remain strong, then... It must be realistic, do you see?"

"Hmm. Hertfordshire... depth of passion... by Jove, yes! Very ingenious, Angie. What a clever little thing you are! But what if Cadman spreads his evil thoughts abroad? He will say that he saw us together, in compromising circumstances, yet we will still be... circum... whatever you said."

"Circumspect. Then you may just hint, to anyone who is so impolite as to mention the matter, that you are in expectation of an announcement soon."

"Hint... expectation... announcement soon... yes, I see. Then we are betrothed? So may I kiss—?"

"No, we are not and you may not," she said crisply, stepping back. "Good night, Mr Sylvester. I will not thank you for a pleasant evening, for I cannot say that it has been anything but disagreeable from start to finish."

So saying, she swept back across the road and into the house without a backward glance.

Her defiance crumbled within minutes. What on earth was she to do?

There was no opportunity for reflection, for as soon as she went upstairs, hoping only for the refuge of her room, Belinda bounced out of the drawing room.

"Oh, you're back already! Was it deadly dull?"

"What are you doing home so early?"

"Oh, I couldn't go, Angie. An apothecary's daughter mingling with the nobs? It's not right. It was very kind of Lady Louisa to invite me, but it wouldn't be right. I said I had the headache, and your mama said I showed great sensibility. Angie, is your gown torn? Such a strange place to tear it! How did that happen?"

"Oh... I caught it as I was entering the chair," Angie said vaguely, pulling her cloak tightly around her.

"How odd! I can't quite imagine—"

"Look, I have the headache myself, after a whole evening with the Sylvesters. I just want my bed."

"Oh, of course! May I get you anything? I make a very pleasant tisane."

"Nothing. Thank you. I just need to lie down."

Even when she had escaped Belinda's questions, there was Sarah to be endured, for she could not unfasten all the tiny buttons on the back of her gown or disentangle her hair ornaments without help. And all the while, there was the effort to be cheerful, to laugh off the torn gown, to pretend that she had passed a boring evening at the Sylvester's house, and had not been tricked into something terrifying and not in the least boring. How many times had she grumbled about long, dreary evenings where nothing happened and the time passed so slowly it was as if every clock had been frozen? She would never again protest at the uneventful hours, for uneventful meant placid and unthreatening, not something that would upend her life in moments.

When Sarah had seen her safely tucked between the sheets and shut the door, Angie slipped quietly out of bed again and crossed to the window seat. Pushing open the window a little further, a wisp of stuffy air crept into the room. It was so hot! There was no freshness anywhere, the trees in the garden rattling dry leaves in the slightest breeze.

She was glad of her little room now, for here she could be alone to wallow in her misery and bewail her miserable situation with no need to pretend. No matter what she said, Rosie would know instantly that something was amiss, and now at least she had the quiet hours of darkness to calm her agitation, and the solitude to consider her situation.

What was she to do? On one point she was determined... that she would not, under any circumstances, marry Randal Sylvester. Yet how could it be avoided? She had postponed the inevitable, perhaps, but if he followed her to Chadwell Park, then she would have her work cut out to get rid of him. Pa could do it in a moment, but she would have to tell him everything and she was deeply reluctant to confess.

It was Angie's policy to get through the vagaries of life with as little trouble as possible. One made mistakes, of course, and got oneself into scrapes, but by telling no one and continuing as if nothing had happened, such difficulties often disappeared of their own accord. Once one confessed, then it was a blot forever more and had unpleasant consequences, such as punishments and being more carefully watched in future.

Here, confession might have the undesirable consequence of tying her irrevocably to stupid Randal Sylvester. Mama, she was certain, would say she had been compromised and the only answer was marriage. As for Pa... a year or two ago, she would have been sure that he would protect her from anything, but now he listened to Mama as often as not, and she would say that the scandal would affect Rosie's chances of a good match and therefore must be squashed at once.

Rosie! Angie wanted her to marry well as much as anyone. She was so beautiful and so good, she deserved the best husband in the world, and Lord Albury might be just the man. For all he had told Angie clearly that he had no serious intentions towards Rosie, they had been spending so much time together lately, and now, a dinner invitation... It was possible, was it not, that with greater intimacy, he had grown to value Rosie for herself and then who knew what might come of that? Could Angie be so selfish as to inflict a huge scandal on the family, just when things were looking so promising for Rosie?

She could not. She had been foolish, perhaps, and had made a bad mistake in trusting the slippery Sylvesters, but now that it was done she must take the consequences.

Now she knew what she must do. She would pretend she found Randal agreeable and she would allow him to pay court to her. That much was inevitable, and although it would be unpleasant, she would do it for the few days remaining to them in Bath. She would allow him to think that they would be betrothed soon.

Perhaps, if she were fortunate, something would set her free from him. Miracles sometimes happened.

But if there were no miracle, and Mr Cadman did his worst, then she would accept her fate. For Rosie's sake, she would marry Randal Sylvester.

She climbed quietly back into bed and sobbed for a long time, until exhaustion caught up with her and finally she slept.

25: A Chivalrous Hero

Mr John Fletcher arrived while B was sitting down to breakfast. B took him through to his study, showed him the boxes of books and left him to trawl through them, while he finished his repast.

He made his way without haste to the Abbey for morning prayers, but the familiar words of the ritual had no power this morning to soothe him. There was a bubble of discontent growing inside him, and he knew very well the reason — in a few days, Angela would depart from Bath for ever, and he would never see her again. It was hard to contemplate.

As for Angela herself, she was young enough to recover from her ill-advised infatuation with him. At eighteen, a girl may fancy herself deep in love, only to discover with the next young man she meets that she had entirely mistaken the matter. She would forget him. Somehow, that thought was worse than anything else.

Still, her letters lay hidden in the pocket of his waistcoat, warming him inwardly. Whatever the future may bring, at this moment she loved him and that was a great gift. She had opened his eyes to the possibility of love, and now he could barely remember how dark and empty his life had been before he met her. Even when she went away, the remembrance would comfort him, like a perfect summer day brought to mind in the depths of winter.

From the Abbey, he made his way to the Pump Room and anticipation sped his steps. Perhaps she would be there today. Would she wear one of her brightly coloured bonnets? Or perhaps the one with the cheerful feather, that bobbed and danced with her every tiny movement? He could not wait to see her smiling face! Surely she would be there?

He could not see her. His spirits plummeted. But wait... Mrs Fletcher was there, in a group of matrons, and Miss Fletcher and Miss Jupp were laughing at some jest of Lady Maria's, so Angela must be here somewhere. He began to look more carefully.

There she was! She had been hidden by a great crowd gathered about her.

Something was wrong. He could not see her face, but she wore a little violet cap... that cap! What had she said about it? ' *When I am really in the dismals, I have an old violet cap that I wear.'*

Angela in the dismals? It was not to be borne! B strode across the room, little clusters of promenaders parting for him. He waded into the large group until he was beside her.

"Miss Fletcher, what is amiss?"

She turned her face to look up at him, and his heart turned over. So pale, so unhappy! And why did she have her arm through that of Randal Sylvester, who was beaming happily around. He frowned a little when he saw B.

"Nothing amiss, Appleby, no. Not in the least. Is there, my

pet?"

My pet? There was something very wrong here, but he could not see how it concerned Sylvester, so B ignored him.

"Miss Fletcher, you are distressed. Let me take you outside to get some air."

"Appleby, you are not wanted here," Sylvester said. "Do, pray, leave Angie alone."

Angie? B had to breathe very hard to control the rage pouring through his veins.

"You mean Miss Fletcher, sir," B said stiffly. "You do not have the right to call the lady by any other name."

Sylvester smirked. "Well now, perhaps I do, eh? Perhaps the lady has granted me that right."

"But I have not," Angela said, detaching her arm from his. "You presume too much, sir."

"Well, if that is not too bad!" Sylvester said, reaching out a hand and then dropping it as she stepped smartly out of reach. "After all that has happened, and everything you said, Angie, I think—"

He never finished the sentence. As much to his own surprise as anyone's, B's clenched fist shot out, connected with Sylvester's jaw with a satisfying thunk and the fellow went flying. Everyone scattered out of range, there were squeals from the ladies, and "I say, sir!" from the gentlemen, but B had never felt so exhilarated in his life. That showed the miserable worm! How dared he be so familiar with Angela!

Only Angela remained at his side, gazing up at him with a look of astonishment. Then her faced creased into mischief, as if she were on the verge of laughing. Instead, she lowered her head demurely. "Thank you for your chivalry, sir," was all she said.

Chivalry! B had never thought of himself as chivalrous before. Polite, naturally, and gallant towards the ladies, he hoped, but chivalry? That was a word for medieval knights of yore, not plain Mr Appleby of Bath. He rather liked it, though.

Digby and Lambert Sylvester had hoisted their kinsman to his feet, and Mrs Sylvester was mopping his face with a red spotted handkerchief. Was that blood? Good heavens, he had caused the man an injury. He had not realised a single blow could be so effective.

"What the *deuce* was that for, Appleby?" Sylvester yelled. "I have a good mind to call you out over it, sir, indeed I do."

"Quite right, Randal," Mrs Sylvester said. "Such an insult is not to be tolerated."

"The insult was to Miss Fletcher, madam," B said. "This man made free with her name, without the least right."

"I do! I do have the right," Sylvester bellowed. "She is my—" Angela gave a squeak, and he threw her a quick glance. "We are... we have... well, we will soon—"

"They are betrothed," Mrs Sylvester said impatiently. "Really, Randal, why can you not say what you mean?"

"Being circum... circum... something," he muttered.

At that, Angela put her hands over her mouth, but muffled giggles were audible.

"They are not betrothed," B said. His rage had dissipated

now, and he felt quite serene. He should, he knew, be ready to shrivel up with shame to have created such a spectacle, and in the Pump Room, too. He would never live it down. But it was not of the least consequence, for Angela was wearing her violet cap and she had to be rescued, that was all there was to it.

"They are!" Mrs Sylvester cried. "It is quite true — they are to marry."

"No," B said, calmly. "That is impossible, because Miss Fletcher is betrothed to me, and I have her letters in my pocket to prove it. Is it not so, Miss Fletcher? I do not wish to display our private correspondence in public, but you can confirm that you have indeed written letters to me of a personal nature."

"I have," she said, a little breathlessly. "It is quite true. Three letters."

The Sylvesters stared at him, for once rendered blessedly silent, as the watching crowd, now considerably larger, muttered in low voices. And then, as if the Sylvesters were not trial enough, Lady Mellish materialised out of the throng.

"What is the meaning of this disgraceful display, Appleby? I hope someone has sent for the constables to arrest you. I was used to think you a man of some integrity, sir, but of late you have turned into a scoundrel of the worst kind, with all kinds of debauchery, and now here you are, brawling in the Pump Room! I am severely disappointed in you."

"And I in you, madam," B said, lifting his chin a little. "I was used to think you a virtuous Christian woman, but you have been so ready to believe every passing rumour, without even taking the trouble to determine whether it might be true or not, that I can no longer consider you to maintain a shred of good principle. I strongly advise you to examine your conscience. Miss Fletcher, let me escort you away from this unseemly mêlée."

He bowed and offered his arm. She curtsied with modestly lowered eyes, placed her hand on his sleeve and together they turned their backs on the gaping watchers and withdrew with dignity.

"I see your stepmother approaching," he said. "It will be best if I do the talking."

"Yes, sir," she said, eyes still lowered.

Mrs Fletcher arrived in a billow of outrage. "Angie, whatever—?"

B held up one hand to forestall her. "Mrs Fletcher, your daughter has been subjected to a distressing scene. I should like, with your permission, to escort her home."

"Whatever has happened? Have you been playing your games again, Angie?"

B cut in before Angela could speak. "There was a minor disagreement with Mr Sylvester, for which Miss Angela was not in the least to blame. She is upset, however, and I believe she should go home at once. If you will permit me—"

"Certainly she should go home. We will all go, although it is most inconvenient." Her eyes strayed to the seats where Miss Fletcher and Miss Jupp sat with Lady Maria and Lord Albury. "This is very thoughtless of you, Angie."

"There is no need for you to alter your plans, madam," B said smoothly. "A chair will convey Miss Angela home in no time, and it would be my pleasure to accompany her, to assure myself of her comfort."

"A chair... and Mr Fletcher is at home just now to take care of her. Very well, then, but straight home, mind, Angie, and no tricks."

"Yes, Mama. Thank you, Mama."

With Angela on his arm, B made a stately progression through the crowds of wide-eyed onlookers and out into the street, where several chairmen lounged waiting for custom.

"Do you want to take a chair?" he said. "Or perhaps you would prefer to walk?"

"Mama said I should take a chair." She raised an anxious face to him.

"That is not quite correct, Miss Fletcher. I said, if you will recall, that a chair would convey you home in no time, which is perfectly true. Your mama agreed with me. I do not think that anyone said that you *should* or *would* take a chair. The shade of the Gravel Walk would be very refreshing in this heat, I believe. If you would like that."

She nodded, putting one hand over her mouth to hide her smiles, but he could see the amusement in her eyes.

He offered his arm again, half expecting her to refuse it, but she was determined to be decorous, resting her small hand on his sleeve trustingly. A burst of pride rushed through him. Here she was, the lady who lit up his life like a small, vivid sun, walking through Bath on his arm. Here and there an acquaintance acknowledged them as they passed by, and he thought that life could furnish no greater delight. It was a memory to cherish.

It could not last long, of course. Angela had too much vibrant energy to remain on anyone's arm for more than the few minutes it took to pass through the crowded ways around the Pump Room. Westgate Street was freer, and here she spun away from him, skirts swirling, her face shining with excitement.

"Mr Appleby, I can never thank you enough for rescuing me from that *horrid* man! He put me in such a fix, and then he said we must marry, and I could not think how to get out of it, but you have done it beautifully. To hit him like that! No one has ever got into a mill over me before. Rosie, sometimes, but never me! And I know how much you dislike to be the centre of attention in that way, yet you never hesitated. And the set down you gave Lady Mellish — that was so, so delicious, and you even bamboozled Mama. You are my hero, sir."

A hero. Chivalrous and a hero... he could let her run on like this for ever. He made some feeble protest, but she would hear none of it, dancing around him on her light feet, arms waving in her enthusiasm and finding a hundred ways to praise him.

"You will have me appallingly puffed up in my own esteem if you continue in this vein, Miss Fletcher."

"And so you should be," she said. "You are a true gentleman, sir, for you are always so polite and correct, and you seem very gentle in your ways, but when a lady needs your help you are a positive lion! The way you somehow divined that I was in a scrape and came at once to rescue me. *'What is amiss?'* you said, as if you could see into my mind and know all my worries. You were splendid, quite splendid."

"Now, as to that, knowing your worries, I confess I could not see your mind, only your hat."

"My hat?"

"Your little violet cap. You once told me that you would wear it if you were in the dismals."

"And you remembered that? What an astonishing man you are, Mr Appleby."

And he could only smile, and bask in her admiration, and revel in the sight of her skipping around him all the way along Westgate Street and up Barton Street, across Queen Square and the full length of the Gravel Walk.

"Will you come in?" she said, as the butler open the door to them. "It is so hot today. A cool drink, perhaps."

"We left your mama and your sister at the Pump Room, and you can hardly entertain me alone," B said. "However, if your father is in, I will have a word with him. In private."

She looked slightly puzzled, but bade him a very pretty farewell and skipped away up the stairs, affording him a brief glimpse of slender ankles.

Mr Fletcher was in, and emerged from his fastness to greet him and take him up to the small room that he called his office. He sent for some ale, and B gave him a succinct summary of what had transpired at the Pump Room.

"Sylvester claimed to be betrothed to Angie?" Fletcher said, in tones of amazement. "She can't stand the fellow."

"Precisely, and I could see that she was being imposed upon in some way, so I dealt it with in the only way which occurred to me on the spur of the moment."

"Which was?"

"I hit him, and told him that Miss Fletcher is betrothed to

me."

"Good God! And is she? Betrothed to you, I mean?"

B frowned. "That is a difficult question to answer."

"I can't see why," Fletcher said sharply. "Either she is or she isn't, but I have to tell you, Appleby, I don't take kindly to men who attach a girl of eighteen without asking her father's permission first."

"No, indeed, and I have not made any attempt to attach her, sir. Rather she has attached herself without any assistance from me."

Fletcher open his mouth, then closed it again with a snap. "You're going to have to explain yourself more fully."

"Miss Angela has, for some reason I cannot explain, conceived an affection for me. She sent me several letters detailing her feelings, which have led me to... take an interest in her. I feel a certain responsibility towards her, a bond, if you will, so I regard myself as... not precisely betrothed, but in some way bound to her. Do you... do you want to see the letters?"

It was curious how reluctant he was to show them to anyone, as if it would somehow break the intimate secret he shared with Angela. But she was not of age, and her father had every right to see them.

Fletcher rubbed his nose thoughtfully. "I dislike reading the girls' private correspondence, but... I suppose I ought to, in this case."

"She is very young," B said gently. "Still in need of a father's guiding hand."

Fletcher grunted, and took the letters B passed to him. He read each one carefully, then began again with the first. Only when he had read them through twice apiece did he hand them back. B exhaled slowly, not aware until then that he had been holding his breath. Fletcher had the right to keep them, and probably they should be destroyed, but B was infinitely grateful to have them back in his hand. Hastily he tucked them away in their pocket.

"That is very clear," Fletcher said slowly. "They are not signed, but this is Angie's hand. And what did you do when you received them?"

"Nothing, except to preach a sermon on the evils of the written word, after which Miss Angela was so horrified that I immediately deduced that she was the author. That drew my attention, as you may imagine, but I give you my word that I have done nothing at all to encourage her, and I have no doubt that the fondness she feels for me now will fade when she leaves Bath. She is very young and impressionable, and will meet many men more worthy of her in time."

The ale arrived, cool from the cellar, and for a while they were silent while the butler and a footman fussed around them. When they had withdrawn, Fletcher said, "You haven't proposed to her, or anything of that nature?"

"No, no. I am not in any position to marry, sir. I have neither income nor career, and very little prospect of either."

"And if you had, would you like to marry her?"

B gave a little laugh. "Oh, if only I could aspire to her hand! If I could but call her mine, I should be the happiest man alive. But it is out of the question. Without employment I am effectively penniless, and even if I could obtain a living, the income would be very small. Not enough to support a wife like Miss Fletcher in a fitting manner."

"You are an educated man, Appleby. You could look beyond the church for a career. Politics, perhaps, or the law. You speak well in the pulpit, so I imagine you would make an impressive barrister."

"What, several years of eating my dinners and then finding a place in chambers? I cannot afford it, and I have no patron to sponsor me."

"And that is what I cannot understand," Fletcher said. "It's your uncle's duty to provide for you, one way or another, I'd have thought. If you're not to inherit, and it seems that bird has flown, then he should at the very least help you establish yourself in a career. And if the church is your preferred choice, then he should buy up an advowson or two, so that you will be able to support yourself in tolerable comfort. What reason does he give for refusing to do it?"

B shifted uncomfortably. "He has not precisely refused."

"Have you asked him?"

"I could hardly do that," B said stiffly.

"No, you shouldn't have to. But maybe he just hasn't thought of it and needs a bit of a nudge, eh? So why don't you ask him outright to help you to a career, and if he refuses to do what's right, I know people up in Yorkshire who'd be happy to have a smart fellow like you working for them. And then, when Angie's a bit older and sure of her own mind — well, that'll be the time to talk about marriage."

26: Of Duty

Angie stayed in her room, where the sultry, airless heat quickly enervated her. All the exhilaration of Mr Appleby's heroic rescue evaporated into misery. He was speaking to Pa there and then, and that could only mean that Pa would know everything, and then she would be in trouble. After a while, she heard male voices downstairs, then the front door opening and closing, then silence.

But not long afterwards, the door opened again followed by the unmistakable sounds of Mama in distress. She had discovered, then, all that had happened in the Pump Room, and no doubt she would lay the blame squarely at Angie's door, as usual. And perhaps she was not so far wrong this time. If Angie had not listened to the Sylvesters, if she had, at any point, recognised the impropriety of it... She had been dreadfully foolish, but at least Mr Appleby had spared her from the horror of marriage to Randal Sylvester.

Silence fell for a long time. Then slow, heavy footsteps on the stairs. A knock on the door, followed by Pa's head, and then the rest of him, as he came into the room and quietly closed the door.

"I've brought you a jug of lemonade, flower. You must be

thirsty."

"Thank you, Pa," she said meekly, waiting as he poured the lemonade into two glasses. Then he sat down on the faded chaise longue.

"We need to have a little talk, Angie love."

"Are you going to shout at me?"

"Now when have I ever shouted at you? I haven't, have I? I've been cross with Will, once or twice, because he's been a fat-headed fool sometimes, but never any of you girls."

She hung her head. "I am a great trial to you, Pa, always in trouble."

He chuckled. "With eight children, there's always one or other of you in trouble." A frown flitted across his face. "Except Rosie. She's never in trouble, and that's not natural, so don't you be worrying about that." He sipped his lemonade. "So, are you betrothed to Appleby?"

"No! Of course not."

"Has he asked you? Suggested it?"

"No, never."

"Ah. But you're in love with him."

"No... at least—" It was an odd thing, but that thought had never entered her head before. He was nothing like her ideal gentleman — why, he could not even dance! — so she had not wondered just why she took such an interest in him. Pity, and sadness for his solitariness, that was how it had started, but now? "I cannot say," she said finally.

"A fine pair you are," Pa said, shaking his head, but his eyes were twinkling. "He doesn't know whether you're betrothed or not, and you don't know whether you're in love with him or not. But then, why did you write to him, flower? What were those letters about if you're not sweet on him? And I've seen them, so tell me the truth, all right?"

"Oh, Pa, he was so sad, so solemn and serious and stern, and it was hardly to be wondered at. He was his uncle's heir for years, and he was betrothed, or as good as, and then all that was lost, and even though it turned out that he was very glad when Miss Meek went off and married someone else, I did not know that then, so I imagined him to be broken-hearted. Anyone would be down at heart after all that. I thought if he had an admirer, it would cheer him up... bring a little happiness into his life. That was all it was, and he was not supposed to know it was my doing, but then he gave that sermon, and it made me feel like the lowest worm."

"But Angie love, you must know how improper it is to write to a single man like that unless you have an understanding, at least. No wonder he's confused about whether you're betrothed or not. He thinks you're head over heels in love with him."

"Well, I never signed my name. Oh! When he said we were betrothed, did he really believe it? Because of the letters? But we are not, not in the least."

"And yet he told who knows how many people at the Pump Room that you were, and you not only didn't deny it, you walked out on his arm. I'm not sure how you can wriggle out of it now, flower."

"Better Mr Appleby than that *horrid* Randal Sylvester."

"I'm glad you mentioned him," Pa said. He rose to refill their glasses, so Angie was given a moment's breathing space to consider her answer. The full version? Or something a bit less that would not show her in such a poor light?

She licked her lips. "What about him?"

"You can start by telling me why the fellow thought *he* was betrothed to you, for a start, and don't give me any moonshine, Angie, because Appleby thought Sylvester must have imposed upon you in some way. Or compromised you, maybe? Because I have to tell you that a torn gown is not something that passes unnoticed."

"You know about that?" she said in a small voice.

"Sarah mentioned it below stairs, more as a joke, it seems, for it was always Julia who used to tear this and that, not you. She saw nothing in it, but Enoch thought it proper to inform me, as you were out on your own last night. I hear that Sylvester accompanied you home, too. Did he cross a line, pet?"

Angie took a steadying breath, and then another. But there was no help for it now, so slowly, haltingly, she related the story of her disastrous evening with the Sylvesters. To her dismay, Pa jumped up and paced across the room, then back again.

"Can this be true? They took you to a *brothel?*"

"To a what?"

"Oh... never mind," he said, waving a hand impatiently. "But are you telling me that they did this *deliberately?* They took you to a place no gently raised young lady should ever see, and— Dear God! I've never heard the like!"

Angie burst into a torrent of tears. "I am so sorry, Pa! I never meant—! I thought... Mr Appleby... they said I was the only one...

oh, Pa, please, please, please forgive me!"

"Forgive *you?* Oh, Angie love!" He sat on the window seat and wrapped an arm around her waist. "There's no blame attached to you, my lovely, not the least in the world. You've been vilely misused, that's the long and the short of it, and I'll not stand for it. Sylvester will answer for this, see if he won't."

"Oh!" she squeaked in horror. "You are not going to call him out? No, Pa, you must not, for what if you should be killed and... why are you laughing?"

"What a romantic girl you are! Would you like that? To have a duel fought over you?"

"No, not at all, not if anyone should be hurt or worse, although I will admit that it was very exciting when Mr Appleby hit Mr Sylvester. I never thought he could be so heroic! He saw that I was unhappy and came directly to my rescue, and when Mr Sylvester kept calling me *'Angie'*, he hit him! And he fell over and there was blood! It is most improper in me, so you need not tell me so, but I enjoyed it enormously."

Pa laughed and shook his head. "Best not tell your mama that, eh? But no, no one is going to fight a duel. That's never been my way of dealing with impudent young men."

"But you *are* going to deal with him?"

"I am," Pa said grimly. "No one treats my daughter like that and gets away with it. But in the meantime, we must see what can be done about Mr Appleby and this supposed betrothal of yours."

~~~~~

"I never knew such a girl for getting into a tangle!" Mama said fretfully. "And just when everything is in such a promising way with
~~~~~

Lord Albury. It would be too bad of you to spoil all Rosie's hopes."

"Let's not worry about Rosie, shall we?" Pa said placatingly. "Let's see what might be done about Mr Appleby."

"Mr Appleby? Mr Appleby?" Mama cried. "Who has not a farthing to his name? Now, Randal Sylvester, on the other hand..."

"No," Angie whispered, her heart thudding painfully in her chest. "Please... no."

"Certainly not," Pa said. "She will never marry that black-hearted scoundrel, never. Did you not listen when I told you what he did?"

"From *love*, Mr Fletcher," Mama said. "He loves Angie so much he was driven to desperate measures. It is a little extreme, I grant you that, but so romantic! And now that it is done, and Mr Cadman is bound to tell the world about it, there is no denying that Angie has been compromised and marriage is the only way to escape the whole family being engulfed in scandal. Are you sure you cannot like Mr Sylvester, Angie? He is extremely eligible, and his father is a baron."

"And that's nothing to the point, Lizzie," Pa said testily. "If Angie were head over heels in love with Sylvester, I'd still caution her against him, because I don't like him. He's no gentleman."

"But if we are to protect Rosie from—"

"Rosie, Rosie, always Rosie!" Pa snapped. "Really, Lizzie, you think of nothing but Rosie! She's not the only Fletcher daughter, and they are all of equal importance to me."

"Of course," Mama said placidly. "I only set so much store by Rosie because she is best placed to make a truly advantageous match, and that would immeasurably improve the prospects for

Angie, and indeed the whole family. I want the best for all the children, just as much as you do, Harry. I am approaching it in a different way, that is all."

"That's all well and good, but right this minute we must think about Angie's future, and what's best for her. She's only eighteen, after all, she's done nothing at all to be ashamed of, so I'll not see her hustled into anything hasty, and certainly not against her will. Sylvester is out of the question, so forget about him. What we need to discuss is Appleby, because he's the one everyone thinks is betrothed to Angie, and don't tell me he's ineligible as to fortune, because he's perfectly well aware of it. Still, he may yet be able to do something about that."

Mama primmed up her mouth, but she said more temperately, "I have always thought him a disagreeable man, and I cannot like his part in the disgraceful scenes in the Pump Room this morning, but his family is respectable, I suppose."

"Right. The question is what we do about getting this betrothal scotched."

"It is difficult to do that," Mama said, pulling a face. "Once a betrothal is announced, however informally, it must stand. Angie cannot cry off now without looking like a jilt."

Pa tutted a little. "Even so, I'll not agree to a wedding unless both parties are happy with it. But it seems to me that neither of them really knows much about the other. They need to talk, and decide what they want themselves before we can make any future plans, and Angie love, you need to be completely honest with him. Tell him the whole truth. You understand me?"

Glumly, she nodded. She would have to confess to poor Mr Appleby not only that she had written those silly letters, but that she was not even in love with him.

Was that even true? It had been true when she wrote them, but now? Her feelings were in such a jumble it was impossible to say.

~~~~~

B went directly to his uncle's house. Mr Fletcher had dangled the prospect of marriage to Angela in front of him, and he was fired with enthusiasm. He would ask his uncle to provide for him, in some way or other. Everyone had expected it when he had married and especially so after little Roger was born. Many people had whispered of it, and thought it odd that nothing was done. And now even Fletcher, with his background in trade and his northern ways, had said the same thing. His uncle's *duty*, that was what he had said, and if a man like Fletcher held to that principle then it must be universal, and he need not scruple to ask directly. His future with Angela was at stake, and he must know, once and for all, what was possible.

His uncle was on the brink of going out again, but he agreed to see him in his dressing room as he changed his attire, greeting him affably enough.

"Well, my boy, and how are you? I have hardly seen you in an age. You were not at Lady Mellish's card party the other night. Pfft, another cravat, Wilkes."

"I was not invited," B said stiffly. "I will be brief, sir, for I can see that you are busy. Wilkes, a moment's privacy, if you please."

Silently, the valet withdrew, and Uncle Maurice turned to look at B fully. "This is very serious, nephew. What is amiss?"

B had not had time to consider how he might judiciously
~~~~~

approach the subject. That was a mistake, he realised, for he would have preferred to be properly prepared with all his arguments arranged in his mind. He hesitated, torn. Part of him was so eager that he wanted to ask his uncle directly, without roundaboutation, for some settlement immediately. Yet the habits of deference ran strong, and his nature was not combative.

"I wondered, sir, if you have any suggestions as to how I may proceed... given my situation..."

"Situation? What do you mean?"

"I have neither property nor income nor career, nor any prospect of getting any without... without some help. It would be better for both of us if I were independent."

"Oh, you will get a living in time, you know. The bishop will come up with something, or one of your well-connected friends. Do not despair."

"Perhaps, but nothing has arisen yet... nothing material," he added punctiliously, recalling the withdrawn chaplaincy. "I cannot wait forever. I thought perhaps... given our relationship and... and your own position in society, you might be able to... to offer me some assistance. After all," he rushed on, seeing the blank look on his uncle's face, "you brought me up to be a gentleman of leisure, without a profession to enable me to earn my own bread. I thought perhaps you might be able to... well, to do something."

"And that is just the difficulty, Barry." B winced, but his uncle went on, "I would love to help you — of course, I would. But professions cost money, a great deal of money, and there is little Roger to be considered, and who knows how many more to come, now that Calantha is expecting again. How can I so diminish my children's futures? The rents will likely be poor again this year, and the work at Lindworthy will cost at least double what we first thought. Lord, the expenses I have to meet, and now that I am married—! She wants another carriage, you know. A barouche like the Fletchers', that is what is in her eye, and how can I say no to such a dear little creature? You cannot imagine the expense of maintaining a wife in a suitable style, my boy."

"No, nor am I ever likely to," B said savagely, anger making him reckless. "Your pardon for intruding, sir. I dare say I shall be able to find work somewhere, as a gardener perhaps. I have some skill there."

"Ha! You are just jealous of that boy of mine," Uncle Maurice said.

"Not in the least, sir. I am, however, disappointed to find you so unwilling to do your duty."

"Duty! You had better not lecture me about duty, my boy, for my duty is very clear — to my family."

"Precisely, Uncle."

So saying, he spun on his heel and left. At that moment, he felt he would not be greatly distressed if he never saw his uncle again.

His anger could not be sustained for long, for it had been clear for some time he could expect nothing from his uncle. He consoled himself with the thought that if his position was no better, it was also no worse. There had never been much chance of becoming a serious suitor for Angela's hand, and that had not changed. And did he really want to win her only through his uncle's charity? Better by far to keep his dignity and fend for himself in the world, even if he lost Angela.

A gardener... he had tossed the idea out at random, but perhaps he could do something with that. Not in employment, for he did not think he could jump from gentleman to under-gardener in one move, but market gardening might be profitable, and he had the skills for it. All he would need would be a modest investment — he might even have enough saved already to lease a patch of land and establish himself.

When he got home, there was a note waiting for him. He read it without surprise. *'Sir, Please be so good as to wait upon me at your earliest convenience. Harry Fletcher.'* Naturally he would want to talk further about the situation, once he had talked to both Angela and Mrs Fletcher.

He put on a fresh shirt and neckcloth, donned his newest waistcoat and coat in Angela's honour, then set out once more for the Royal Crescent.

27: A Betrothal

"Do I have to, Pa?" Angie said, in what she hoped were suitably pleading tones. But sometimes Pa was implacable.

"I'm afraid you do, flower, and no games, you understand? Appleby has to know everything that you've told me. I will tell him what Sylvester made you do, because you shouldn't ever have to talk about that again, but you must explain the letters to him. He thinks you're deep in love with him, and it's not fair to the man."

"But he might be angry with me," she said in a small voice.

"He might be, and with some justification, but it's best he knows the truth. So be honest with him, and when he knows everything, we'll all sit down and talk about what's best to be done now. If he's still around, of course. Maybe he'll want nothing more to do with you, and that would resolve the problem rather well, don't you think?"

Angie was not sure she agreed. To Pa, every little difficulty was just a problem to be solved, like a delay in the arrival of a ship full of silks, or a sticking point in a business deal. But this was her whole life at stake. She might end the day irrevocably betrothed, or not betrothed at all. And then there was the question of Mr

Cadman, and what harm he might or might not do. Or the Sylvesters, for that matter. Would Randal want revenge on Mr Appleby for knocking him down? And swirling through all of it was the biggest unknown of all — Angie herself, and what *she* wanted. She knew very clearly what she did not want — Randal Sylvester. But as to whether she wanted Mr Appleby, she could not say. Her mind was too muddled to know anything for certain.

She sat in the drawing room pretending to sew. Mama had her own elegant piece of embroidery, but although she looked across at Angie occasionally, and no doubt saw that the needle was still, she said nothing. Johnny was away on business of his own. Rosie and Belinda were hunched over a small table in the window, composing a letter to Ricky in Sagborough, and arguing about what could be said and what left out, to keep the whole to a single sheet. Belinda was keen to fill the page with the glorious tale of dinner with Lady Louisa, for even though she had not gone herself, Rosie's report of the great names mentioned and all about the family home of Chaseley Court would go down well in Sagborough, she was sure. Rosie thought that was less interesting than the forthcoming Grand Gala at Sydney Gardens Vauxhall. Both of them threw glances at Angie now and then, but they knew without anyone saying so that there was something strange afoot, and it was not to be spoken of.

The doorbell sounded, and Angie jumped. Voices in the hall below, then footsteps on the stairs to Pa's office, then silence. A long, unbearable silence.

The door opened and Angie jumped again. Pa appeared, beckoned to her and dutifully she rose and followed him out.

"He's in the office waiting for you," Pa said. "In you go."

"Alone?" she said, aghast.

"There are things to be said between you that no one else should hear, Angie love. I shall be in the drawing room if you need me. Off you go, now, and remember — be honest. You owe him that much."

She went, creeping into the office like a little mouse. He was wearing another new coat in a rich wine colour, with a lovely embroidered waistcoat, and he was smiling as she entered the room. He should not smile like that, it was unfair when she felt so guilty already, and now she was going to make him unhappy. Or angry. She would hate it if he were angry with her.

"Miss Fletcher." He bowed, the smile if anything wider.

"Mr Appleby." She licked her lips, then fell silent. What on earth could she say?

"There is something you wish to tell me," he said encouragingly. "So your father said."

Still she stood, unable to speak.

"Something to do with the letters?"

"Yes. The letters." Suddenly, her knees were shaking and she plumped down on a chaise longue, while he sat on the desk chair nearby, gazing at her expectantly, still smiling. "Mr Appleby, I am afraid you have been misled. The letters I wrote... you assumed I was expressing my own feelings, but... but... it was not so."

He was puzzled now, not understanding her meaning. "Not... your own feelings? Then whose?"

"No one's. I... I made it all up. I—"

She was too agitated to sit still, but when she jumped to her feet he rose, too. In that small room, he loomed over her and made her feel like a child.

Flopping down onto the chaise longue again, she rushed on, "You were so sad, you see, and it seemed to me that women had treated you very badly, so I thought that if you believed that someone were in love with you, it would bring a little happiness into your life. That was all. I wanted to... to make you smile, and..." She could not keep the tears at bay a moment longer. "I am so sorry... so very sorry. It was such a foolish thing to do."

"You do not love me?"

She shook her head.

"You never loved me?"

"N-no."

"And yet you did this to... bring happiness into my life?"

"Yes. I am very sorry."

"Oh, Miss Fletcher, please do not cry." He moved to sit beside her and curled one arm round her waist. "Hush now. There is nothing to cry about. Hush, hush."

But all she could do was to weep into his smart new coat and cling to his lapel and murmur, "Sorry... so sorry," repeatedly.

When the storm of weeping had abated somewhat, she found herself still being held by one strong arm, while his free hand stroked her hair. Was he kissing the top of her head? He was! It was such a comfort to be held so, as if she were a child... no, not at all like a child. The tightness of his arm, those kisses, and the endearments he was murmuring...

She raised her head, and at once the endearments ceased.

"Are you feeling better?" he said softly, smiling at her, and that made her want to weep all over again.

"You are not angry with me?"

"Angry?" he said, surprised. "Heavens, no!"

"Oh. Disappointed, then?"

"Perhaps, but it always seemed too great a blessing to be real, that a wonderful person like you could ever fall in love with a dull old stick like me."

"You are not a dull old stick!" she said indignantly. "You were very far from dull when you hit Randal Sylvester."

His lips twitched. "Ah yes, my moment of chivalry and heroism. I shall never live it down."

"Do you regret it?"

"Not in the slightest. For you, Miss Fletcher, I would do anything."

She could only stare at him, her heart beating uncomfortably fast. It was hard to breathe, suddenly.

"Miss Fletcher, you asked me if I were angry or disappointed to discover that those letters were... not what I thought them. I want you to know that I am grateful to you for writing them."

"Grateful!"

"Truly. I was stumbling through my life half asleep, I think. When my uncle married, I blamed Calantha for all that I had lost. She told me she had no designs on Uncle Maurice, and then she married him anyway."

"They fell in love," Angie said.

"They did, but I could not understand that then. All I saw was her betrayal. And Elspeth Meek, who pretended to love me, and that was all a lie. So I wrapped myself in my bitterness, and resented all young women as flighty, frivolous creatures. I have been adrift, waiting for something or someone to rescue me. And then you came into my life."

"I am flighty and frivolous, too," she said in a small voice.

He laughed, which she felt as a deep rumble in his chest since he still held her tight. "You are light-hearted. There is a difference. And although you never loved me, you wrote those letters from the kindest, most charitable of motives. You *cared* about me, Miss Fletcher. I cannot think of anyone else in my whole life who has actually cared about me, or did anything for me purely to make me happy. Not my father, nor my uncle, nor Elspeth Meek. Even Lady Mellish, who offered me a chaplaincy, did not care enough to ask me whether the rumours she heard were true. But *you* cared. You — young and lovely and light-hearted as you are — brought sunshine and joy into my life. It is a great gift that you have given me."

"Ohhh," she breathed. Something shifted inside her, as if a smoke-grimed window had been cleaned. She could see him clearly at last. "Then I *did* make you happy! The letters worked."

Another rumble of laughter. "Yes, they worked, and better than you could ever have imagined. When I looked at you — looked at you properly, I mean, and not through my bitterness, I realised what a woman could and should be... generous and unselfish and loving, and infinitely lovable. I *do* love you, Miss Fletcher. I love you so much I feel... oh, as if I might burst with happiness. You make me want to smile all day long."

"Ohhh."

There were no words. She could not even say if his words made her happy, or if she felt anything like love in return. Who could say what love was? What was this strange giddiness that had swept over her, rendering her incapable of speech or even thought?

She could not move, did not even want to move. He *loved* her! It was astonishing!

His free hand cupped her cheek. He was so close to her, leaning down, nearer and nearer... She could have stopped him. One word, a quick twist of her body, and she would be free of his grasp.

Instead, she closed her eyes and waited...

Soft. Warm. The masculine scent of him. His lips gentle on hers, his chin slightly rough.

He pulled away, and she was sharply aware of her disappointment. Was that it? Her first kiss, to end so soon?

A shaky little laugh escaped him. "I ask nothing of you... expect nothing. You will leave Bath behind... leave *me* behind, and in time you will find someone worthy of you. But for a short time, while I have your letters in my pocket, I can pretend that you are mine, that we are betrothed. Is that all right?"

And then he kissed her again, kissed her properly, until Angie hardly knew where she was or who she was or anything at all beyond the raging maelstrom of emotions, swirling too fast for her to determine what it was she was feeling.

But it was all right. It was very much all right.

~~~~~

B could not tell what the Fletchers were thinking. He could not tell what he was thinking himself, for his mind was as jittery as a rabbit, hopping this way and that with no control from him.

The four of them had gathered in the drawing room, Mr and Mrs Fletcher, Angela and B himself, still quivering inside from that kiss. Was Angela quivering, too? She was smiling, but then she smiled a great deal. Was it a different smile? Was she as shaken as he was after that shattering kiss? Surely she must be.

"— do you not agree, Mr Appleby?" Mrs Fletcher said, with her bright smile.

"I... I beg your pardon, I was not—"

She gave no sign of impatience. "You have told the world you are betrothed, so it would look very odd if you act as if you are not betrothed."

"Yes."

"Our proposal is that we maintain the fiction of the betrothal while we remain in Bath, and then, after a few months, it can be quietly dropped. Do you see?"

"Yes. I see." He must sound like an idiot.

"Get to know each other better," Fletcher said. "Then see how things stand."

Mrs Fletcher threw him a quick glance. "Angie is too young to commit herself to anyone just yet," she said smoothly, "and since there is no great affection between you..."

His mind drifted away again. A few months... for a few months he would be truly betrothed to Angela. He smiled.
~~~~~

"Do you understand, Mr Appleby?" Mrs Fletcher said.

"Yes. I understand."

Mr Fletcher chuckled. "Dinner tonight, Appleby. We eat at six. Don't be late."

"No, sir. Thank you, sir. Ma'am."

"We shall see you later, then, Mr Appleby," Mrs Fletcher said.

"Yes. Oh..." He finally recognised the dismissal in her words, and made his farewells. Angela rose and curtsied demurely to him, but her laughing eyes shone. He gazed at her a little longer than politeness decreed, trying to commit her expressive face to memory. All too soon, his memories would be all that remained of her.

In a daze, B walked home to Gay Street. John Fletcher had left, but there were heaps of books all over his study, on the desk, on the floor, on every surface, so he went out into the garden and sat on a seat, gazing out at his neat rows of vegetables, remembering.

Eventually, Higgins came looking for him, and B meekly followed him into the house, allowed himself to be dressed in one of his new coats and walked the short distance to the Royal Crescent.

It was perhaps the strangest evening of his life. In other circumstances, he would have accounted it a dull affair, for there were no guests beyond the Fletcher family, no great entertainment arranged, not even a rubber or two of whist afterwards. However, in the state he was in, his mind in total disorder, he was grateful for a few hours where nothing at all was expected of him.

Mrs Fletcher made a few efforts to drag him into conversation at table, but finding him unresponsive, she left him to his own thoughts. Angela was equally silent. But the rest of the family went on as if they were not there, discussing the news from Yorkshire brought in the day's mail, or the prospects for rain on the day of the Grand Gala, or the snippets of life amongst the nobility gleaned from Lady Louisa.

When the ladies withdrew, Fletcher and John Fletcher talked easily together over the port, mostly of B's father's books that John Fletcher was evaluating. They were, he said, all old and some in poor condition, but his father agreed that they would buy whatever B wanted to sell.

"If they're old, they'll look the part in the library at Chadwell Park," Fletcher said with a chuckle. "It would never do for people to think I bought them by the yard."

"I have no idea of the value of any of them," John Fletcher said. "I tend to read books, rather than buy or sell them, and I should hate to undervalue them and give you less than they are worth. May I ask Mr Quarman to take a look at them? He would have a better idea of value, or he will know someone who will."

"Of course," B said, not really interested. What would they be worth anyway? A pound or two apiece, perhaps, if the binding were good, and a few hundred pounds in his pocket would be a useful sum. Enough to help him establish his market garden, anyway.

Fletcher, ever the businessman, wanted to know the details of the market garden project, but B was hard pressed to answer any of his questions. He would lease a piece of land outside Bath, and use his own garden as the seedbed for the larger project. He guessed he would need a couple of boys to tend the vegetables, under his supervision, and a man to take the produce to the market twice a week. Beyond that, and as to the costs involved, he could as yet make no precise estimate. The idea had come to him only a matter of hours earlier, and would need some careful research.

"An interesting prospect, Appleby," Fletcher said thoughtfully. "I like the sound of it. If you need advice or simply someone to discuss your ideas with, I'm your man. I'd be happy to loan you funds to get started, too, if you wish it."

"Thank you, sir, but with my own savings and the little extra I will have from the sale of the books, I should be well set, initially. I shall start in a small way, but the garden will grow over several years until it is established and profitable."

"It certainly should be profitable," Fletcher said, smiling at him. "Everyone needs cabbages, after all. Well now, shall we join the ladies?"

Then there was music and the delight of listening to Angela play and sing, and a game of chess with John Fletcher, which his father watched carefully, asking no questions but taking it all in.

It gave B the oddest feeling. He felt as if he had been picked up bodily and dropped into some other family altogether, one with a living mother not a ghost, a father who actually talked to his children, relations who wrote to them regularly, and children with brothers and sisters and friends, real friends like Miss Jupp, who had travelled all the way from Yorkshire to spend the summer with her bosom friend.

B could not think of a single Bath friend who would so much as cross the street to spend time with him. What did they know of him? Which of them had ever seen his garden, for instance? Yet the Fletchers had. That dinner gave him the most disorienting sensation, as if they were *his* family, as if they wanted him there, as if they were his. It was nonsense, of course, for they were just warm, open-hearted people, but for a few short hours they opened their arms to him and he felt as if he truly belonged.

They all came down to the hall to see him out at the end of the evening, when he made Angela blush by kissing her hand. Did it remind her, as it did him, of other, sweeter, kisses? He hoped so. Then he walked home, astonished to find when he arrived that he was wet, for he had barely noticed the rain.

And then to bed, where he lay awake until the sky lightened, thinking of Angela and smiling.

28: An Apology

Angie could not determine what she felt. There had been a rightness to Mr Appleby's kisses, on that point she was certain, and there was, in a strange way, a rightness in being betrothed to him. At least she was safe from Randal Sylvester! Throughout that evening, when Mr Appleby was there, she felt unusually calm. She had begun the day in despair, thinking she would have to marry Randal, and she had ended it betrothed to Mr Appleby.

And kissed! She had been kissed, and it was everything that her sisters had whispered to her. She had thought they exaggerated, but if anything they had not gone nearly far enough. It had been... sublime.

Still, it was odd, for the kisses they described which had swept them away to some earthly paradise had been with men they loved. Allie had talked about kissing Jack Ewing in that way, and she was head over heels in love with him. And Ted's wife, Cathy, who was not at all given to hyperbole, had said that one could tell it was true love by whether his kisses made one's toes curl. Had her toes curled when Mr Appleby had kissed her? Hard to say. She had been in such a dithery, light-headed state of mind it was impossible to determine just what her toes had been doing.

Mr Appleby had been almost silent the whole evening, so she could not tell whether he was happy or miserable or merely bemused by the day's events. He had smiled at her sometimes, which surely meant he was not completely unhappy. She could hardly remember it now, but when they had first met, he had frowned whenever she caught his eye. He had not frowned at her for a long time.

And now she knew the reason — he loved her! In all the astonishing events of the last few weeks, that was surely the most astonishing of all. Despite all her outrageous behaviour towards him, and she could see now that her letters at least were beyond the pale for a respectable young lady, he had not only left his earliest antagonism behind, but he had even come to love her. A man like that, to fall in love with her! He was not a silly boy, blushing scarlet when she so much as looked at him. He was not a practised flirt, with smooth words to beguile her. He was not a desperate fortune hunter, pursuing her with poems and flowers, while dreaming only of her dowry. No, Mr Appleby was a sober, responsible man who disliked flighty young women intensely, and yet somehow, by some strange miracle, all that had been overcome in his mind, and he loved her.

When she retired that night, she sat beside her window with the soft night sounds around her as the house slumbered, and thought with deep gratitude of Mr Appleby and his love... and his kisses. Especially his kisses.

~~~~~

The next day was Sunday, and it had been arranged that B would accompany the Fletchers to church. He presented himself early at the Royal Crescent, and had the delight of Angela beside him for the walk to St Swithin's. Being Sunday, she was not dancing about
~~~~~

as she went, but her steps were so light and graceful, he could almost imagine her twirling merrily. She wore the prettiest little bonnet today, with pink ribbons and a cluster of little pink flowers to one side, their petals fluttering in the gentle breeze.

"What do the dainty pink flowers signify?" he said. "I know that the violet cap is for when you are in the dismals, and I believe you said that bright colours are to cheer you up, but what about pale pink?"

"Pale flower colours mean that I am serene and happy," she said solemnly, although her eyes were twinkling.

"I am glad of it," he said.

"So am I," she said, smiling up at him so heart-warmingly that he had an almost overwhelming desire to crush her in his arms and kiss her again and again. Would he ever have the opportunity for another kiss? It seemed unlikely. Four days, that was all he had left. In four days' time, she would leave Bath, and... that would be the end of this glorious and unforgettable interlude. He sighed.

Still, he would have his market garden to occupy him. His days would be filled with industry, and he could not help a shiver of delight at the prospect of growing all manner of vegetables and soft fruits on a scale previously unimaginable. He already had one or two likely places in mind where he could rent a field to start with, and could expand later if things went well. There would be no time, he hoped, to dwell on Angela, far away from him.

Outside the church, the congregation gathered to smile and be smiled upon, for the ladies to display their newest bonnets and the gentlemen their fine coats, and for the latest gossip to be exchanged.

B was displeased to see Lady Penelope Whittleton approach Angela.

"Miss Fletcher!" she called, waving from some distance away. "Here you are, Miss Fletcher! I hoped I would see you today, and on the arm of your paramour, I see."

"He is not my—"

"Oh, tush, now, no false modesty, if you please, miss. We know all about it. But what a to-do yesterday! We missed the excitement, sadly, but the Pump Room was like a shaken hive when we arrived, and we heard every detail, you may be sure. And to think you once told me he was the most boring and respectable man in Bath."

"Did I?" Angela squeaked, looking surprised.

"Indeed you did, and yet he turns out to be something of a bruiser. Drew the fellow's cork, too. How delicious! I imagine there is not often a mill in the Pump Room here." She laughed heartily. "How sorry I am that I never saw it, for it would make such a good story for my—" She coloured abruptly, then said hastily, "...for all my relations buried in the countryside. *'Nothing ever happens in Bath,'* they told me. Well, this will show them. Good day, Miss Fletcher. Appleby."

A good story for my...? And she was not talking about letters to her relations. Strange. But on one point, he was too honest to deny the truth of her words.

"I suppose I was," B said musingly.

"What, something of a bruiser?"

"The most boring man in Bath."

She looked puzzled. "I *cannot* believe I ever said you were boring, even when I was most at outs with you. Respectable... I said you were— Oh!" Her hand flew to her mouth. "Oh dear! I believe I *may* have said you were stuffy."

He laughed again. "And so I am, Miss Fletcher. At least, I was until I... erm, became a bruiser and drew Sylvester's cork. How does a lady learn such expressions, do you think?"

"By having brothers who enjoy a good mill now and then, I expect," Angela said promptly. "My oldest brother, Ted, was said to be very handy in a mill and Will displays to advantage, too, but naturally I know nothing of such things."

He chuckled. "Naturally. Ah, Lady Mellish, how are you? But I need not ask, for I can see that—"

"Yes, yes, but never mind all that," Lady Mellish said, in some agitation. "I have been considering... examining my conscience, as you suggested, Appleby, and I have sinned grievously. I can only hope you can forgive me for listening to all that was said to your detriment, and believing it to be true. But this book... you cannot have written anything so... so *wicked!*"

"I did not write *The Errant Prince,*" B said quietly. "Upon my word of honour, I did not."

And that was when he realised who must have written it. *A good story for my...* book? Of course! Lady Penelope Whittleton knew the Prince of Wales and his cronies intimately. Who but she was better placed to write a scurrilous book about them? So that was why she had left Brighton so hastily. He almost laughed out loud. But then she must have started the rumour that he had written the book, no doubt because he was the most boring man in Bath. That too was almost funny. With difficulty, he turned his attention back to Lady Mellish.

"I realise now you could not have written that book, and it is greatly to my regret that I ever thought otherwise," she said. "I have known you as a man of the utmost rectitude for twenty years now, and shall not throw your reputation to the wind merely on hearsay. I have been telling everyone I meet that it could not have been your doing. And Miss Fletcher…" She looked at Angela thoughtfully. "A certain gentleman has been telling some very unpleasant tales about you, but I have applied the same rule. I know you to be a girl of very pretty manners who would certainly not be involved in any dealings of a disreputable nature, and so I told him, very plainly, and I am telling all my acquaintances the same. I do believe I shall cut Cadman altogether. Nasty little man! So you see, your words had a great effect upon me, and the position of chaplain is yours, Appleby."

"Thank you for your confidence in me, Lady Mellish, but I cannot accept."

Her eyes narrowed. "Two hundred not enough? Three hundred a year, all found."

"I have made other plans."

"Oh." Her eyes flew to Angela and back again. "Of course. Four hundred and a cottage on the estate somewhere. The gamekeeper will not object to living above the stables, I am sure. That is my final offer, Appleby."

"I thank you most sincerely, but the position would not suit me, I fear. I have been for too long dependent on the good offices of others. It is more than time that I began to stand on my own feet. I am going to become a market gardener."

Her mouth opened, then closed again with a snap. Without another word, she spun on her heel and strode away.

"Her remorse did not last long, did it?" Angela said cheerfully.

The congregation had begun to drift away to enjoy breakfast, and most of those remaining were waiting for the commencement of Sunday school. B's uncle was still there, however, in the centre of a noisy group of friends. He spotted B and Angela, and bounded across to them.

"Barry!" B flinched. "Just the man I wanted to see. I have been considering what you said, about helping you to establish yourself, and I think I see a way of doing it which will be of great benefit to you without any detriment to dear little Roger. It is quite a cunning scheme, which a chance remark by my dear Calantha put in my head. *'That house in Gay Street is far too big for a bachelor,'* she said. *'It is a family house.'* I was much struck, for it is very true, and while you live in it, it makes me no money, anyway. If I were to sell it altogether and give you the money from the sale, I should be better off, in not needing to keep up that allowance I give you, and you could rent rooms somewhere — much more suitable for a single man. The proceeds of the sale would enable you to live comfortably that way, you know. And if..." Here he glanced at Angela. "If you should happen to marry a woman of fortune, then you would be very well set up. Very well set up indeed."

B was too shocked to answer. Lose his lovely garden? Allow a family to move in, who would no doubt lay turf and paths all over his vegetable beds?

"What about his garden?" Angela cried. "Mr Appleby loves that garden."

"Pooh to that," his uncle replied. "What is the point of a

garden in town? Live in the country if you want greenery about you. What is a garden for, except somewhere to sit in hot weather, with a few flowers to cut for the house? Ah, my dear Calantha is growing impatient. I bid you farewell, Miss Fletcher. Nephew."

And away he trotted, leaving B in gloom.

"What a horrid man!" Angela said. "Will he do it, do you think?"

"I cannot say. But if he does, then there is nothing to anchor me to Bath. I could go anywhere in the country."

"You could come to Hertfordshire," she said, bouncing on her toes a little. "You could set up your market garden there, for there is land enough for any number of cabbages to be grown. Do not look so downhearted, Mr Appleby. Are you in the dismals? Shall I lend you my violet cap?"

That made him laugh. Somehow, Angela always cheered him up.

"Shall we go in and begin Sunday school, Miss Fletcher? And perhaps we might try a small change today, by allowing the girls to attend the reading classes, if they wish."

"Teaching girls to read, Mr Appleby? How radical you are become."

"Indeed, but you see there is a young lady of my acquaintance who put forth some excellent arguments for the idea, and she has entirely convinced me of the merits of it."

"She sounds a very wise young lady," Angela said solemnly.

He nodded. "She is a great deal wiser than I once gave her credit for, and is a very remarkable young lady altogether."

Angela blushed and lowered her head and they entered the church side by side.

~~~~~

Angie was practising on the Audleys' rather fine pianoforte the next morning when Bryant entered the room.

"The master and mistress would like to see you in the drawing room, miss," he said.

Now what? Angie had hoped that their last few days in Bath might be a little less fraught.

Pa and Mama were not alone. An elderly man rose at her entrance, tall but not stooped although he was several years older than Pa. His grey hair was fashionably styled, but his clothes, while expensive, were those of a country squire. He examined her closely, but his gaze was neither unfriendly nor, as sometimes happened with men of that age, lascivious. He seemed merely curious.

"Ah, come in, Angie love," Pa said. "This is Lord Trescowe, come about that business with Randal Sylvester."

"You are his father," she said as she rose from her curtsy. Lord Trescowe! Was he cross with her? He did not look especially cross. Tired, perhaps.

"For my sins," he said, with a rueful smile that made him look much younger. "What I ever did to be saddled with such a great booby I cannot imagine. There is no idiocy in my side of the family, nor his mother's, so I must only conclude that his nursemaid dropped him on his head at some point. He was always in trouble at home and in town, so we rather thought that a sleepy place like Bath would suit him. No one can get into trouble in Bath, surely.
~~~~~

But Randal has managed it. Although one thing I will say for him — he has excellent taste." He looked Angie up and down again, and then smiled at her. "Charming, quite charming. I can see why the boy lost his head, for anyone would. Was that you at the instrument just now? I thought so." He sighed. "If only Gaston had brought home someone like you, Miss Fletcher, instead of— But that is water under the bridge, and however attractive the prize, Randal had no business to subject you to such a dreadful ordeal. May I offer you the apologies of the entire family for my son's despicable behaviour?"

She curtsied in acknowledgement.

"Do sit down, Miss Fletcher," Lord Trescowe said, "for I must explain one thing to you, at least. Randal, it seems, was duped too. He believed, you see, that the objective was solely to place you in a predicament, whereupon he would heroically rescue you." Here he sighed again, lifting his eyes heavenwards. "Foolish boy! But he had no thought of making the affair public and believed the meeting with this Cadman fellow was mere ill fortune. In fact, that nasty little incident may be set at the door of Mrs Lambert. Now there is a deceptive woman if ever I saw one. To listen to her rattle away nonsensically, one would think her devoid of any brains at all, but no, she planned the whole thing. Well, I can do nothing about her, for she is Lambert's responsibility, but Randal I can and will deal with. He is presently occupied in packing up all his belongings and settling his accounts in Bath, and I shall have him on the road by nightfall. A few weeks to reflect on his manifold sins in Gloucestershire, and make arrangements, and then I shall ship him off to his cousin in Ireland. He can do little damage there, one must devoutly hope. He will not trouble you again, Miss Fletcher."

Something inside Angie relaxed. She had not realised how

much the prospect of seeing Randal again had disturbed her, but knowing she need not was blissful relief.

Lord Trescowe scratched his nose thoughtfully. "I wonder... is your sister at home? Lady Trescowe cannot leave the house these days, but she reads the society pages of the newspapers avidly, and I was much berated for returning from town without so much as a glimpse of the Yorkshire Rose."

"Rosie is out at present, my lord," Mama said. "Perhaps you would care to dine with us tonight? We will be joined by a few friends who leave Bath tomorrow — Lord Albury and his sister, Lady Maria Landers. Do you know them? And Lady Louisa Horsfell, their aunt, who lives in Bath."

"Louisa Horsfell? Ha! I cannot think how many years it is since I saw her. Those Landers sisters were the talk of London in their glory days. Louisa was not the prettiest, but there was something about her that her sisters never managed. Too insipid by half. Louisa was never insipid. I did think of her myself at one time, but Horsfell got to her first. I know Albury slightly. His father and I do not always see eye to eye in the House, for he is far too inclined to vote against the government, but there we are. Some men are stubborn like that. Thank you, Mrs Fletcher, I should be delighted to dine with you, and carry a report of the Yorkshire Rose back to my good lady."

"Should you like a sketch of her to take to Lady Trescowe?" Angie said. "I have one or two that are not too unlike."

He beamed at her. "What a kind thought! Thank you, Miss Fletcher, and if you have a likeness of yourself, too, that would be delightful, and bring pleasure to an elderly lady."

~~~~~
~~~~~

B was in a quandary. He would hate to lose the Gay Street garden. It had not only been his refuge for years, but it would have helped him establish his market garden. He could sow a few seeds at home to see whether they took before risking a larger sowing, or he might grow a few special varieties in small quantities within its sheltering walls, better protected from the vagaries of the weather than an open field.

He could not afford to buy the house himself, but he wondered if his uncle might give him the house outright.

"That would be the same to you, and I would not have to move," he said.

"But then what would you live on?" his uncle said, in reasonable tones.

It was a good point. He would no longer have the generous allowance he had depended on for years, and would have no other income. It would make the market garden a desperately risky venture. If he failed, he would be destitute.

Yet without the house, what was there to keep him in Bath? Nothing at all, except for habit and a few friends, and his own foolishness in clinging to the familiar. If the Fletchers could uproot themselves, surely he could do as much. He could move anywhere in the country. Hertfordshire, his heart whispered. But he could not impose himself on Angela. If their betrothal were a true one... but that was not something he dared consider.

Where else could he go? Yorkshire, perhaps... but no, that would never do, for the soil and weather would be different. Produce he might grow easily in Somersetshire might fail altogether in the north. It would have to be the south — the same county, or one adjoining. Gloucestershire or Wiltshire, perhaps.

Bristol was a growing city, one he knew well, and must surely need fresh produce. Yes, he would consider the outskirts of Bristol.

But a new home, with no familiar places, no friends, no garden and worst of all, no Angela... it was unutterably depressing. When he had thought of establishing himself in a career, he had never imagined he would lose everything else.

29: A Grand Gala

The day of the Grand Gala arrived. The summer saw several of these great events, with the excuse of celebrating the birthday of one or other of the Royal Family. The King and the Prince of Wales were the principals, but the Duke of York, the Duke of Clarence and the Princess Amelia also had birthdays conveniently timed for the inhabitants of Bath to enjoy. The Gala was to feature fireworks, a concert, a military band, brilliant illuminations and appropriate decorations, according to the notice in the *Bath Chronicle.*

B dined with the Fletchers, as was becoming a habit, and then accompanied them to Sydney Gardens Vauxhall. They were too many to fit the carriage, so the ladies were to be driven, while the gentlemen walked through town, across the Pulteney Bridge and then joined the throng making their way to the Gala. By the time they arrived, B's starched shirt points were already wilting in the sultry air. Far off in the distance was the slightest rumble of thunder.

The ladies arrived, the party showed their tickets at the gates and were admitted. Within the gardens, all was peaceful, the paths lit by a multitude of coloured lanterns, with music playing in the distance. B found Angela by his side as they walked along, her feet taking little jumps and her eyes shining with excitement. Every now and then she twirled round altogether, her eagerness too great to be contained.

But then, to his surprise, she took hold of his arm and adjusted her stride to his. "I shall miss all this when we leave," she said, and her voice sounded almost sad. "There are no Grand Galas in Hertfordshire, or fireworks or military bands. There will be no you, either, and Mama and Rosie will be away, so we cannot even have a ball."

There will be no you... She would miss him! Hope bubbled up inside him. *She would miss him!* What had she said? Something about Mama and Rosie...

"They are going to Essex, are they not? To some friends from London."

"Yes, our neighbours from Grosvenor Square. They are having a great gathering at their country estate. Mama is excited for Rosie, naturally, but she still has hopes of Lord Albury. I cannot see it, myself."

"He was very attentive to her at dinner last night," B said.

"His manners are impeccable. Although... it is strange, because when we first arrived in Bath, he took care not to distress Rosie by any distinguishing attention, yet last night, he seemed quite happy to sit and talk to her."

"She likes him, I think."

"One would have to be very hard to please to dislike him," Angela said. "Still, it is more than that. Something has changed between them, as if they were uncertain before but now they are courting properly, and to be truthful, I have never seen that in

Rosie before. She has always been indifferent to her many suitors, but now she is beginning to see Lord Albury in a different light."

"Well then, perhaps your mama will get her wish and they will make a match of it yet," he said easily. "Should you like to listen to the musicians for a while? The others have gone on ahead, but I know where the supper boxes are."

She agreed to it, and so they stood for a while, she absorbed in the music and he absorbed in watching her. Even though she jigged about slightly from time to time as the music caught her in its spell, she still held his arm with both hands. He savoured the moment, storing the memory.

The air was unnaturally hot and still. The first drop of moisture alerted him. "It is starting to rain."

"Are we near the supper boxes? If we run—"

Even as she spoke the slight moisture became fat drops, and the crowd gathered around the musicians began to move in all directions.

"I know a place," he said, grabbing her hand. "Come on!"

They ran. All around them were the squeals of the ladies and the urgent shouts of the men, but Angela laughed as he towed her along. They did not run far, only behind the musicians' stand, where a deep overhang sometimes provided shelter for stalls for food. It was empty now, and no one had followed them. They were alone, a line of lanterns casting a multitude of colours over them. Angela laughed with exhilaration as the rain drummed on the roof and made a watery curtain all around their hiding place.

The downpour soon diminished to a soft patter above them, and now it could be heard that the stalwart musicians played on.

Angela began to dance. B sighed with contentment — to watch her dance one last time was an unexpected grace. Another memory to squirrel away to sustain him through the desolate years to come.

"I wish I could dance with you," he said wistfully.

"But you can," she said at once, mischief lighting up her face. "Stand like this." She held her arms out wide, as if she were hugging a large tree. When he complied, she touched her hands to his. Then, with an exclamation, she stripped off first her own gloves, then his, tossing them to the ground. "Again," she said, holding out her arms to him. Their hands touched, warm skin to warm skin, and a shiver of delight rippled through him. "Now stand still," she said.

And she began to dance. It was not any dance he recognised. The steps were familiar, sometimes, but the movements were her own invention. She danced this way and that, she bowed low and stretched high, she spun and arched and swayed, but she always held one hand firmly to his. Sometimes the left hand, sometimes the right, but she never once let go of him.

He was enchanted all over again. He hardly knew where he was, for the world receded from his mind and all that existed was Angela, smiling, dancing with him, touching him...

Whatever happened to him in the future, whatever of good or evil might befall him, he would always remember this night and be glad.

Her movements slowed, and then stopped. She stood, her right hand resting in his left hand, staring at him as if mesmerised, her breathing ragged. Gradually, in tiny little steps, she moved so that she was against his chest, their joined hands behind her back so he was holding her. He pulled her tight against him, as she stretched her face up to his.

Then she kissed him.

He could not say how long they stood thus, lost in their own little paradise. He knew only that there was not an ounce of reluctance on her part. Whatever she did was done with energy and enthusiasm, and so it was with kissing. Oh, that it might never end!

But even Angela could not go on kissing indefinitely. She sighed, and rested her head briefly on his chest, before tilting her face up to look at him, mischief in her eyes.

"I like being betrothed."

Warmth flooded him. She liked it! She liked *him*. "So do I," he murmured, his voice sounding oddly husky.

"Do you? And yet, one day it will end, and that day cannot come soon enough for me."

The pain that shot through him was almost unbearable. Not yet! Please, no, not yet!

She must have seen the anguish in his face, for she cried out, "No, no! Not like that. I meant only that much as I like being betrothed, I shall like being married much better." She tilted her head to one side. "Now you look shocked. Did you not think— Oh! Perhaps you do not want to marry me."

"I want to marry you more than anything in the world," he said fiercely, his voice so low it was all but inaudible. "I never imagined... it would be beyond anything wonderful! Should you truly want that... for us to marry?"

"Of course, but it is quite impossible," she said, in startlingly cheerful tones.

His spirits plummeted at once.

"Because you have not asked me, of course." She bounced expectantly on the balls of her feet. "Well?"

He opened his mouth, but no words came out. He cleared his throat, and tried again, but there was only an odd gurgling sound.

She laughed, shaking her head. "I shall just have to do it myself, that is all there is to it. Mr Appleby, would you do me the very great honour of becoming my husband?"

"Yes. Oh yes!"

"So you can speak after all. I was a trifle concerned for a moment."

"Angela Fletcher, you are a dreadful little minx!"

"I know. It is impossible to resist teasing you. If you could have seen your face! But you will laugh about this one day, trust me."

"Angela, I—"

She pulled a face. "No one calls me Angela, except Mama when she is cross with me. Everyone calls me Angie."

"I like Angela — you are my angel, you see."

She burst into laughter. "It is a singularly inappropriate name. May I call you Barry now?"

He winced. "No! I hate being called that."

"But it is your name!" she cried. "I really cannot call you Mr Appleby all the time — not in private, anyway."

"It is *not* my name," he said sadly. "When I was baptised, my father decided that I was to be called Barachel. It means *'blessed'* apparently. But the parson got confused, since it was just after Easter, and named me Barabbas instead."

"*Barabbas?* The nasty thief who was released by Pontius Pilate instead of Jesus? What a horrid name to give a baby."

"My father thought so, too, so he decided that I should be called Barry henceforth. But I have always hated that name. To be honest, I hate all three names — Barachel, Barabbas and Barry. Why could I not be plain Edward or William? Or a proper saint's name, like Mark or Luke or Matthew."

"Then change it," she said. "People change their names all the time. You need only put a notice in the newspaper. *'Henceforth Mr Appleby of Gay Street will be known as Mr John Appleby.'* Something like that."

"Christian names are strange sacred things, given at baptism. I am not sure the bishop would approve."

"Why not ask him? I think the rain has stopped. Shall we go and tell the others our news?"

"Angela... Angie... are you quite sure about this? Marriage is a big step to take and you are still young. Take some time to think about it."

She turned to face him, laying her hands on his chest as she gazed up at him. "My very dear Mr Appleby, for so I will call you until you have a name that you like — yes, I am very sure. I once thought that I knew precisely what I wanted in a husband. The man I loved would be handsome and rich and would dance divinely."

"I fail on every point," B said, wrapping his arms around her once more.

She chuckled. "Not quite every point. Lady Louisa said something very wise to me when I told her of my requirements. *'When you see a man gazing at you with utter adoration in his eyes,'* she told me, *'he will be excessively handsome to you.'* And..." She lowered her eyes shyly, and then glanced up again, full of mischief. "And she was quite right. When you look at me in that way you have, as if I am the most amazing creature in the entire world, then you are the handsomest man I have ever seen."

"But at other times I am not handsome?" he said teasingly.

"When you used to frown disapprovingly at me, I did not think you at all handsome then. But when we were dancing just now, you looked at me and... I could not *breathe*. But as for the rest of my silly requirements, it seems to me that they are irrelevant. We are good for each other, you and I. You were too serious before, with your black clothes and your frown, and I was too frivolous. You are becoming a little more light-hearted, I hope, and I am learning to be more sensible. Shall I tell you something odd, something I have never told anyone before? Sometimes I feel as light and insubstantial as thistledown, which terrifies me, because what if a puff of wind should carry me away altogether? I might never find my way home. But you anchor me to the ground. Nothing can blow me away when I am with you. So I should like to stay with you for my whole life, so that I will never be blown away and lost."

"Oh, Angie, my love, there is nothing I should like better," he whispered. "I love you so much, my sweet girl."

"And I love you, too, my darling. How strange that all this started because I wrote those foolish letters, as if I were in love with you. And it came true! It really happened, and I fell in love with you but I did not realise it until just now when you looked at me that way — with adoration in your eyes. That was when I understood my own heart, and knew myself to be entirely yours, my love."

He held her very tight, and wondered what he had ever done to deserve such joy.

~~~~~

Pa was not very encouraging. "I've no objection to Appleby himself, Angie love," he said, when they were having their breakfast the next day, "but you're very young to be settling down. Besides, he's no money, and I'll not have him setting himself up as a gentleman on your twenty thousand."

"You would not withhold my dowry?" she said in alarm.

"No, I'll not do that, but I want to see what sort of income he can come up with before I'll agree to it, and even if he inherits a fortune tomorrow, I want you to wait at least a year before you marry."

"Do you think I might change my mind?" she said.

"Well now, you've been known to change it once or twice before." But he smiled affectionately at her as he spoke. "Marriage is a serious matter, so you want to make absolutely sure you're not making a mistake. You've only known the fellow a few weeks, after all."

"I can wait a year," she said calmly. "We will have the rest of our lives together, after all."

Pa's eyebrows rose. "He's a good influence on you, I'll say that for him. I thought you'd fly up into the boughs at any check."
~~~~~

"We are good for each other," Angie said. "He calms me down and I lighten him a little."

"Good, because he was too serious before. Let's see what happens with this house of his, and if his uncle sells it from under him, well, he can come to Hertfordshire and I'll help him set up his market garden there. Once he knows what he's doing, then we can talk about a wedding, if you still want it. But just at the moment there are too many uncertainties."

Mama had said nothing very much about Mr Appleby, although her expression was not entirely disapproving. He had neither fortune nor title, and was not a fashionable buck like Will, but perhaps she thought he was good enough for Angie. Or maybe she believed Angie would lose interest in him before long.

Now she gave Angie a long look, but merely said calmly, "What are your plans for today, Angie?"

"If you can spare me, I should like to say farewell to Mr Bravington."

"An excellent idea. Rosie has netted a purse that you may take to him, to thank him for his kindness towards you."

"And for the ball," Angie said, with a sigh of happiness, remembering.

"Of course, dear," Mama said complacently. "You will say everything proper, I am sure. I would go myself, but the packing, you know..."

"I will come with you," Johnny said. "Quarman has some fellow coming from London to look at Appleby's books in an hour or so, but I will look in on Bravington first."

In the hall, as they prepared to depart, Pa caught them and

said in an undertone, "Don't forget to ask one more time about the Grosvenor Square house. I'd love to surprise Mrs Fletcher, and maybe Bravington will soften if you're leaving, eh? Lease or buy, either would suit me."

They agreed to it, and walked the short distance in the rain to Mr Bravington's house.

"Does it always rain in Bath?" Angie grumbled, as they shook off raindrops in the hall.

Mr Bravington's man smiled. "This has been an unusually dry summer, miss."

"Has it, indeed? Then I should hate to see a normal summer."

They found Mr Bravington hunched over the chessboard with Mr Appleby, who jumped up with a beaming smile at Angie's arrival. Mr Bravington, however, looked miserable.

"I am very pleased for you, my dear," he said, as Angie bent to kiss his cheek, "very pleased indeed, and I wish you joy, naturally, but must you take Appleby away from Bath? Why can you not live here? Then I could have the delight of your skills on the spinet and his skills on the chessboard. That would make an old man very happy."

"We both wish it could be so, sir, for I love Bath as much as he does, but Mr Appleby the Elder is to sell the Gay Street house, and without that there is nothing to keep us here, excepting only your company. And your spinet, which I shall miss very much, I assure you."

"Yes, but why would he do such a thing? That house is perfect for the two of you. Whatever is the man thinking? Why would he not simply give you the house, Appleby?"

"I must have an income to live on, sir."

"And what income will you have from the proceeds of the house? Fifty a year? A hundred at best?"

Mr Appleby's eyebrows rose. "Is that all? And he saves the three hundred a year of my current allowance."

Mr Bravington's face darkened. "Your uncle is a villain, sir, and I do not scruple to say so. He thinks you will live like a lord on Miss Fletcher's dowry, so he need not do anything for you. Pass me that writing box from the table. I have a letter to write."

~~~~~

For their last evening in Bath, there were no dinner guests besides Mr Appleby. The family gathered for the last time in the elegant drawing room, and Pa had ordered champagne to be poured.

"We have cause for celebration tonight," he said, beaming at them genially at them from his position in front of the fireplace. "Two causes, in fact. Firstly, Angie and Appleby are officially engaged to be married, for the notice has gone off to the *Gazette*, the *Bath Chronicle* and the *Sagborough Chronicle.* Secondly, we are the proud owners of a house in Grosvenor Square..." Mama squeaked in excitement. "...for Bravington has agreed to sell to me. I have been trying to persuade him ever since we arrived in Bath, but I never understood before today why he wouldn't, since he'd never go back there. It appears the Bath house and most of his income is only his for his lifetime, left to him by his sister. The London house was all he owned, the last tie to his marriage, and he kept it for sentimental reasons. But now he has a more compelling reason to sell, for the proceeds will partly pay for the purchase of Mr Appleby's house in Gay Street, which is to be a wedding present to the two of you."
~~~~~

Angie stood as if stunned. "He would do that for us?" she whispered.

"He's done it already. The papers are signed and sealed. I've been dashing about talking to attorneys and bankers all day, but it's done. Mind you, he'll expect you to live in it when you marry."

"That is precisely what we most wanted," Mr Appleby said. "Sir, I hardly know how to thank you for—"

"No, no, no," Pa said. "None of that, if you please. All your own doing, you know, Appleby — yours and Angie's. Seemingly, Mr Bravington can't manage without someone to play chess with him, and someone to play music for him. So that's all worked out very prettily. Is it the dinner hour yet? I'm sharp set this evening."

"Before that, there is one more cause for celebration," Johnny said.

"Oh, you have a valuation on those old books of Appleby's, have you?" Pa said. "So how much is that little lot going to cost me?"

"About twenty-five thousand pounds. Possibly thirty." The shocked silence in the room was absolute. "Sorry, Pa. It seems that Mr Appleby Senior was not just a reader of books, he was a collector of rare and valuable items."

"Thirty thousand pounds?" Mr Appleby said in strangled tones.

Pa laughed. "Don't worry, I'm good for it."

"Some of the rarest items could be sold off separately," Johnny said. "There is a second edition of *Philosophiae Naturalis Principia Mathematica* in very good condition that Quarman's London colleague was very excited about. That one alone is worth thousands."

"Thousands of pounds for an old book in Latin?" Pa said. "Well, what a day of wonders this is."

Angie was unusually silent over dinner and afterwards. It was hard to take in. They would have the house in Gay Street to live in, they would have money to live on, and Mr Appleby would have his beloved garden. Pa was adamant that they must still wait the full year before they married, but she could cope with that. Besides, two weddings in the family in one year was enough for the moment. Julia was married already, and Will would be married soon. Perhaps Rosie would make Mama happy and secure Lord Albury before too long, or she might meet a handsome young lord at the Armitages' house in Essex. There would be time enough for Angie to leave her family and become Mrs Appleby.

She accompanied her betrothed to the hall as he was leaving, and even the servants were tactful enough to leave them alone for a moment.

"Are you pleased?" he said, taking her gently into his arms and planting the lightest of kisses on her forehead. "Shall you like living in Bath?"

"Oh, yes! The shops, the winter assemblies, the galas in the summer… there is always something happening in Bath. But what about you? You have no need to worry about your market garden now."

"I might do it anyway," he said, in surprised tones. "Now that the idea has lodged in my mind, I find that it has put down very strong roots. I love gardening, and always wished I had more space for my endeavours. Now I can turn an entire field into an extension of my garden, and if it takes me years to turn a profit, we will not starve in the meantime. I have been idle for too long, my love, and now I am filled with energy and enthusiasm."

"You do not mind waiting so long to marry? You will come and see me in Hertfordshire?" she said in sudden fear. "You will not get so caught up with your market garden that you forget about me?"

He silenced her in the most delicious way, so that for a long time she forgot all about the market garden and the long, dreary year until they could be together for the rest of their lives. When eventually he lifted his lips from hers, he was smiling down at her in that heart-stopping way of his, that made her dizzy with joy. He *loved* her! How amazing it was that she could inspire such a feeling in him!

"As soon as I have put my affairs on a more stable footing, I shall come to Hertfordshire to see you, my little love," he said softly. "I cannot stay away from you for very long."

"Will you ask the bishop if you might change your name?" she said.

"I have already written to him," he said, "and I have thought of a new name for myself. How do you like the sound of Benedict? It means *'blessed'* just like my original name."

"Benedict. Benedict. Ben." She rolled the name around her tongue. "I like it. May I call you Ben?"

"If you must, but I should prefer you to call me *'my darling'* or *'my love'*, as you did before."

"My darling," she said, reaching up to kiss him. "My sweet love." Another kiss. "My beloved. My adored one. My hero. My dashing knight. My own. My dearest, most wonderful man. Is that better?"

He sighed. "Much, much better."

He held her very tight, and kissed her again and warmed her down to her very toes. She still could not tell whether they curled or not when he kissed her, but now she had her whole life to find out.

THE END

The next book in the series is *A Michaelmas Truce*, wherein grumpy Madge Paton's battles with neighbour Morgan Plummer get them into hot water. You can read a sneak preview after the acknowledgements. For more information, go to my website at marykingswood.co.uk.

Thanks for reading!

If you have enjoyed reading this book, please consider writing a short review on Amazon. You can find out the latest news and sign up for the mailing list at my website at marykingswood.co.uk.

Family trees: Hi-res versions available at my website under Extras.

A note on historical accuracy: I have endeavoured to stay true to the spirit of Regency times, and have avoided taking too many liberties or imposing modern sensibilities on my characters. The book is not one of historical record, but I've tried to make it reasonably accurate. However, I'm not perfect! If you spot a historical error, I'd very much appreciate knowing about it so that I can correct it and learn from it. Thank you!

The great houses: Most of the houses I describe in the books are creations of my imagination, or 'generic' styles of a particular era, but sometimes I base them on real houses. These are the principal houses of this series:

Chadwell Park, Hertfordshire: based on two separate designs from Vitruvius Britannicus and Georgian Architectural Designs.
Chadwell Manor, Hertfordshire: invented.
Grosvenor Square, London: based on several designs of real

houses.

Royal Crescent, Bath: based on plan of no 20.

Chaseley Court, Huntingdonshire: based on Fountains Hall, near Ripon, Yorkshire, but I added a couple of wings and a gallery.

Isn't that what's-his-name? Regular readers will know that characters from previous books occasionally pop up, or are mentioned. The Fletchers stay in the Bath home of the wealthy Leo Audley, previously seen in *The Chaperon.* There is mention of Elliot and Evie Armitage, their ward Violet Barantine, and the Tranter brothers, seen in *The Orphan* and also in *A Spring Dance.*

About the series*:* A family grown rich in the wool trade. The landed gentry they've displaced. And the gentle daughter whose beauty will open the door to an even greater prize - the nobility.

The Fletcher family is moving from Yorkshire to a mansion in the south of England. After generations in trade, can they escape their roots and be admitted to the leisured world of the gentry?

Their new home is Chadwell Park, in Hertfordshire. **The Mercer's House.**

Book 0: The Mercer: the rich merchant and the poor widow. *(A novella, free to mailing list subscribers).*

Book 1: A Winter Chase: the wild daughter and the reluctant clergyman.

Book 2: A Spring Dance: the flirtatious son and the prim paid companion.

Book 3: A Summer Game: the mischievous daughter and the strait-laced gentleman.

Book 4: A Michaelmas Truce: the cross spinster and the even crosser bachelor.

Book 5: An Autumn Courtship: the intellectual son and the flighty socialite.

Book 6: A Christmas Betrothal: the beautiful daughter, the unhappy son and the lost lover.

Any questions about the series? Email me at mary@marykingswood.co.uk - I'd love to hear from you!

About the author

I write traditional Regency romances under the pen name Mary Kingswood, and epic fantasy as Pauline M Ross. I live in the beautiful Highlands of Scotland with my husband. I like chocolate, whisky, my Kindle, massed pipe bands, long leisurely lunches, chocolate, going places in my campervan, eating pizza in Italy, summer nights that never get dark, wood fires in winter, chocolate, the view from the study window looking out over the Moray Firth and the Black Isle to the mountains beyond. And chocolate. I dislike driving on motorways, cooking, shopping, hospitals.

Acknowledgements

Thanks go to:

Allison Lane, whose course on English Architecture inspired me.

Cara King, whose course on Regency dance taught me about the minuet and much more.

Dr Octavia Cox, whose podcast on the class of the Bingleys in Pride and Prejudice clarified my thoughts about the Fletchers.

Sarah Waldock, whose book *A Regency Miss's Guide to Bath* ensured that my characters had a lovely stay in that city.

Shayne Rutherford of Darkmoon Graphics for the cover design.

My beta readers: Charles Crouter, Melissa Forsythe, Pat Oen, Rosemary Paton, Melanie Savage

Last, but definitely not least, my first reader: Amy Ross.

Sneak preview: Book 4 of The Mercer's House: A Michaelmas Truce: Chapter 1: An Unexpected Arrival

HERTFORDSHIRE, THE FIRST DECADE OF THE NINETEENTH CENTURY

JULY

Morgan Plummer was bored. Chadwell Manor was silent, the family all out, the servants tucked away in the kitchen wing, and the children... he had no idea where the children were. Not his responsibility, thank heavens.

He had spent the morning knocking balls around the billiard table to improve his carom shot, which had always been his weakness. It was dull work, but then the Manor was a dull place these days. His brother Owen was a splendid fellow, naturally, but dry as a bone and without a spark of liveliness in him. Everything had been fine until Father had died and Owen had decided that economy was to be the order of the day. Now even the Park was sold, and they were all squeezed into the Manor like cattle, and the billiard table had to be taken down every time Sarah held a dinner party.

Everyone was miserable under the new arrangements, he thought savagely, hitting the cue ball so hard that it flew clean off the table. Sarah had been so proud to be mistress of the Park, and understandably resented giving up its modern elegance for the decaying heap that was the Manor. Michael was still miserable after that business with the heiress, and surely it was time he came out of the dismals? Letitia — well, Letitia was always ill-humoured. She had been a wailing, unhappy baby and now she was a wailing, unhappy woman. There was no doing anything with her, and that husband of hers was no better, always on about *'my brother, the marquess'*. As for Patricia, who knew what went on in her empty head? What a family! James was the only one of the lot of them that Morgan could honestly say that he liked.

It was James who put his head round the screen that separated the great hall from the entrance hall, a cheerful smile on his face. He was always smiling these days.

"Good morning, Uncle Morgan. Is Mother about?"

"Out. All out. Gone to Ware for the day."

"Have they?" James said vaguely, although he must have been told of the arrangement. He and Julia dined at the Manor most evenings. "Well, no matter. I shall talk to Mrs Hoskins. I need a ham, and perhaps a leg of mutton or a goose, if she has one. Oh, and some of the fish I brought yesterday."

"Holding a dinner?" Morgan said, brightening slightly. Dinner at the rectory might be more fun than the morose affairs at the

Manor.

"Not us, no. It is for the Park. Some of the Fletchers are back."

"So soon?" Morgan said, feeling a spark of interest. "Bored with Bath already, are they?"

James laughed. "Not bored. Outraged would be nearer the mark. Miss Whittleton's reprobate of a father turned up, and since she cannot bear to be within a hundred miles of him, Will Fletcher has brought her here, together with her aunt, Mrs Greenwood. Naturally, there is very little food in the house, and half the servants off to visit their kin. Tell Mother, will you? I expect she will invite them to dine soon."

"If I remember," Morgan said, struggling to recall who Miss Whittleton was. Was that the woman Will Fletcher was set to marry? And who was the reprobate father?

James laughed. "Hmm. Well, I shall tell Jefford. He will remember."

"What about the rest of them? I thought they took the house in Bath for a month."

"So they did, and they are staying on. There is too much pleasure in Bath to be foregone, seemingly. Oh, but Miss Paton is here. She has no faith in the servants running the Park to her exacting standards, so she is here to keep them up to the mark."

"Ha! That termagant! I thought we had got rid of her for a while," Morgan said, but he felt a spike of excitement all the same. Miss Paton might have a barbed tongue, but at least she had a brain in her head and could argue her points with energy.

James smiled, and shook his head at him. "You two! You are like a pair of dogs fighting over the same bone. What is it that riles you so much about her?"

"She is an odious, smug, puffed up fool of a woman," Morgan said at once. "Irksome female, far too opinionated. Never knows when to be silent. The most disagreeable person in Hertfordshire. Why could she not have stayed in Bath and given God-fearing folk a rest from her irritating ways?"

He could continue in the same vein for hours, but with a laugh, James held up his hands in surrender, and went off to the kitchens to see what he could scavenge for the Park. Morgan topped up his brandy glass thoughtfully. Perhaps he would walk up to the Park and see whether her short stay in Bath had made the woman any less irritating.

~~~~~

Madge Paton looked with distaste around the servants' hall of Chadwell Park, where Polly, the kitchen maid, was frantically tidying away the remains of tea and cakes scattered over the long table. "Well, I can see you've been having a fine holiday here while I was away. Drinking the best tea, no doubt, and sitting at your ease all day. Have you done any of the jobs you were set, Mrs Graham?"

"Yes, madam," the housekeeper said, twisting her apron in her hands. "The carpets are all beaten, the linens are sorted and the window cleaning's under way. If you could but have sent word ahead, madam, but with most of the house under holland covers—"

"A letter was sent, but we made all haste to be here before the Sabbath. Best part of three days on the road, to be greeted with nothing but disorder. Well, we'll have to make do, I suppose. Send hot water up to Miss Whittleton and Mrs Greenwood at once
~~~~~

and—"

The apron became even more twisted. "The boilers aren't lit, madam. Anthony has gone to light them, but there won't be enough for baths yet."

"Hmpf. Ewers, then," Madge said, more gently. "We must look after Miss Whittleton, you know, because she'll be mistress here one day."

"We're right pleased to have her here," Polly said, eyes shining, holding a precarious pile of cups and saucers. "Master Will's young lady... so excitin'! Will the weddin' be here? Cos we thought it was to be Bath."

"Get those cups to the scullery, and never you mind about a wedding," Madge said. "Is that one of the family's tea sets, Mrs Graham?"

She flushed pink. "We had them out for washing, madam."

"Hmpf. Well, make sure nothing gets broken. Now then, Mrs Sharwell, let's think about dinner. What do you have in the meat safe just now?"

Mrs Sharwell was not the greatest cook in the world, but with a guiding hand she could produce a tolerable meal. Not that Madge was particularly concerned to impress Eloise Whittleton, who might be a distant cousin to the Marquess of Carrbridge, but was only a poor relation, after all. Although Eloise was very ladylike and would doubtless make a gracious mistress of Chadwell Park, in time, Madge privately thought that Will could have done much better for himself. With his looks and the Fletcher fortune, he should have aimed a little higher than a poor relation, however elegant.

Half an hour inspecting the larders satisfied her that dinner wouldn't be a total disaster. She'd given Mrs Sharwell a few hints as to the type of dishes that would be acceptable. It was a pity there was no fish to be had until next week, but they would have to make do.

Madge had joined the Fletcher household years ago to help her sister Edith with the children. Gradually Edith had left more and more of the management of the house to her, and when Edith had died, Madge had expected to run things for ever. But Harry had chosen to marry again and move the whole family to this grand pile in Hertfordshire and a more gracious style of living. What Madge missed more than anything, though, was running her own house, and with Harry and Lizzie still in Bath for a few weeks, she had the pleasure of being fully in charge again.

The kitchen was in a separate wing of the house, so Madge made her way back to the main part of Chadwell Park, where the low ceilings and dark walls of the servants' domain gave way to the elegance and lightness of the family rooms. She would rather die than admit it, but the house pleased her very well. Their Sagborough house had been large, stretching over five floors, but the rooms had been modestly proportioned, and fitted up with solid furnishings that were designed to endure for many generations. Chadwell Park, on the other hand, was all high ceilings and delicate plasterwork and gracefully curvaceous furnishings, and although there were only two principal floors, the rooms sprawled luxuriantly, one flowing into another. Madge ought to feel like an interloper in such grand surroundings, but somehow there was a rightness to it that she acknowledged. The Fletcher family might have their roots in trade, but they had winched themselves up a notch in the world, and despite the antagonism of the aristocracy, this was where they belonged.

Madge walked slowly through the three principal saloons, taking note of the furniture and chandeliers shrouded in holland covers, a layer of dust coating every surface. Then she climbed the gently curving stairs. On the upper floor, all was bustle, as a maid rushed past with towels and sheets and pillows, and two more heaved an ancient box along the landing. Madge took one end of it, and read the faded lettering.

"Mrs Greenwood's... this first room, Mary. Young Mary, hold the door open. There now, just set it down on the rug here. Is Miss Whittleton's box up yet?"

"Yes, mum," Mary said, bobbing a curtsy. "Both of 'em, in her room."

Madge looked with critical eyes around the room. The bed was stripped, the furniture was still draped in holland covers and the same light film of dust lay everywhere. "Hmpf. Lots of work to be done here."

"Mrs Graham said to start with Miss Whi'leton's room, mum."

"Quite right."

The room next door was only marginally better. Bedding was piled on a chair, Mrs Greenwood's maid struggled to fold holland covers as Eloise and Mrs Greenwood wrestled sheets onto the bed.

"The maids can do that," Madge said sharply. "Let me send for some tea—"

"No, no, no," Mrs Greenwood said. "You want us to sit about drinking tea while there is work to be done?"

"You're guests," Madge said. "No need for you to work."

"We are used to it," Eloise said with a smile. "Besides, we have taken the servants by surprise, so it is only fair that we help out."

"Surprising them is not the issue," Madge said sourly. "These rooms should have been kept ready, with just the covers to remove. Look at the dust in here!"

"Good," Mrs Greenwood said. "Nothing I like better than flicking a duster around. Off you go now, and leave the bedrooms to us, Miss Paton."

Madge reluctantly went back downstairs. She found one of the footmen precariously perched on a ladder in the saloon, attempting to remove a cover from one of the chandeliers.

"No point trying to get the saloons habitable before dinner, John," she said briskly, "or the dining room, either. The parlour and breakfast room will do for today. I can give you a hand."

Just then, a whirlwind tore through the entrance hall. "Aunt Madge! Aunt Madge! How are you?"

The whirlwind hurled itself at Madge, almost knocking her off her feet.

"Good day to you, too, Julia," Madge said, disentangling herself and straightening her cap. "I'm as well as anybody can be who's been jounced about in a carriage for three days. No need to ask if you're well, young lady. If your stepmother were here, she would say, *'Decorum, Julia!'*".

"But she's not here, is she, and I never was very good at decorum. Where's Eloise? Still upstairs?"

"Making up the beds," Madge said, rolling her eyes. "See if you can drag her away from there. It's hardly fitting for the future mistress of this house to be doing the maids' work. Is James with you? And what has become of Will?"

"James has gone to the Manor to get some decent food for you, otherwise you'll be eating rabbit stew, and Will has gone to the stables, naturally, because the horses are far more important than mere people. I'm sure he'll be here soon. I'll just pop up and see Eloise..."

And with that she was gone in a swirl of skirts. If John had not been watching interestedly from his perch on the ladder, Madge might well have laughed, for there was no doing anything about Julia. She had always been a hoyden, and marriage to James Plummer, the local clergyman, had not made her any more ladylike.

As for Will, there was no doing anything about him, either. Much as he adored Eloise and would put her wishes above all else, his horses rated a very close second. Naturally he had gone to the stables, and who knew when he might emerge from there?

"Why are you still up there?" Madge growled at the footman on his ladder. "We have two rooms to get ready before dinner, and with lolpoops like you we'll be hard pressed. Come on, come on! Shift yourself."

Some steady work saw the parlour readied for habitation, and they had moved on to the breakfast room when Keeble sidled in with an apologetic cough.

"Mr Morgan Plummer is here, madam. Are you at home?"

"Ha! That man! Well, if he expects us to be sitting about

making polite conversation while he drinks his way through our brandy, he's very much mistaken. On the other hand, if he can fold holland covers, he can come in."

Morgan Plummer's grinning face appeared in the door moments later. "Well, well, well, Bath had enough of you, Miss Paton? Packed you off home, have they? You must have kicked up a rare old dust, to have to leave so hastily."

"There were reasons," Madge said with dignity. "Are you going to stand there like a statue, or will you help John with these covers, while I shift this mountain of dust? Less than a month since I left, and look at the state of the place!"

With a long-suffering sigh, he tugged half-heartedly at a cover on one of the chairs. "And what would you find to grumble about if everything were perfect, eh? Admit it, you love to grumble."

"I admit no such thing," she said briskly, picking up a feather duster. "I should have liked very much to sit at my ease after such a journey. Three days on the road, and resting only in the hours of darkness, to get here before the Sabbath. Not a wink of sleep have I had since we left Bath, and I'd be in my bed now if I had my way. Have you never folded anything before, Mr Plummer? Look how disorderly you leave these sheets. I should have done it myself, I dare say, if I wanted it done properly."

"So you should," he said cheerfully. "So you may, if you wish, madam. Far be it from me to offend your fastidious eye with my inept folding. Is there no brandy in this house to offer a thirsty guest? You, fellow — find me some brandy, will you?"

The footman scuttled away, as Madge rolled her eyes. "Useless man that you are, Morgan Plummer! But all men are useless when there is work to be done. God put men on this earth to plague women, and that's the truth. If you're not going to make yourself useful, you can keep out of my way."

"With pleasure, dear lady," he said, grinning, settling himself on the window seat and folding his arms. "Do carry on. I should hate to interrupt your endeavours."

It was fortunate that Will appeared just then, or Madge would have been tempted to throw something at her unwanted guest.

"This place is a shambles," Will said, his face thunderous. "Half the grooms are missing, the stalls are unswept, the coach is still sitting in the yard where Murgatroyd left it, and he and Young Murgatroyd are having to see to the carriage horses themselves. And that wretched, wretched dog—! See what he did to my boots? A perfectly good pair of boots ruined. It is not good enough, Aunt Madge. That animal has to go, no matter how much Rosie weeps and says he just needs training. He is beyond redemption, I swear it."

"We'll see about the dog later," Madge said. "I like it no more than you, but Rosie's fond of the creature and your father always lets her have her way. Too soft by half, he is. He spoils those girls rotten."

"I have seen the dog tied up, for now, but we need a cage of some sort for him. But where are all the grooms, that is what I want to know. Ah, Keeble," he added, as the butler appeared with Mr Plummer's brandy. "Where have the grooms gone? There seems to be no one in the stables at all."

"Matthew and Tommy are over at the farm helping their father, sir. I've sent Toby across to fetch them back. Young Bill has taken Emperor to the farrier. And Dan Pritchard..." His face clouded.

"Yes? Dan Pritchard?"

"Dan went off to visit his mother two weeks ago, sir."

"Two weeks! That is a long holiday."

"It was only to be a week, sir. Mrs Pritchard lives on the other side of Ware, so it could hardly be less. But he's not back yet, and Mrs Graham met someone in Ware the other day who is from the same village as Mrs Pritchard, and seemingly the boy never went to his mother's at all."

"So he has just vanished, is that it?" Will said.

"Mostly likely spent all his money on drink," Madge said, with a sniff.

"I don't think so, madam," Keeble said. "He was always a good, sober young man, and past the age of such foolishness. I'm more concerned that he's met with an accident somewhere."

"Well, whether he has drunk himself to oblivion or fallen into a ditch, I am not sure what we can do about it," Will said. "I am going to change my boots."

So saying, he stomped out of the room.

On the window seat, Morgan Plummer sipped his brandy, chuckling at them. Irritating man!

END OF SAMPLE CHAPTER of *A Michaelmas Truce;* for more information or to buy, go at my website at marykingswood.co.uk.

Printed in Great Britain
by Amazon

19133257R00222